Eurotrash

Dare Pender

Eurotrash

By Dare Pender
Copyright 2013 © Dare Pender

www.darepender.com

ISBN: 9-780615-811932

DEDICATION

To my darling husband with his never-ending
encouragement on this new chapter in my life.

CONTENTS

CHAPTER 1

If there was one thing that Everlee Marvin "William" Joseph Crenshaw was good at it was playing poker. And he was just as good at making babies. What he wasn't good at was staying around. He was committed just long enough to make sure his children safely carried his name. Although he was never a steadfast father, he would visit his offspring while touring and playing professional poker. All of his daughters had different mothers and all lived in different states. It kept things neater that way.

When he was around his girls he was a warm and generous man, but his scatter plot of baby-mamas realized he had a seemingly larger calling that did not include them. He preferred to be selfish with his time, but generous with his money and DNA. William Crenshaw was too great to belong to just one woman. When he did leave a woman, he would leave her feeling like she was the only woman on the planet. That was part of his charm, in addition to his stately good looks, perfect hair and slender build. The mothers of his daughters always left room for William in their lives. Sometimes it was the hope that one day he would come back, stay and settle, correcting what would otherwise be considered a mistake. Despite his daughters being raised by single mothers, and one stray father, they were well-provided for and got everything they needed- except a full-time dad.

His first born daughter was Everdine Crenshaw. He had met and charmed her mother at a high stakes game in Savannah, Georgia, where she served as her daddy's good luck charm. She was heiress to a old cotton empire in the Southeast. Since being an unwed mother was worse than wearing white after Labor Day, Everdine's mother was sent off to live with relatives in Atlanta to have her daughter. That's where she was mostly raised.

Everdine was the quintessential southern debutante. She attended cotillion faithfully growing up, went to private school and earned a degree in mathematics and chemistry from an Ivy League university. She was as smart as she was beautiful, and dressed up her famous Crenshaw curves with pride. People were drawn to Everdine due to her long, wavy strawberry-blonde hair, faint freckles and limpid, blue eyes, as well as her outgoing personality. She imparted immediate warmth with a perfect smile and Crenshaw dimples- the same dimples her father used to charm women wherever he went. She was friendly, charismatic and never met a stranger.

Growing up she saw her father a few times a year and they would bond over cards. William thought it was most important for his girls to know how to play a solid game of poker. He made a fortune playing poker, making sure he took care of his girls financially and always sent gifts on special occasions. From the time she overheard her father on a phone call mention something about Willadine getting into Duke, she knew she had to do the same so she could meet her sister. With a name like Willadine she knew it had to be her half-sister. Her dad never spoke of his other children or significant others, keeping his relations perfectly siloed. Everdine's mom had alluded to the possibility that William had more children, but trying to forge any kind of relations with them would be futile. Everdine's mother was also ashamed that her youthful indiscretion would allow her to have something in common with these other women.

It was at Duke University where she became acquainted with Willadine Crenshaw, her half-sister. In true Crenshaw form, Willadine was highly intelligent, had Crenshaw curves, but was hidden underneath her unruly, coppery hair and black rimmed glasses that covered her verdant eyes. Willadine was socially awkward and found comfort between the covers of books. Unlike her sister, Everdine, who wore fine clothes that snuggled her body, she wore baggy clothes making sure not to give a clue to the salacious curves beneath.

Willadine found ease and certainty in numbers, which explained why she majored in economics and physics at Duke. Unlike Everdine, she grew up in a sparse Appalachian mountain community in North Carolina and didn't partake in the fineries of being a woman like her sister. An early gift of encyclopedias from her father sealed her fate as the brain trust of the family. Her rural upbringing imparted her with a strong, billowy southern drawl and her dad would often tease her that she had a bad case of lazy jaw.

William Crenshaw had met Willadine's mother when he was passing through a mill village in North Carolina on his way to a tournament. Their meeting was quite serendipitous. His 1967 Cadillac convertible broke down and she was working at her father's garage as a mechanic. William was so impressed with her acumen, beauty and femininity- all while covered in grease, holding a wrench and wearing coveralls. He made a date with her after he picked up his car and they spent a wonderful passion-filled night together, staying up and talking and making love until the sun came up. Of all the mothers he spent the most time with Willadine's. When Willadine was five he recognized her ability to count cards and would occasionally take her with him to a few private card games.

Everdine had requested Willadine as a roommate on her dorm application to Duke and they were inseparable after that. Both sisters realized that they were only six months apart in age when they first met and openly cussed their father for his roving ways. Both also shared a love for math and butchering the French language. William was so pleased when they told him they had found each other and he would visit them when passing through. Willie and Ever, as they like to be called, were amazed at the differences in their upbringing and diverse backgrounds. They both had very strong-willed, curvaceous mothers, which said a lot about the kind of company William kept and whom he chose to procreate with.

Ever and Willie were graduating from college in a month and had posh internships lined up with an international agency in New York City. They were in the middle of packing up their apartment, excited to take their place in the real world, when William Crenshaw showed up at their door.

"Oh Daddy! What a surprise," Ever said. "Come in."

"Anything wrong, Dad?" Willie asked.

"Girls, I can't tell you how proud I am of you both and what you've accomplished. I know it wasn't easy having an old man like me on the loose. I came here to give you both a present and to share something with you." William was never one to mince his words and he always came quick to the point.

"I want to give you both a gift this summer. You have worked so hard in your studies and you deserve to have some fun. I'm sending you both to Europe after you graduate and have taken the liberty of registering you for the Euro Cards Tour. Your participation is optional. Since you are my daughters I had no problem arranging your entry. I have an apartment in Geneva and you can use it as a base for your travels. All of your expenses will be covered."

"Wow, Daddy, that is amazing. We have to make arrangements with our internship to start at a later time. Hopefully, that won't be a problem," Ever said.

"What do you think Willie?" She asked. "Does it sound like fun to you?"

"I think it will be amazing," said Willie. "We need to work on our French anyway."

"Thank you so much Daddy," both girls crooned in unison as they gave him a hug.

"There is one other thing girls. I have another daughter over there and I'd like you to try and find her if you can. Her name is Marvadine and I have not seen her since she was five years old. I met her mother on a farm outside of Macon, Georgia and that is where they lived until she was five or six. Not long after that the checks I sent her mother started coming back. A poker buddy of mine told me she moved to New Orleans for work and things may not have been so easy for Marva and her mom. Her mother is French Creole and grew up around Jefferson Parrish and likely has relatives there."

"Daddy we always wondered if there was a Marvadine. Does that mean she is the same age as Willie and me?"

"Yes, you girls were all six months apart. I know....I know...it's crazy on my part to be so reckless and I hope to goodness she is doing okay. I love all of my girls. A private investigator I hired told me a little about Marva's background. She lived around the Tremé and Ninth Ward neighborhoods of New Orleans. Her mom was working as a home-care nurse and took care of the maid that worked for her parent's family when she was a child. That area of town can be kind of rough and her mother didn't have an easy way of life. I also learned that Marva attended Tulane on a music scholarship, but dropped out to join the Air Force. She finished her tour in while stationed in Germany and stayed over there. My P.I. told me she was touring around, playing with a brass band and singing. Here is a list of contacts and locations you can use to find her while over there.

The Euro Card Tour will take you to many of these locations anyway if you decide to play in the cities listed here."

"Of course, we will try to find her," Willie said.

"Yea, Daddy, you can count on us."

The kindness of his daughters was more than he could bear. "I'm sorry I wasn't there for you as much as I should have been. You girls deserve so much more. I hope you forgive me one day for the mistakes I made," he said, wiping away his tears.

"Daddy, you were always there if we needed something and we are truly grateful for what we did have."

"Ever is right, Daddy. We never doubted your love and we always knew if we needed you all we had to do was call."

William pulled himself together and gave his girls a hug. "Your mothers did such a wonderful job raising you and I could not be prouder of how well-rounded, smart and beautiful you are. I love you both more than anything."

"We love you, too," Ever replied.

CHAPTER 2

With the excitement of graduation behind them, Willie and Ever boarded a plane from Raleigh to Geneva, via Paris. On the long flight both girls practiced their card skills with Texas hold 'em, blackjack and seven card draw, their personal favorite.

"What do you want to do first when we arrive, Everdine?"

"I think I'd love to go shopping and maybe get my hair done. Wouldn't a trendy European hairstyle be a good way to start our summer?"

"That sounds great. I'm not sure how much progress they would make with my frizzy bird nest I have here," Willie joked.

"Well, Daddy told us we need to pick out a minimum of four cocktail dresses and one evening gown for our tournament events, so that would be a good start."

"You'll have to help me pick out dresses, I've never worn a cocktail dress before. You know so much about fashion and style."

"You'll be a pro by the end of the summer. I'll give you a complete makeover and this will be your summer to sparkle."

"Oh, I can't wait. We may even meet some men, too. Well you might, anyway," Willie said with a false enthusiasm. She had been shy her whole life and was very awkward around the opposite sex. Deep down she wished she could be as outgoing and beautiful as Everdine. For her, love was something she witnessed happening to others.

"Willie, once we get you a new wardrobe and tame your hair with some product, you will have men eating out of the palm of your hand. You have all of the assets, we just need to present them differently. You've got those Crenshaw curves, but they are hidden under layers of baggy clothes. Just leave it to me, sister."

"We never talked about this, but Ever, did you uh....did you do it yet, you know....sleep with a guy?"

"No, I haven't. I think people just assume I have because I was always popular. I've come close, but it just wasn't right. I'd love to lose it this summer with a tall, dark and Swiss hunk." Both girls break out in a fit of giggles.

"I thought you did, too, with all those guys paying such close attention to you in college. How far have you gone?" Willie asked.

"You know I would have told you if I did. I've made out, mostly. The first time was in high school. His name was Andrew and we were both seniors. We had known each other since middle school. I was tutoring him in trigonometry and we would study together. One time when his parents were out of town we were at his house and he kissed me. I was so nervous I felt like my stomach had turned upside down. A few days later I went to his house to watch a movie and we were kissing on his couch. His hands were all over my breasts on top of my shirt and then he laid down on top of me, fully clothed. His breathing was so loud and out of control I thought he was going to explode. While he was on top of me, kissing me, I could feel his erection." Ever smiled at that memory.

Willie was in awe hearing her sister. "Did you touch his penis? Did he touch you?"

"No, not then. We both hadn't any prior experience. A week later we went on a date and went parking in his car. We started making out and again his breathing was so heated and erratic. He completely fogged the windows in two minutes. This time his hand went under my shirt into my bra and felt my breast. He was groaning so loud and kissing me. He asked if he could see my breasts and I decided to show him. I pulled off my shirt and took off my bra and I thought he was having an asthma attack. He told me how beautiful my breasts were and asked if he could kiss them. I said yes. He nervously kissed and fondled my breasts and then I heard him almost growl and I think he came in his pants! Lordy he was so excitable."

"Oh my goodness. Did you go out again?"

"Yes, one last time. He came over to my house a few days later when my mother was in Savannah visiting her parents. We were on my bed making out, both of us nearly naked. He was wearing boxers and I just had my panties on. He was laying on top of me kissing me all over and paying a good amount of attention to my breasts. He asked if he could touch me down there and I said yes. His hand skimmed down my stomach and then he slid one finger inside me. It was a bit of a shock, but felt good. He then asked me if I wanted to touch his penis. I said yes and he laid on his back and slid his boxers down. He had a huge boner. Again, he was nearly breathless and told me to touch it. I reached over and put my hand on it and he immediately started coming all over his stomach."

"Wow!" Willie said, hanging on to every word Everdine spoke.

"That was it. After that we didn't go out anymore, but remained close friends. I was afraid of doing something I would end up regretting. Mother was always lecturing me about boys and getting pregnant. That boy had such a short fuse I don't think we would have ever been able to get that far anyway. After that I just decided I wanted to wait until I was in college or more responsible enough to handle what comes with having sex. A lot of guys were intimidated by me, though. This will be our summer of love, Willie!"

"I hope so. I have never even kissed a boy and would love to meet someone. Unlike you, I didn't have guys lined up at my door, so my momma never had to lecture me on boys, even though she made sure I was on birth control from the start."

"I did have the opportunity to date a lot of guys, but I'd always think of how sad mom was sometimes at being a single parent and didn't want to get serious. I never had a good example of what a healthy relationship was like. She opined that it was natural to be curious at my age, but didn't want me to act on it. I'd just block it out as much as I could. What did your mother say about men, Willie?"

"Oh gosh, just about nothing. She'd only say that one day I would make some man very happy."

"I'm sure you will. What a nice thing to say. My mother was only cynical when it came to men."

"You know, Ever, I always assumed you lost your virginity when we met in college. Guys were always so drawn to you."

"I was so glad to finally meet you and I wanted us to have our time. I did date a few guys seriously- remember Langston? I think I was too outspoken for most guys. Also, the thought of falling in love scared the hell out of me- still does. It was fun enough hanging out with you and studying; Otherwise, I would have gone to way too many keg parties." Both girls laugh at that thought. They both had such a heavy course load with double majors and partying was not a priority.

"That is funny we are so different on love. I can't wait to fall in love. For me, I guess the prospect of it not having been so attainable makes me want it more."

"You have no idea how gorgeous you are do you, Willie? Any man would be crazy not to fall in love with you."

"You are the best sister! I'm so glad we are starting out on this adventure together."

"Me, too!" Both sisters shared a quick hug.

After chatting for hours, watching a movie and sleeping a little, their plane arrived in Paris. A quick check through customs and the girls rushed to make their connection to Geneva. Once they were settled in their seats their attention returned to their father.

"Did you ever go with daddy to any poker games?" Willie asked.

"Mother wouldn't let me travel with daddy. She was worried I would encounter some unsavory characters and just worried in general. Did you go with him?"

"Yes, I went a handful of times. I first went with him when I was five or six. He had me counting cards for him a few times," Willie giggled.

"No way! Did you ever get caught?"

"Not one single time. Those men didn't fathom that a little girl could count cards. I use to signal him with my hair."

"What was it like to watch him play cards?" Ever asked.

"He was amazing to watch. I learned a great deal from him, although, I didn't quite share his passion and thrill for the game. He always romanticized poker and traveling to Europe. Now here we are."

"Yes, he did. That is the reason I studied French. Hearing him talk about Paris, Monte Carlo and Geneva made me want to learn the language."

"Me, too," Willie said. "The first private poker match I went with daddy to had a few businessmen from France and Germany. Several kids were in tow for this match since it was in the summer. One of the men brought his son along and he was probably twelve. I had the biggest crush on him- a serious case of puppy love. We played poker while our fathers were playing and used our toys as currency when we ran out of pennies. I bled the poor boy dry. I won his toy cars and book, Le Petit Prince.

He was so upset. I remember wanting to give him back his toys, but our fathers were adamant about us keeping our bets. One of the rules of playing cards, I guess- never back down or welsh on a bet. I was able to sneak him back his cars, but kept the book. In fact, I brought it with me. It's what inspired me to learn French."

"That is amazing Willie. You have seen a whole other side of daddy that I would love to have seen."

The girls arrived in Geneva shortly after lunch and took a cab to their father's apartment. Neither girl had traveled to Europe and they both reveled in the new sounds and sights that welcomed them. So many new experiences awaited them in Geneva.

The drive from the airport to the apartment only took fifteen minutes. The sights of their new city and surrounding mountains greeted them along the way.

When the sisters arrived at their father's apartment inside the Hotel Valle they discovered a lovely welcome basket. He had thought of everything. It included vouchers for boutiques where they could shop, invitations to the Euro Card Ball, a helicopter ride over Geneva and the surrounding Alps, and bottles of wine, chocolate, champagne and other goodies. Anytime William Crenshaw did something he didn't think small.

The apartment was beautiful with large windows and views of the Alps. It had two master suites, complete with en suite bathrooms. The furnishings were muted, yet cozy. A white palette was accented with pops of color throughout the apartment. It was obvious that their father had it professionally decorated.

Not long after they arrived they had a visitor at the door. Both sisters were anxious with excitement since they did not know a soul in Geneva.

Ever opened the door to an older man, appearing to be in his fifties. He was dressed in a black suit, white shirt and black tie, and had graying hair at his temples.

"My name is Bernard Valentin. Mr. Crenshaw hired me to drive you during your stay in Geneva."

"Hi there Mr. Valentin. My name is Everdine Crenshaw." Ever extended her hand to the driver and he took her hand and posed as if to kiss the back of her hand.

"Please, Mademoiselle, call me Bernard. And you must be Willadine Crenshaw," he uttered with his thick French accent.

"Yes, sir," she said, extending her hand, "please call me Willie."

Bernard took her hand, giving it the same careful treatment as he did Everdine's. He obviously had excellent training and manners.

"But, is not Willie the name of a man? I should prefer to call you by your given name, non?"

"I like Willie, but if you have to, you may call me Willadine."

"Oui, Mademoiselle."

"So where are you taking us, Bernard?" Ever asked with too much excitement.

"I shall take you wherever you like to go, Mademoiselle. My services are at your request, courtesy of Mr. Crenshaw. As long as you are in Geneva, I will be your chauffeur. I understand you just arrived and may be exhausted from your trip. How may I help you today?"

"That is so nice of you. I think Willie and I would like to get some lunch and then see a little of the neighborhood before turning in. We would normally love to walk, but we are kind of tired after our long trip. What do you think Willie?"

"I would also love some lunch and to see the neighborhood. How exciting! This will be my first ride in a cab."

"Very good ladies. I will be waiting at my car in front of the building, so just come down when you are ready. And please, call me Bernard."

"See you in a minute, Bernard." Ever's eyes got huge and they both screamed and jumped in each other's arms as soon as they closed the door behind him. They went to freshen up in the bathroom and changed into some nicer shoes, more suited for dining and not hauling luggage through airports.

Both girls were astounded to find Bernard standing beside a black Mercedes limo. He opened the door, welcoming them into the car. Again, they were moved by their father's generosity and jarred by the lifestyle he was privy to.

"Ladies, what kind of food shall you like to have?"

"I think we want something casual, right Willie?"

"Yes, very light."

"Very good. I know just the place." Bernard drove for about 10 minutes and took them to a small bistro with a lovely view of Lake Geneva. Although Everdine was more worldly than Willadine, she had never experienced such a magical place as Geneva and marveled at the lake being cradled in front of the

Alps. The sisters just absorbed the beauty in silence, trying to take in as much as they could.

After lunch Bernard gave them a guided tour of their neighborhood and also showed them were the best shopping was located. They could not wait to get a new wardrobe and try out some French perfume. It was early evening when Bernard returned the sisters back to their apartment. He made plans to take them shopping the next day and then cordially departed. After such a long trip and an exciting first day in Switzerland the girls went right to sleep.

As they were stirring out of their bed at 9 a.m. the buzzer to the apartment sounded. The concierge informed them they had a delivery to send up. In a few minutes a lady was at their door with two bags of groceries and some fresh bakery items for breakfast. But more importantly, she came with fresh coffee. They didn't even have time yet to see what was in the kitchen.

"Bonjour Mademoiselles. I am Irena and I do the cleaning and shopping twice a week for Mr. Crenshaw. He has instructed me to bring fresh groceries to you. Here on the counter is a note pad and if you need anything, please write it down and I'll be sure to get it on my next visit. You may also call me. Thank you and welcome to Suisse."

"Thank you so much," Willie said as Irena left the groceries and her card on the counter before leaving. Willie and Ever were still trying to figure out this part of their father's life. Until their trip to Europe they had only seen him on their turf. They never really thought much about what William did when he wasn't visiting.

Bernard picked the girls up after breakfast and took them shopping all day. They were amazed at how many lovely clothes they found. They bought several cocktail dresses and matching shoes, perfume and finer ensembles for when they were at the poker table. Tomorrow evening was the reception for the Euro Card Tour and they were not sure what they should wear. In the middle of having a discussion on what is appropriate attire Bernard interrupted them.

"Pardon, ladies, I could not help but to hear your dilemma. For tomorrow's reception you should wear a cocktail dress. You will get to meet all of the other players on tour and will be served drinks and hors d'ourves. There will also be a band and floor for dancing. I hope this answers your questions."

"Thank you, Bernard. You are such a big help and a joy to have around. I don't know what we would do without you."

"You are welcome, Miss Everdine. I assure you the pleasure is all mine. Also, you will need an evening gown for the ball this Saturday and for the Finale."

Bernard helped them to their apartment with all of their packages and the girls gave him a hug before he left. He was not accustomed to such a show of affection, but enjoyed it. The girls were young, innocent and had such an indomitable enthusiasm. They were growing on him and he imagined if he had daughters he would want them to be just like the Crenshaw girls. William Crenshaw was a good friend of his, and one to which he was deeply indebted. He promised him he would look after his girls while they were in Geneva.

The next day Ever and Willie were nervous about the cocktail reception. They had forgotten about getting an appointment at a salon and found it very difficult to find someone that could take them on such a short notice. After calling all over Geneva they decided to ask Bernard if he could help.

"Ever I'm calling Bernard. Your hair will be fine, but mine is a hot mess."

Willie dialed Bernard's number and he was surprised to hear from her.

"Yes, Miss Willadine how may I help you?"

"We are in desperate need of a hair stylist. We forgot to make an appointment and we would like to get our hair done before the reception tonight." Willie said concerned.

"Yes, it may be difficult to find someone at this late hour. Let me make a few calls and I'll see what I can do. You will hear from me soon."

Willie and Ever were praying that Bernard could get them in somewhere. They were desperate- especially Willie and her wild locks. In less than two minutes Bernard rang her back.

"Oui Madame, I have found a stylist for you and Miss Everdine. I shall pick you up in five minutes."

The sisters were waiting on the sidewalk for Bernard when he arrived. Such kindness could not be left to chance they thought. When they arrived at the salon both girls were immediately carted off to their stylists. The man who was attending to Willadine just shook his head when attempting to run his fingers through Willadine's hair.

"Never have I had such hair in this salon," he exclaimed.

Willie felt so uneasy. She had dealt with her frizzy, reddish hair her whole life and only dreamed of having smooth, long hair like Everdine. Her only recourse was to let it grow and keep it locked up in a pony tail or thick braid.

While the girls were having their nails done they both had their heads wrapped in towels getting a deep conditioning treatment. The two stylists were across the room arguing and pointing at Willadine. Their discussion seemed very heated at times and finally they came over to talk to her.

"Listen, Mademoiselle. We really don't have enough time to straighten your hair with a relaxer before your event tonight. The chemical would also smell bad. We would like to cut long layers and then use a product on to define your curls so they fall nicely. You will look sexy."

Although Willie was disappointed, she could not argue. It wasn't the first time she came up against her hair and lost. After another hour the girls were ready to leave the salon and get ready for the cocktail reception. Ever's hair looked fabulous and sleek. They had cut some layers in her hair and blew it out smooth and gave her big soft waves that cupped her face and shoulders. Willie looked like a babe with her long, layered, curly look. They used some smoothing cream and a diffuser with a finishing spray to get her hair to form perfect, compact curls. They twisted her hair around at the ends and pinned it up into an elegant up-do with a few escaping tendrils. With this hairstyle her eyes took center stage and it made the freckles across the bridge of her nose stand out.

Bernard bestowed many compliments on their new hair styles and dropped them off back at their apartment. Willie could hardly believe what she saw in the mirror. The swept up curls bounced light off Willie's hair, showing her natural auburn-golden highlights. Ever was use to this kind of treatment and was in her element. The biggest decision now was choosing what dress to wear to the reception.

"What do you think the other girls will be wearing, Ever?"

"I don't know, but we will look very demure in whatever we choose. I think you should wear the dark purple, single shoulder dress. With your hair up like that it will really show off your face, shoulders and beautiful skin. I wish I had your skin. It's stunning."

"Thanks, sissy. Well, if I'm going to be showing a little leg with my dress then you had better wear your short one, too- the black strapless one. Your legs are to die for."

"Well you have the exact same legs I do except mine are just one inch longer."

Both sisters giggle and finish getting dressed. Willie was about five and a half feet tall and Ever was just a tad more. They put on very light evening-toned make up and simple accessories. Willie replaced her glasses with contacts and dressed up her emerald eyes with some mascara. Ever was right- they both had stunning curvy legs, the kind that men wrote songs about and fought wars over. One thing was for certain, the Crenshaw curves were dangerous tonight.

CHAPTER 3

Bernard picked the girls up promptly at 7 p.m. and drove up the mountain to a palace nestled in the foothills of the Alps with sensational lake views. The palace was steeped in elegance and romance, bidding a night that the sisters would not forget. The girls were escorted inside and checked in at the registration table.

"Mademoiselles we have you checked in and would like to invite you to participate in our roulette dance. It is just a way for us to share our generosity to those in need."

The girls agreed, but had no idea exactly what they were agreeing to. They were certain they could spare a contribution to charity since their father had been so generous to them with this trip.

"Great Mademoiselles, here are your numbers for the roulette, so do not lose it. We will collect you later."

"Merci," replied both Willie and Ever. They entered the beautifully appointed ballroom of the palace and were shocked. All eyes turned to them as they entered through the ornate, Baroque period doors. Where were all the women? Both girls stopped in their tracks, visibly dazed at the sea of men before them. Handsome men. Gorgeous men. European men. Ever pasted a polite smile on her face and nodded at the men, who raised their glasses to them. She stepped forward into the room and Willie remained a statue, feet firmly planted, mouth gaping, Switzerland's first petrified woman. Ever leaned over to Willie and calmly prodded her with a firm smile.

"Just follow me Willie and we'll go get a drink. I'm sure we came into the wrong room or something, but it would be impolite to turn and leave."

"I'll be fine. I've just never seen so many men in one place before. They look so nice. Very nice."

Everdine pulled Willie over to the bar and ordered a champagne for them both. They clung together and took up a conversation with one of the other guests, Gerard, from Belgium. Both girls thought that if the other men here were equally as boring as him they would not have to worry about succumbing to their good looks. Slowly, but surely, other women began to trickle into the ballroom and they felt more at ease.

While Everdine was chatting up a small group of men, Willie caught the gaze of the most handsome man she had ever seen standing across the room. Her heart stopped beating when he returned her gaze and smiled. She immediately blushed, thinking that his warm reception was intended for someone else nearby and looked around to check. Nope! Dark hair styled in a small pompadour framed his sculpted face and firm lips. His shoulders were perfectly square on his tall frame and his face looked rugged and handsome with a slight cleft chin. Willie thought that he could very well be the perfect male and that somewhere Greek gods were weeping. He turned to her again, smiling with cerulean blue eyes, nodding at her, causing Willie to blush and scatter.

"Everdine, come here," she motioned to her sister. Ever excused herself and joined Willie. "Don't be obvious, but look at that man standing over there by the fireplace," she said with her back turned to him.

"Wow, he is dreamy and I love his curly hair. Look at his dimples when he smiles"

"What?....No..he doesn't have curly hair," Willie said, turning around to look. "It's the man beside him. The one curly is talking to." Ever saw him, but had her sights on the man he was talking to. He was angelic looking with his beautiful raven-colored hair. His eyes were piercing and made his whole face light up. Best of all, she noticed, was how he filled out his suit.

"Oh Willie, your guy looks so serious, but he is very handsome. Why don't you go talk to him?"

"I could never do that. He is definitely someone to admire from afar."

"You are acting so silly. I was talking with Veronique, the location coordinator for the tour, and she said that only three of the women here tonight are on the poker tour, so the other women you see here are from the Ladies Auxiliary helping out with the charity event. I can't believe there are so few women on tour."

"That just means more men for us," Willie giggled.

"You mean more men that you can admire from afar, right?"

"Oh stop it. I need to go on the veranda and get some fresh air. See you in a minute." Willie walked out to the veranda, grabbing a glass of red wine on the way. What she saw in front of her was a sensory overload. The sun had set over the Alps and the lights of the city and valley below were dancing around the lake. The air was heavy and cool as the night fell, filled with sweet smells from the garden surrounding the veranda. Willie was amazed that at this moment, this place, this was her life.

Every year Anton and Gabriel Delacroix came to the same cocktail reception and saw the same women. The two handsome brothers discussed which women they would like to bed and keep between their sheets for the summer while on tour. Although business engagements would not allow them to participate in as many tournaments as they would like, they still enjoyed the plethora of willing ladies such tournaments attracted. For them it was about sex and nothing else. It was hard enough to run the family business while playing in tournaments, and being encumbered by a relationship was out of the question. For them, the Ladies Auxiliary was nothing more than a source of beautiful, consenting women, willing to serve their needs in exchange for a few nice meals and attendance to the best parties across Europe. It was time to start charming the ladies and Anton zeroed in on the new face wearing the dark purple dress that had stared at him across the room. He noticed how she blushed when their eyes met earlier and it intrigued him, as well as her plentiful curves.

Willie was enjoying the view and tranquility of the surroundings on the veranda. The vagaries of the temperate climate had her unprepared for such cool evenings and her bare arms felt a light chill. When she heard foot steps behind her she froze, unable to turn and see if it was him, the most beautiful man she had met eyes with moments ago. Her timid nature around men prevented her from acknowledging his presence. He stopped very close behind her, causing the hair on her neck to stand. He was so close she could smell his woodsy, fresh cologne. Nervously, she brought her hand to her neck, clutching at it.

"The most beautiful things in the world cannot be seen or touched.....," he said with a seductively beautiful French accent.

"....they are felt with the heart," Willadine finished his quote, and with a smile, turned to see from the corner of her eye the handsome man she had admired from afar.

"Yes, ma chère, that is correct. I have been using that quote by Antoine de Saint-Exupéry on ladies for the last five years and you are the only one who recognized it. Hello, my name is Anton Delacroix." He moved beside her, holding his hand out waiting to greet her.

She was able to make a half-hearted, nervous laugh. "Hey there," she said, holding her hand out, "my name is Willadine." Anton took her hand and and brushed a kiss over the back of it. Willie dropped her head, blushed and pulled her hand back instinctively.

"You are American, oui?"

"Yes. My sister and I are on the tour this summer," Willie said, rubbing her arms and looking toward the view, unable to meet his eyes. Just being in his presence made her heart race. His smell and his voice wreaked of sex appeal. She had never been so drawn to a man before and it was unsettling how her insides clenched being near him.

"Please, ma chère, take my coat," Anton said, placing his jacket over her shoulders, letting his hands run up and down her arms. His warm, masculine-scented jacket closed around her, embracing her senses.

"Thank you," she said coyly.

"Will you and your sister be playing in Monte Carlo in a few weeks?"

"Yes, we are so excited since it is our first time visiting."

"There is a lot to do there and I'd be glad to give you a tour if time permits."

"That would be lovely." Willie was thankful that it was almost dark enough to camouflage her flushed face. She could feel her knees growing weak beneath her. Even though it was dark on the veranda, the lights were just bright enough to make out her rosy cheeks. Anton had never met anyone like Willie. For someone who was so beautiful, she seemed unsure of herself and quite bashful. From afar she looked fairly common, but up close her prepossessing features were unmistakable. Her eyes were the most luscious green color with splashes of amber mixed in. He thought it was comical that the one lady wearing the least revealing gown held his attention over more scantily clad women. How her porcelain face took color when blushing was endearing.

"I should go back inside and check on my sister. It was very nice meeting you, Anton." She slid his jacket off and held it out for him. "You are welcome to keep it if you need to."

"Thanks, but I'll be fine inside." He slid his arms in the jacket. "Oh, your collar needs to be adjusted," she said motioning to his jacket where it clipped the collar of his shirt. "Do you mind fixing it for me?" Anton could easily take care of it himself, but he wanted her to.

"Sure," Willie said. She reached up on her tiptoes, her hands guiding under his jacket around his neck. Using both hands she was able to smooth out his lapel and collar. The proximity to his glorious mouth was paralyzing. Anton didn't bend down enough to accommodate their height difference. He wanted to feel her close to him. He could see her eyes focusing on his mouth and feel her hitched breathing against his neck, which instantly made him hard. He could tell she was attracted to him. As much as he wanted to kiss her, he knew it was too soon.

"It was very lovely to meet you...Willadine, and I look forward to seeing you on tour." He extended his arm back toward the ballroom and she took the lead. She definitely was not like any woman he had ever met. She seemed very simple and very down to earth. Anton went back inside and dished to his brother about the sisters on tour.

"Gabriel, I just met the woman I am going to bed while on tour. She is a little shy, but has a body to die for. She's here with her sister. It couldn't be more perfect."

"Yes, Veronique introduced me to the other sister. Her name is Everdine and she seems like a very lovely young lady. The other men have been crawling all over her, so I arranged with Veronique that we all have a little brother-sister connection for the roulette dance."

"You are so damn clever, Gabriel."

"Don't you get tired of the same routine every summer, Anton? We meet the ladies, sleep with them, go our separate ways and then do it over again every summer. This is getting old."

"Speak for yourself, brother. I'd much rather have a warm, voluptuous woman in my bed than going it alone."

"Now that doesn't mean I'll turn away an opportunity if it presents itself. Americans are very easy from what I've heard."

"That's the spirit, Gabriel. Bed them and then beat their sweet little asses in poker." Both men shared a deep laugh and turned their attention to the emcee.

"Ladies and gentlemen! Welcome to our annual cocktail reception kickoff for the ECT. We are supporting a great cause this evening with our roulette dance and will begin the game shortly. For those of you that are new to the tour I'll explain what this entails. When you checked in you received a number that corresponds with a number on the roulette board. The Gentleman that has put his name on the number of the roulette board that matches the number you were given when you entered will share a dance with you this evening and will also be your date for the Poker Ball this Saturday evening if you are inclined to do so. Let's begin the festivities."

The crowd broke into a round of applause and a panic-stricken Willie looked at her sister. "You mean we have to dance with a man? I just don't know if I can do that, Everdine."

"Willie, you need to put your big girl bloomers on and just breathe. You'll never fall in love if you don't put yourself out there. Don't waste this beautiful dress, your killer legs, great hairstyle, and most of all, this magical night. You can do this." Willie told her sister about meeting Anton and how she nearly melted at his feet. As long as she didn't have to dance with Anton she would likely survive dancing with with another member of the opposite sex.

Her sister was right and Willie knew she had to gather up all of her steel resolve and start taking some chances. Easier said than done. All of her life she excelled at the black and white areas- it was the gray areas that scared the hell out of her. Her gray areas were matters of the heart and understanding men.

Before the girls realized it they were the last two ladies to be selected in the draw. To Willie's horror there were only two men left, Anton and his brother Gabriel.

"Ladies and Gentlemen, the last selection in our roulette draw is a brother-sister duo on tour this summer. Anton Delacroix and number 36. Which one of you two ladies is number 36?"

Ever had to nudge Willie forward to claim her tall, handsome prize. And since her and Gabriel were the only two left, they politely acknowledged each other. The emcee announced the first dance and the small band at the front of the room started playing La Vie En Rose.

"Mademoiselle, s'il vous plait." As Anton led Willie to the dance floor he thought it akin to leading a lamb to slaughter. This coy, little, American minx would be calling his name in bed after the ball on Saturday. By the looks of her sister, Gabriel may even get lucky tonight.

Across the room Everdine and Gabriel were dancing very closely. She was so taken by his devilish good-looks that she didn't notice how he was encroaching on her person in every way possible. She couldn't get enough of his dark, curly hair that spilled over his forehead, his cerulean blue eyes and broad, full lips. When he laughed he had the most gorgeous dimples and slightly cleft chin like his older brother.

Willadine was so nervous she had to fight the urge to throw up. When Anton took her hand she felt butterflies throughout her whole body. He put his arm around her lower back and as she lay her hand on Anton's upper arm a gasp of air filled her lungs involuntarily. Oh my! He was large and taut underneath his tuxedo. She began to wonder what he would look like naked and started blushing furiously and thought maybe she'd better imagine him in a swim suit first. It horrified her that he may guess where her thoughts were headed.

"What are you thinking, ma chère, that has added such color to your cheeks?"

Willie could not look into his eyes. She turned her head to the side and let her eyes wander the room. The shock of having this hunk of a man in her arms was too much. It was all she could do to control her breathing.

"I'm just not a very good dancer or at least it's not something I prefer to do. Having a night out is great, but I'd much rather spend the night at home in bed."

As if on cue, the lights dimmed and Anton pulled her closer, leaning down to speak. "I know exactly how you feel ma chère, but we can't leave yet. It would be impolite, non?"

Willadine was frantic thinking he may have misunderstood her. She could never take this man to bed- that much she knew. "No Anton, that is not what I meant. I'm so.."

Laughing, he interrupted her before she had a chance to self destruct. "Ma chère, please, I was only making a joke," he said pulling her even closer. "You are such a bundle of nerves my sweet, little lamb," he said in a low growl. "Someone needs to kiss you senseless, and as much as I would like to, I'm afraid you would catch fire." His words of ardor stirred up butterflies in Willie's stomach. Shocked would be too light of a word to describe what was happening with Anton.

"You are a very beautiful woman Willadine and the tone of your skin is the envy of every woman here. Surely you have been told this many times," he said, stroking the back of her small hand with his thumb.

Willadine could hardly construct a coherent thought. There were too many firsts happening this evening that she didn't know where to begin. "Th..Thank you, Anton. You are very sweet. My friend Kevin use to tell me my skin looked like bread dough and I never knew what he meant exactly. Maybe all of these years I had a false impression." All Anton could think was that this woman had a false impression of him. No woman had ever called him sweet. Sexy, yes. Callous, yes. Insatiable, yes. And his all-time favorite- bastard, yes.

"So were you and this Kevin very close?"

"Yes, we were inseparable throughout high school and then we went off to different colleges and just fell out of touch." Kevin was her best friend and study buddy. They were in the Beta Club together and shared a love of math. She always thought that if she had a brother, he would be just like Kevin.

Anton was thinking that she may have had her heart broken and that explained her coy behavior. She was guarding her heart. Too bad that he would break it all over again this summer.

"I can assure you, ma chère, your skin is far from the likes of bread dough." Anton laughed silently at the thought. "It is as pale as a gardenia," he said, bringing their joined hands up to her jaw, skimming her cheek with his thumb. "And just as soft," he whispered, returning their hands. "And just as sweet," he said, brushing his lips briefly across her temple.

His lips set her skin on fire. She had never felt such pressure in her throat, her chest and between her legs. Just the thought of his lips touching her in any place sent desire pulsing through her body. She had to get away from him, but was too frightened to move. Maybe she didn't want to move. She wanted to feel his lips again and again. Without realizing it she was stroking Anton's upper arm, appreciating every muscle that her hand caressed.

Anton longed to have his hands all over her body. He wanted to see her naked and taste her smooth, pallid skin from head to toe. Never had he wanted a woman so much. He had been with plenty of women and there was always a mutual desire, but what he felt for Willadine was a wildfire. He had an erection since he first spoke with her on the veranda.

The song was coming to and end and Anton softly kissed Willadine on her forehead, holding her close. They reveled in the scent of one another. She stepped back and finally met his gaze. For a moment there was no one else in the room. The honesty in her expression nearly stunned him. Her piercing green eyes could see right through him. At first he thought it was sweet that she was too shy to look him in the eye- now he knew it was lethal. Their eyes were drawing each other, lost in pools of desire and passion. Realization of what this woman did to him brought on fear. For the first time in his life Anton was afraid of a woman.

As the next song started Anton took the opportunity to pull himself together and remembered that he was in charge and he called the shots. This woman would be taking no liberties with his emotions.

"Thank you for the lovely dance, Willadine. May I get you a drink?"

"I..."

Before she could answer they heard a ruckus across the room. "You scoundrel! Get your filthy hands off me." The outburst was followed by a smacking sound. Everdine had smacked Gabriel across the cheek. Both Anton and Willie looked on, astonished. "Oh my word. I have to go to Everdine."

Willie turned heel and followed Everdine out to the veranda. She was fuming mad. "Ever, what's wrong?"

"I'll tell you what's wrong. That filthy frenchman tried to feel me up on the dance floor. It never fails that if a woman has curves in all the right places a man feels like it is an open invitation to explore. He groped my ass in front of everyone and humiliated me. I hate him."

"Oh Ever, I'm so sorry."

"Do you know what he said to me?"

"No, what?"

"He said that if I didn't want to go to bed with him tonight there were plenty of women here that would." Everdine scowled and deep down she knew it was true. He was a gorgeous creature. Any woman could get lost in his twinkling blue eyes and firm arms.

"I told him that no self-respecting woman would ever do that and that the only way he could get a woman to look up to him was if he was lying on top of her."

"Noooo, Ever, you didn't say that."

"You're damn straight I did. He's lucky he can still walk. That French bastard!"

"I am so proud of you, Ever. I wish I had half of your bravado."

"I just need to cool off and calm down before I go back in there. Enough about Gabriel. How was it with Anton?"

Willie thought that was a great question. How was it with Anton? It was exciting, thrilling and mesmerizing, but she knew she had better tame her answer a bit. "It was very nice. I didn't throw up on him and he was very pleasant to be around, but he scares the hell out of me."

"Did he try anything with you? I will kick his ass, too."

"No he didn't, Everdine. He was actually very sweet. There is something about him that I just can't put a finger on."

"Probably that his brother is a pig."

Both girls giggled and went back inside for drinks and hors d'ourves. While Everdine was babbling about everything under the sun, Willie stole a few glances at Anton across the room and he returned the sentiment. She was in deep trouble with this man. Anton knew she was not very experienced and she wasn't typical of the kind of lady he was attracted to, but he was irrevocably drawn to her. Across the room Anton raised his glass to Willadine and she proffered him a smile, confirming her quiet allure to him. Just as Ever was beginning to calm down, Gabriel strolled over to Anton with two women on his arm wearing nothing but scraps of fabric. Ever got a glimpse of him and spat out another scowl and then grabbed Willie's arm. "Come on, Willie, let's leave. I can't stand to be in the same room with him."

"Of course, Ever. Let's have Bernard take us out for some real food." Ever didn't understand how she could be repulsed by someone and turned on by them at the same time. There was no question how gorgeous he was with his dark, wavy hair and charming smile, but his foul mouth and roving hands did little to elevate his handsome face.

CHAPTER 4

Willie and Ever were waiting in front of the palace for Bernard to bring the car around when Anton approached them.

"May I speak to you in seclusion Willadine...I mean, in private, please?" Willie looked at her sister for approval and she shooed her away to talk.

Anton placed his hand around her waist and led her a short distance from Ever. "Ma chère, were you going to leave without saying goodbye to me?"

"I'm sorry, Anton. I had a wonderful time meeting you tonight and dancing. Everdine is kind of upset and I didn't want to leave her alone," she said, still dancing around his eyes.

"Of course, I understand. Sometimes my brother can be the ass of a horse, you know."

"Yes, I heard," Willie said, with a firm mouth.

Anton lifted her chin with his thumb and index finger and tucked a strand of her fallen locks behind her ear. "Hey, chérie, look at me. I am not my brother, understand?" Willie placed her hand on his arm and glanced up to meet his eyes. "Yes Anton, I understand." As soon as their eyes connected the pull between them was magnetic. Anton was not expecting to be so stirred up over her, but he couldn't stay away.

"Good. According to the roulette we have a date for the ball on Saturday night. What time shall I pick you up, chérie?" He stroked her cheeks with his thumbs, rendering her awestruck. "Your sister can ride with us, too," he added.

"Is it okay if I call you tomorrow and let you know? I'd like to give Ever some time to simmer down."

"Oui, chérie." Anton pulled a contact card out of his wallet and placed it in Willie's palm, folding her fingers over the card and kissing the back of her hand. "I look forward to hearing from you. Good evening, ma chère. Sweet dreams."

"Goodnight, Anton."

Stroking her face with his right hand, he kissed her sweet and long on her other cheek. To Willie it felt like he was making love to her face. He dropped her hand and walked back up the stairs to the palace.

Willie joined her sister who was just as awestruck. "Oh my gosh, Willie, he likes you a lot." She just smiled at Ever while some color came to her cheeks. "You like him, too, don't you?"

"I'm afraid I do, Everdine. All he has to do is speak, really, and I'm unable to form an intelligent thought. He has this sexy accent, he smells incredible and when he touches me.....oh, I am so screwed."

"Too bad his brother is such a jerk," Ever said, shaking her head.

Bernard pulled up and opened the car door for the sisters. "Ladies, did you have a nice time this evening?"

"We did, Bernard. Thank you," Willie answered.

He got in the limo and started driving back down the mountain. "Do you wish to go back to the apartment or shall I take you somewhere?" Bernard asked.

"I think we need some ice cream, Bernard."

"And maybe some cake, too." Everdine added.

"Very well ladies. Tough night, was it?"

"Indeed it was," Ever mused.

Bernard meandered his way down the mountain and into the city while the girls continued talking. "What did Anton want with you while we were waiting?"

"He wanted to tell me goodbye and ask if he could pick me for the ball on Saturday. He said he would like to take both of us if you are interested. I told him I'd call tomorrow and let him know."

"That is wonderful, Willadine. He seems like such a gentleman."

"He is, but I'm so nervous around him. We're very different. He is handsome, worldly and sophisticated, and I'm....I'm just Willadine."

"That's right, Willie, he is different and that does not mean he's better. Money and possessions don't make up for love and experiences. You graduated from the top of your class and no amount of money or world class can buy that."

"Everdine did I ever tell you that you were the best sister in the whole world?"

"It never hurts to hear it again." They both shared a laugh and leaned on each other, locking arms until the limo came to a stop.

"Ladies, we have arrived at the Italian Bistro. I recommend the cinnamon gelato, but you really can't make a bad choice. It's all delicious." The girls medicate the excitement of the evening with three scoops of gelato and got some tiramisu to go. By the time they arrived back at the apartment they were pooped.

"Well you sure screwed yourself with the American, didn't you?" Anton chided his brother. "What happened exactly that you made her so angry she struck you?"

"I completely misread her, or misunderstood her- that's what happened. I thought with a body like that she was a done deal and when I put my hands on her beautiful, round ass, she let me have it. She was not as accommodating as I'd hoped. What about you and the other sister? I hope you had more luck."

"She is not anything like I thought or expected her to be, either. I definitely want to take her to bed, but it will require some work. She seems very coy, but there is such an honesty in how she carries herself. She is different from any other girl I've met. Since you royally pissed off her sister, you need to fix it or we'll both have a very boring summer."

Anton and Gabriel hadn't accounted for the Crenshaw sisters as their summer conquests. As both brothers plotted and planned on bedding Willie and Ever, the sisters were none the wiser.

Jet lag, parties, shopping and sexy frenchmen had taken their toll on the girls and they went to bed as soon as they got back to the apartment that evening. Willie lay awake trying to reconcile how fast she became so smitten with Anton and had trouble understanding why he seemed to be interested in her. She couldn't stop thinking about his sexy accent, dapper good-looks and the way he smelled when she danced closely with him. Everdine on the other hand was confused. Yes, Gabriel acted like a pig, but she was still attracted to him. There seemed to be so much tension between them that she thought briefly about giving him a dose of his own medicine. That would show him.

A beautiful Geneva morning greeted the girls after a long night's sleep. The ball was only two days away and they still had to find a dress for the occasion. Irena arrived to clean the apartment and brought some fresh croissants.

"Thanks for the croissants, Irena. I don't think Willie and I will ever get tired of chocolate croissants and coffee over here."

"You are welcome, girls. Enjoy your day." Irena left the girls to savor their breakfast.

"Are you still upset about last night, Everdine?"

"No, I'm over it. I can even be cordial to Gabriel, but if he values his limbs and the small thing between his legs, he had better not touch me."

"Ha! Now that's a vision. What about the ball? Do you want to go with Anton and me? I will call him at lunch and let him know."

"Last night Sven from Sweden asked me out, so maybe I'll call him and see if he wants to go to the ball. I think you and Anton should go together- without a third wheel."

"I'll be so nervous. I was tossing and turning all night thinking about him. You'll have to help me pick out an evening gown. I have no idea what to get. That reminds me, Bernard made us an appointment at the salon Saturday morning so we'll have plenty of time to get our hair done."

"We need to get ready to hit the shops then. I'll see if Bernard can pick us up in an hour."

As the girls were getting ready someone rang the door. A gentleman is stood in the hall with two vases of flowers. "Please, come in," Ever said.

"Oui, madame. I have a delivery for Miss Everdine and Miss Willadine."

"Set them down on the table." Everdine directed him over to the dinner table. The delivery man set the flowers down and Everdine tipped him a few Francs.

"Willadine, the bouquet of white flowers is for you and this bouquet of yellow roses has my name on the card."

"You must have made quite an impression on Sven or maybe they are from daddy. You read your card first Ever."

"Okay, let me look." Ever's eyes got as large as golf balls as she read the card.

"What is it Ever? Tell me."

"It's from Gabriel," she said, a little stunned. "Here goes. Dear Everdine, I apologize for my reprehensible behavior last night. You are a lovely lady and I hope you please forgive me. Truly, Gabriel. He also left his phone number."

"That is a sweet gesture, Everdine. He sounds very sincere."

"It is very thoughtful, but I'm still keeping my distance from him. Like I said, I have no problem being cordial to him. Now read your card."

"Goodness. I'm so nervous. I've never had a guy send me flowers before. Dearest Willadine, It was such a pleasure meeting you last night. Your beauty, smile and touch are missed. I look forward to seeing you Saturday evening. Yours, Anton."

"Wow, Willie, he has it bad for you. That is so sweet."

"I think I'm going to be sick. Should I call him now or at lunch time?"

"You really should call him as soon as you get the flowers. That would be appropriate."

Willie took in a large breath of air and then exhaled. "I'm going to my room to call him. Be right back."

"You'll do fine. Remember to breathe," Ever joked.

Willadine nervously punched in Anton's phone number and paused before sending. Two rings.

"Oui, Delacroix"

"Hi Anton, it's Willadine"

"Ma chère, how are you doing today?"

"I'm doing great. Thank you so much for the beautiful flowers and sweet note. You're a very dear man."

"I like to hear you say that. How did you sleep, ma chère?"

"A little restless, but I slept late. How about you?"

"About the same, I'd say, but I had to work this morning. What are you and Everdine doing today?"

"We are going shopping for evening gowns and then we're spending the night at home making fondue."

"That sounds like a perfect evening. So what do you say about Saturday night? Shall I pick you up?"

"Yes, I'd love to accompany you to the ball, Anton. Everdine won't be riding with us since she may have a date for the ball lined up."

"Wonderful, ma chère! I'm meeting some business associates for dinner Friday night and I would love for you to be my date. I hate to mix business and pleasure, but I don't think I can wait until Saturday to see you again. What do say, chérie?"

"Well....I...I..uh..sure. I'd like to see you too, Anton."

"Great. I'll pick you up at seven Friday evening."

"See you then. Bye, Anton."

"Goodbye, chérie."

Willie walked back to the living room with a huge grin on her face. She really liked Anton, but deep down inside she was worried about how far this could go. Would it be more than just a summer fling? She remembered the conversation her and Ever had on the plane ride over and she was not sure now that she could give her self to a man at all. Her anxiety was through the roof.

"So, you were talking for a while, what did he say?"

"Oh dear! He asked me to go to dinner with him tomorrow night. He's meeting some business associates, but said he can't wait until Saturday to see me."

"Willie, that is fantastic. I'm so happy for you. I decided to send Gabriel a text message instead of calling. I just said thanks for the flowers and apology accepted- no hard feelings. It actually feels good not to have this hanging over me."

"I'm going to need your help shopping for a dinner dress for my date with Anton. I would be so lost without your help, Everdine."

Ever wrapped her arms around Willie and gave her a big squeeze. "Come on little sis, Bernard is waiting for us."

"I'm not that much younger than you," Willie commented as they made their way out of the apartment to Bernard's car.

The girls went through miles and miles of evening gowns at Globus, a shopping mecca in Geneva, and narrowed it down to a few contenders. Willie found a low cut, dark green silk gown that hugged her body perfectly, but she was worried that showing her ample cleavage will be a bit too much. She didn't want Anton to think she was a tramp. Ever talked her into it since it would go great with her hair and it's really the only evening gown with such a beautiful cut and color. She also had the goods to pull it off. Everdine decided on a slate blue, goddess-style gown with a slit up the side. It draped her figure perfectly.

"Alright Willie, now we just need to find you a dress for your dinner date tomorrow night. I think I have the perfect dress in mind. We need some kind of shirtdress made of a fine fabric. The style is perfect for the business side and the fabric will make it elegant enough for evening wear."

"You're the boss, Ever."

The girls consulted a sales associate and were immediately shown no less than five dresses fitting the description. The one

that caught their eye was a black sateen shirtdress with half
sleeves, double-breasted fitted bodice, medium cut front with a
scoop hemline and short slits up the side. It fell about four
inches above the knee and was perfect with the heels she bought
several days ago. Willie tried on the dress and both her sister
and the sales associate agreed it was the perfect one.

After a long day of shopping Bernard drove the girls to the
grocery store and they got everything they needed to make
cheese fondue. During the car ride the girls discussed the
Delacroix brothers and Willie's date tomorrow evening. Bernard
could not help but to listen in on their conversation. He didn't
want to intrude on their fun, but he was concerned that the girls
may allow themselves to be taken advantage of. He decided he'd
do some snooping of his own.

The girls enjoyed a bottle of wine over dinner at the
apartment and Ever tried to find out just how smitten Willie was
with Anton. She had never seen her sister excited over a guy.
Ever!

"Willie, do you think you would sleep with Anton if got
that far?"

"I feel such a strong connection to him. I can't explain it.
But, if he did want to sleep with me I don't think I could resist.
As much as I am fond of him, I just don't know if it has
longevity. I've been asking myself how I would feel, knowing
that we would not be together after the summer, and even
knowing that what we have may not be enduring. I may still do
it. I seem powerless when it comes to him. I swear Ever, I have
never been so drawn to a man like I have to Anton Delacroix."

"I don't know what to tell you Willie. It's scary and
exciting at the same time. I can't say I'd be immune to charms
of his brother if he'd shown me more respect. They are both
very provocative men."

Willie yawned. "I'm ready to go to bed now. I have to get
up early and work off this cheese fondue. I've been eating so
rich since we arrived and I don't want to gain weight. Do you
want to go jogging with me in the morning or would you rather
sleep in?"

"I think I'd rather sleep in. Goodnight Willie. Sleep well."

The sisters gave each other a hug and retired to their suites.
Willie called her mom first and told her about Monte Carlo and
what a great time they were having. She also told her about
Anton and how smitten she was. Willie described to her mother
how he looked a lot like the tall, dark and handsome Dolce &

Gabana model. Her mother said he sounded like a real man and
Willie could not agree more. As soon as Willie's head hit the
pillow she was asleep. Sometime around eleven-o'clock Willie's
cell phone rang.

"Mmmm Hello."

"Oh ma chère, you are already asleep, non?"

"Hi Anton. I'm fine."

"I should let you go back to sleep. I didn't realize it was so
late."

"No, it's good to hear from you. Is anything wrong? Have
our plans changed?"

"Non, chérie. I just wanted to hear your voice before I
went to bed."

"That is very sweet Anton. I'm glad you called."

"Me, too, chérie. I thought about you today."

"You did, huh? I thought about you, too, and how excited I
am to see you tomorrow."

"I hope you have pleasant dreams tonight, ma chère.

"I will now. You, too."

"Yes, sweet girl, I will. See you tomorrow evening,
chérie."

"Goodnight Mr. Delacroix."

Hearing his voice made her insides jolt. It still felt like a
dream to her, having the attention of this beautiful man. She
wondered if her naiveté prevented her from seeing this for what
it was. Maybe there was some unspoken rule of dating sexy
European men she was not privy to.

CHAPTER 5

Willie went to bed with a smile that night and woke up with an even bigger one. Anticipation of seeing Anton tonight made her completely giddy. Everdine was still asleep when she went for a run. Geneva was such a beautiful city and they had been so busy they hardly had time to see much of it. Their first tournament was in Monte Carlo and they planned to stay two weeks there and make a vacation out of it. On Tuesday they would take the train from Geneva to Monte Carlo.

By the time Willie finished her run and workout Ever had already fixed breakfast and coffee was almost finished brewing.

"How was your run?"

"It was very nice. I went by the lake and the views are amazing. Did you hear back from Gabriel after texting him yesterday?"

"I did, actually, right before I went to bed. He just said 'thanks' and that he hopes I'll save one dance for him."

"That is hopeful, then."

"Yes, but I'm not looking for trouble. Just give me the fun without the trouble. Maybe Sven will be the one. He's pleasant, has a gorgeous body and I don't think I'll have to worry about falling in love with him."

"I'll have no problem falling in love with Anton and that is worrisome. He called me last night after I was asleep."

"Are you still seeing him tonight. Did he cancel?"

"Yes, we are still on for tonight. He said he wanted to hear my voice before going to bed and that he was thinking about me."

"Willadine, this is crazy. You never dated anyone and as soon as you step foot in Europe you practically have a husband lined up. That's amazing."

Willadine hadn't ever thought about marriage. It wasn't something she really considered since the mere thought of having to talk to an attractive man made her nauseous. She just wanted to enjoy the feeling while she could, no matter how long this thing with Anton lasted.

The sisters spent the day at Salève, the mountain that backed up to Geneva. They took a gondola up and hiked down the mountain. By the time they arrived back at the apartment it was time for Willie to start getting ready for her date with Anton. Ever planned on styling her hair and making sure she looked perfect. Willie could not help but wonder that if she and Ever had known each other in high school if she would have been as socially awkward growing up. Ever knew about so many things: boys, hair, clothes and relationships. They had each other now and that was all that mattered.

"He should be here in a few minutes. Are you sure I look okay?"

"You look sexy and sophisticated, Willie. You will make him drool." Before Willie could take another look in the mirror the door bell rang. She opened the door to find Anton just as handsome as she remembered.

"Hi Anton, come in."

"You look stunning, ma chère. Flowers and chocolates for my lovely date," he said, leaning down to kiss her on the cheek.

"Thank you so much. That was very thoughtful of you." Seeing him in the flesh made her heart jump.

"Here, I'll put those in some water for you," Everdine offered.

"Thanks, Everdine."

"Gabriel wishes to send his greetings, Everdine."

"That's sweet. Please give him regards."

"I'll do that. Are you ready to go, chérie?" he said, turning to Willie. "Yes, let's go."

Anton took her hand and led her out to his car. "Willadine you look so beautiful in this dress. I'm a very lucky man."

"Thanks Anton, you look very nice, too. Your tie is very sharp."

"Here, let me help you into the car. The seats are very low to the ground." Anton took her hand and guided her in the passenger seat.

"Thanks. This is a nice car. What kind is it?"

"Wow, to think I spent so much money on this Aston Martin and a beautiful lady does not even recognize it," Anton said, smiling.

"I'm so sorry Anton. We just don't have these cars where I'm from in the States. It really is a lovely car and if it helps, you should know that I'm very impressed," she said with a smirk.

"Now someone is fibbing. I don't believe you are impressed for a minute, ma chère."

"Well it is a nice car. So tell me what kind of meeting or dinner this is tonight. Are you meeting clients?"

"We are meeting some associates- gentlemen I form silent partnerships with from time to time. We pool our resources together for the sake of restructuring specific types of manufacturing operations, buying and selling. Our specialty is that we have holdings in several facilities that manufacture with steel and wood parts- mostly in furniture. It gives us leverage when restructuring new prospects that can benefit from these connections."

"That sounds like a fascinating business to be in; hardly boring."

"Yes and it pays the bills." They both laugh. "Chérie, what kind of work do you do when you are not playing poker?"

"Seeing as how Ever and I just graduated, we haven't done much working. We had an internship at an international agency lined up in the New York City, but then our dad surprised us with a summer in Europe on the poker tour. We were able to relocate our internship to Geneva starting this fall, so it worked out even better."

"Fabulous. I live in Monte Carlo, but also have a residence in Geneva that I share with my brother when we are in town. So where are you and Everdine from?"

"Everdine is from Atlanta and I'm from a small town in the Appalachian Mountains of North Carolina. She is my half-sister." The more she talked to him, the more at ease she felt. It was like a fairytale having this picture perfect man showing her attention and she was willing to follow along.

"So your parents are divorced then?"

"No. Our father was something of an enigma. He was never married to either of our mothers and traveled around all the time. Even though he wasn't around much, he took very good care of us and made sure we knew how to play cards."

"You must have had a very hard upbringing because of your circumstance. Was your mother very strict raising you alone?"

"My mother is a very vivacious, charismatic and strong woman. I wish I was more like that, but she was strict. My mom was worried I'd make the same mistake as she did- young, single and pregnant. She made sure that I was on birth control as soon as I was in high school, even though there wasn't a boy within a hundred yards of me. I was too shy to really think about them in a non-platonic way."

"What about this Kevin fellow? He was around you, non?"

"Not like that. We were just friends and he was more like a brother to me. What about you Mr. Delacroix? Someone as handsome as you with such an impressive car is certain to have a lot of girlfriends."

"I like your sense of humor, Willadine. Yes, I have had many girlfriends, but my relationships have not been serious. I'm what most would call a professional bachelor, but at thirty-two years old it has become tiresome. There is only girl I'm interested in right now, chérie." Anton glanced at her with a closed expression. Willadine blushed and smiled at the thought of being exclusive with him. She didn't know how to handle that kind of declaration and Anton could hardly believe he had made such a declaration.

"You just don't know what you're getting into," she joked, "Once you do, I'm sure you'll run for the hills."

"Non chérie, you are very special. Anyone can see that. I want to thank you for coming out to dinner with me and I apologize ahead of time if it is too boring. Another thing...I have never brought a date to our dinner meetings, so be prepared for some stray comments."

"Okay, I'm not nervous at all," she joked and wondered what exactly was going on inside Anton's head. Anton was thinking the same thing. Part of her appeal was how honest she was and how void of pretense her look and demeanor was. Most women he dated were very layered and seemed to confuse sex for intimacy. He felt like he knew exactly what he was getting with Willie and he liked it. For the first time he admired a prospective date's intellect. His plans for the summer were changing.

They arrived at the restaurant and the valet parked his car. It was an upscale French restaurant and Willie was certain she had never eaten in such a nice establishment before. She really wished they knew more about each other before meeting any friends or business associates. Once they entered the restaurant Anton waved at his guests across the dining room. Willie was shocked to see that there were no women at the table- only men.

"Anton," she whispered. He leaned down, resting his hand on her lower back. "Oui, chérie?"

"Did the others bring dates?"

"They don't usually bring dates, so you may be the only one. Is that a problem ma chère?"

"No, not at all."

"Chérie, they will like you just as I do." He took her head between his hands and kissed her cheeks. "Come, let's meet my associates."

Her hand was clutched tightly in his as Anton led her over to the table where his business associates were. All of the men stood to greet them and Anton pulled her chair out for her, getting her seated. As Anton expected, there were a few comments that he may be softening up by having a date with him. Two of the men were older and one looked as though he may be Anton's age. The men talked business politely through wine and the first course and engaged Willie in small talk. Anton excused himself to say a quick hello to a friend he saw across the room and Willie was left with the polite strangers.

Their conversation turned to a problem they were having with a manufacturing operation they were acquiring, namely logistics and production.

"Excuse me, sir," Willie interjected. "Yes, young lady," the older gentleman from Paris replied.

"I could not help but to hear your problem and I'm curious- have you thought about dividing your manufacturing operations strictly by agglomeration with your US-bound furniture in particular?"

"We are looking into some locations on the East Coast when we expand distribution. What did you have in mind Miss Crenshaw?"

"If you take, for the sake of example, partially constructed units, utilizing what is best and most affordable here, ship them to your US market and have them finished up there, taking advantage of local economies of scale, and agglomeration opportunities, thereby reducing shipping costs, tariffs and getting tax breaks for job creation, then that may be a viable option for restructuring. The vagaries of the labor unions here can make or break such a deal. Also, there is no way to beat the southern states on labor costs should you want to ship pieces in bulk and have them assembled there."

"I think you have a good grasp of our problem, but we really need to crunch the numbers. What is your background, if you don't mind me asking?"

"I'm from North Carolina and grew up around the furniture industry there and I also studied manufacturing economics in college. But, I have not worked in such a capacity, so I hope you don't mind the intrusion."

"That is fascinating. If we give you the particulars on this operation can you crunch the numbers for us and come up with several proposals based on the scenarios you discussed? Of course, we'll need externalities factored in, too, and not just the savings. We try to operate with a conscious when possible. I know Anton will be relieved to have a plan of attack."

"Well, uh...I...you...." Willie didn't know how to respond as Anton returned to the table.

"...I apologize for the interruption. It was good to see that you were keeping Willadine entertained in my absence." Anton said, sitting down at the table.

Willie was so nervous that she excused herself to the bathroom. Why did she have to say anything at all, not knowing much about their business relationship? She was bored, but this was something Anton could get really upset about. What would he say about her interference?

When she arrived back at the table the gentlemen were on another topic and their evening was winding down. Anton had his hand on her leg the whole time, stroking the exposed skin of her thigh with his thumb and didn't say anything about her meddling. This only made her more timid about being alone with him after dinner.

"Well, gentlemen, it was great meeting with you all tonight. I'm excited about our new strategy," Anton said, as everyone stood to leave. "Willadine, it was a great pleasure meeting you and we look forward to seeing you again. We'll be in-touch. Anton, this one is a keeper."

He looked over to Willie and smiled. "I could not agree more."

They walked outside to the valet and Anton took her aside and wrapped his arms around her and pulled her to his chest.

She let her hands rest lightly at her side, not sure how to react or what she should say. All she could think about was how good he felt and smelled. She decided to clear the air about conversing with his associates. "I'm sorry I interjected myself into your business. I hope you aren't upset about it. I was just trying to understand what they were talking about."

"Au contraire, ma chère. You completely amaze me and surprise me," he said, stroking her cheek with his thumb. "Thanks to your plan of action I have the necessary backing. Is there something you want to tell me?"

"What do you mean?"

"Well my business partners back there wanted to know why I didn't tell them my girl... uh..my friend was a business shark. Where did you gain your experience, chérie?"

"I studied manufacturing economics in college, along with physics and a little French on the side."

"Well, they were very impressed with your acumen, as well as myself. You proved not only to be smart, but beautiful and sexy, too. There is still so much I don't know about you and I look forward to us getting to know one another." Anton cupped her cheeks with his hands, caressing her cheeks and diving his fingers into her hair, kissing beside her mouth, trailing kisses across her face.

Willadine's eyes rolled shut and her lips opened, showing signs of excitement, as did the wet panties between her legs. "Anton, may I touch you?" Willie asked between her arrhythmic breathing. "Oui, chérie."

With Anton's permission, Willie's hands surveyed the sculpted man in front of her touching his upper arms, running them down his biceps. With each passing her intake of air increased. Anton's lips moved down to her neck in a slow and sensual motion fueled by Willie's breathing. Her hands moved up over his shoulder into his thick, dark hair. This was new to her, this feeling like she couldn't get enough of him, like she would explode. She was practically panting.

"Chérie, you must calm down or we both will be in trouble." Willie didn't realize how hard she was breathing. He held her in a close embrace where she could feel every muscle in his chest and his huge erection against her stomach. "See what you do to me, chérie?" He whispered in her ear. Willie was so turned on that she let a few moans escape from deep in her throat.

"Come Willadine, I need to get you back home."

The valet brought his car around and he drove Willadine back to her apartment, talking along the way. "So what did you do today, ma chère?"

"I went for a run this morning by the lake and then Ever and I went hiking around the Salève."

"You must be tired then."

"No, not too much."

"I forgot to ask you why you decided to study French. Any particular reason?"

"Yes," she smiled, remembering fondly a moment from her childhood. "When I was a child I got a copy of Le Petit Prince and it was in French. I spent every free hour translating it so I could understand it. My dad always traveled a lot overseas and spoke so fondly of France. When I was older I decided I wanted to learn French."

"That is sweet, ma chère. When I was a child my mother would read that book to me and it was very special. She passed away when I was 10 and I lost the book not long after. It was a hard time for me."

"I'm sorry Anton," she said, placing her hand on his strong leg.

Anton parked in the garage under her apartment building and walked her up. She didn't want their evening to come to an end. "Anton would you like to come in for a drink?"

"You need to get your sleep don't you, chérie? You must be exhausted."

"I don't want you to leave. I didn't get to have much time alone with you. Just 30 minutes?"

"How can I say no when you ask so nicely?" The chemistry between them was omnipresent as Anton held her hands in his.

Willie led him into her apartment where they found Everdine in the living room watching TV. "Hey Everdine, did you have a nice evening?" Anton acknowledged her with a nod and short greeting and she responded in like.

"I just spent the day recovering from our hike earlier."

"Do you want a drink with Anton and me?"

"No thanks. I'm going to bed soon anyway." Ever went to her suite leaving them alone.

"Anton, would you like wine, juice, mineral water or ice tea?"

"I'll have some white wine, please."

Willie poured them both a glass of wine and joined Anton in the living room, handing him his glass. "Would you like to go to my suite, Anton? If Everdine comes back out she'll have more privacy that way. I also have a nice seating area back there."

"Sure, ma chère."

"I'm doing it for selfish reasons, of course. My feet are sore in these shoes and the lace on these stockings is very itchy."

"Well I can't argue with that, madame."

Willie took Anton's hand, walking him to her suite. She had a queen sized, four poster bed and a small seating area with a sofa and coffee table. It also had a walk-in closet and en suite bathroom, making it on the larger side as far as European bedrooms go.

Anton sat on the sofa outside her walk-in closet and they both set their wine down on the coffee table. Willie slid her shoes off, carrying them toward her closet and tried to undo the clasp of the garter in front. After struggling too long, Anton came up behind her, placing his hands on her hips. "Ma chère, allow me."

Willie just stood there, momentarily paralyzed, as Anton's hands slid down her front legs and with a hand on each thigh, his fingers found their way under her dress and he snapped the garters with the greatest of ease. "I'm getting the back now, chérie."

Anton stepped around in front of her and plied her with kisses from her cheek down the silky smooth skin of her neck. He bent down as his hands slid down over her hips around to the backs of her legs and snapped the garters free.

"Chérie, you have fabulous legs." Willadine was almost shaking with nerves, wondering how far they would go tonight. She hoped he would finally kiss her on the lips. She wanted to kiss him in the worst way, but was afraid to make the first move. He went back to the sofa and she changed into a t-shirt and yoga pants.

He knew that if he wanted to he could have her right now. She would be his. That was part of his charm after all. Drive the women crazy with lust until they throw themselves at you. There was something so different about her, though. He knew she hadn't been with many men and there was such a comfort just being around her. There were no expectations from her and he liked that. All of the other women knew what he was about and they willingly played the part. With Willadine he found freedom, but he felt an attachment. That part was unique to him.

They sat on the sofa for a few minutes drinking wine. Anton took her feet in his lap and giving her a massage for several minutes. "You know chérie...." He looked over and she was sound asleep. She was beautiful; angelic even. He carefully laid her feet aside and went to her bed, turning her covers down. Just looking at her sleeping on the sofa did sexy things to him. Returning to the sofa, he gently picked her up and carried her over to the bed, laying her down and pulling the covers up. She still had hair pins in, which he removed and set on the bedside table.

"Sleep well my beautiful chérie," he said, kissing her briefly on the lips.

"Mmmm....stay with me," she whispered in a love-struck slumber. Internally, Anton was having a struggle with staying. There was no question that he wanted to, but there were some things that were beyond his control if he did stay. It was decided too soon. He had never denied any request from a woman and he wasn't about to start tonight. He took his shoes and socks off along with his jacket and dress shirt and placed them over on the sofa. He unbuckled his belt, stopping to debate whether or not to take his pants off. That was the shortest debate he ever had in his life. If they ended up making love, then so be it. This week he had defied all that was reason when it came to her. Courting a woman was new to him, but the kind of woman Willie was almost commanded it. He took his slacks off and slung them with his other clothes on the sofa and crawled into bed beside her wearing nothing but his black silk boxers. "I'm here, chérie," he whispered, kissing her temple. He snuggled up behind her, holding her close and went to sleep.

CHAPTER 6

The early morning light shone through the outline of the heavy curtains and Willie began to stir a little, the hair on his chest tickling her cheek. Anton had been awake for twenty minutes watching her sleep with her curly mop of hair scattered on his chest. She was breathtaking.

The scent permeated her nostrils, warm, peppery and musky. It was arousing. When she opened her eyes and realized she was laying on Anton's chest she was afraid to move. Then the second realization hit- her legs were snaked around through his. Third- where was her hand? It was resting on his thigh, merely inches from his manhood. At that she stiffened like a board. Anton immediately knew she was awake.

"Bonjour, ma chère."

"Good morning, Anton." He moved her unruly hair to the side and kissed her forehead and she grazed his chest with her hand.

"I better go to the bathroom." She slid out of bed, going to her bathroom and first glancing in the mirror. Her hair was all over the place. Well he might as well see what he is getting into she thought. After using the toilet she washed her hands, brushed her teeth, puts some deodorant on just in case. She skirted back to the bed and got under the covers getting a view of the gorgeous body that was beside her and under her all night. Wow.

Anton kissed her on the forehead again and she wanted badly to kiss his chest. "May I kiss you here Anton?" She placed her hand on his chest.

"Chérie, you needn't ask every time you want to touch me. In fact, last night your hands were all over my body."

"No, Anton. Really?"

"Oui, ma chère. Okay they were, but not in the place I wished them to be."

Again, her face lit up a lovely shade of pink. It was not something she could help. Any time he threw sexual innuendo at her she blushed.

She leaned in to kiss him in the center of his hairy chest. "So tell me what you are blushing about chérie?"

Just the though of what she was blushing about made her even more flushed. "Anton, no. Redheads blush a lot anyway," she said.

"I better go to the bathroom, too, before I'm not able to." He eluded to the growing bulge in his boxer shorts.

"I have washcloths and a pack of travel toothbrushes under the sink if you'd like one. Just make yourself at home."

"Merci," Anton said, getting up, making his way to the bathroom. Willie tried not to stare at him, but it was too tempting. She had never had a well-endowed, half-naked man in her bed before. After a few minutes he returned to the bed and crawled under the covers facing her.

"I love your hair Willadine. It is so pretty and wild," he said, pushing her hair away from her face with his slender fingers. "Thanks," she said nervously, placing her shaky hand on his waist as they lay on their sides facing each other.

"Chérie, why are you so nervous around men? Tell me, please. Especially after we spent so much time together last night," he said caressing her hair.

"Anton, I've never...." She stopped herself before she finished the sentence. There was no way she could tell him she was a virgin. Think quick, Willie. "Never what, chérie?"

"Uh, well, I've never......felt such a strong connection before and I've always been shy." It wasn't what she was going to say, but it was the truth. The last time she felt something for a guy was when she was tutoring a football player at Duke. After a few weeks she had developed feelings for him, but came over to tutor him one morning and he had a girl in bed with him. Only that time the feelings were unrequited. This was completely different.

"Yes, I feel it, too. You are sure that's it ma chère?"

"Yes, Anton. You are amazing, sweet and so handsome. Why wouldn't I be nervous?" She managed to say all of that without making eye contact with him.

"Chérie," he said, tilting her chin up, "I feel the same about you." Anton held her face up and kissed her so gently on her velvety lips, so soft and smooth. It was everything she hoped it would be. Finally. She melted into the bed. Just as he was taking his lips away, Willadine deepened the kiss and added flame to the fire. This was not his usual style with women, but he knew she would be unique, he just wasn't sure how. Normally, he would have her naked and bedded, but he knew with Willie it would only work if she set the pace.

He rolled almost on top of her, supporting himself on one elbow, their tongues and lips going around and around. His hand moved down her rib cage to her hip. Sliding his hand underneath her shirt he started back up her side, not touching her breast, but going as close as he possibly could. This drove Willie crazy. It felt like a lightening bolt straight down the middle of her body. She was moaning and breathing so loud between their kisses. His erection was pressed to her leg and at this point she wanted him to rip through her virginity. Anton had never, in all of his years of lovemaking, experienced a woman as ripe as Willadine. It dawned on him how empty his sexual endeavors had been compared to what he was experiencing with her and they had barely gotten started.

Unexpectedly, Willie rolled him over on his back and was now laying on top of him, her legs between his. Maybe he'd underestimated her. She was nipping at his ear and jaw, putting him on notice. His hands slid down her back and cupped her buttocks. She gasped at his commanding touch. Her tight, round ass felt amazing. He started to move her slowly back and forth a little, sliding her over his erection. Both of them were struggling to breathe between the heavy kissing. He was moving her a little faster now. She had never felt anything so amazing and they weren't even naked.

With every push of his hands he could feel his erection sliding between her luscious lips, covered by her now sodden yoga pants. His hips were curving up to meet her as he pushed her back and forth over his erection. How he wanted to tear her clothes off and dive in to her hot, wet pussy. The thought drove him mad. He was close to the edge already and Willie was even closer. He moved back and forth with a nice pace now and

Willie was moaning into his chest now, the feeling too great. She was becoming louder and louder. Her sister would definitely hear them. At that moment she was bucking her hips with him and screamed loudly into his chest. "Anton, Anton," she groaned, mewling and almost in tears. He grabbed her and held her so tight and close as he came in his shorts, releasing his own pleasure, growling with each release.

How in the world did this happen to him? She was sighing as she came down from the orgasm, babbling almost incoherently, rolling on to her back. "Oh my god, that was an orgasm," she said. He could not make out the rest.

They just lay there in silence, taking in the feel of each other, their breathing returning to normal. "Chérie! What do you do to me? I've never....this is a first." He stopped before finishing his sentence. There was no way he could validate what just happened with words and Willie didn't want to either. They were both taken by what just passed between them. "It's a first for me, too," she replied.

Anton leaned over and kissed her before going to the bathroom to clean up. He looked at himself in the mirror and just shook his head. How did this happen? How had this colloquial, English-speaking, beautiful bumpkin touch him so deeply where no other woman had?

When he came out of the bathroom he got dressed and Willie was straightening her clothes and had pulled her hair back in a ponytail. "Would you like some coffee?"

"Oui, I think I have enough time."

Willie could not wipe the grin from her face and she was fine with that. They went out to the living room and Everdine was not there, but left a note that she went for a run. Being the sweet sister that she was, she made coffee before she left. They were sitting at the kitchen bar, a calm feeling surrounding them.

"Chérie, you have had the most glorious smirk on your face for the last 10 minutes. If you keep it up your face will stay that way, you know."

Willie just smiled even bigger down into her coffee, not saying anything.

"Oh you think it is funny, chérie? Just wait until you have to explain why you are smiling so big." Anton put his coffee down and walked over to her, grabbing her head with his hands, kissing her cheek, taking in her wonderful scent.

"You drive me mad, Willadine." He took a step back after realizing how potent the air was between them. It would be so easy to wind up back in bed with her and not see the light of day for another 24 hours.

"So what time will you pick me up tonight?" Willadine asked.

"Is 7 p.m. okay?"

"Yes, fine. If you like we can take our limo and Ever and Sven can ride with us."

"That will be fine since I think Gabriel will need our company car anyway. As much as I hate to leave you I have a lot to do today. Chérie, I had an amazing time with you last night and this morning."

"Me too, Anton. It was.....it was." Willie couldn't find the words.

"Shhhh." He kissed her temple before she could finish and her words were lost. The way he whispered to her in his low, throaty, French-accented voice did things to her. She walked him out of her apartment and they stood and closed hands. He leaned down, kissing her on the cheek. "Goodbye, ma chère."

He turned and walked toward the entrance of the building at the end of the short hall and Willie started to feel a little panicky as he was walking away. "Anton....bye," she shouted, her chest aching. He could recognize the uncertainty in her voice.

"Ma chère, come here," he said striding back to her, pinning her against the wall with his hips, grasping her face and kissing her like she was his last breath. Earth stood still and she had no idea for how long. His tongue probed hers and she could feel the kiss all the way down to her toes. When she was with this sexy, virile man nothing else existed.

"Forgive me for not giving you a proper Goodbye, chérie." With one last passing of her lips and tongue with his, he kissed her hand and turned to leave. There stood an awestricken Everdine in the hall by the entrance, decked out in her running attire. "Bonjour, Everdine. Nice to see you," Anton said as he passed her, opening the door, exiting the building.

"Willadine!" Ever gasped. "You have to tell me everything. Come on let's go inside." Anton's kiss almost rendered her stupid.

Anton sat in his sports car unable to move. Never in all of his experience with women had he ever slept in the same bed with one and not fucked. He had to admit that as far as sexual encounters go, that was by far the most erotic, soul-reaching experience he'd had. Some things she said made him consider how experienced she was. Remembering how she screamed when she came, with her head buried in his chest, gave him an erection all over again. He rested his head on the leather-clad steering wheel. For the first time in his life he didn't know what to do. He already found himself courting her and truly liked it. This wasn't supposed to happen.

Back at his apartment Gabriel was there saying goodbye to a woman who was about to do the walk of shame. "I see you had an exciting evening, Gabriel."

"For some reason it wasn't as exciting as I thought it would be. I drank way too much and didn't even get laid. I can't get that damned Everdine off my mind and I'm sure it's only because I can't get her where I want her."

"I understand the attraction of the Crenshaw sisters."

"Where were you last night, Anton? Or should I ask who you were with?"

Anton smiled, remembering his night with Willadine. "I was with Willadine."

"Well I'm glad one of us got laid. I knew I picked the wrong sister."

"Non, non my brother you better take a step back. We did not have sex, but it was the most exciting night I've had since I can remember. There is something very special about her and I'm going to have to rethink my plans for the summer."

"Fuck! You are falling for her aren't you?" Gabriel said. Anton's lack of a response answered the question for him.

CHAPTER 7

Willie and Ever drank coffee and ate croissants while Willie dished out all of the details about last night. "Tell me everything," Ever said.

"We didn't have sex, if that is what you want to know."

"No, Willie, I want to know what the 'but' is, as in, we didn't have sex, but," she emphasized the last word. Willie took humor in her sister's reaction.

"We went back to my bedroom and drank some wine. I changed into some comfortable clothes and we were sitting on my sofa talking. He was rubbing my feet and I must have fallen asleep. He carried to my bed and tucked me in. I vaguely remember asking him to stay and he must have gotten undressed and slid in the bed with me. I woke up wrapped in his arms on his chest and it was the most heavenly feeling. God was it fantastic waking up with him."

"And...anything else?"

"Yes." Willie grinned and started blushing. "I had an orgasm."

"WHAT! You're kidding! But no sex, right?"

"Right. He didn't even touch me last night. After we woke up we both freshened up in the bathroom and stayed in bed to snuggle. He finally kissed me on the lips and that was my undoing. We were going at it, completely hot and heavy. He was laying on top of me and then I rolled him over and I was laying on top of him, between his legs. I was completely clothed and he had his silk boxers on. He grabbed my butt and slowly started sliding me back and forth over him until we both climaxed together. It was the most mind-blowing experience. I can't wait until we actually make love."

Everdine just sat there with her mouth gaping. "Willie, that is amazing. So hot. When I saw him kiss you in the hall it was like he owned you, possessed you."

"He does. One hundred percent."

The girls cleaned up and called Bernard for a ride. They had a spa and hair appointment lined up and would spend most of the day getting ready for the ball.

Bernard opened the limo door for them and they continued their conversation. "Anton said we could all ride in the limo together if you like. He drives this little sports car and it is not exactly ideal in a gown and high heels."

"That's great. What kind of car is it?"

"Ashton...something- like a man's name. He wasn't thrilled that I didn't know to be impressed."

"Do you mean Aston Martin?"

"Yes, that's it- a convertible."

Everdine broke out laughing. "Willie, that's probably a $300,000 dollar car."

"Oh my goodness! That's what he meant by wasting his money because I didn't know what kind of car it was. Oops!" Everyone in the limo laughed, including Bernard.

The girls got everything under the sun done to them at the spa- hands, feet, face and waxing on every part of their body imaginable. Although Everdine was use to the spa treatment, all of it was new to Willadine. Even in college she just didn't think it was practical or even necessary since the guys weren't exactly lined up at her door. The ones that were lined up were there for Everdine. Now she wanted to look perfect for Anton. She wanted to drive him wild tonight.

The hair stylists did a great job with Willadine's hair. They combed her hair out with a natural relaxer so there was no chemical smell. Then they blew it out as straight as they could. Next, they used a flat iron to get it perfectly straight and then used large hair rollers to get big, smooth waves. She was completely shocked looking at herself in the mirror. For the first time she really felt like a desirable woman.

Back at the apartment Ever and Willie helped each other get in their gowns and make last adjustments to their make up. They both struggled into their gravity-defying high heels and finished up with a spritz of perfume.

"How do I look Everdine?"

"Anton is going to flip when he sees you. You really are gorgeous Willie. Just....wow gorgeous. And your cleavage.....it looks spectacular."

"Goodness Everdine, you are going to make me cry. Your figure looks amazing in that dress. Sven better keep you close tonight. Another thing- Gabriel will be green with envy when he gets a look at you."

Ten minutes before the limo was supposed to arrive Willie got a call from Anton. "Hello, Anton."

"Hello, ma chère. I have a business emergency that I have to take care of with a conference call. I'll get a ride to the ball with Gabriel so I don't keep you and the others waiting. Do you mind riding alone with Ever? I'm so sorry, chérie. I hope you are not too upset."

"No Anton, that's fine. I'll see you there."

"Again, I'm so sorry. See you soon, ma chère."

Willadine was so disappointed when she got off the phone with Anton. All of her insecurities came flooding back. She and Anton just met a few days ago and still didn't know each other very well. Trust was still developing and she told herself that she was just being paranoid.

Ever and Willie walked down to the limo where Sven and Bernard were waiting. Sven was practically drooling before they got in the limo. Willie explained to Bernard that Anton would meet her there and that they should go on without him. It was a short drive from the apartment to the Mandarin where the ball was being held. Bernard pulled up and helped the ladies out of the limo. Sven and Ever walked ahead of Willie and Bernard asked her if he could have a word with her.

"Willadine, I understand you may be a little fond of Anton Delacroix."

"Yes. I like him a lot, actually."

"Your father and I have been good friends for a long time and I promised him I would look out for you and your sister when possible. Please don't take this the wrong way, but Mr. Delacroix has a reputation among the ladies, as does his brother. I'm not trying to tell you what to do, I'm just making you aware. You are a smart, beautiful young lady and need to make your own choices, but I would feel bad if you didn't know what you may get involved with."

"Thanks, Bernard. I appreciate your concern. He is unlike any other man I've ever met and It may be that my heart gets

broken, but it is something that I have to figure out myself."
Willie hugged Bernard and headed into the ballroom.

Upon entering the ballroom a million eyes were on Willie.
She was a bit nervous by the attention she was getting. She
didn't see Ever or Sven through the sea of dancers and made her
way to the other side of the ballroom to the bar. She was a
bundle of nerves, which could only be treated by a stiff drink.
After thirty minutes and two martinis she thought better of
getting a third and walked out on the terrace. This is not at all
how she imagined her evening going. She walked back in to the
ballroom and found Everdine.

"Where is Sven, Everdine? Did you guys already dance?"

"We did dance and when he realized I wasn't a quick study
he went on to greener pastures. Seriously! We arrive and after
one dance he wants to peel me out of this dress. Do I have tramp
written on my forehead?"

"Yikes, who says romance is dead? Well I still haven't
heard from Anton and am not sure what to think."

"Give him some more time, Willie. He seems to have his
act together. In fact, he may be the only one that has his act
together."

In a matter of minutes the girls were surrounded by a bevy
of men, plying them with drinks. After almost an hour and no
word from Anton, Gabriel walked up to them and told Willie that
he was in the hall and still on the conference call and that she
should not wait for him. Seeing Everdine look so stunning made
Gabriel ache. She was so sexy and he knew the only attraction
was that she was not an easy conquest.

"What do you want to do Willie," Ever asked. "I came
here to dance and I want to dance," Willie replied.

With her courage being fortified with alcohol Willadine
accepted an invitation to dance from a very handsome Italian
gentleman and Everdine was in an animated discussion with
Gabriel. There was little chance that this evening would be
boring, after all. Willie's impromptu date got her another drink
and she was a little on the tipsy side- a side which she had never
been on. After another dance with the Italian she decided she'd
better collect her sister before another fight erupted between her
and Gabriel.

"Come on Ever, stop fighting with him. Let's drink and
dance," she slurred and stumbled a little.

"You see that Gabriel? Your brother stood my sister up
and now she is sad and drunk."

"Ever I have to go to the bathroom, but I'll be back soon. Ya'll be nice to each other. The Italian is getting a little too fresh, so you and I can dance together when I get back."

Willie left them arguing on the dance floor as she made her way to the bathroom outside the ballroom down the hall. Going to the bathroom in a long gown can be quite a challenge even when sober, not to mention wearing heels. She checked her make up and was glad to see her hair was still holding up and she looked fine. Disappointment didn't even begin to describe how she felt. If it hadn't been for Anton then she would not have spent half a day at the salon. She walked down the long hall, vowing to get Anton off her mind before she started crying. She missed him, ached for him.

Before she was half way to the ballroom she looked up and Anton was standing at the entrance. She stopped when she saw him. He looked so handsome. "Ma chère," Anton said, marching toward her.

"Chérie, please, please forgive me. One of our plants just went on strike in Le Havre. I'm so sorry."

"It's fine, Anton. I understand. I really missed you," Willie said, doing little to hide her disappointment.

Anton's eyes grace Willadine's figure, taking in her luxurious curves. "Willadine you look stunning. I feel like such a fool for making you wait. Your hair, your dress...you are so beautiful, chérie." He took her cheeks in his soft hands, lifting her head and planted a supple kiss on her lips. Her hands closed over his wrists and she deepened the kiss. Anton pulled back and his eyes meet hers. "Do you know how hard it was to concentrate on work today? You were all I could think about. This morning was amazing. It's you Willadine....all you."

She closed her eyes, savoring his words. "This has to be a dream, Anton."

"Non, chérie," he closed in and kissed her again.

"Anton, we'd better get back to the ballroom. Ever and Gabriel were having a heated discussion when I left."

"....well maybe if you weren't so pigheaded and arrogant."

"The only pig in here is you, chérie."

"You had no problem putting your hands on this pig at the reception, now did you?"

"Obviously, I must have been weak, drunk and desperate."

"You are nothing but a vile piece of eurotrash."

Everdine raised her hand to slap Gabriel across the cheek, but he caught her hand. "Not this time, chérie." He yanked her wrist pulling her close, grabbing around her waist with one hand and the other hand snaking around the back of her neck. His mouth plowed into hers roughly and without apology. She was completely powerless in his charge. She pushed her free hand against his shoulder. For a brief moment she gave way to his desire, and her own, going limp in his arms. He then pushed her back. "Why don't you think about that, chérie," he said, turning to leave. Ball patrons looked on, stunned.

"Not so fast you bastard," She grabbed his lapels with her hands, pulling him down to her and invading his lips with hers. Kissing him like her life depended on it. His eyes were closed, relishing the thought of Everdine taking control of him, getting hard thinking about her naked. One stinging slap across his cheek brought him back to reality. "Why don't you think about that, you jerk," she said storming out of the ballroom. God was she beautiful, he thought as he stood there watching her leave. He simply had to have her no matter what.

"Anton, I'll be right back." Willie ran after Ever and stopped her in the hall.

"Ever wait! Are you okay?"

"I'm just fine, Willie. It's that asshole, Gabriel, that has a screw loose." She scowled at the thought of him. "How dare he grab me like that? I'm so mad I could just scream."

"I'm so sorry, Ever. Is there anything I can do for you? Why don't we go back to the apartment and get some Italian ice cream on the way home. I'll go tell Anton."

"No way, Willie. You look amazing and should enjoy your night with Anton. I'll make Bernard have ice cream and cake with me and I promise I won't wait up for you." Ever calmed down enough that Willie felt comfortable letting her go.

"Call me if you need me, Ever."

"I will."

Ever greeted Bernard in front of the hotel. "Finished so soon, Mademoiselle?"

"Yes, Bernard, and the only thing that will salvage this night is three scoops of cinnamon gelato."

"Oui."

Willie walked back into the ballroom where Anton was having an animated discussion with Gabriel, until Gabriel threw up his hands and walked away.

"Pardon, ma chère. He will go back to Monte Carlo first thing in the morning. I told him that they are both like a chemical reaction and should stay away from each other for their own safety."

"Yes, they should," Willie giggled.

"Now, chérie, I would like to have a dance with you and try out this fabulous dress. Will you please honor me this dance?"

"Yes, Anton I'd love to."

Anton took Willie's arm, leading her to the dance floor. His hands slid down her sides at her waist and gently caressed around to her back in circular motions. Willie rested her hands on his upper arms, dreaming about his firm, naked body. She hoped this would be the night she gave herself to him. Just being in his presence gave her that bolting feeling deep in her body. He wanted to kiss her so badly he was salivating practically. Her pert lips and sweet mouth invited him. His fingers traveled up her body, his thumbs resting on her cheeks and he delivered a slow, deep kiss on her sinuous lips.

"Chérie," he whispered between kisses on her cheek, "stay the night with me. Let me make love to you."

Willie thought she would faint at his invitation. "Yes, Anton, I want to make love to you."

He grabbed her hand and lead her off the dance floor before the song ended. As they were about to leave a very scantily clad woman jumped in front of them.

"So you're the one sleeping with Anton, are you? All of the ladies were wondering who would get to share his bed this summer."

"No, we haven't slept...." Willie tried to respond, but was cut short by Anton.

"Leave her alone, Anaïs. She is none of your business," Anton barked.

"You see, young girl, I was the one sharing his bed last summer so I know what awaits you. Just don't make any long-term plans with him and you'll be fine."

Willadine nervously looked at them both, trying to figure out what was going on.

"You knew exactly what you were getting into, Anaïs, so please keep your disparaging remarks to yourself."

Anton walked out with Willadine in hand, steaming all the way until they got to the limo. He thought he should explain his past to Willadine, but without letting her know just how strongly he felt about her. They were safely ensconced in the limo on the way to his apartment. "Willadine, I need to explain some things to you about my past."

"I already know, Anton. A friend of the family that lives here and is familiar with you and your brother told me that you both have a reputation with the ladies and that I should be cautious."

"That's great," he sarcastically replied, "and yet you still want to be with me?"

"My response was that I will make my own careful decisions and even if it means getting my heart broken it's a chance I'm willing to take."

"Willadine, you have to know that I do care about you and things are so different with you. I've never had this kind of affinity with another woman before and I can't make promises, but I'm willing to explore what can be."

"Anton, that is all I want."

"What your friend and Anaïs said was true and I have to be honest with you. I was having a strictly consensual sexual relationship with these women and nothing more. I always used protection and never had sex without it. I was never interested in having more." He lightly stroked her arm while they talked.

"I don't have a choice at this point, Anton. I can't stop thinking about you. If I don't......have you I'll go crazy."

Anton brought Willie in for a deep kiss in the back seat of the limo. He trailed his kisses down her neck, sliding her gown off her shoulder and continued his wrath of passion on Willie's body. He leaned her down into the seat and slid the gown off both shoulders, exposing her buoyant, perky breasts. His mouth immediately found respite on her nipples, making her moan with wild abandon. He knew his feelings for her were deep and cutting right to his heart. This woman could tame him if she wanted to and that scared him.

"Chérie, you have the most tantalizing breasts," Anton said with one hand kneading her full breast, pinching her nipple between his fingers and then his mouth.

Just as she was about to come unglued the driver spoke over the intercom, "Sir, we are at your apartment."

Anton helped Willie upright in the seat, sliding her dress back over her shoulders. His outburst of ardor made her weak in the knees and Anton had to help her to her feet getting out of the limo.

Once they were in Anton's apartment, a high rise building on the outskirts of the city, he made them a drink and wanted to broach one more topic before making love to Willadine. "Have a seat, Chérie," he said, motioning to the sofa. "Before we go to my bedroom I do want to ask if you are still on birth control?"

"Yes, both Everdine and I have an implant. We decided to do it at the same time in college since we would often forget to take the pill. Her mother had the same philosophy in birth control. Here it is." She lifted her arm and ran her finger over a small match-like shape beneath her skin.

"I see," he said, coming closer to her on the sofa. "I think you know I want to have an exclusive relationship with you, and I think you want the same with me, oui?"

"Yes, Anton. Only you."

"Then would you mind if I didn't use any protection?"

"No. I don't mind as long as you are clean."

"Of course, I'm clean and I take it you are, too?"

Wille gave an incredulous chuckle at him asking if she was clean. "It's uncanny that I've been on birth control so long, but have never had sex. I'm glad to finally be able to use it."

"What do you mean, chérie?"

Willie became nervous, realizing her slip and her hands started fidgeting at his tone. "Uh...I kind of thought you knew or had an idea from our time last night that, that....well, I haven't had sex before."

"Non, ma chère I didn't think for one minute that someone as lovely as you could be without having sex. So last night when we...uh...you've never done that before either, fooled around or had an orgasm?"

Willadine shook her head right and left, looking down before turning up to him. "Anton you are the only man who has kissed me and has seen me without clothes."

"You mean you have absolutely no sexual experience?"

"Only you. I was a late bloomer and guys were never interested in me like that."

"I just don't believe this," Anton said, clasping his hands behind his neck.

"You can use a condom if you like since it's my first time. It's okay Anton. I want this more than anything."

"Non, chérie, I can't do this. I will break your heart and take the one thing from you that you can't get back. You are too special and you should do this with someone you want to be with for a long time."

Willie stood up and placed her hands on his shoulders. "Anton, no. Don't say that. I do want to be with you a long time. I wanted you from the moment I first saw you across the room at the palace."

"Willadine, I can't do this. You deserve so much better than me. I've never had a long relationship and don't know that I can commit to you the way you want." Tears start forming in Willadine's eyes. "But you just said a minute ago that you wanted to be exclusive with me. How does me being a virgin change that?"

"I may be able to give you a month or a half-year, who knows, but I can't promise beyond that. I've never done this and don't want you to throw away something so special."

Willie could tell that Anton was serious and she was about to lose him. She was crying harder now. "Anton I want you to make love to me and even if you tell me that tomorrow we are through I still wouldn't change my mind. I want to feel this with you and have this together. Please!"

"Chérie, non." he wiped her tears with his thumbs. This was the hardest thing Anton had ever done and went against every desire of his being. He wanted her more than any other woman, but he wasn't a monster, after all.

"You said you didn't want to break my heart, well this is breaking my heart. Is it because I'm not good enough or experienced like all of your other women? Am I too plain for you?"

"Never! Don't say that. I told you being with you fully clothed the last time was the most exciting experience of my life. You should go now. I'll walk you down to my driver." Anton was afraid that if he didn't get her out of his apartment he would take her anyway.

"No, Anton. You don't have the right to care for me anymore and you are nothing but a liar," Willie said between sobs. "If this is how you are ending things between us, by being a coward, then you should stay where you are most comfortable-in your ivory tower."

Anton placed his hand on her back. "I'm so sorry, Willadine. I never wanted to hurt you, but you have heard from two people what will happen if you stay with me. I'm sorry. I want to but I don't trust myself."

"Can you call my driver, Bernard? I'm too upset to speak to him and I don't know where I am." After handing Anton her phone, Willie folded her head between her hands and let it all out. Anton got up and walked across the room, telling Bernard where he could pick Willadine up.

As Willie stood by the door, she turned back to him one last time, taking her phone. "I'm going now Anton and if you don't stop me then this is the last time I will speak to you. Maybe I'll go out and get some experience this summer and you'll change your mind then."

"Chérie, please don't say that. I care for you, but this can never work." Anton's eyes swelled as he watched her leave. Nothing about what just happened felt right. He was so unsure of himself that he had to turn her away even though it was the last thing he wanted to do.

Willadine waited outside in front of Anton's apartment when Bernard pulled up. He saw how upset she was when he opened the door for her and grabbed her arm. "Mademoiselle, what is wrong? Did Delacroix hurt you?"

"He just broke my heart is all," she managed between sobs.

"I will kill him."

"No, Bernard, it's not what you think. I really like him and wanted to stay the night with him, but when he found out I had no sexual experience he ended it. He is too much of a coward."

"It is probably for the better, Willadine. Your sister has two quarts of gelato at home, so you should be in good spirits."

"Thanks, Bernard."

"My pleasure, Miss Willie." He drove her back to the apartment, allowing her to collect her thoughts.

"Take care and call me if you need anything." Bernard was secretly pleased that Anton broke it off with Willadine, but didn't like seeing her so upset. He thought maybe Anton did have an ounce of decency despite his reputation.

CHAPTER 8

Willadine entered her quiet, dimly lit apartment with no sight or sound of Everdine. She headed back to her suite and started to undress and put on something more comfortable. Something that would grow with her and the quart of ice cream she was about to eat. In a way she was mourning something she never had. She knew he felt strongly for her and she felt as strongly for him. There was such clarity when she did look in his eyes that it scared her and grazed every nerve in her body. There was no denying the animal attraction between them and now that she had a taste for it, her only taste, she didn't know what to do about it.

Willie walked back out to the kitchen, searching for the much needed quart of ice cream when Everdine came out and joined her.

"Why are you back so soon? Did everything go okay?"

As soon as Ever caught sight of Willie and her puffy, red eyes she knew that it was not okay. "Willie what did he do to you?"

Having to explain it yet again brought on a fresh new round of tears. "At the ball he said he wanted to make love to me and then he broke it off with me after we got back to his place because he found out I was a virgin," Willie said, crying through the word virgin.

"That bastard. What is it with him and his brother wanting after easy women? I'm so sorry, Willie. Let's grab that ice cream and a couple of spoons and talk about it on the sofa."

"So tell me how this came about. Did he not know you were a virgin before?"

"I guess not. He didn't know that as far as my sexual experience went, he was responsible for all of it. On the way to his apartment we made out in his limo and he had my dress down. He was kissing me all over and it was the most incredible feeling. We got to his apartment and were discussing birth control and I made a comment about how it is funny that I've been taking it for so long, but have never had sex. It just kind of slipped out."

"Well why did that matter to him? He should have been happy about it."

"I agree. He even asked if we could be exclusive before talking about birth control and then afterwards he copped out, saying he would only break my heart and I deserved better."

"What cowardly bullshit!"

"That's exactly what I said."

"Don't worry about him Willie. There are so many other handsome men here who will love you for who you are and not some idea that you have to open your legs for every man that walks."

"Yea, that should be fun finding Mr.Right, or in my case, Mr. Not Right Now.

Both girls laugh at what seems to be a running joke since they landed in Europe. "So what was going on with you and Gabriel at the ball? That kiss you two shared heated up the whole room."

Everdine just rolled her eyes at the mention of Gabriel. "He is a prick, that's what went wrong. I don't even know how the argument got started, but you were right, that was one heavy kiss. I thought I was going to pass out, but I couldn't let him have the last word." Ever was proud of how she handled Gabriel, even though it left her with wanting more.

"You really showed him."

"I just don't know how I can hate him so much and still find him so freaking sexy."

"There is no denying that the Delacroix brothers are attractive. They are just very stupid when it comes to women."

"Amen, sister!"

Anton was hurting and angry as he paced his apartment. She had only been gone thirty minutes, but he was already missing her. She was right- he was a coward. The thought of making love to her carried too much emotion for him. He got a taste of what it would be like earlier that morning when they made out with their clothes on. Her without clothes and in his bed would have sent him to the crazy house. He felt like he had been hit by a bus when it came to her. Since the first time he met her on the veranda of the palace he felt drawn to her. If she was a tornado, she would have swallowed him up. That's how strong it was. He was cursing himself because her beauty, honesty and innocence were what made him fall for her and here he was rejecting her because of the very same things. He was such an ass, he thought.

"What's wrong brother? You look pretty angry," Gabriel said as he strolled through the door into the living room of their apartment.

"Willadine and I are finished." He said the words, but he didn't believe it yet. Deep down he knew he was far from finished with her, but he just didn't know how.

"It wasn't because of me and Everdine, was it?"

Anton laughed at that assertion. "Non, my brother. I brought her here and I was going to make love to her, but I found out she has no experience at all when it comes to men."

"Sex, you mean?"

"Oui. I was her first kiss and first everything so far. I could not risk taking that from her when I don't know if I will be with her a month or a few months from now."

"How did she take it?"

"She was devastated over it. I'm afraid that she is going to do something stupid with another man to prove a point."

"Well, I guess that's not your business now, is it?"

Anton's jaw hardened at the thought of Willie in another man's arms and bed. This was not going to work for him at all. He had to change the subject.

"Why are you and Everdine always fighting? Every time you are in the same room she ends up slapping you."

"That woman drives me up the wall. She needs to relax more."

Anton got a huge laugh out of that. Relax was the opposite of what took place when they were together. "Let me tell you brother, you are not the man for the job of making her relax. You are the one to get her blood flowing and her heart racing. She is a beautiful woman and I can see you are attracted to her."

"Like a brick in the head. That is what describes my attraction to her. She is very attractive and after the kiss she gave me tonight I'm not worried about her lack of experience at all."

"Hmm...these Crenshaw sisters really did a number on us, didn't they?"

"Yes, but Anton, I really think you have a good chance with Willadine. I know she made you happy. Maybe you should reconsider. She could be the one."

"The thought of her being with another man makes me wild, but I'm also afraid I'll break her heart and she deserves more. I have never been able to give more."

"You also have never felt the way about another woman as you have Willadine. You can make it with her, Anton. Just think long and hard, because what you had with her was special. This bachelor lifestyle is getting old."

The next few days flew by as the girls were packing to leave Geneva. The first stop on the poker tour was Monte Carlo and Everdine was so excited, Willadine less so. She was not ready to see Anton again so soon. Her heart needed time and distance.

"Ever, I've been thinking and I know we have two weeks in Monaco, but I'd like spend the first week trying to find our sister. In the information that dad gave me I saw that her band played in Salzburg, Milan, Munich and Zurich this time last year. I may start with Milan since it is closest to Monte Carlo, work my way around, then join you for the tournament the second week. Is that okay with you?"

"Of course. I'll miss you, but I think it works out perfect. You need some time away don't you?"

"Yes, I do. I'm afraid I'll break down and cry if I see him. I was really falling for him and it hurts still." Willie had more than fallen for him. She thought she was in love with him. Why wouldn't she be?

"I understand completely. I know dad will also appreciate it if you can make progress on finding Marvadine, too. Has Anton tried to call you since the ball?"

"No, but he did send a text asking if I got home okay."

"How did you respond?"

"I didn't. I wanted to tell him to fuck off, but I don't have half the confidence and courage that you have."

"I think it is smart to ignore him. The last thing you want to encourage is him contacting you every other day just so he can string you along."

"That is true. Oh, I almost forgot. I have something that I need you to pass along to Anton when you get to Monaco. It is an old copy of Le Petit Prince. The book reminds me of him and I just don't want it anymore, but I know it would mean a lot to him."

"Are you crazy, Willie? Why would you even care what he wants?" Ever couldn't believe how generous her sister was sometimes.

"I know it's odd, but I really want him to have it. I do care for him a lot and I think it would mean more to him to have this book. For me it is just a reminder of him."

Willie remembered the conversation about his mother and how she would read the book to him and it really touched her that he shared something so intimate. Now all that book would do is serve as a reminder of how they first met on the veranda and the quote by Antoine de Saint-Exupéry they shared: The most beautiful things in the world cannot be seen or touched, they are felt with the heart. Well her heart was brittle, weak and aching for the man that swept her off her feet and then left her in a free fall.

"Sure, Willie, I'll give it to him."

The following morning Bernard picked the sisters up to take them to the train station. It could be several weeks before he saw them again. He knew that William would be very proud of his daughters if he could see how they carried themselves. Both of them were intelligent and well-mannered. But if they were anything at all like their father at the poker table, then they would come back to Geneva with substantial winnings.

Bernard helped the ladies load their luggage in a cart and made sure they called him to keep in touch while they were traveling. He could tell that Willadine was still nursing a broken heart over Anton and thought it smart of her not to go to Monte Carlo where she would certainly run into him.

"Alright ladies. We must bid adieu now. It was a pleasure meeting you and driving for you. I'll be in London for two weeks, but will be checking my voicemail should you need anything. Take good care and let me know when you will be back in Geneva."

"Thank you for everything, Bernard. We'll miss our late night ice cream runs with you," Everdine said. Both her and Willie gave Bernard a hug and a token kiss on each cheek. They thought of him like the father they wish they'd had growing up.

He was very good to them and they would miss his fatherly advice.

Both the girls were taking different trains out of Geneva. Willadine's train to Milan was a straight shot with no connections, but Everdine had almost a nine hour journey with several connections. Luckily, they both had laptops to keep them occupied. With a hug goodbye, and promises of email and text messages, the girls parted ways as Everdine caught her train first.

Willadine was a bit nervous about traveling by herself since she had never traveled outside the South. It was exciting, but seeing and being around so many people made her very nervous. She checked her emails while waiting for her train and saw one from Byron Blaise, one of the businessmen she met at dinner with Anton. Byron must not have known that she and Anton were not seeing each other anymore. It felt awkward for her to think of her and Anton together since it was such a brief period, but her feelings said otherwise. How should she handle this? She could email Byron back and let him know that her and Anton were not seeing each other, but Anton may not appreciate that. It would be best if she let him tell Byron that she would not be working on this project. She thought a simple text message would be best since she didn't have his email address.

She exhaled, held her breath and typed out a text message to Anton.

To Anton: Got an email from Byron about the project. Thought it best you tell him I'm not involved anymore. Thx, Willadine.

Willie didn't expect a response from him anytime soon, so she put her phone away and got out her laptop. Her train wouldn't arrive for another hour. Her phone made a ping sound and she nervously checked her text message.

To Willadine: Do you not want to do it anymore? Would be a great opportunity for you and we do need your local industry knowledge. Your cut would be 2.5%. How are you doing? I miss you. Merci, Anton

He didn't not understand how much it twisted her heart when he asked her how she was doing. Willie was starting to tear up and she knew this would not work out well if she had to have contact with him while working on this project. She would just ignore any personal questions because she was sure he did not really want to know how sad, depressed and hurt she was.

To Anton: I'd love a distraction right now. But it would be too much to work with you at the moment. Sorry.

To Willadine: You'd be working closely with Byron and David, not me. I don't need to be involved. Although they are backing the project the goal is to take your findings and get financing from a bank so we can use our capital on other high risk projects.

To Anton: That sounds fine. You don't have to pay me; Since I'm so green the experience is payment enough.

To Willadine: We're required to pay you by law and it is never a good policy to do this kind of work without pay. No budging on this.

To Anton: OK. I'll take it with Byron from here.

To Willadine: I miss you chérie. Will you be in Monte Carlo this week?

To Anton: Please only ask about work related tasks-if you must. This is hard for me.

To Willadine: I'm sorry, chérie. Take good care.

There was the coup de grace. Shove the knife in and twist it. He had no right to be calling her Chérie, Willie thought. Deep down she craved any kind of contact with him, but it hurt to see him acting like nothing had happened between them. The night he kicked her out of his apartment was the worst night of her life and carried pain that she would not soon forget.

Anton knew it would be difficult to have Willadine involved in the project, but her cool, self-preserving manner bothered him. She did not belong to him emotionally or physically, but in his heart she still belonged to him. This is what drove him mad. This is what kept him up at night. How could he walk away from her when thoughts of her bore on him constantly? He had desired many different women in the past, but never had he desired just one woman- Willadine.

Willie boarded her train for Milan and started working on the numbers for the restructuring project. This would be the largest spreadsheet she had ever created. She had lots of time to download all of the necessary data from the government websites on labor, costs and employment. She would delineate each local economy in play and use techniques to determine national share and productivity. Supply chain costs also had to be brought in. Byron had already sent her numbers on current labor and transportation conditions and he would send his son David to meet her in Milan with a remote VPN key and work laptop. Her first task should be to fully understand the product and manufacturing process. This was something that was hard to do remotely. She emailed Byron that she would be able to have a rough draft by the end of the week and would email him with any questions. She already felt better knowing that she would not have idle time to sit around and moon over Anton.

Everdine's train pulled into Monte Carlo early in the evening. She was glad to have gotten some sleep on the train. She let Willie know she arrived okay. It looked like the whole Municipality of Monaco was busy with tournament preparations. There was a social mixer tonight at her hotel and she thought it would be nice to attend after a long, hot shower and a change of clothes, of course.

She went to check in at the hotel reception and they were having problems finding her reservation. Even after giving them her reservation number they could not find it. The hotel manager came over to assist her and told her that because she didn't check in before 6 p.m. her reservation was lost. A stunned Everdine stood at the counter in disbelief. She was told that the whole town was booked out due to the tournament and other events. That was two weeks that she may be out of a room. She was livid and didn't see anything in her confirmation that she was required to check-in by a certain time. They took her name and phone number and promised to call if there was a vacancy. It didn't make sense at all.

Reception kept her luggage for her while she got on the phone at the bar and spent the next hour calling every hotel and pension in a 20 kilometer radius. Not only was the poker tournament taking place, but a jazz, culture and food celebration of the city was happening all week that had people traveling in from all over. After three glasses of red wine she may as well have been drunk dialing. In fact, she was ready to start calling strangers asking for help. In a gesture of exasperation she asked out loud to bar patrons if any of them wanted to share their hotel room. That gave them the wrong impression, though. Even scarier were the ones that showed interest.

Across the bar she saw none other than Gabriel Delacroix chatting up two tall, gorgeous brunettes. He was such a dick she thought and he obviously didn't know she was in the bar or he would have run away already. As a true indication of her desperation she walked over toward him and tapped him on the shoulder. When he turned and saw her he jumped back spilling his wine on his shirt and holding up his hand in a defensive motion. She giggled at his reaction. The wine was certainly in effect because nothing about Gabriel made her want to laugh. It was good to know he was frightened of her. All he could think was how beautiful she was when she laughed. It brought such a lightness to her dreamy blue eyes.

"Don't be silly, Gabriel. I'm not going to slap you." He could tell she'd had one too many glasses of wine.

"It was my brother that pointed out that you can never be in the same room without slapping me."

"There is some merit to that, but it's not as though you were undeserving."

"What do you want? You can see I'm kind of busy," he said, motioning to the two smiling beauties. Gabriel was on edge around her, but seeing her made his pants swell when he thought about how she kissed him at the ball. He also loved the way she filled out her t-shirt.

"I need your help. Unfortunately, you are the only person I know here."

"You are right, it is unfortunate. What help do you need?"

"Well, the hotel deleted my reservation because I didn't check in on time and I just spent the last hours calling all over the area looking for a room and they are all booked out. Since you live in this area I thought you may know of a place where I can get a room?"

A smile slighted Gabriel's face and he wondered if he should dare to add insult to injury. Of course, he should. He planned on having as much fun with her as her drunken state would allow. "Do you remember the intersection you came through before arriving at the hotel- the really big one?"

"Yes, I do." Ever was so surprised he was willing to help her. Maybe she didn't give him enough credit.

"If you go to that intersection you'll see a few ladies standing at the corner. They are all wearing short dresses and high heels." Ever nodded, thinking it may be some kind of concierge service. Gabriel continued, "Go stand with those ladies and when a car pulls up to the curb and someone asks you if you are available tonight, say yes. That may get you a room for the night at least."

Once Ever realized what he was getting at she was furious. She motioned like she was going to slap him and he spilled his wine again when both hands went up. "You goddamned bastard. Fuck you!" She slapped his arm and charged off as he was laughing. How is it possible that this man could make her even angrier at him than she already was?

Ever left Gabriel and went back to where she had been sitting, her head about to go up in flames. Starting on her fourth glass of red wine, Ever was not feeling her best. She was hungry, tired and about to cry. She lay her head down on the bar for a moment and thought of what she could do. Gabriel was a creep and she couldn't believe she ever doubted it for a second. As she was getting ready to leave Gabriel approached her, but at a distance.

"If you really are desperate maybe we could make a wager on a game of cards for accommodations."

"Yes, I'm desperate, so if you are serious this time, what did you have in mind?"

"Where is Willadine?"

"Willie won't be here until next week, so it's just me."

"We play a round of cards, seven-card draw since it is just us. If you win then you can sleep in my bed."

"But what if I lose? That still leaves me without a place to stay."

"Non, chérie. Now we are at the crux of the wager. If you lose, then you have to sleep with me in my bed."

"Sleep or have sex?"

"I don't run a charity, ma chère. You will have sex with me, of course, and also sleep in my bed."

Everdine thought that maybe she shouldn't be making wagers when she was drunk, hungry and tired. This could backfire in a big way.

"You called me a pig last night. Surely you have no problem finding a woman more suitable to your tastes to take on such a chore with you."

"Oui, but maybe I find your temper irresistible. Calling you a pig was said in a passionate debate and I don't believe that or I wouldn't be making this wager."

"Well, that's an understatement since I don't have casual sex. I had actually hoped to while in Europe this summer, but I refuse to sleep with someone who has no respect for women."

"That is too bad. Are you confident in your card playing or are you a turkey?"

Everdine could not help but to laugh at his misuse of the saying. "You mean chicken, and no, I'm not afraid. A little drunk maybe. I have no doubt that I can beat your pants off Gabriel, but there has to be a few conditions."

God her smile and laugh were intoxicating. He wanted to see more of that. He'd also like to see her pink, pouty lips wrapped around his dick. "Yes, you are very good at beating things. My face knows first-hand of this. Go ahead."

"Here are my conditions:

    1. We play the best of five hands.

    2. If I win then I sleep in your bed and you sleep on the couch.

    3. If you win I will only make love to you once- have sex, I mean.

    4. If I win, then you will stop being mean to me.

    5. If you win, then you will stop being mean to me.

    6. You will wear protection and I'm not giving you a blow job in the unlikely event I should lose."

He found her confidence to be utterly sexy and he could not ignore the fact that he always seemed to have tight underwear in her presence. Other women did not have the same appeal since he had met her and he could not wait to see how she was in bed. One thing was for certain, he would be having sex and not making love. It's not something he did. Ever.

"Chérie, it sounds almost like a truce and I like it that either way my pants are coming off. In light of your conditions, I have a few of my own.

    1. If I win, you will wear lingerie of my choosing for the special evening- and trust me it will be special.

    2. If I win you will not slap me anymore

    3. If you win you will not slap me anymore.

    4. I will take you to dinner on the agreed upon evening and you need to allot me a whole night for our special time together.

    5. If you win I will still be sleeping in my bed beside you and not on the couch."

Ever's eyes glazed over at the though of having a whole night with Gabriel and what he would do with that time.

"I don't object to your conditions, but if you would stop being mean to me then I would not need to slap you. And, your idea of a special evening makes me want to puke."

"Well, chérie, I think we have an agreement. Shall we shake on it?"

Everdine stuck out her hand to shake with Gabriel. He took her hand in his, brought it to his mouth and gently kissed the back of it. Shocked by the pulse of electricity that went through her at the touch of his lips, she immediately snatched her hand back. Why did she feel like she just made a deal with the devil?

"Lets get your bags then, Chérie, and I'll take you to my apartment. You can take some time and freshen up, have dinner and then we can get started. You are walking so tipsy I may need to carry you."

Gabriel's apartment building was adjacent to the hotel and one of the taller ones in Monaco. They were able to reach his building with a short walk. Upon entering he told the concierge that Everdine would be his guest for a week and to give her anything she needed. Immediately, she was skeptical of his generosity. She didn't even have to guess that he had a penthouse apartment. If he was anything like his brother, then only the best wares would do. Once they arrived at the penthouse level Ever noticed the foyer floor was made of beautiful black marble and the apartment was appointed with modern architectural features and a wall of windows. The views were jaw-dropping.

"Wow, Gabriel. The views here are fantastic. Your apartment is beautiful. Maybe I should have negotiated for two weeks instead of one."

"Chérie, you don't want to know what you have to do to me to get a second week. Let me show you around." She wasn't entirely sure she wouldn't enjoy it. Gabriel's apartment was gorgeous. No wonder women threw themselves at him. It just made her wonder even more why he was going through the trouble of this silly wager when he truly could have any woman he wanted. Then it hit her. He couldn't have her and it ate at him knowing that there was one woman on the planet who would reject his roving hands and gorgeous lips. The revelation made her a bit uneasy, even in her drunken state. Then she thought for a moment how sad it was, because, if he had treated her with respect and kindness, she would likely be throwing herself at him like all the other women.

"My brother and I rent our apartments at a very reduced rate because they are a part of a real estate development we invested in. Our business does very well, but we'd never be able to afford such a place as this if we had to actually buy it. Lastly, here is the bedroom where we will spend our special night, chérie, so better go ahead and get a good look. The bathroom is through here. You may go ahead and unpack, hang your clothes and freshen up while I order dinner. Do you need anything?"

"No, Gabriel, but thanks. Is it okay if I take a bath? This tub is way too tempting. In fact, I would have made a wager just for the tub alone."

"Yes, make yourself at home and don't forget that I will do the same, oui?"

"Okay," Ever said with a healthy dose of trepidation. What exactly did he mean by that? She was sure she'd find out soon and whatever it was it would likely make her want to slap him. Considering that she had already slapped him three times and doused him in wine within a week's time, she was lucky that he would even brave having her stay with him.

After languishing in the jet tub at her leisure she got dressed in her most comfortable clothes and joined Gabriel in his expansive living room. It was so airy and inviting that she almost felt at home. She was glad to see he had changed out of his wine-stained dress shirt and into a very tight black v-neck t-shirt that left nothing to guess when it came to showing how muscular he was. He wasn't bulky or anything, just perfect, Ever thought.

"Please come have dinner, ma chère. I took the liberty to order for you and set the table on the balcony."

Ever looked out and saw a beautiful table set with candles, wine and food. She was shocked. She hadn't pegged him for the romantic type at all. He was full of surprises. "This is breathtaking. I bet all of your girlfriends love eating here. If you need me to get lost for a few hours this week so you can entertain a lady, just let me know."

Gabriel gave her a deadpan look. "I don't have girlfriends and I don't feed women in my apartment- I just fuck them here." It was yet another reminder to Everdine that she was an eternal optimist and to never give Gabriel the benefit of the doubt. He was a pig. A sexy pig.

"What an awful thing to say, Gabriel."

"You think that is awful, do you? All of the women I fuck willingly throw themselves at me because of what they think they can get from me. They want money and all of this," he said, gesturing around with his hands, shaking his head.

"So that is what you have resigned yourself to? How sad."

"Okay miss high and mighty- where is your boyfriend then?"

"Maybe if men would get past my looks and stop thinking I'm just a pair of nice tits with legs, and consider that I have a brain, I would be planning a wedding by now. Despite having the brains to attend an Ivy league school, I still had to work harder to prove myself just because of how I looked, so forgive me if I'm not aroused by all of your worldly possessions. I've dated some nice guys, but they just weren't up to par."

"Well I think we can agree you and I are oil and water and to that we know there is no solution."

"Of course there is, Gabriel. All you need is an emulsifier."

"So you are a rocket scientist?"

"Can we eat now?" The thought of another argument made her head spin, so Ever thought it best to speed things along.

Gabriel walked out on the balcony and she followed him until she got to the folding glass doors. She had never been in such a tall building despite living mostly in Atlanta and never aspired to be. Gabriel took his seat and waited for her to come past the door but she wouldn't.

"Come, chérie. Let's eat"

"Gabriel, I'm not use to heights. I've actually never been in a building this tall and this balcony is so open."

"Dear lord! The only woman that could make the devil cry is afraid of heights. That is silly. I'll help you." He got up and came around to where she stood. "Face me and I'll walk out in front of you so you don't see over the railing. Okay?"

"Okay, but please go slow. You promise?"

"Yes, chérie, I promise."

Gabriel stood in front of Everdine, offering his hands. "No, I can't take your hands. I need to place my hands on your waist. Sorry, it's just a trust issue."

"That is fine, chérie, do what you must."

Everdine put her hands around his waist, sliding them around to the middle of his back and made slow shuffle steps sideways. He placed his hands on her shoulders and gently stroked her with his thumbs. He was only a few inches away from her and she didn't know what she was most afraid of: being so close to him or being so many stories off the ground on a sliver of concrete. He smelled wonderful, she thought. After about ten feet the balcony opened up and the table was tucked in the recess before the glass window of the living room. Anton pulled her chair out for her and pushed her safely under the table. Now that she was sitting down she really could enjoy the view without having to look down.

"It's incredible up here. Do you eat out here a lot?"

"Oui, when weather is nice, which is often."

"It's an artist's dream up here. If I was a painter I'd spend hours out here capturing it all."

"You have a good eye, chérie. I use to love making art, but have not picked up any chalks or coals in ten years. Reality got in the way."

"Don't you mean women and work?" Ever said with a smile.

"Oui. Both are full time jobs. Besides, it is much nicer to experience a woman in the flesh than hanging in a frame on the wall. You have a very beautiful smile, Everdine."

"Thank you," Ever said, her demeanor turning serious. "My favorite painter is Dufy. After seeing his artwork in books I always wanted to come here and see the same landscapes he did."

"And now you're here. How is your salad?"

"It's exactly what I needed, thank you The wine you selected is amazing and I don't even drink white wine very much. Even though I should be drinking water I can't help myself."

"What is your favorite wine?"

"I love Italian red wine. Thick, spicy, southern Italian wine suits me best. My favorite grapes are Aglianico, Nero D'avola, Primitivo and Negroamaro. French wines are more expensive in the U.S. than Italian wines, so I don't know them really well. Willie and I took an Italian cooking class together and learned a lot about the wine regions of Italy."

"Now you are in the South of France, so we will educate your palate on French wines. I think you'll be very pleased."

"I tried a Bourgogne in Geneva and really liked it. I'm sure I'll love the French wines. I've never had any problems stepping out of my comfort zone." Everdine took a minute to think about what she just said and maybe it was an understatement. Sometimes she thought she would cut off her nose to spite her face. If anything she was too reactive and often wished she was more passive like her sister.

"I agree with you one hundred percent, chérie. So what are your plans after the tour is over?"

"Willie and I will do an internship in Geneva at an international agency working on some economic development projects. We'll see where that leads us to when the time comes. What kind of work do you do, Gabriel?"

"I work with my brother in our development corporation. I do a lot of the leg work, location scouting and heavy planning.

Our main focus is small scale manufacturing with some real estate mixed in. Many decisions can be made on a visual inspection. I just do whatever is needed of me. It works well for us."

After dinner Everdine went into the bedroom and called Willie while Gabriel cleaned off the table. She didn't tell her she was staying with him, only that she has temporary arrangements until next week. If anyone knew she was staying with him they would worry about the onslaught of WWIII. Willie told her about the project she was working on and Ever was worried that Anton may use it as a way to keep her in his grasp. Poor girl, she thought. Willie said she would send her some data and number crunching to do for the project so she could put the proposal together faster.

Ever joined Gabriel in the kitchen to see if she could help him and also broach the topic of paying for her meal. The one thing she would not be able to stand is if he paid her way. It was a power issue more than anything.

"How much do I owe you for dinner?"

"What do you mean? You want to pay me?"

"Yes, remember- you don't run a charity and I prefer to pay for my expenses."

"Non, chérie, that won't happen in my house, so get over it quickly."

Damn he was so stubborn and full of double standards. He probably wants me indebted to him she surmised. He could see she was still thinking about what to say next and he though he'd better snuff it out quickly. "If you even think of paying me for food then you can spend the night on the corner with the other ladies. This is not an issue."

"I have never met someone so pigheaded in my life! Do you strive to make all women miserable or is it just as simple as breathing for you."

"Say what you like chérie, but when women leave me they are far from miserable. Many often leave with a smile."

"Whatever Gabriel! Then tomorrow evening, if you will be home, I'll cook dinner for you. You just have to show me how to work the range."

"I have never used the range in here, but I'm sure it can't be that difficult."

"You don't cook?"

"Non, ma chère. I believe in deferring to people who are best at what they do. In this case a chef is better at cooking."

"I can't believe you live in one of the most exciting culinary regions and don't cook. I love to cook, so it is settled then that I will cook dinners while I'm here."

"Well after I win our bet tonight you may want to poison me."

"Dream on, hot stuff!"

CHAPTER 9

All of the wine Ever had was catching up with her. She
was regretting having to play cards in such a condition, but it was
good practice for the rigors of the poker tour. Gabriel set up the
dining room table for their card game. He was sure to have only
water for Everdine. She was pretty drunk he thought, but this
should be a lesson to her. She needed to be put in her place,
which was in his bed, right beneath him.

"So chérie, we are at the moment of truth. Shall we play
cards?"

She just scowled at him and sat down at the table. Before
they started she looked around to make sure there were no
mirrors or reflective surfaces where he could cheat. She was
ready to show this piece of eurotrash how to play cards.

"A real gentleman would offer me a place to sleep without
such conditions."

"I think you know I am no gentleman- at least not when it
comes to you."

Ever just shook her head in disbelief. "That's for sure."

"Here are the cards, chérie. Please inspect them and shuffle
them to your satisfaction." Ever took the cards and looked over
them. They had a colorful provincial design on the back with a
black background and gold trim, which she thought was very
elegant. Ever finished shuffling the cards and put them back in
the middle of the table.

"You may cut the deck and deal if you like," Ever offered.

"Sure, but why don't we make this a little more interesting.
How about we incorporate the American strip poker into our

games. We have five rounds and that should give me a nice glimpse of what I stand to win. What do you say?"

This guy had no idea who he was dealing with, or maybe he did. Ever loved a good challenge, but even more she loved the element of surprise. She wanted to floor him.

"Silly Frenchman, I don't need a childish antic to take my clothes off." To her own surprise, Ever stood up, scooted out of her shoes. She slowly unbuttoned her jeans and pulled down her pants, folding them over the chair beside her, almost tumbling over in the process. She then lifted her soft, white cotton t-shirt over her head and folded it over her jeans. In her drunken state she didn't remember what kind of undergarments she wore. A quick look down and she was satisfied she had on a matching white lace bra and panties that she bought in Geneva. She danced around in a circle to give Gabriel a tour of what was at stake. "Do you like what you see frenchie?"

Across the table Gabriel looked stone-faced. His mouth was tight and no expression escaped his face- a look likely perfected from years of playing poker. His eyes absorbed every nuance of her salacious body. Never had he experienced a woman like her. Fire and ice. She made his blood boil and his passion sing; he had to have her. Those Brazilian cut panties gave him a glimpse of the ass he grabbed at the reception and it was more luscious than he had imagined it would be. Her breasts looked full and natural in her demi-bra, which was not something he was use to. She was simply exquisite. Never had he been so excited by a woman. By the time most women came to Gabriel they were already prone. Although Ever had a gorgeous body, he loved that she didn't back down to anyone and she played her own game. She was worthy of respect and admiration, but right now all he wanted to to was fuck her until the sun came up. He swallowed the huge lump in his throat. Unfortunately, the huge lump in his pants would be around for a while.

"Well, it seems as though you are calling my bluff, chérie. I do like what I see, but would like it even more if the lips were sewn shut and the hands tied behind the back. My cheeks would be a lot safer anyway."

Gabriel stood up and had to shift in his bulging pants before taking them off. He folded them and put them on top of Ever's stack of clothes, revealing red satin boxers. Ever was starting to feel sick about being so brazen. Yet another time where she bit off more than she could chew- especially seeing what those red boxers were struggling to contain. Oh my was he large. Her reactive personality was about to land her in some big trouble. Gabriel pulled his shirt up over his head and placed it on top of the stack of mounting clothes. He did a cute little dance in a circle like Ever did, which made her giggle. "Now, do you like what you see, chérie?"

Ever didn't have nearly as good of a poker face as Gabriel. Her lips parted and her mouth fell open as her eyes took in the beautiful man before her. She traced her parched lips with her tongue. Her chest was rising to the rhythm of her racing heart. Never had she been in the presence of such a sexy creature. He was a piece of art she thought, with his sculpted arms, chest and abs, but what caught her attention most was his legs. She had a weak spot for men with great legs. But the nail on the coffin was his copious chest hair. Her fingers were itching to play in it. She loved the way his dark, curly hair flopped over his forehead when he tried to push his hair back.

"Well?" he prodded, even though he could tell she was very attracted to him.

"You look gorgeous, Gabriel. No complaints here. I definitely need to sew my mouth shut, though."

He was pleased, yet surprised at her reaction to him. Her honest appraisal was not what he expected considering how hard it was for to use restraint in her presence. "Want to up the ante, chérie? How about I slip out of my boxers and give you a glimpse of your new best friend?"

Gabriel started to pull down his boxers and Everdine gasped and extended the palms of her hands. "No Gabriel, don't do that." She looked away quickly. Both of them had already seen more than they had bargained for. "What a pity. No sweet dreams for you."

"I need to go to the bathroom first- be right back." Being in Gabriel's presence was a sobering experience. Every ounce of her body jolted at the sight of him half naked. She needed to rein in her focus to make sure she won tonight. She knew he was attracted to her and she wanted to taunt him until he could not stand to be around her anymore. A splash of water on her face gave her a new resolve. Game on.

"It is nice watching you go, chérie, but I can't wait to see you come. And I mean that."

"You are so crass, Gabriel."

Gabriel started dealing out the cards when they heard a voice. "Où es-tu Gabriel?"

All Gabriel could manage was a four letter word before Anton strolled into the open living and dining area and got a glimpse of his brother and Everdine almost naked at the table. Everdine stood up and lurched for Gabriel's black shirt and put it on in record time. Not before Anton got a view of her sweet ass. He wondered if Willadine's ass looked as gorgeous. He could remember how it felt the morning they made out.

"I am so sorry, Gabriel. I didn't think you would have company during the week. I'm a bit worried about you two. Should I call the police? You know what? I don't want to know. Have a nice evening."

Anton turned and left in a state of shock.

"Although I love seeing my shirt on you, I'd much rather see you without it. Shall we play?" Gabriel did like seeing her in his shirt. It turned him on more than he let on.

Ever took Gabriel's shirt off and gave him another scowl, muttering pig under her breath. As Ever looked through her cards she didn't feel too good about her hand- it would be up to the luck of the draw. As she studied her cards she noticed that Gabriel put aside two cards to be discarded. Maybe he was trying to rush her. She continued to think of a strategy and decided to go with three cards. She placed them down and hoped she would at least end up with two pairs to stand on. To her dismay she only had one pair of tens to Gabriel's three jacks. Round one lost.

Round two was her turn to deal and it went just as quickly as round one, and just as unsuccessful. Round two lost. Gabriel dealt out round three and Everdine felt much better about this hand. She had three of a kind and two of a kind, and discarded only two cards. Despite not getting any luck from that draw she won her hand, which caused Gabriel to utter cuss words under his breath. Round three won.

Round four was lackluster and could be risky if she wanted to go big and she did. She was after a flush and traded in two cards. Gabriel didn't give anything away with his poker face, but Ever tried to act disappointed at her draw when it was actually better than she had hoped- a flush and a pair. He only had a pair. Round four was hers. Her excitement was about to boil over. They were tied two games apiece.

Gabriel dealt round five and she felt a little mixed about her hand. What bothered her more was the way Gabriel looked at her as though he could see right through her. She decided to go big like she did in the previous round and drew four new cards. Gabriel only drew one card. She knew that wasn't a good sign.

"Well, chérie, shall we show our hands?" That smug bastard knew he had won.

"Sure, I'll amuse you." Ever placed her cards down, which only revealed a pair of threes. "Mmmm," Gabriel said before laying out his hand that included a straight.

"Fuck!"

"Yes, Indeed," he replied.

Gabriel helped Ever get ready for bed and tucked her in. Her long adventurous day had surpassed her and she was asleep before her head hit the pillow. He had some work to finish with Anton and needed to do that before turning in even though it was after midnight. Anton's apartment was across the foyer. They were the only two that occupied the floor.

"It is good to see that you are dressed now. You want to tell me what's going on other than you have a death wish?" Anton and Gabriel never had a problem talking to each other. They often knew what the other was thinking before words came out of their mouths.

"Everdine had problems with her hotel reservation and needed a place to stay for a week and I thought it was best to settle her problem with a few rounds of poker and a wager. Of course, I won."

"So the woman who has struck you twice already is going to stay in your apartment for a week? Are you crazy? You two can't be in the same room without showing an act of violence. What about Willadine?" Anton shook his head.

"Correction: she will be staying in my bed. You don't want to leave out where she slapped me and threw wine on me today in the hotel bar, either." Gabriel laughed at how angry he had made her then. "We also made a truce in our wager, so hopefully that will keep the violence to a minimum. Sorry, but she didn't tell me where her sister was."

"You are playing with fire, brother. These Crenshaw sisters are potent. If she agreed to this then you both are crazy and deserve each other. But, I can't help but to think that you met your match with her."

"I may just agree with you on that. I came over to see how the project was going. Everdine told me that Willadine asked her to take a set of the data and work out the calculations so she

82

would have time to go over it thoroughly. Are you okay working with Willadine?"

"Byron and his son will be working with her closely, not me. She does not want to see me or talk to me, which I understand. I can't deal with that right now."

"I know I can't convince you otherwise, so I'll drop it. David or I will be making a day trip to Le Havre by the end of the week to get a better understanding of supply chain issues. This is something that Willadine may want to do, too."

"Yes, I thought about that. She should see what the failing operation looks like. I'll have Byron or David take care of it, but it would be ideal if she could go with you."

"Well I have to go to bed now. Wish me luck."

"I'd love to be a fly on the wall when she wakes up. Good luck."

The sight of Everdine sprawled out over his bed made him thirsty. She was like the last drink of water and he didn't know how long he could go without tasting her before he'd pass out. She looked stunning when she slept with her strawberry hair cascading over her back and her leg snaked over top of the covers showing her voluptuous behind. He could stare at her all night, but even better than that he would be sleeping beside her for the next week. He undressed and crawled in beside her and had the best sleep he'd had since they'd first met.

Everdine slowly woke with a splitting headache and the events of yesterday were all coming back to her. Her hands were tangled in the mass of dark, curly hair resting on her stomach. Great- she thought- he has wandering hands even when he is asleep. "Get up, Gabriel. Come on." Gabriel just groaned and stayed right where he was, grabbing her tighter and snuggling his face deeper into her stomach. It's not like she could push him off. He was at least 8 inches taller than her and stronger. "Move Gabriel! I have a headache and I need to get up."

Gabriel popped his head up, smiling at her, and then kissed her stomach. She pushed at his shoulders and growled at him even though his playful, sweet smile nearly melted her. "You are such a man-whore."

He belted a low heartfelt laugh that Ever thought was way too sexy in her state.

"Now dear, remember that as part of our agreement I will be nice to you and you will not slap me. I think kisses are nice, don't you? Maybe we need to come up with a little punishment for breaching the agreement."

"As good as that sounds, I would not even know how to punish you."

Not letting me touch you, he thought, would be the worst punishment. "Alright my little drunkard, what would you like for breakfast? I'm having bakery items delivered. Would that suit you?"

"Yes, Gabriel, that will be just fine, thanks." Ever scooted out from the bed looking around for her clothes, feeling a little self conscious with Gabriel's eyes glued to her. She was wearing her undergarments and crossed her arms across her chest.

"Uh...do you know where my clothes are? And, stop staring at me."

"Oui, chérie," he said in that husky laugh of his. "They are on the dining room chair. But please don't get dressed on my account."

"That is exactly why I'm getting dressed. If it wasn't for you being here I'd be walking around naked since I usually sleep without clothes on." She wanted to ruffle his feathers.

"You mean like this?" Gabriel pulled back the covers and turned over to flash his sculpted, naked ass to Everdine as he leaned on his side. "Oh my God, Gabriel. You were naked beside me all night?"

"Did I not tell you to make yourself at home because that is exactly what I was going to do?"

"I never know what mood you are going to be in, Gabriel. So, here goes," she said, shaking her head.

Everdine turned her back to Gabriel, standing at the foot of the bed, took off her bra and covered her breasts with one arm and turned and threw the bra at Gabriel. It was all over with. He sprung up from the bed in his bare-naked state to chase her as she ran toward the living area to find her clothes. He scooped her up from behind with one arm around her waist like she was a sack of potatoes and carried her back to the bed with her screaming and laughing all the way. "No, Gabriel. Stop." She said between hysterics.

He threw her on the bed and she landed and rolled to her stomach. He wrapped the blanket over her and flipped her over on her back so she was covered, pinned her arms above her head and plowed his lips into hers. If there was any way this kiss could be more puissant than the last one they shared it was a hundred times more. It was the kind of stuff they launched rockets to the moon with. Judging by the sonance of pleasure coming from them both reason had to be found. Ever didn't want him to stop kissing her, but she was terrified that at some point he would not be able to stop.

"Gabriel...Gabriel....we need to stop," she said as his lips took pleasure down her neck. He kissed her lips softly, taking her eyes in his. He saw passion, hunger, fear and something else. It was the something else that startled him. "Right. I'll go make coffee."

Gabriel got off the bed in the most casual manner, erection and all, and strolled into the kitchen to make coffee. Ever was about to die inside she wanted him so much. He put on the khakis that he took off last night playing poker and brought Everdine her clothes and left her to get dressed while he arranged breakfast. This was going to be more difficult than he anticipated.

"Here is some juice and pain reliever for your head." He smiled and motioned for her to sit down. "Everdine, you had a lot to drink last night and I need to know if you are still in cooperation with our agreement. At best I could give you a re-match."

"Gabriel I knew exactly what I was doing last night and I never renegotiate on a wager. My word is my honor. Are you having winner's remorse?"

"Oh no, I think you know I don't. One special night is the deal and that's is exactly what it will be."

"You can call me Ever if you want to. That is what everyone calls me."

"And you call your sister Willie, non?"

"Yes. Ever and Willie."

"Sure. Maybe we should go ahead and decide on a date for our special night. I was thinking about Saturday. This week will be busy depending on how the project goes. I also have to make a day trip to the north of France. Does Saturday sound okay with you?"

"Yes, that will be fine," Ever replied, sipping her coffee, thinking it surreal that she was discussing the date they would have sex.

"Here is the keycard you'll need to get into the building and apartment. I also have a contact card with my numbers and email on them should you need to reach me for anything- you can call or text. Give me your number, too, and I'll let you know what time I'll be back at the apartment for dinner"

"Sure, that's very nice of you."

"I have to go to some meetings this morning. Can I give you a ride somewhere?"

"I have this map of Monte Carlo and if you can just circle where I can find a market, a spa and a department store that would be a big help."

"Let me see this so-called map. Okay, here is our apartment." Gabriel made a square around the apartment on the map. "You will find shopping here by the casino, Métropole, and also here at La Condamine, with some boutiques. And the spa is here, Les Thermes. It is best to make an appointment, so better call first."

"Thank you, Gabriel."

"I have to shower and get ready to leave and then I'll drop you off at La Condamine to start, oui?"

"Oui." Ever said with a smile.

Everdine waited by the wall of windows in the living room overlooking the Mediterranean. She wondered if Gabriel was dazzled everyday waking up to this view. What a beautiful existence she thought.

"Are you ready to go, sweetie?"

Ever found his attempt at American endearments very cute. "I like it better when you call me chérie."

"You do, huh? Then let's go, chérie."

The limo drive through town was pleasant enough. Gabriel had already taken several calls and was apologetic about it. She was the one who felt like an intruder. As the limo came to a stop Gabriel got out the car with her to say goodbye.

"You call me if you need anything, oui?"

"I sure will."

"If I have time for lunch I may try to call you and make sure you didn't empty your bank account."

"I will be fine- I promise."

"Oui." Gabriel leaned in close to her and gave her a firm hug and a kiss on each cheek. Ever rested her arms around his waist, insecure about his amorous intentions. He paused in front of her face and placed a hand on each of her cheeks and searched her eyes for any clues as to what he was about to do. He kissed her gently and thoroughly on the lips until the sounds of traffic brought them back down to earth. Ever was a willing participant in this kiss. They were both up against a power much stronger than either of them could ignore. Ever was at the point where she didn't want to ignore it anymore. Gabriel kissed the back of her hand and was whisked away in his limo.

As his limo drove away Gabriel had a new plan in mind and it didn't stop at getting Everdine in his bed. He wanted her more than for just a night, which he imagined would be much harder than getting her in bed. He no longer wanted to have sex with her or fuck her- he wanted to make love to her. The chemistry between them was explosive and he had no doubt that when they did make love she would be the last woman in his bed. He'd never met anyone like her or had so much fun with a woman before. He loved how playful and spontaneous she was. Her complicity in their kiss is what really convinced him. He felt it to the tips of his toes. It surprised him at how much he enjoyed having her in his apartment and how easy she was to be with. Most other women outright annoyed him in the seldom occasion he brought them to his apartment. His intentions had changed.

Ever walked away from the limo in a haze. Who was that man that dropped her off? It's as if she woke up beside a new Gabriel this morning. He was gentle, sweet, kind and sexy- nothing like the rude, demeaning, whorish man she knew him to be. She loved the new Gabriel, but it was disquieting not knowing when the old Gabriel would make an appearance. It was a problem she easily solved with optimism. Perhaps a little encouragement would keep new Gabriel around.

After a round of shopping she called Willie. It was time to tell her exactly what had transpired with Gabriel. Willie was speechless.

"Say something, Willie."

"Does Gabriel have a death wish?"

"That is exactly what Anton said to him. He has been trying to find out where you are, by the way."

"How is he?

"He looked sad, but that could have been due to him walking in on me and his brother nearly naked playing cards. Really, he was sad. I hope he comes to his senses." Deep down Willie did too.

"I think you should try a new approach with him. He's a good guy Willie- just afraid of love. Talk to him on a friendly basis like you are over him and throw in the occasional social event to make his curiosity boil over. Keep it friendly, but not personal. I guarantee you that after a week he will come running to you."

"Do you really think so?

"I'm one hundred percent sure of it.

"Then I'll give it a try- maybe tonight, texting him when he is getting ready for bed."

"That will be perfect."

"So you and Gabriel really are going to have sex?"

"Yes, we are. Saturday night unless he finds out I'm a virgin and then high-tails it like his brother."

"Don't tell him unless he asks you specifically. I'm serious."

"I agree with you. This morning he was so sweet, like a different man from the Gabriel I knew. I have no idea what's gotten into him. I'm cooking dinner for him tonight. Oh- I didn't have time to give Anton your gift yet. I don't know when I'll see him next, but I can give it to Gabriel to pass along since he will see him at work."

"It would be best if you gave it to him on the weekend."

"We'll do. Keep me posted on your progress with Anton. I'll finish the labor projections you wanted for the project tomorrow. I'm too hung over today."

"No problem. Let me know how you and Gabriel are getting along."

CHAPTER 10

Shopping while hung over didn't set too well with Everdine. She bought a new bikini and some other intimate apparel, fresh ingredients for the dinner she was making tonight and a special gift for Gabriel. Getting him a gift made her a little nervous since they hadn't really known each other very long and the short time they did know each other they were throwing insults, wine or hands at each other. When she saw it she knew she had to get it and knew just the right way to entice him. She had gotten a text from Gabriel that he would have to work through lunch so he could be home in time for dinner. Finally, he called her at 5 p.m.

"Chérie, how have you been today? Are the shops of Monaco safe now?"

"Yes, Gabriel. Everything is safe. I had a great day. What about you?"

"Just too busy with work. I'd much rather spend the day with you. I'm finishing up on my last call and I should be home by 6:15. Is that okay?"

"It's wonderful. I'll have dinner ready so we can relax this evening."

"I can't wait. See you soon, ma chère." Gabriel got off the phone and had to do a reality check. He had a woman at home waiting on him with dinner and he liked it.

Everdine thought she should go ahead and set the table on the balcony where Gabriel loved to eat. If she hugged the wall closely or even crawled on the balcony floor she should be able to do it. It wasn't nearly as bad as she thought it would be. Dinner was coming along just in time for when Gabriel was expected home. She made mussels and pasta with a garlic, lemon-butter sauce, chilled roasted asparagus in a vinaigrette sauce and toasted baguettes. By the looks of the kitchen you'd have thought the Battle of Marseille had taken place.

As soon as she'd brought the last of the food and wine to the table Gabriel walked in the door. It was hard for her to believe how much she looked forward to seeing him today. Scary, even.

"Ma chère, I have missed you today. Just a little."

"I missed you too, Gabriel. Kind of." They were both trying hard at the concept of being nice to each other.

This time she initiated a kiss, just to test the waters. She was still expecting the mean Gabriel to make an appearance at anytime. She reached up and rubbed his cheeks and gave him a kiss on each side and then grazed his lips very lightly. Gabriel pulled her in and slowly enjoyed the feeling of his lips on hers, pausing to enjoy her taste and smell before finishing deep with his tongue.

A stirred up Ever had to steady herself before speaking. "Come on, I have dinner prepared on the balcony if you are ready eat. Also, don't go in your bedroom. I have a surprise for after dinner"

"How did you get the food to the balcony?"

"It took a lot of crawling and mind tricks before I finally became comfortable with going out there, but I think I'm use to it now."

"That's fantastic. You really shouldn't have gotten a present you know. It is very unnecessary."

"It's more of a present for me than it is for you, so don't get your hopes up. I also appreciate your hospitality- even though it comes with strings attached."

"Well, we better start eating then."

Everdine walked carefully out to the balcony and her and Gabriel enjoyed a leisurely dinner and stimulating conversation together. He had let all of his walls down and she loved what she saw when he did. There was so much more to him than the sleazy bachelor she thought him to be. It was hard to keep their agreement separate from what was taking place between them and that worried Everdine. After spending two hours eating and talking with Ever over dinner, Gabriel was ready to see his present.

"Before I show you I need to set it up first and it will only take a minute. Wait a minute and a half before coming to the bedroom, okay?"

"The clock is ticking," Gabriel joked.

Ever went into the bedroom and made sure the pastels, pencils and charcoals were set up neatly beside the easel and drawing pad. She stripped off all of her clothes and only had a narrow silk scarf to drape over her lower front. She laid on the chaise and struck a pose right out of the 18th century, laying on her back with her legs bent at the knee and laid to the side, with one arm looped up resting above her head, which was tilted and gazing toward the easel and the other arm bent at the elbow, resting on her waist.

A few seconds later she heard Gabriel's footsteps into the room and she was so nervous. Her heart felt like it was beating out of her chest. How would he react?

"Very nice, ma...."

Gabriel stopped when he arrived at the easel and pastels and realized that a nude Everdine was lying before him. His heart was beating the same as hers. All of the wind must have been knocked out of him because he couldn't breathe or move. There was no other woman like her and for him revelation lead to realization. He was lucky that he was able to capture that splendid, unique moment on paper. Never had he seen such a beautiful woman. His mouth went dry as his pants began to swell, looking at Ever's sexy, curvy body.

Gabriel picked up a charcoal and started drawing feverishly, not even rolling up his sleeves. His eyes glowed and his curly hair was jumping around on his forehead. He was breathtaking and it was that moment that Everdine knew she could not turn back her feelings for him. From this point on she could be crushed just like her sister. Being weak was not a state she was familiar with, but it seemed every time Gabriel took more of her heart the more exposed and weak she felt. Both Ever and Gabriel paralleled each other with these new, raw feelings they shared.

Gabriel finished his art work and covered it with another sheet from the pad and turned it facing backwards on the easel. He darted into his bathroom to wash his hands and then came and kneeled beside Ever on the chaise.

"That was the best present anyone has ever given me, chérie. You are so beautiful and you amaze me every moment I spend with you."

"You are being very sweet today, Gabriel. I like this side of you a lot."

Gabriel grinned and smiled with his eyes. "You have no idea woman. I do need to talk to you, so get dressed and join me in the living room."

"You know Gabriel, if you want to make good on our bet tonight I don't mind."

He took her to his lips in a shared sensual kiss. "Non, chérie. I have special plans for us Saturday. Didn't I tell you it would be special?"

Everdine thought back to that conversation where he said he fucked women in his bed, but she wasn't sure how that could be special. Maybe to him, but not really to her. She was truly confused now.

She joined Gabriel in the living room and he was sitting astride a white leather, tufted bench style sofa with no back to it. It was a combination of several squares and rectangles, creating nice conversation areas for parties, she imagined. Very modern. She sat on top of it facing him with her legs crossed.

"You are a very good cook- one of your many talents. Thanks again for dinner. The gift you gave me was very special Everdine, but you really should not spend that kind of money on me. You put a lot of thought into it and that means a lot to me."

Before he could go on Everdine had to tell him about her money. "Gabriel, there is something you don't know about me. I'm very well off financially even though I don't live like I am. My father set up a large trust fund for all of his kids and he is paying for this trip. But I'm also sitting on old cotton money that my great grandfather left my mother and me, as well as some technology stocks. That money is so old it has dust on it and it's never been touched. I don't even know how big it is now, but please let me do something nice for you if I want to because I'm sure there'll be other times."

"Thank you for your generosity. The reason I wanted to talk to you is to apologize for the way I've treated you."

"What do you mean?" His demeanor was very serious- a side of him she had never seen.

"Before today I was very rude to you and made all kinds of ugly comments and I'm ashamed of that. I never made such comments to any woman and you are so undeserving of that treatment."

"Why just me, Gabriel? I don't understand."

"I wish I could tell you, but I guess I just never met anyone like you. I was insanely attracted to you the moment I saw you and I'm not use to women putting me in my place. I had no idea how to handle you."

"Here, let me show you how to handle me. You put your hands around my waist and pull me close to you." Ever put Gabriel's hands on her waist, scooted forward on the bench and wrapped her legs around him and placed her hands on his shoulders.

"Now this is the part where you are supposed to kiss me." Gabriel didn't need to be asked again. He opted for fire this time and he and Everdine were devouring each other. He loved to nibble on her lower lip and she his upper lip. Everdine could not get enough of his tongue. If she didn't have him soon she would explode. Gabriel laid her back on the bench, kissing down her neck. Ever untwined her legs and placed her feet down on either side of the bench to give him all the access he wanted.

His hand slid down her firm stomach while his mouth took hers again. Slowly his fingers made their way under the waist of her shorts and played in her arousal, finding her sensitive bud. Ever made a little sound in the back of her throat when he touched her sensitive area and her heart was racing.

"Chérie, you taste so good. I can't get enough of you." He continued kissing down her neck.

"Then don't. Let's go to the bedroom. I want you so much, Gabriel. It's driving me crazy. I've waited so long for this."

"You don't understand chérie. I want it to be special. We had a deal and agreed on Saturday."

Gabriel continued kissing her soft skin and took small nibbles on her collar bone. Both of them could not control their breathing. Everdine grabbed Gabriel's hand and put it on her breast, moving it over her hardened nipple. He stopped kissing her and just lay his head on her chest. "You are trying to kill me, non?"

"No, it is you who is trying to kill me. Can't we just fool around and do everything but that?"

"Chérie, once I start with you like that I won't be able to stop. You know this."

Ever let out a big sigh. "Do what you like my dear frenchie, but don't think for one minute I'm going to make it easy for you. It's getting so hot in here sometimes I may have to wear the lingerie I bought with only you in mind."

They were both sitting upright now, keeping temptation at bay.

"But chérie, I told you I was going to buy lingerie for our night together."

"Well Gabriel, I was kind of hoping that we'll have more than one night. I'll be here for a week."

He didn't want to discuss the future too much with her. He wanted more than one night and he was glad to see she also was open to more.

"Yes, you are right. We have until Tuesday. So tell me about this lingerie."

"I've just never had someone to buy it for and wanted to. It was quite a turn on looking through it in the store knowing it would be you who'd take it off me."

Gabriel groaned and rolled his eyes at the thought of her in lingerie. This was going to be the test of all times not having sex with her until Saturday.

"I like to cuddle with you when I talk to you and the furniture in here is not very cozy. Let's go to the bedroom. I promise I'll behave."

"You, behave? No way, chérie. What is wrong with this that we are sitting on?"

Everdine got up from the tufted bench seating area and held out her hand for Gabriel. "This is great for talking to strangers or maybe having sex on it, but not so good for intimate conversations. Come on, I'll show you." Gabriel agreed. He'd had sex on the seating area plenty of times and rarely made it to the bed with women he did bring home.

She led him to the bedroom and motioned for him to get on the bed with all of the pillows. Gabriel's bed was large with a floor to ceiling tufted headboard in khaki colored fabric. The pillows were stacked up against it. He slid off his shoes and crawled up in the bed and sat against the pillows and eyed her suspiciously. Everdine crawled up beside him and threw her legs across his lap and put her arms around him. "See how nice it is to talk and be so close, comfortable and be able to lean back? I can also kiss your cheeks better," she said, pressing her lips his cheeks. "Why do you always smell so good, Gabriel?"

"Let me change the subject, chérie. Are you telling me that with all of the boyfriends you've had you never bought lingerie for them?"

"No. It just wasn't the same."

"How many men have you slept with, chérie?"

His direct question made her uneasy about the truth. Time to evade and direct the question back to him. "I'm sure not nearly as many partners as you have slept with."

"I hope not, chérie. But that still leaves a lot to the imagination."

Everdine's jaw dropped at his comment. "Tell me! How many have there been?" Suddenly, she was jealous at the thought.

"You really don't want to know, chérie. It's a lot. Maybe as many as I can count on my fingers. Maybe more. Is that answer enough for you?"

"I suppose. It just means that every woman gets to have sex with you but me."

"Earlier you said you had waited so long for this. In what way, chérie?"

Goodness, he was such a chatty Cathy tonight for some reason. Ever was wondering why he was asking so many questions about her past sexual experience. It was obvious that he had more than enough experience. She didn't want to go through what her sister went through with Anton, so back to ducking and dodging.

She was able to change the topic and her and Gabriel stayed up into the wee hours of the morning talking about anything and everything. They shared stories from their childhood and also their most intimate thoughts and feelings. In a span of less than 48 hours Gabriel became someone she could not live without. He most certainly felt the same about her, too.

It was 10:30 p.m. and Willadine decided to take Everdine's advice and send Anton a text message before going to bed.

To Anton: Are you asleep yet? Can you give me a call tonight or tomorrow morning if you have time?

Within ten seconds after her text she received a call from Anton. That was a good sign, Willie thought.

"Hello, Anton. I hope I didn't wake you."

"Non, chérie, I was just lying in bed looking over some emails before lights out. Is something wrong?"

"No, not exactly. Are you aware of what's going on with Everdine and Gabriel?"

"Oui, I saw them last night when I stopped by."

"You don't think they'll kill each other?"

"I don't think we need to be worried." Anton didn't say that with very much confidence.

"You don't sound very convincing, Anton."

"Well, it is hard to know what is going on with them. When I stopped by they were playing poker and were almost naked. Your sister was pretty hammered, but they both seemed content."

"Oh, she didn't tell me that. That's okay, though. I know it's because she thinks I'll worry about her. She called me today to tell me she would be staying there until a room at the hotel became available."

"I live on the same floor as Gabriel, so if something happens I'll call you in secret, okay?"

"Thanks, Anton."

"So how is the project coming along if you don't mind me asking?"

"No, I don't mind you asking and I need to apologize to you for my text message. It was very immature. You were the first man to ever hold me in such a cherished regard and I just.... I just.... had to accept that you and I will never have an intimate relationship or anything other than friendship. There, I got that out of the way."

"You don't need to apologize for anything, Willadine. I think any feelings you may have had were justified. Since I have you on the phone I wanted to tell you that on Friday there is an opportunity to see the manufacturing and shipping ops in Le Havre. I think Gabriel is going and the charter plane can pick you up on the way. Would that be okay?"

"Yes, I'd love to go. Are you going, too?"

"No, not this time. So where are you, Willadine?"

"That's too bad. Just a minute Anton........Vi ringrazio, cari..... I'm in Milan right now."

"You speak pretty good Italian. Are with with someone?"

"Yes, I'm staying with an old friend who was an exchange student at Duke .....È cattivo ragazzo.....sorry for the interruption. I'm looking forward to the Le Havre trip and thank you again for having such faith in me to work on this project. I really mean that."

"I should thank you, chérie. Be safe and take good care."

"You, too. Bye, Anton. Sleep well."

Willie ended the call and thought it went very well. She liked Ever's idea of trying to normalize her relations with Anton.

Hearing his voice again was torture, though. It was like silk to her ears. It also made her realize that she still burned for him. She still wanted him. Desperately.

This was not working out for Anton at all. He had not slept good since he ended it with Willadine and talking to her again only made him miss her even more. She sounded like she was doing well and moving on, but it didn't make him feel any better. Today when he was supposed to be taking part in a conference call he was in deep thought about her supple lips and having his hands on her ass again. And who was this friend she was visiting? Anton was worried that she would make a decision in haste and regret it later. He planned on keeping close tabs with her- as close as she would allow anyway.

Gabriel worked some in his home office after he and Ever stayed up until early morning hours talking. The pastels Ever bought him proved to be very therapeutic. Seeing Everdine asleep in his bed made him feel like he was looking in on someone else's life. He was still trying to grasp how his life had changed so profoundly in the last week, and particularly, the last few days. After he brushed his teeth he took off his clothes and joined Everdine in bed.

He was warm, hard and soft all at the same time. Sometime during the night Gabriel came to bed naked, just like her. She didn't even know what time it was, but she knew she wanted to explore this gorgeous man while she had him at an advantage. She scooted over as close as she could get and wrapped her arm and leg over him and snuggled in close to his chest. She could feel his length growing against her draped leg as she kissed him on the side of his chest. She moved her leg down and let her arm slide down, trying to be careful not to wake him. Her arm came down lower and she could feel it. He was so hard. Her heart was galloping as she placed her hand on top of his rock hard length. She took in a loud, involuntary gasp, but didn't move her hand away. She was too mortified at her own audacity to move, and if Gabriel had not said something she may have hyperventilated. "Be sure to exhale, chérie," he said in a low, sleepy voice.

If the room wasn't dark he would see that she was several shades of pink from being mortified and embarrassed. The size of his erection was staggering and she was afraid to move her hand now. "Did you bite off more than you can chew, ma chère?"

"I'm sorry to wake you Gabriel. I...I was just curious," she said, taking her hand away from him.

"Oh no you don't," he said, catching her hand and putting it back on his erection.

For the first time Everdine was frightened that she may get what she wanted. He took her hand under his and rubbed it up and down his length. They were both nothing but heartbeats and heavy breathing.

"I can already tell that neither of us will get any sleep if we don't do something. So you want to play a little, chérie?"

"Yes, Gabriel. Please."

"Music to my ears."

Gabriel pinned her hands over her head with one hand, rolled to his side and kissed her like she was his only salvation. His lips trailed down her neck onto her breast while his free hand roamed between her legs. He grazed his palm over the warm apex between her thighs and she was about to combust at his touch. She was hot, electric and wild.

As Gabriel kissed and worked her nipples with mouth and his fingers found her clitoris. "Do you trust me chérie?"

Trust you- I'm in love with you- she thought to herself.

"Yes, Gabriel, I trust you completely." The words were intoxicating to him, He didn't know why, but having her trust impassioned him. He'd never even cared to have a woman's trust before.

"I'm just going to play a little so don't be worried."

He rolled on top of her, spreading her legs, nestling in between them. Supporting himself with one elbow, he gripped his hardened length he teased her with it over her clitoris and around her opening, imbuing himself with her moisture. Gabriel knew he was in a very precarious position. He could take her now if he wanted to.

"Oh Gabriel," she moaned, "that feels so good. Please don't stop." He was growling something in French, which she was too euphoric to translate. He then rested his weight on both elbows and started to move over her clitoris with his erection, her arousal providing easy movement on top of her. The weight of his body moving back and forth over her was maddening. "Gabriel there is so much pressure. I'm going to explode." She was wild and erratic and Gabriel knew she was on the brink and so was he. Never had Gabriel had such a licentious woman in his bed. He rolled to the side and stroked her clit with his thumb and eased a finger inside her, moving with a slow, steady rhythm until he could feel her shaking.

Everdine was moving with Gabriel, trying to find relief together. She moaned torturously. "Oh Gabriel," she screamed, digging her claws into the bed as she came, her body arching up off the bed. He followed right behind her, stroking his penis until he came.

Gabriel rolled on top of Everdine, not caring about the mess between them. His face buried in the pillow beside her, he mumbled, "Tu es aimés chérie...." Everdine wished she could understand what he was saying. Her French was a little out of practice since her and Gabriel spoke mostly English together. It didn't help that he was talking into a pillow. "What did you say, Gabriel?"

"Nothing, chérie. I'll clean up. You stay in bed." Gabriel cleaned them both off with a washcloth and then crawled back into bed. They stayed up for an hour talking while he held her in his arms.

When Everdine woke Gabriel was spooned in behind her, her head resting on his bicep, his other arm around her waist. There was no greater feeling than being in his arms. His scent was home. She didn't want to know what it would be like not to touch him or smell him everyday. "Mmmm...this is heaven."

In an equally sleepy state Gabriel answered, "Oui, ma chère. Tu es ma ciel." Gabriel kissed her cheek, turned her over and pressed his lips to hers. "Good morning, beautiful."

A luminous smile graced Everdine's face. "Yes, it is good. Last night was out of this world. So sensual."

"Yes, chérie. Do you want to get coffee started while I get ready to leave? I have a lot of errands today and also have to fly to Geneva to pick something up."

"Of course, I'll get breakfast started. Ever put on some tight sweatpants and a small white t-shirt. She planned on working from Gabriel's apartment today, getting the data finished for Willie.

Over breakfast the two were cordial, but the air was heavy with contemplation. Gabriel couldn't help thinking there was something Everdine wasn't telling him. He needed to get her to talk. The comment she made yesterday about waiting so long and the way she responded to him last night left him with questions. It was also very clear that their relationship had taken a sharp turn and the uncertainty was very cutting.

Everdine was wondering what Gabriel had said to her in French after he pleasured her. She thought she'd heard a love in there somewhere.

"Chérie, yesterday when you said you were 'waiting so long for this', what did you mean? I asked you yesterday, but you didn't answer."

It would be hard to evade him, but she would try. "I don't know. I guess any time longer than I have to wait to make love to you is too long. I wanted you since the first night we met. While we are on confessions, what did you say when your head was buried in my pillow last night?"

"I probably said something like stay on your side of the bed from now on silly girl." Everdine thought he was so adorable when he was being sweet.

"Don't be ridiculous, Gabriel. Tell me."

"Yes, ma chère, me and my ridiculous self have to go now, so you think long and hard about what you meant yesterday. There are a lot of things to be discussed, Everdine, and I expect answers when I get home tonight." He didn't like at all how evasive she was sometimes.

Gabriel got up from the table with a tight line across his forehead. All he could think was how stubborn this woman was. She wore her expressions on her face and he could tell there was something she was not forthcoming with. He grabbed his briefcase and walked out the door, saying goodbye. Frustrated, Everdine followed right behind him.

Anton was about to make a call waiting for the elevator when they came bounding out into the foyer, screaming at each other. He decided based on previous experience it would best to end his call.

"...... don't you dare walk away from me like that."

"I'm sorry, were you saying something? Because I didn't hear you say anything, even after I asked you specifically to tell me what you meant," Gabriel growled.

"You want to know what I meant? I'll tell you. I meant you should have fucked me already. Is that good enough for you?" Anton's mouth gaped.

"No, it's not. And stop talking that way."

"You are the one who made the wager so that I'd have to sleep with you and now you don't have the balls to do it."

"You should know I have the balls to do it, chérie, since your hands were all over them last night. You oversexed little vixen!"

"You ass!" Ever brought her hand up across his cheek before he could stop it. Anton watched on in horror as these two were at it again. Willie was right that they did need looking after.

After Gabriel soothed his cheek with his hand, the fire jumped between their eyes. He grabbed Everdine and brought her in. His hands pulled at her waist and then he grabbed the back of her neck and tore his lips into hers, his tongue dug out her mouth as they were taking their last breaths with each other. He edged her back against the foyer wall and continued his assault on her mouth as he moved his arms down and brought her legs up she wrapped them around his waist. Finishing the kiss, he set her back down and held her like his life depended on it, one arm around her shoulder, the other arm cupping the back of her head, holding her close to him as he leaned down to her ear.

"I'll tell you what I said last night, chérie," Gabriel whispered in her ear. "I said, you are my love, my heaven." With that, he sweetly kissed her lips and stepped into the elevator with Anton. Ever rested against the wall panting with her eyes closed, relishing his touch, his kiss. Damn!

It wasn't efficient enough to say that sparks flew when Gabriel and Ever were together- it more resembled a volcanic eruption. As beautiful and powerful as it was, it was bound to do some damage. "Glad to see you two are getting along better now," Anton smirked. Gabriel just shook his head. "This woman will be the death of me. I'm mad about her, though."

"Willie and I are both worried about you two staying in the same apartment together. If it becomes too much we can surely find other accommodations for her."

"No way. I'd go crazy if she ever left."

"Yes, because the way you two are carrying on now is perfectly sane." Anton looked baffled at his brother.

"Fire and ice. It will get better this weekend, I promise. I have errands to run and can drop you off by the office unless you need the car."

"That will be fine. I wanted to see if you could go to Le Havre tomorrow with Willadine. Byron's son may be able to go, though. He's been in Milan this week getting Willie set up with a VPN."

"Already planned on going, so I'll be glad to take Willadine with me."

"Great."

Anton got out of the limo and walked to his office. He found himself thinking of any excuse to call Willadine. She did want to have updates about Everdine and Gabriel and he could also relay flight plans to her, even though his secretary usually did that. Once he decided it was okay to call her, Anton anxiously dialed her number.

"Hmmmm .....hello."

"Hello Willadine, It's Anton. I'm sorry, chérie, did I wake you?"

"Yes, but it's okay. I didn't get in until late last night and I need to get up anyway." Willie yawned as she rolled over in bed.

"So you went out after we spoke on the phone?"

"Yes. You know how late they get started in Italy. I worked for 15 hours yesterday and just needed to get out. Is anything wrong?"

"I wanted to give you your flight information for tomorrow morning. The plane will arrive at 9:15 and you'll go to the private aviation area for boarding. Gabriel will be flying with you. Maybe you can convince him that he and Everdine are going to kill each other if they don't sleep in separate quarters."

"What happened Anton?" Willie sounded worried.

"They were fighting at the elevator when I was waiting there this morning. He said some ugly words and she slapped him, but then they kissed and may have done more if there was a bed in the foyer."

"Oy! It really is a sickness what they have, isn't it?"

"Yes it is, but it may be best if you don't mention it to Ever since I think they will be fine today. You wanted..."

"Just a minute Anton......Grazie per il caffè. Mi puoi dare il mio abito?...sorry, go ahead Anton."

"You wanted me to give an update and that's it. Did you just say robe?"

"Uh....yes."

"Is there a guy in there with you?"

"Yes, my friend Giovanni that I went to Duke with. Remember?"

"Yes, yes, I do. So why do you need a robe?"

Willie was getting a little annoyed that he felt as though he had a right to question her, but happy that he still cared. "It is very hot up here in the rooftop apartment and I didn't sleep with any clothes on under the covers last night. Giovanni brought me some coffee from downstairs and I asked him to give me my robe on his way out. Not that it's any business of yours, Anton."

"I'm sorry, Chérie, you are right. Please forgive me. I still care about you as a dear friend. I just thought you were staying at a hotel."

"It's fine Anton. I still care about you as a friend, too. There was an issue at the hotel and Giovanni offered me this apartment."

"I see. Have a great day Willadine and don't work too hard."

"Thanks for the call Anton. It's good to hear your voice."

Blood was boiling and thoughts were flying. Anton wanted nothing more than to go to Willadine and yank her out of Milan. Why was she parading around in front of this Italian like that? She was always so shy around him, Anton thought, but with this Giovanni she seemed perfectly at home. He had to clear his head and not get distracted by thoughts of her.

Preparations for his date with Everdine on Saturday kept Gabriel busy all morning. He wanted everything to be perfect. He made calls to Geneva for the special gift he was going to pick up in the afternoon and left no detail untouched. Everdine had over an hour to cool off since their spat in the foyer of his apartment, so he thought a text message would be a nice gesture.

To Everdine: How is my favorite slugger? I hope you know how crazy I am about you.

To Gabriel: Sorry about this morning-I'm crazy about you too-so very much! It's hard not being able to express how I feel about you until Saturday. Last night was wonderful!

To Everdine: You can always tell me how you feel chérie. Want to have a late lunch together?

To Gabriel: I wish I could tell you- don't want to scare you. Lunch would be great. I can make something at home.

To Everdine: I'll be home at 1:30.

She absolutely loved cooking for Gabriel. Maybe it was the southern girl in her, but when she saw him enjoying what she had prepared for him it made her heart swell. Her attraction to him was something she never denied. The first time she met him she would have gladly spent the night with him if he hadn't been such a jerk. Being in close quarters with him had somehow changed things. It was no longer about the one night of passion they would share. It was about how she felt now and how she would feel after they had sex. A bet is a bet, but she could start to feel a sliver the heartache for what was to come after they had their night together.

Gabriel admitted to Ever that he loved coming home and seeing a woman cook in his kitchen. What he didn't tell her is that it was just her he loved seeing in his kitchen. Never had such a simple act, such as having her prepare lunch for him, brought such clarity to his life. It was like she belonged to him. The rush he got when he came up to his apartment, knowing that she was there waiting for him turned him on. Right now, they both just had to survive until Saturday.

After a calm lunch both Gabriel and Everdine agreed to back off their affectionate pursuits until it was time. The tension was just way too high and Ever respected Gabriel's wish to wait until Saturday as agreed. Neither of them liked arguing with the other, but having such unrequited feelings left them sexually frustrated.

"I'm leaving for Geneva now and I'll be back early evening if all goes well. Thank you for the lunch, chérie. I love it when you cook for me." Gabriel stood up and walked over to Ever. He looked so handsome in his crisp white dress shirt and black slacks, she thought.

"Thank you, Gabriel. I love to cook for you, so it works out perfectly. Have a nice flight and see you tonight."

"Can I just get a hug, chérie? No kissing since we know where that will lead."

"Of course. You better give me a hug before you go." Everdine moved forward as Gabriel wrapped his arms around her back. Her arms laced under his and she gently caressed his back and laid her cheek against his chest. His scent was heavenly. Gabriel noticed her breathing growing faster on his chest. They both just stood there in each other's arms and let the feeling, warmth and love emanate around them. He stroked the back of her hair. It didn't matter if they kissed or touched, the desire was still the same. Just being in the same room was enough to ignite the passion that had been building since they first met.

Ever and Willie spoke on the phone for a long time going over the data and ideas for the best possible outcome for the restructuring project. Willie was enjoying Milan, but missed her sister. All of the calculations were complete and now they were putting it all together for different financial projections based on which labor markets and manufacturing centers that would be utilized. According to their calculations the biggest savings would shave off $3 million in manufacturing, labor and shipping costs, but they felt the other option, saving $1 million would be best in the long term due to political and social reasons, as well as externalities.

Willie was glad that Gabriel would be flying with her tomorrow to Le Havre. She had told Ever that Byron's son, David, had been pursuing her heavily and she didn't like it. She had to practically fight him off once and didn't trust him. It was a huge relief that Gabriel would be there to act as a buffer.

Gabriel arrived at the apartment shortly after 7 p.m. It had been a long, exhausting day for him and he was looking forward to spending the rest of it with Everdine. He had been spending time at work all week on a special surprise for Ever. He also had a few questions he wanted her to answer, but didn't want to risk them getting into another fight. They sat on his patio, enjoying a gorgeous sunset, a glass of wine and holding hands. Gabriel thought it would be a good time to get to get her to open up.

"How many serious boyfriends have you had, Everdine?"

"I don't think I've really had one that I would call very serious since high school- fun maybe. What about you? How many girlfriends? Ever thought the best way to keep his attention off her would be to answer him with more questions.

"Why have you never had a serious boyfriend?" Gabriel knew what she was doing and he would not let her get away with cheap answers.

"There were a few guys in college that I dated, but I don't think they appreciated how outspoken I was. I didn't want to fall in love either, so that kept my relationships from getting serious."

"And falling in love would be so bad, ma chère?"

"Academics always came first with me. Let's see, Gabriel..... how many women have you been in love with?"

"I had one or two serious girlfriends when I studied at the University of Zürich, but wasn't in love. That was a long time ago. With work it's hard to find the right woman to cultivate the right kind of relationship with."

"I understand that. I guess my worst fear is that I'll end up like my mother and that is why I don't see anything wrong with wanting to separate love and sex."

"What happened with your mom?"

"My dad was passing through town playing poker and he swept my mom off her feet. She ended up getting pregnant, but he wouldn't marry her or give up his lifestyle. She always kept hope that he would eventually settle down and waited for him. She wasted her whole life on a love that was never returned."

"Willie's mother never married, either?"

"No, she didn't. Our father seemed to have a stronger relationship with Willie's mom and I wouldn't be surprised if they ended up together after all."

Gabriel thought it was time let the conversation take a serious turn. It was important that she could trust him enough to tell him anything.

"Do you know how much I love spending time with you, chérie?" He brought her hand to his lips, kissing her palm.

"If it's as much as I like spending time with you, then I do know. You are the most wonderful man I've ever met, Gabriel," she said, looking directly at him with a stomach full of butterflies.

"Wonderful enough to call me a boyfriend?"

A huge grin spread across Everdine's face. "I'd be lucky to call you my boyfriend. Are you asking?"

"Oui. I've never felt so strongly about a woman before, Everdine, and I don't want you separating love and sex with any other man but me right now." She loved how he could be funny, yet serious, at the same time.

Gabriel stood up, pulling her up with him and buried his lips in hers, cupping the back of her head with his hands. She tasted so sweet and her lips were softer than silk. He couldn't wait to taste the rest of her Saturday.

"Come, girlfriend, it is time to go to bed. I have an early flight and you have a day at the spa, correct?"

"Yes."

This time Gabriel wore some black silk pajama bottoms to bed and Everdine wore a sleeveless, pink cotton negligee. They kissed very briefly and Everdine scooted as far away from Gabriel as she could on the bed. The temptation was more than she cared to test. Sleep finally came.

She dreamed she was falling and tried to steady herself. The sudden feeling of her stomach giving out ended in a loud thud on the marble floor and a tingling pain on the side of her head. By the time Everdine realized she was on the floor Gabriel had turned a bed lamp on and was at her side in a flash.

"Ma chère, are you okay?"

"Yes," Ever said in a groggy voice, "I dreamed I was falling."

"Well, chérie, your dream came true. Do you hurt anywhere?"

"No I don't think so."

Gabriel turned her bed lamp on and helped her up and that is when he saw the blood on the floor, and blood that was trickling down her night gown. "Oh mon Dieu." Gabriel said in shock. "Chérie, you have a cut on your head. I need to take a look."

Gabriel pulled her hair away and saw where the gash was. She must have caught the edge of the star shaped nightstand on her temple when she fell. The amount of blood was ghastly. Gabriel stripped off Everdine's pillowcase, folded it and held it to her head applying pressure to it. "Chérie, you sit here and hold this and we'll get ready to go to the hospital. You will need stitches."

"Are you sure Gabriel? It doesn't even hurt."

"Trust me, I'm sure. Sit here and I'll get some clothes for you and clean this up. He called his brother to come over and help."

In a matter of minutes Gabriel helped Everdine put on some clothes while keeping pressure on her cut and got dressed himself. He was cleaning the blood off the floor when Anton came in.

"I could hardly understand you," Anton said as he sauntered into Gabriel's bedroom. He had a quick look at Everdine and the floor and almost passed out. "Oh mon Dieu, you two are trying to kill each other. What happened here, Gabriel?"

"Calm down brother and don't always think the worst. Everdine had a nightmare and fell off the bed, cutting her head on the nightstand." Gabriel seemed to have gotten over his initial panic after seeing the blood.

"The reason I called you over is because I need to take Everdine to the clinic for stitches and you'll need to fill in on the trip to Le Havre. The plane leaves in a little over an hour."

"I can just have David fly with Willadine. He was going to go anyway before you decided to go. Since I'll be in Geneva overnight Saturday it will be easier if he goes."

"No," Everdine shouted. "Please don't send David."

Both men turn to Everdine, surprised by her outburst. "Why?" They both asked at the same time.

"I..uh....don't think Willie would like it."

"What is going on, Everdine? I need to know." Anton's voice was stern and Ever knew she had to tell him. "Anton, you need to remain calm and talk to Willie before you say anything to David. Let her explain..."

"Dammit, Everdine, tell me," Anton demanded.

"Okay. David came on to her when he went to Milan to meet with her about the project and made a few passes at her. You know how shy she is, so it was very hard for her to deal with him. She ended up staying with an old friend of ours because she didn't feel safe staying alone at the hotel."

"I will fucking kill him. Why didn't she tell me?" Anton slammed his fist on the dresser and was pacing back and forth in Gabriel's apartment, gripping his hair with his fingers.

"The last time she confided in you it did't go too well. Maybe she doesn't trust you. Just talk to Willie and get the whole story before you say anything to David or do something irrational. I thought she handled it fine. She made me promise not to tell you."

"I need to go so I can catch the flight. Everdine, I hope you are feeling better. Thanks for your help on the project. I'll catch up with you later, Gabriel."

"See you, brother. Remember to keep your head screwed on."

"Yes, I'll probably do just as good as you two did the other morning at the elevator. Anton casted his steely eyes at them and left the apartment.

Gabriel drove Everdine to the emergency clinic making sure to be extra careful and slow. "How are you doing, chérie?"

"I'm doing fine. Thanks for your help, Gabriel."

"Of course, it's only natural to care for you, ma chère." When they pulled up to the clinic Gabriel took a call on his phone. Ever was worried about keeping him from his work. If he was inconvenienced he didn't let her know.

"Gabriel, I can take a cab back to your apartment. I know you are busy and I would feel bad about keeping you from your work."

"That is nonsense, Everdine. I want to be with you today, so don't worry about it. I've already cleared my schedule."

"You really didn't need to do that, but I appreciate it."

"Oui, I did need to do it."

Gabriel got Ever checked into the clinic and helped her fill out the paperwork. They only had to wait fifteen minutes before being shown back to a room. A nurse came in to do an assessment of Ever's injury. She asked Gabriel what relation he was to the patient and it warmed Everdine's heart when he said he was her boyfriend. Her heart was all a flutter until the nurse asked her if she was on birth control and when was the last time she had her cycle. Ever's face immediately turned red. "Why would that matter?" Ever asked the nurse.

"Ms. Crenshaw we may need to give you an antibiotic and do a scan or x-ray of the injury. That is why we need answers to these questions."

"I use an implant birth control method in my arm and I haven't had my cycle in over a year due to my birth control."

"Good. When was the last time you had intercourse?" The nurse looked at a stunned Everdine and then glanced over to Gabriel who was looking with anticipation at Ever. "Well, there is no possibility at all that I could be pregnant if that is what you mean." Everdine didn't want to tell the nurse that she was a virgin with Gabriel in the room. She also didn't want to tell a lie. She had been able to skirt around that dilemma so far and Gabriel just assumed she'd had sexual relationships before.

"And you are sure- so no intercourse in the last few months then?"

"That is correct." Never had Everdine been so embarrassed. She was sure that the nurse thought she was insane. After all, to look at Gabriel is to have sex with him. He was such a hunk. She almost wanted to scream out that they were going to do it on Saturday.

The doctor cleaned the wound area and sent her home with ten stitches. Luckily, they were the dissolvable kind covered with a liquid protectant, so she didn't need to have them removed. What made her most excited was the doctor telling her she could have quick showers, but not to submerge her head completely in water. Ever didn't feel like she was at the height of beauty. She was also excited that she would be able to make her spa appointment before lunchtime.

CHAPTER 11

Willadine was excited for the opportunity to tour the manufacturing operations in northern France. Gabriel explained that she would get a complete overview of the production process from raw materials to finished product. She brought her luggage with her since she would be going to Torino next. In her search for Marvadine in Milan she discovered that there were cafes in Lyon and Torino where Marvadine was singing regularly.

It was time to board the private jet to Le Havre. Willadine was nervous about flying with Gabriel. She had only seen him when he was with Everdine and had spoken to him over the phone once regarding the project. He was extremely charming and just as handsome as Anton, and maybe that was why she was nervous.

Willadine was greeted by the captain of the plane when she boarded. He told her that the travel plans had changed and that he would be flying her to Monte Carlo instead. Willie didn't know what to think, but she needed to find out what was going on. The captain told her she had a few minutes to make some calls if necessary. She checked her phone and had a message from Anton.

To Willadine: Had to fly to Le Havre to make changes in our team/project. Will talk to you tomorrow. Since your sister's accident I thought you may want to see her.

Willie's heart sank. What happened to Everdine? She frantically called her sister and the phone rang three times before being answered. "Oui, Delacroix"

"Gabriel?"

"Yes, Willie, how are you?"

"I'd like to speak with my sister."

"It will be a few minutes. She is washing the blood out of her hair and it is taking a while."

"GABRIEL what happened to my sister? Is she okay?"

"Oh, yes, ma chère, she is fine. She got stitches this morning and the doctor told her she could clean up in the shower."

"Why did she need stitches? Are you two trying to kill each other again?"

"Oh, I guess Anton didn't tell you. No, we are not killing each other. Ever had a dream this morning and fell out of the bed, cutting her head on the nightstand. I took her to get stitches and decided to take off work today just to make sure she was fine."

A wave of relief flooded through Willie. Her sister was fine and that is all that mattered. She did want to go to Monte Carlo and try to talk some sense into her though.

"I didn't know. Anton only sent me a text that he had to take care of something in Le Havre himself and that I was flying to Monte Carlo so I could visit with Ever."

"He'll be back tomorrow. I know Ever would love to see you. I'm taking her to a spa appointment at 11:45 and I'll let them know you'll be joining your sister. Is that okay?"

"Wow, of course. Thank you so much and see you soon."

Utter shock crossed Willie's face after she got off the phone with Gabriel. What had her sister done to him? Obviously, she had him wrapped around her little finger. What a difference a few days made. Maybe Gabriel was the one that needed saving instead of her sister. Regardless of who needed saving this was something she had to see for herself.

By the time Everdine finished cleaning up and got dressed it was time for them to pick Willie up from the airport. She was so excited that her sister was coming to Monte Carlo. Maybe she could stay a few days. The girls squealed in delight as they saw each other at the airport and it was very touching for Gabriel to watch. He whisked them away to the spa and made a few calls while they were getting pampered.

Anton was not a man to be messed with. He was fuming mad all the way to LeHavre. When he learned that David had been harassing Willie under the auspices of work he decided swift action was needed. It only took a few calls to find out that David had quite a reputation for taking advantage of women he worked with. By some accounts he should have been in jail for rape, but proof was hard to make in most cases. David obviously knew how to work it to his advantage so it looked like the women were compliant. The thought of this man having his hands on Willadine made him blind with anger. He knew how shy Willie was and how she may seem like the perfect victim to him. Anton delivered his message in a clear, calm tone to both David and Byron. He made sure Byron knew what a liability this could be for him in the future when his son behaved like this toward women and then the gloves were off. Threats flew from both sides. David made the comment that he thought Willadine was rather enjoying herself when he groped her and that was all it took for Anton to tear into him like a windmill in a tornado. With a punch connecting to his jaw, David went down quick. Anton told him to stay away from Willadine and left. He still had business to take care of in Geneva before going back to Monte Carlo.

The girls took time to catch up with each other while getting treatments at the spa. Ever made sure everything was waxed and smooth. Willie did the same, but didn't know why. It wasn't like she had anyone to impress. They both got their hair and nails done, too, with great care taken for Everdine's stitches. When they finished they met Gabriel in the lobby talking to a beautiful brunette.

"As you can see I have two dates today," he said to the lady, offering his arms for both Ever and Willie. "Well they are certainly lucky," the woman said. "Just a minute Gabriel, we have to pay," Ever said. The lady behind the counter said the bill was already taken care of.

"Gabriel, how much do I owe you?" Willie asked. "It is my pleasure to treat you both," Gabriel stated. It really was hard to argue with him. "I'm the one who benefits from such beautiful ladies for dinner, so it is only fair that I pay."

After a whisper to her sister, Everdine let Gabriel know that they were taking him out to dinner. They went back to his apartment to drop off Willie's luggage and relax some before deciding on where to go for dinner. Gabriel was really surprised at how much he enjoyed himself with the girls. It would have never crossed his mind in a million years that he would get pleasure out of doing something so simple and banal with a woman. Perhaps it was anticipation of seeing what Ever looked like under her panties after getting everything waxed. He saw on the itemized bill that they both got a full bikini wax and the thought of Ever's bare pussy in his head made him dizzy with lust for her.

Conversation during dinner was stimulating and educational. Gabriel learned more about their unique relationship and how different their upbringing was. Willie was basically a farmhand growing up and picked tobacco through high school so she would have enough money for living expenses in college despite having a scholarship and a healthy trust fund from her father. She also let them in on a secret that she had made and operated a moonshine still for her father. He made sure her activities were within the letter of the law so she would not jeopardize her future with legal issues. It was legal to make moonshine and drink it on your own property, but it was illegal to transport it. There was also the issue of taxation. When a new sheriff was elected Willie had to stop making it because her father told her he was unsympathetic to moonshiners. Gabriel also discovered that Everdine had a desire to make her own perfume and that was why she majored in chemistry. She ended up siding with practicality instead and decided to work in economics. He was amazed at how driven, smart and level-headed they were despite their uncommon . upbringing.

The limo ride back to the apartment was quiet. With lots wonderful red wine and a big meal, they were sated and relaxed. Willie's phone rang and she answered it before checking to see who was calling.

"Hello"

"You fucking bitch. I will kill you. What did you tell your boyfriend?"

His anger was so pronounced that Willie didn't recognize the caller to be David.

"Who is this?" Gabriel was sitting beside her and could hear the conversation.

"This is David you stupid whore."

"I have no idea what you are talking about David."

"Oh really! Your boyfriend Anton kicked me off the project today and took a swing at me. If I ever see you again I will...." Gabriel had heard enough and grabbed Willie's phone.

"Listen to me you piece of shit. If you come anywhere near her I will take care of you myself and enjoy doing it. You call her again and we will press charges. Stay the fuck away and be thankful you are still able to walk and talk." With that Gabriel hung up the phone, seething.

Willie was in tears. She had not said anything to anyone about David except for Everdine. She was glad to have this monkey off her back but felt guilty for all the trouble it had caused.

"I'm so sorry, Gabriel. I didn't mean to cause any trouble. I have no idea how Anton even knew about David. Anton is probably so angry with me. I swear I didn't do anything to encourage David."

"Ma chère, we know that. Calm down." Gabriel took out a handkerchief and wiped her tears. "When I had to take care of your sister this morning I needed someone to fill in on the trip to Le Havre and Anton was going to send David. Everdine insisted that you not go with David and Anton finally got her to tell why. You are not at fault here."

"He is right, Willie. David is a criminal and you are not to blame."

"If I hadn't started working on this project then Anton wouldn't have any issues with David. This is my fault and now the project is in jeopardy."

Gabriel couldn't stand for her to think that way. Ever also tried to allay her fears about Anton being mad.

"Willie there is something you should know. We did some checking up on David and he has done this kind of thing before with female colleagues, but even worse, he is accused of rape. We are glad Everdine told us, otherwise this could have ended very differently. We should make a report to the police so he can't do this to another woman."

Willie just gazed out the window, tears falling silently. This trip to Europe was not at all what she had thought it would be. Her whole life she'd had control of her emotions and feelings, but not this time. She was willing to give her whole self to Anton, but he rejected her and now she was in an emotional blizzard. When they got back to the apartment she was exhausted and Everdine was also tired. It was then she realized she had nowhere to sleep and hadn't even thought to book a hotel room- not that any were available.

"You two look tired and I am also worn out. I'm going to get a hotel room and maybe we can meet for breakfast. Sound good?" Willie tried to sound perky even though she was anything but.

"Not so fast Willadine," Gabriel sputtered. "Anton will not be back from Geneva until tomorrow and you can stay in his place tonight. It is right across the hall. I'll call him and tell him once I put my girlfriend to bed. Besides, there are no hotel rooms available right now- just ask your sister."

"He is right, Willie. I spent hours on the phone trying to find a room before I sold my soul to the devil." Everdine smiled and kissed the back of Gabriel's hand as she said it. He kissed the back of her hand in return. Willadine could tell by the way he looked at her that they needed some alone time and she didn't want to argue, so she agreed to go to Anton's apartment. Gabriel took her luggage and walked her over to his place. It looked identical to Gabriel's, even down to the white, tufted bench seating in the living room. Must have been a designer special, she thought. Anton's room had a slate blue and warm grey color palette and was almost sterile it was so clean. Willie felt very nervous being in his apartment without him, but then thought she'd be even more nervous if he was there with her. Gabriel told her to make herself at home and help herself to the kitchen, shower or whatever she needed and then set her luggage down before he left.

Looking around Willie thought his place very much reflected the kind of person he was- cool with warm undertones. He had shown her his warm side before, as well as his cool side. She didn't know if she could ever be just friends with him and having to pretend she was fine around him was eating at her already. She'd make sure she was up early and out of his apartment before he arrived home.

After helping herself to two glasses of Anton's wine, she brushed her teeth, put on her cotton camisole on and crawled into his bed. Anton's scent permeated the pillow and she just melted into it. More than anything she still wanted to make love to him. She got hot recalling how he made her climax back in Geneva. She wanted to feel all of these things with Anton and only him. With Anton's masculine scent hugging her senses she fell asleep.

Gabriel looked at Everdine's stitches before she got ready for bed. He wanted to make sure everything looked fine and she wasn't getting an infection. Her hair covered the stitches, much to her relief. Her head was a little sore and she was tired. She knew Gabriel had to catch up on some work, so she decided to go to bed.

"Chérie, let me tuck you in bed and I'll just lay down with you a minute to make sure you are not too close to the edge."

"Gabriel I can never thank you enough for the kindness you showed my sister and me today. You were so sweet and it means so much to me. Thank you." Ever reached up and kissed him softly on the cheek, slipping her lips over to his and continued her very own personal thank you. Their kiss picked up intensity and she tried to devour him with her lips and tongue, standing beside the bed. There was one way she wanted to reward him for his kindness and she was hoping he would allow her. As her kisses trailed down his neck she felt the huge bulge in his pants against her stomach. They hardly had any time alone today and she wanted to make up for it. She gently unzipped his pants as he was sucking on her neck and then she lightly dropped to her knees. With both hands she unbuttoned his pants, looking up at him. The fire was lit. "Chérie, you don't have to do this. I know you are tired."

"Please, Gabriel, I want to do this. I need to feel you. Let me know if I'm not doing it right." With that Ever eased down his pants and bikini briefs and got sight of her new best friend, as Gabriel referred to it the other night. He was magnificent in size and Ever wondered what he tasted like. His penis was warm, soft and hard in her hands. She took him in her mouth and Gabriel moaned in pleasure. She took him in as far as she could and made circular motions around his shaft with her tongue. His tip was so smooth and soft and she loved licking and caressing it between her lips. She could taste the excitement oozing out and it turned her on to know that he was so aroused. His hands cupped the back of her head and held her steady.

"That feels so good, chérie." Her hands moved with her mouth and she caressed his testicles. That sent him over the edge. "I'm getting ready to come chérie, so you better stop." Everdine moved her mouth over him faster, back and forth, as deep as she could go. "I'm coming, Ever," he groaned. His warm liquid sprung into the back of her throat and she slowly continued to bring him down, swallowing what he just gave her. She was able to hold back her gag reflex.

"That was amazing, Everdine. So amazing. You drive me crazy." She gave him a quick kiss before going to the bathroom to get ready for bed. She was exhausted, but really wanted to take care of him.

"Chérie, is there anything I can do for you?" Gabriel asked as he kissed her soft mouth. "You can tuck me in bed. We have a big day ahead of us tomorrow, right?" She smiled at him and he returned the sentiment.

"Yes, sweet Everdine, we do have a big day tomorrow. How does your head feel?"

"It's fine. I took some aspirin after I brushed my teeth."

"Let's get you into bed now before you get any other ideas."

Gabriel walked over and pulled down the covers to the bed and tucked her in and then came in behind and spooned her. "I'm only going to stay for a little bit and then check in on work."

"Thanks, Gabriel," Ever murmured as she slipped away. Gabriel caressed her shoulder and her hair, kissing her where his hands graced. She was sound asleep and beautiful. "Je t'aime ma chérie." Gabriel brushed his lips against her forehead and went to his office to catch up on work for a few hours and then he'd hopefully be in bed by midnight.

Anton arrived at his apartment at 5am, tired and ragged. He had to do damage control from kicking Byron and David off the project and made sure all interested parties knew that he was in charge and handling the restructuring. He dropped his briefcase by the door and staggered into his bedroom. After a quick shower and change into clean boxers he was ready to climb into bed. What he saw gave his heart a jump. There was someone in his bed- a woman. He could see through the dim light and mass of curly hair that it was Willadine, beautiful Willadine. Gabriel must have let her in and forgot to tell him. He knew he'd had his hands full today, as well. Even though Anton considered crawling in bed with her, he thought better of doing something that would likely end in a confrontation. Instead he thought he would stay up for another hour and make coffee and hardboiled eggs, and take care of a few emails. At 6:30 he thought he heard her moving around and he walked back to his bedroom.

The side lamp was turned on and he could see her clothes laid across the bed. Willie came out of the bathroom, dripping wet with a towel over her head, drying it as thoroughly as possible with both arms moving the towel around her hair. Anton stood there motionless, taking in her naked, damp body.

He breasts were full, round and perfect and he wanted to suck her nipples to a hard peak. Then he would take care of the glistening drops of water on her tight pussy by licking it clean. She was completely waxed down there and it made him rock hard. Her body was unlike any other he had seen, curvy and firm and in no way lacking. He had enjoyed many women, but none like her.

Willadine was audibly startled when she brought her towel down and saw him standing there. She slowly wrapped the towel around her body. Anton could only excuse himself. "I'm so sorry, chérie, I didn't know you were staying here until an hour ago and I thought I heard you wake up and came in to talk to you."

"I'm the one that needs to apologize. You must be exhausted Anton. I'll be gone in a few minutes."

"No, Willie, please don't go. I made you coffee and eggs and the bakery items will be brought up soon. Please stay and make yourself at home. I'd like to sleep a few hours and then we should talk."

"That's very sweet, Anton. Thank you. I'd like to stay for breakfast."

"You'd also do me a favor by keeping my brother at bay should he come over wanting to talk. I forwarded my calls to him, so he should be awake any minute now."

"Of course, Anton. Is there anything I else I can do for you?"

"A hug would be nice."

Willadine tensed and nervously reached up around Anton's neck to hug him. His scent was heady and pulled at her insides as she lay her head against his shoulder. Everything about him was perfect. Anton felt his way around her back and pressed her against him and buried his face in her damp hair. He just held her close and filled himself with her smell and touch. "I'm so sorry he put his hands on you Willadine," Anton whispered. "Anton.....I"

"Shhhh....we'll talk later, chérie." Anton drew back and gave her a lingering kiss on her cheek and left for the kitchen to set the table for her. Willie got dressed and met Anton in the kitchen. "I'll see you in a couple of hours. Help yourself to anything you need in the house, chérie."

"Sleep well, Anton." As he walked toward his bedroom Willie thought how she would love to go and take a nap with him. She was still weary from all of the activity yesterday and waking up early to avoid Anton proved fruitless. Wille decided to hold off on breakfast and went to Anton's office and laid down on the couch. It looked much more comfortable than the tufted bench seating in the living room. It was big, plush and cozy. She imagined Anton took many naps on this sofa.

CHAPTER 12

"Willadine, wake up, chérie. It's 10:00."

Willie rolled over on the couch and was greeted by Anton.

"Goodness, I didn't mean to sleep this late." She jutted up on the sofa.

"It is okay. You needed to sleep. I just wish you'd have told me and you could have slept in my bed."

"Oh no, Anton. I saw how spent you were when you came home this morning. You needed your bed more than I did."

"Well I would have gladly shared it with you. We are adults, you know."

Willadine just looked away at his insinuation. Being intimate with him in any way would send her running for the hills.

"I didn't eat breakfast yet or have coffee. What about you?"

"Non, shall we eat together?"

"Yes, that would be great."

Anton led Willie out to the balcony and they enjoyed their breakfast in the warm, morning sun. Anton was being so welcoming and sweet to her that she was starting to worry. It was time to talk about what had happened with David and Anton was careful introducing the topic.

"You should already know that I kicked David and Byron off the project. Chérie, why didn't you tell me that David was harassing you?"

"It was very hard to talk to you at that point and still is. I just felt like I was an outsider and had no authority to complain I guess. David made it sound like you brought me on this job for one reason."

"How many times did he touch you, chérie?"

Willie just bowed her head and tears started rolling silently down her cheeks. "It's over with Anton. Can't we just forget about it?" Anton got up and walked around to her pulling her up into his arms, holding her close.

"Did it happen more than once?"

"Yes."

"How did it happen?"

"Oh my God, you think I let him do this to me?" Willie backed away from Anton and ran into the living room to get her luggage and leave. He followed close behind her.

"Non, chérie, I'm just trying to understand how he was able to do this. How he operates. Please don't go. I feel horrible that I put you in this situation with him. Please."

An upset Willadine turned around and stared at Anton with red eyes.

"Okay, I'll tell you everything, but don't judge me Anton." Willie sat down on the banquette in the living room.

"I'm not judging you, Willie. I promise."

"Well, it started when he came to Milan to set up my VPN for the project. We were discussing work at the hotel lounge and he insisted on walking me to my room. I thought he was just concerned for my safety. When I got to the room and was trying to work the key, he grabbed my butt. It was shocking and I told him to stop. He just apologized and said he was reading the wrong signals and said to forget it ever happened and left. The next day he said he wanted to go over the projections with me in the office of his hotel room. He was walking around the room talking about the project and then as I was sitting in the chair his hands came down on my shoulders from behind and he kissed my neck. I was so stunned. He said that since I was in his hotel room I must have expected it. Then he grabbed my wrist and tried to put my hand on his privates. That is when I kicked him and ran out of the hotel room. After that I decided to stay with my friend from college who lives in Milan. He is very nice and very gay, and I didn't have to worry about my safety. That night David said I should come back to get my laptop and he promised he wouldn't try anything. I told him no. He said that you would think it was all my fault if I said anything to you and if I didn't come and get my laptop he would say something to you himself.

I brought Giovanni with me, to his surprise, and got my laptop and left. That is all."

Anton's face was hardened. "I should have killed him when I had the chance."

"There is one more thing Anton," Willie said with tears streaming down her face much faster now. "He called me yesterday and said he was going to kill me. I don't know what to do."

Anton stopped pacing the room and knelt down to Willie, wiping her tears away. "Chérie, I promise you he will not come anywhere near you. He would have to get through me first. Gabriel and I will take care of him, so don't worry. I don't think he meant it. You should have told me. I would have believed you, Willadine." Anton folded her in a hug and held her for a few minutes.

"You will stay here so I know that you are safe. Now that we have that out of the way I need your help with something, Willie."

"Of course, Anton. I'll do anything for you."

"Good. For the next few days I need your help on the project. Since Byron and David are no longer backers we will be making the pitch to the bank. We'll need to turn every dollar twice and go through every single detail. I let David handle this so I'm not up to speed on what you have done thus far. Do you mind being holed up in the apartment working on this until I'm satisfied with what we have?"

"I'm all yours Anton....well...I mean use me how you.....no, I mean I'll stay as long as necessary." Willie was completely flustered.

"I love it when you blush, Chérie."

"Can I have ten minutes to talk to Ever?"

"Oui, let's go over there and say hello."

Anton and Willie walked across the foyer and rang Gabriel's door and he welcomed them in. The men went out on the balcony to talk and the girls were in the kitchen trading secrets like international spies. Willie told Ever that they had to work through the project and it would likely be tomorrow before they would be able to see each other. Anton came back in after speaking to Gabriel and led her back to his apartment. They spent the next hours just printing out and organizing data.

Gabriel and Ever had spent most of the morning laying in bed together. He let her know that today was hers only and hinted at the special plans he made for a picnic and then a romantic evening together. After his brother left they showered and got ready to leave. Gabriel told her to wear something comfortable and casual; a skirt would be nice. Ever melted at the prospect of him putting his hands under her skirt, so she complied, finding a skirt that hit just above the knees. He grabbed a blanket out of the closet and they left the apartment. On the drive out they stopped at a market on the side of the road and he came out with a picnic basket. Willie was impressed.

As Gabriel drove away to their destination his hand slid up her leg. Being in the little sports car didn't give her much room to spread her legs, but Gabriel had all the room he needed.

"Are you wet for me yet, chérie?"

"Oh yes," Ever said.

"I want to check for myself." Gabriel's long fingers slid up her thigh, beneath her skirt and panties and over her throbbing folds. Ever gasped at his touch. Slowly his fingers found their way between her wet lips and he started stroking her and gently pushed his middle finger into her. He'd never felt a woman so tight before. It was heaven. His fingers lapped around in her moisture massaging her clitoris, gently stroking her as the pressure built up. Ever was on the verge of an orgasm. "Gabriel. I'm close," She said panting, her chest heaving at his circular motions.

""Come for me, chérie."

"Yes, Gabriel. Oh yes," she managed to get out as she came, arching her back and throwing her head back on her seat. She just held his fingers pressed against her wet, swollen pussy as she came down from her orgasm. It was all Gabriel could do to stay on the road. He growled at the sight of her coming beside him. "You are the most beautiful woman, chérie."

When they arrived at the picnic site it was up a country road with an old house with large garden grounds and an old greenhouse made of stone and glass. It was much bigger than any greenhouse she had ever seen at a residence. The fields around the house were wild and full of flowers. Ever was in heaven. "This is so spectacular, Gabriel."

"Wait until you see the view." Gabriel grabbed the picnic basket and blanket and led Everdine around to the back of the house. What she saw was an unspoiled panoramic, distant ocean view that went on for miles.

"This is amazing. Do you know who owns the property?"

"Oui, a very good friend. Come, let's go have a picnic and enjoy ourselves."

Gabriel picked a spot among some olive and lemon trees and spread the blanket out. He poured them a glass of wine and set the glasses down on top of the picnic basket.

"You know how amazing it was to have your mouth on me last night, chérie?" He hummed so closely to her ear.

"Mmmm. It was amazing for me too. You are a gorgeous man, Gabriel."

"Well now it's time I return the favor. I've been dying to know how you taste, chérie. And now I get to taste your orgasm." He planted a deep, gentle kiss on her lips and continued down.

"But Gabriel, you just gave me....it's my turn to.."

"Shhh..." Gabriel moved down to Ever's feet, sitting on his knees. He grabbed her ankles, pulling her legs down before slipping her panties off and spreading her legs. He ran his hands up her legs and then he lay down on top of her kissing her slow and torturously, gently fingering her hair. She could feel his erection pressed against her. He unbuttoned her blouse, pushing it back and unfastened her bra in the front, exposing her creamy, plenteous breasts. He could see her chest rise and fall in excitement.

"I want to taste you, chérie. All of you." Gabriel's lips went straight to her breast and he took the taut nipple between his lips and teeth, teasing her with his tongue. His hands slowly caressed her breast, squeezing it softly so he could get more of it in his mouth. She was so excited he thought she would come before he even got to taste her. He gave the same treatment to the other breast before kissing his way down her stomach to the top of her lovely, bare mound. "I like what you did down here yesterday at the spa. It is very sexy"

"Hmmm," was all Everdine could manage. Gabriel started out by planting small kisses at the top of her swollen mound. She was so ready for him. His tongue dove between her parted lips over her clitoris and Ever was out of control, writhing and mewling all over the blanket.

"You have to be still, chérie."

"I can't Gabriel. It feels unlike anything......"

He continued his skilled work on her wet folds, holding her hips down and lapping his tongue over her and inside her, taking her clitoris between his lips, sucking it.

"Gabriel.....Gabriel!"

"Oui, chérie."

Casting his tongue very swiftly over her, she came apart before him and he finished her off. She lay still trying to compose herself, her face flushed and heart racing.

"Gabriel that was....it was...the best thing that's ever happened to me."

He laughed at her enthusiasm and could not get over how excited she was about oral sex. "Chérie, have you ever had oral sex before?"

Ever was a bit nervous telling him, but it was kind of beyond the point of honesty now. It was all real now she would tell him the truth. Besides, a bet is a bet and he would have to sleep with her regardless of if he new about her lack of sexual experience.

"No Gabriel, that was the first time for me. I had no idea it could be so amazing."

"So yesterday when you gave it to me, that was also your first time doing it?"

"Yes."

Gabriel laid down beside her and stroked her hair around her face. Again, he was wondering if she was as experienced as he had thought. She never really answered his questions, but just kind of danced around them. Her reaction to his intimate gesture was honest and unscripted.

"That was very good to have been your first time. May I ask why you've never had oral sex before with any of your boyfriends?"

Everdine thought a little about how to answer his question. "I guess it's hard to explain, but the relationships seemed lopsided. I didn't want to do that with someone who only cared about himself- I didn't want to be used. I just felt that a mutual respect should be there, even if the feelings were not the long-lasting kind. Does that make sense?"

"Yes, very much so. We are the same in that account. But for you this goes back to separating love and sex?"

"I never really had the need or desire to be in love with a person for sexual purposes. I've always been afraid of being close to someone and developing trust was not easy."

"So I take it that you must trust me in that regard, chérie?"

"Gabriel," she said turning her head to look at him directly, "I trust you with all my heart."

He suppressed a low growl and pulled her over so her head was resting on his chest.

"You are mine, Everdine," he whispered. "Oui," she responded.

They enjoyed a leisurely lunch and talked about everything form religion to politics. She realized that they had a lot more in common than she could have imagined. She learned about Gabriel's upbringing and his time in college, as well as his plans for the future. It surprised Ever to hear him say he was tired of the bachelor lifestyle and wanted to settle down.

"Come chérie, we need to get going. Would you like to come back here again?"

"I love it here. This would also be a great spot for you to draw. Maybe I could model nude for you."

"Then it is settled. We will come here often." Gabriel said with a laugh. The expression on Ever's face turned downward thinking about not staying with Gabriel when a hotel room became available. She wondered how long this charade would hold. Was he just making the best of this situation? Then Gabriel spoke as if he could read her mind. "Chérie, I want you to stay with me the whole time while you are in Monaco. Please say you will."

"Maybe after you get me in bed tonight you may change your mind," she joked.

"I promise you that could never happen. Besides, Anton is out of his mind with guilt over Willadine and this creep David. He is also taking David's threat very seriously and I doubt he will let Willie out of his sight. You both may be around longer than you thought."

"Oh, well that's a change."

"Yes, I hope he has finally come to his senses. I know he is crazy about her."

As Gabriel was packing up the picnic basket he thought about his and Everdine's wager. Why did it bother him that this was the pretense under which he would first sleep with her?

"Everdine, I need to talk to you about our wager."

"Are you backing out?"

"Not exactly." He could see the panic in her eyes. He took her in his arms, caressing her shoulders. "Chérie, I want you to sleep with me because you want to and not because of the wager. I know we would not be in this situation if it had not been because of our bet, but I think you know my feelings for you are the long lasting kind. I don't want our future to start under a sense of servitude."

Panic was replaced by nausea. He was talking about the future when all she was thinking about was the next week. She had fallen for him, but had told herself that his behavior was just part of the ruse- including being his girlfriend. She had no idea he was thinking beyond their time together in Monte Carlo. That changed everything. She knew she would miss him terribly when she had to get her own hotel room and was already dreading the day they would have to be under separate roofs. It made her sick to think about it. Now he was telling her that he wanted something beyond the two weeks they would have in Monaco.

"Everdine, is something wrong?"

"You said future....our future."

"Oui, usually one takes a boyfriend for an indefinite period of time, which means there is a future. What did you think I meant when I asked to be exclusive with you? Don't you want the same, chérie?"

"Well, yes, Gabriel I do.....but..I guess I misunderstood you. I just thought you were making the best of our time together. I've just been trying to accept my feelings for you and counted on having my heart broken after our week together. I didn't know how serious you were."

"I've never been more serious in my life." Gabriel brought her in for a kiss, languid and deep, resting his hands gently on the sides of her head. If his testament to her was determined by this kiss then she had no doubt. Her tongue and lips were lost in his and she could feel the pressure mounting in her groin. When he nibbled on her lower lip desire shot right through her. He could not ever imagine feeling another woman's breath on his lips. His heart sung every time he thought about her. Seeing her and touching her awakened his whole body.

"When you said you never felt this way about a man before were you amusing me or was that for real?"

"Oh goodness, Gabriel, of course it was real. I've never shared such intimacy with another man as I have with you and I'm not talking about sex. I'm talking about what is inside." She placed her hand over his heart to make her point. Gabriel gave her another kiss and rested his forehead against hers. She was so in love with him.

Both Gabriel and Ever were quiet with anticipation about their special evening. There had been so much build up to this night. Both were nervous, but for different reasons.

Anton and Willie poured through all of the data sets and brought in some new parameters due to the need for more flexibility in their presentation to the bank. They wanted to present two options, one being very lean with no accounting for externalities of politics and the local economy, and the other option being more sympathetic to economic vagaries. It was past time for lunch and they needed a break.

"Okay chérie, we need to get out, eat a little and move around a bit. We've been working hard for hours and we have a lot more work to do later. What do you say we grab a quick bite down at the Beach Club and go for a swim to rejuvenate?"

"That sounds perfect. Cool water is just what I need right now. I'll go change."

Willie changed into her dark green bikini with gold strings that she bought in Milan. It was the first bikini she ever owned and it took lots of assurance from Giovanni to convince her it was the one. She'd never worn such a tiny bathing suit before and she went through great lengths to not ever have a reason to wear one. Although she slimmed down a lot in college, she was never comfortable with the attention her Crenshaw curves received. Anton guided her down to his car and ordered their lunch on the way so they would not have to wait once they arrived. He also made sure they had a tent down by the water.

Lunch was brought out when they were shown to their tent. Anton took the liberty of ordering for her and salad with grilled salmon could not have been more appetizing. "This is so delicious, Anton. Do you come here a lot?"

"In the summer months I do come to swim. I prefer to swim in the ocean and not so much in pools."

"I'm the same way. Growing up in the mountains I always swam in the river or in the creek near our cabin. We would make a dam out of stones in the creek bed and the water would pool up. It was like having our own paradise, except for the snakes that would inevitably skim over the water. I remember the water tasting so sweet. After working in the fields we would go straight to the river and jump in. Nothing felt better."

"That sounds like a wonderful childhood memory. What kind of fields do you speak of? Do you mean making sports on the field?"

"No. I worked in tobacco when I was a child and teenager. Up until I went to college, actually. In the summer months we would top the tobacco and by late summer it was still hot when we primed tobacco."

"So you were a farmhand?"

"Well I never really thought of it that way, but yes, I guess I was." She didn't know why, but Anton's reference to her as a farmhand seemed condescending. It was the truth, though. She didn't know why she felt ashamed. Maybe it was his silver-spoon upbringing that made her feel uneasy.

"Was your family very poor growing up, chérie?"

"No, not at all. My dad took very good care of us and I have a large trust fund. My mother felt it was important that I knew what hard work was like so that maybe I would appreciate my education and circumstance later, I suppose. I went to college on a scholarship and used some of the money I saved in tobacco farming to pay for living expenses. I didn't even need to use my trust fund for school."

Anton felt his heart expanding the more he spoke with her. Never had he met such a simple, beautiful woman whom he held so high on a pedestal. He knew he would never meet anyone like her and wanted to make sure they reconnected. He was a fool for turning her away.

"Willadine you are a remarkable woman." He looked at her with a sincere longing when he said it.

"Thanks, Anton." Maybe she had misjudged his assessment of her. It was just hard to tell what he was thinking and after he rejected her the first time she was treading with caution.

"How about a swim now?" Anton said with way too much excitement.

"Yes, let's go."

"First, ma chère, we must put on sunscreen. You have such lovely, fair skin and I know it will burn, so turn around."

"You're right. I didn't even think about that."

Willie took off her t-shirt and shorts, throwing them on the platform lounger in the tent. Anton did the same. She was surprised at how tailored and small his swim trunks were. The dark orange color went great with his olive colored skin and dark hair. They were more like low cut shorts, but with a three inch inseam and not the banana hammocks men usually wore in Europe. She was just glad he didn't wear knee length board shorts like men did in the U.S. Anton had amazing legs and she could stare at them all day in those shorts. He looked like Adonis with perfectly toned abs, obliques and a wonderful rear. Anton was equally pleased with her in a bikini. Her waist was small compared to her full butt that spilled out from her bikini bottom and beautiful, plump breasts. He could not get enough of her shapely legs and had to be careful because there was not much room for growth in his shorts.

Willie turned around so he could rub sunscreen on her back. It was a perfect excuse to touch her and he would enjoy every minute of it. She held her hair above her head with both hands while Anton made large, circular motions with his hands over her back, neck and upper arms. He went down the side of her ribs and she could feel her breasts tingle.

"Turn around and I'll get your neck."

Willie turned to face him and she could feel Anton's addled breathing. Her body was simply amazing. He wanted to sleep with her so badly now it hurt. Seeing her firm nipples through her bikini didn't help his bulging erection. He had to shift so it wasn't as noticeable.

"You are all covered now. Shall we go to the water?"

"Don't you want sunscreen, too?"

Anton never wore sunscreen because he didn't burn with his skin tone. They would only be there an hour at the most, but he wanted to feel her hands on him.

"Yes, I better at least get some on my shoulders and arms. Thank you, chérie."

Since he was too tall to reach, Willie sat on her knees on the platform lounger, making room for him in front of her. Anton sat down in front of her and she began to rub the sunscreen on his shoulders. Her touch was magic to him. Her hands were small, but strong, and they seemed to move fluidly over his muscular back. He could feel all of the tension draining from his shoulders.

When Willie ran her delicate hands over his sculpted shoulders she imagined how it would feel to taste his skin there and trace his muscles with her lips.

"Chérie, that feels amazing. My shoulders are tense from work the last few days and I haven't had time to get a massage."

"Maybe tonight after we finish I could give you a massage. I have some wonderful white musk oil that is very relaxing. I rub it on my shoulders because the scent helps me sleep."

"That would be great if you don't mind."

"Not at all. That's what friends are for. I'm glad we can spend time together as friends and not have to worry about it being more. It's very liberating, actually."

"Oui," Anton said, his reply not matching his conviction. He wanted to be more than friends and gaining her trust back would not be easy. Willie was keeping it friendly and cordial like Ever recommended, acting like she was not phased by the thought of just being friends. Pretending that Anton didn't affect her was like falling off a boat trying not to hit water. Seeing him in his sexy swimsuit was torture. Any woman with a pulse would respond to how good he looked.

"Let's go move our bodies, chérie" Anton said, holding his hand out. Willie took his hand, feeling her insides melt as they walked down to the beach. He took her straight to the water's edge and the cold water made Willie jump back.

"Oh, that is way too cold."

"Non, chérie. It is refreshing. Come!"

"You go first."

In a snap Anton picked Willie up and carried her to the water. She screamed at him grabbing on to him for dear life, wrapping her arms and legs around him. Anton didn't mind that his face was buried in her boobs and his hand was supporting her delicious, round bottom. The sooner he was in the water the sooner he could hide his budding excitement.

As soon as they were up to his waist in water Anton was preparing to throw her. "Let's see if you can fly now, Willadine."

"No Anton, please don't." He saw the alarm in her eyes and stilled.

"What is wrong ma chère?"

"It's a little scary," her small voice sounded off.

"You are serious?"

"Yes. Let me go in slowly."

As soon as Anton started to lower Willie slowly into the water she put her hands on his shoulders and put all of her weight on him, trying to dunk him in the brisk water. Anton turned over, using her own weight against her and took her under. She clung to him with all the strength she could gather and he brought them back quickly above the water. They both choked through a few laughs, sputtering some water before their gaze settled on each other. Anton's desire for her was marked by his punchy breathing and his gaze tore from her eyes, caressing her lips. Willie wanted so badly for Anton to kiss her and was practically willing him to do so. As they both came down from the heightened sexual awareness surrounding them, Willie scurried out of his hold and acted as if nothing was amiss.

Anton was so close to kissing her and almost did. He knew she wanted it as much as he did, but their unique living and work situation forced him to act with rationality rather than what was between his legs. Exercising that much control around Willie was not something he would be able to maintain. She decided to break the tension running between them.

"Do you think there are any sharks in here?"

"Just swim beside me and you'll be safe. We can get some laps in together."

"I'd love that."

Willie and Anton swam laps for twenty minutes back and forth in front of the beach. The view of the mountain behind them was incredible. She could see why Anton loved it here. It was paradise. She was ready to bask in the sun a little before they had to go back to work. Her next trip to the beach would be with Everdine. She could just imagine them spending the day at the beach drinking cocktails.

"Anton I'm going back to the tent to lay down."

"Oui, chérie. I'll be there in fifteen minutes or so. I'd like to swim a bit more."

On the way back to the tent Willie noticed that all of the women had their tops off and she felt like a prude. If she weren't with Anton, then she'd consider taking her top off, too. She pulled the curtains back on the tent, allowing the warmth of the sun's rays to enter. It felt amazing to have the warm Mediterranean breeze dancing over her skin. It only took a few minutes before the warm air lulled her to sleep.

He stood there dripping wet, struggling to exhale, astonished at how beautiful Willie looked. She lay like an angel before him with her salt-laden curls spread out on the lounger, rosy cheeks and the most gorgeous pair of barely covered breasts he had ever seen. They were perfectly round with perky nipples that pointed to the sky. This woman had given him painful erections since the first time they met on the veranda at the palace and if he didn't find relief soon he would explode. He took advantage of her afternoon siesta and soaked up every inch of her with his hungry eyes.

Anton dried off, keeping his eye on Willadine. He decided to get his shorts on to cover his obvious affection for this woman and then crawled on the lounger beside her, and tried to wake her up gently. She was sleeping quite soundly and he felt bad about waking her, but they still had a lot of work to do. Laying down on his side next to her, he stroked her shoulder.

"Chérie, it is time to go." His lips brushed her shoulder as he slid his fingers down her arm. "Come, ma chère, wake up," he said stroking her shoulder. In an instance Willie flew up in the lounger, gasping for air. Her chest heaving violently before realizing that it was Anton beside her. Relief was strewn across her face and she placed her hand over her heart, which felt pinched at the moment.

"Chérie, it's ok. It's just me. Come here," Anton said pulling her in, lightly embracing her. His open hand circled her back and his other hand clutched the back of her head and he adored the softness of her skin. "It's okay Willie, I'm here for you." The feel of her breasts pressed to his bare chest was enough to make him nearly pass out. He felt so close to her and didn't want to move. As she pulled back he gave her a kiss on the temple.

"I'm so sorry, but I've been stressed out about this whole thing with David." Willie sat with her arms crossed over her chest looking for her top, suddenly feeling conscious.

"Would you mind handing me my clothes?"

"No, not at all." Anton reached over the chair in front of the lounger and snatched her clothes, handing them to Willie. She stood up on her knees and faced away from Anton and shimmied into her shirt. The view of her round ass barely being covered by her bikini made him drunk with lust.

Willie finished getting dressed and they packed up and left the club, driving back to the apartment. "I had a really nice time swimming today. I hope we can do it again when you have more time."

"I did, too, Willie, and I promise I'll make time."

Willie valued how warm and attentive Anton was acting toward her. It was obvious he still cared about her in a way that spoke to being more than just friends. Even if he did come to his senses and want to try again she wasn't sure if she could trust him enough to fully give her heart. If she thought she could have sex with him and not fall in love, then she would do it in a heartbeat. At one point she would have slept with him regardless, but now that she had a taste of the heartache he caused her, sleeping with him was out of the question. As soon as they returned to the apartment they took turns showering and then got back to work on the proposal.

CHAPTER 13

When Ever and Gabriel returned to his apartment he asked her to wait in the living room while he disappeared into his bedroom. He took a quick shower and got dressed in a stone colored linen suit, crisp white shirt and brown Fratelli Rosetti shoes. A quick comb through his curly locks and a splash of his best cologne and he was ready.

Gabriel came up behind Ever, putting his arms around her waist. "After I take you to dinner tonight I have a special surprise for you. On the bed you will find the clothes I have laid out for you to wear tonight, including the lingerie I had the pleasure of selecting. I hope you like everything." He kissed her sweetly on the cheek and told her he would be at Gabriel's if she was finished getting ready early. The man could fill out a suit.

Everdine went into his bedroom and looked at what Gabriel had picked out for her and tears came to her eyes. He had put a lot of thought into this night and she was sure it would be one of the best nights of her life.

Gabriel rapped on Anton's door, hoping to catch him at a good time. He just needed to touch base with him on the project and also make sure he was not interrupted this evening.

"Hello brother, come on in."

"I hope I didn't disturb you."

"No, we are knee deep in work right now. We took a break and went for a swim at the club earlier and need to push on through until we have everything ironed out."

"Do you think you'll be ready to present in Paris by Tuesday?"

"We'll certainly try and it looks good right now. By tomorrow afternoon I'll know for sure."

"That is pretty good, then. I am taking Ever out for a special evening and just wanted to make sure you didn't get it in your mind to come over before lunchtime tomorrow."

"I'll be sure to keep to myself and also tell Wille. It is getting pretty serious over here isn't it, Gabriel," Anton said, cocking an eyebrow up.

"Yes, quite so. I've never been more serious about anything else in my life. What about you and Willie? You'd be crazy not to try and patch things up."

"Yes, crazy. I just don't know how receptive she is about being more than friends after what I did to her. She has it in her mind that we are good friends and that is how she treats me, seeming very happy to do so. She practically treats me like her brother."

"Ouch. I recommend turning the heat up just a little and take her on a date. Did you open her present yet? The one that Ever had me give to you from Willie while she was in Milan."

"No, I completely forgot about it. It's buried under a mountain of paperwork in my office right now. I'll get it Monday when we go into work."

"Good luck with Willie and try not to get too wired over the project. We have a good plan and a good reputation. The bank will back us."

"Alright, see you tomorrow and good luck with Ever tonight- no fighting."

"Don't worry, we'll be far from it tonight."

Gabriel walked back over to his apartment and Everdine still wasn't finished getting ready. He went through each detail of the evening in his mind. This was the night. The night he would make love to Everdine for the first time and for the first time he would not just be fucking. He was excited and nervous about the surprise he had for her. For him it was the only way that she would believe that tonight wasn't just about making good on a bet. It was important that she know his feelings for her superseded getting her in bed.

Her hair and make up were finished and it was time to get dressed in the clothes Gabriel bought for her. She thought having her hair in a chignon in the back to the side would look pretty with the dress he picked out for her. The lingerie he wanted her to wear was sensual and tasteful. It was a black silk and lace, plunge bustier with garters and stockings and some matching Brazilian cut panties. It almost made her wonder if he had help from another woman putting it all together. That's not something she wanted be thinking about. The lingerie fit her perfectly and looked amazing. She knew it would drive Gabriel crazy. The black dress was full length with a slit up the side and a V-line in the front with goddess straps. The bustier was perfect and did not show despite the dress being cut as low as it was. Looking at herself in the mirror turned her on knowing what Gabriel was going to do to her tonight. The excitement gave her butterflies. Time to go get her man.

She grabbed her clutch and joined Gabriel in the living room and his gaze was fixed on her. He knew she would look amazing, but knowing what he knew about their evening made it even more special. She took his breath away.

"Wow, Everdine. You are the most stunning woman I've ever laid eyes on. You look so beautiful. Everything looks like it fits perfectly."

"Thank you, Gabriel. I'm impressed with your impeccable taste. You look pretty amazing yourself." Gabriel was the kind of man that exuded a presence when he walked into a room. He could be wearing rags and he would still be that impressive. His dark, wavy hair and olive toned skin looked regal with anything he wore and people were automatically drawn to him. She felt proud to be in his company and that he called her his girlfriend.

"I have a small gift for you before we go, chérie."

"You don't need to give me a gift, Gabriel. You've already done so much for me, sweetheart."

"Come here and turn around."

Ever stood right in front of him and he gave her a kiss on the cheek, stepping behind her. Something was different about him today she thought. He looked at her as if he held her in a different regard. It was as if his eyes were saying things, but the words failed to pass through his lips. She could hear him messing with something when his arms came around in front of her and he fastened a necklace around her.

"Here, Chérie, you better put these in yourself," he said, handing her the earrings.

The shock on Ever's face was lucid. She didn't know what to think about Gabriel. Maybe he was ill.

"Gabriel, I can't accept this jewelry. I'm sure it is way too expensive. This wasn't part of our deal, so you really don't need to do this."

"This is my special evening to you and I want you to have this necklace and earrings. Forget about the deal, Everdine. This is about my feelings for you. These blue diamonds match your eyes perfectly, chérie. Please accept them."

Ever swallowed a huge lump in her throat. "Thank you so much, Gabriel. They really are stunning. I'm a very lucky woman." She fought back tears at his generosity and then put on the cushion cut blue diamond earrings and matching pendant necklace. The pendant was surrounded by white pave diamonds and was the most beautiful piece of jewelry she owned. It was hard suppressing the joy she felt for him. Ever pulled Gabriel down to her and gave him a string of kisses on his neck.

"I love the necklace and earrings, Gabriel, thank you. I'm sorry, but I didn't get you a gift."

"You have already given me a gift that meant more to me than you realize with the art supplies. Later you will give me the best gift I could ever receive." He kissed her hand, knowing she was thinking about when they would make love.

"Shall we go ma chère?"

"Yes, Mr. Delacroix."

They could have driven 500 miles and Ever wouldn't have noticed. There was a calmness about them as they both sat in their own quietude, driving through Monte Carlo. Everdine felt that the evening held some kind of grandeur that she was not privy to. Regardless of what happened her sights were firmly set on the prize and that was finally making love to Gabriel. If what they had already experienced with each other was any indication of how their night would end then another trip to the emergency clinic may be in order.

Gabriel pulled up to an older building perched on a hill above the winding road. It looked like it could be from the 18th century. Ever loved learning about all of the architecture styles in Europe. He came around to help her out of the car. Her high heels were no match for his low-to-the-ground sports car.

"It's spectacular up here. It seems like everyone has a view in Monte Carlo."

"Yes, sometimes it really does," he mused. "Come, let's go inside."

She took his hand as he led her inside the centuries-old building. Once inside Ever noticed all of the paintings on display.

"You said that Raoul Dufy was your favorite artist and I wanted to bring you to this gallery that has a great many of his works. We have the gallery all to ourselves tonight so let's take our time looking and then we will have dinner on the rooftop."

"This is the best surprise ever, Gabriel. You completely amaze me." She reached up and kissed him pointedly on the lips.

"Well I hope it's not the best surprise, but it's a good start then."

"The first night I met you, Gabriel, I thought you were....despicable," Ever said through glassed over eyes, "and now... I don't think I could live without you."

"Chérie, you don't have to. Give me another kiss," Gabriel said, drawing her in.

Ever ran her hands up his lapel and over his shoulders as they shared a seraphic kiss.

She spent over an hour looking at the Dufy artwork and others that were on display in the gallery. On the rooftop they enjoyed a leisurely, candle lit dinner and watched the sun set over the Mediterranean in each other's arms. As she stayed in his arms, taking in his clean, woodsy smell she was felt it was time to take the next step.

"Let's go home, Gabriel. Make love to me."

He clenched her even tighter to his body. "Chérie, there is nothing more I'd rather do. Come with me- I have your last surprise on the second floor."

Gabriel took her hand and led her to the second floor where they saw more paintings and lots of oil pastel works. He slowly brought her around to see all of them, stopping before they got to the last few. They came upon a charcoal drawing of a woman casting her eyes out a window over a balcony and the woman looked like Everdine. It was titled The Dreamer.

"Is that..."

"Oui, chérie, it is you."

The next drawing had a woman asleep in bed with her hair tangled all around her face and her hand laying on the pillow beside her. Everdine recognized herself in the warm earth tone hues of the pastels. This piece was titled The Temptress.

"They are beautiful, Gabriel," she said with pools forming in the corners of her eyes.

The last drawing instantly made Ever's breath hitch. It was her posing nude on the chaise the day she gave Gabriel the art materials. The lines were finely drawn with charcoal with every shadow and highlight perfectly showcasing her round breasts and curves. Ever let pass a bevy of adoring tears. Never had she been so moved and awestruck. Gabriel was right behind her and pulled her in close so her back was flush against his chest. She wiped the tears off her cheeks and looked down to see the title of the drawing and it read The Wife. She drew both hands over her face and turned around as Gabriel got down on bended knee.

He took her hand in his as she cried, shaking her head in disbelief.

"Everdine Crenshaw- I knew from the moment you first slapped me that I had to make you mine." Ever laughed through her tears at how many times she's slapped him. "I have shared, laughed and felt more in the short time that I've know you than in my whole life. The day I drew this portrait of you is the day I knew I couldn't live without you. I love you with all my heart, Everdine. I can't live without your spirit, touch and passion. Will you be my wife, chérie?

A thunderstruck Everdine sobbed into her free hand while Gabriel clung to her other hand. She managed to finally speak. "How do you know Gabriel? We haven't even slept together yet. What if you're disappointed?"

"There is no way I could ever be disappointed with you. I know you don't think we'll have a problem in bed, either. If we do I'm sure you'll beat the shit out of me. Everdine, I've been with enough women to know that you are the one. You are the one for me. It's crystal clear. Marry me; be my wife, please."

"Yes, Gabriel, I will marry you." Gabriel slid the ring on her finger unnoticed and then scooped her up into his arms, both were dropping tears now. "You've made me the happiest, horniest man alive. Let's go home."

They practically ran down the stairs with Ever's high heels giving her a lot of grief. When Ever was tucked in the car she realized she hadn't even looked at her ring. Holding out her hand she splayed her fingers against her open hand and marveled at the blue diamond that matched the necklace and earrings that Gabriel had given her earlier. The pristine cushion-cut blue diamond was surrounded by a halo of pave white diamonds that extended all the way around the platinum band.

"I've never seen such a beautiful ring, nor did I know blue diamonds even existed. This is just spectacular, Gabriel."

"I'm glad you're happy with it, chérie. I know couples usually pick out rings together, but when I went to Geneva to look at stones I saw these blue diamonds and they reminded me of your deep, blue eyes. A perfect match."

"That is so sweet, Gabriel, and I'm glad you picked it out yourself. I don't think I could have done it."

"Do you want to call your mother and tell her?"

"No, not right now. I need time for this to sink in. When I believe it myself, then I'll tell her."

"Well, you better believe it Miss Crenshaw. Maybe consummating our relationship will help or would you rather wait until our wedding night?"

"If you make me wait any longer people may be injured. I don't think I can wait unless it is something that is important to you."

"Uh....no. I just wanted to give you the option." Ever's chest strained knowing she had to tell him she had never had sex before. At this point it obviously would not change how he felt about her since he proposed already. She decided she'd tell him once they got back to his apartment. Now that their relationship had taken a serious turn she thought he should know the truth.

It was nearly ten o'clock before Willie and Anton called it a night. They finally had two proposals that they both felt comfortable with and they were sure the bank would appreciate the different approaches they outlined. Although Willie loved numbers, it was exhausting trying to meet Anton's demands for creating every possible outcome with the data. He was a perfectionist and she admired that about him. He didn't stop until they reached some kind of numeric nirvana.

"Anton my eyes are crossed I need to get some fresh air. I think I'll change and go for a walk. I'll probably be back in 30 minutes."

"Willie, may I go with you? I really need some fresh air, too."

"Of course. Excuse me for not asking you."

"Non, please, I understand. You have been with me the last 24 hours and probably need a break. Am I so tough to work with?"

Willie couldn't tell him that she had been salivating over him since they got back from the beach club. He wore a half-buttoned dress shirt with his sleeves rolled up. To him and anyone else it may look all business, but to her it was an invitation to admire his masculine forearms and swarth of chest hair in view. It was of no effort on his part to look so sexy. He could very well have bathed in sex appeal. Every time he would lean in close beside her to discuss the presentation on the laptop his smell and closeness would cause her stomach to wrench. She really just needed a break from being so turned on the last five hours. Even though she thought her and Ever's plan to bring Anton around was working she could not forget his words when he said he would break her heart. She knew deep down that's exactly what would happen. It would crush her to lose him again.

"You are amazing to work with, Anton. I've learned so much from you and I'm lucky to get this kind of experience. You probably need a break from me though, bugging you with questions all night."

"On the contrary, chérie. It is quite refreshing to work with you and I think we make a really good team. I've had many assistants over the last few years as the business has grown and it never worked out. I'm very particular about details and it is hard to find someone who understands that. Not only are you a very hard worker, but you ask the right questions and are extremely detailed."

"That's very kind of you to say, Anton, thanks. Shall we change and then get our wiggles out?"

"Wiggles?"

"Yes, wiggles. The desire to move your body in a certain way- to wiggle." Willie twisted her body demonstrating what a wiggle was and Anton rather enjoyed it. Although his English was nearly perfect, she forgot that some vocabulary may be challenging for him.

Willie changed into her snug blue, running shorts, a high cut striped yoga tank top and her running shoes. She clipped her hair up in the back so it wouldn't stick to her neck. While she waited for Anton to finish changing she looked for water bottles in the kitchen to take with them. A full day of work and time at the beach made her very thirsty. Looking through his kitchen cabinets she was amazed to find nothing out of order and every cup, plate and bowl was lined up perfectly- too perfect. It appeared that Anton was a neat freak. She spotted two identical water bottles on the top shelf beside the refrigerator and stretched as high as she could to reach them. With no step stool in sight she halfway climbed on the counter underneath the shelf to reach the water bottles. Although Anton enjoyed the view of her hiked up shorts and full, round ass, he was afraid she would end up in need of stitches like her sister if she climbed any higher.

"Come, chérie, I can reach that for you. Let me help you down," he said making a few strides to reach her.

Anton gripped his hands around her small waist and helped her ease off the counter back on the floor, brushing against his chest as her feet planted. He declared to himself again how stupid he was to break it off with her. Working with her the last 24 hours he realized how much in common they had. If he was going to get her trust back he needed to create some chaste intimacy between them and try flirting. He hadn't had to flirt with a woman in as long as he could remember. It was never necessary. Most women he met flirted with him and partaking in such niceties was never an issue. When Everdine told him that Willie didn't trust him it bothered him to the point of sleeplessness. He wanted desperately for her to trust him so he could have a second chance. He decided to make the most of the time they had together.

"Thanks for getting the water bottles down. Your house is kept so neat. I take it you are obsessive about keeping everything in order?"

"Non, but my maid is. She is obsessive compulsive when it comes to cleaning the apartment. In fact, every day I come over to this painting here against the wall and tip it slightly so it is uneven and every time after she leaves it is perfectly straight again. I think she carries a level in her cleaning bag."

"You are so mean, Anton. That poor woman," she laughed.

"So where would do you recommend we go?"

"The casino park and waterfront are very romantic and beautiful at night. Why don't we go there?"

"Sounds great," Willie said, nervously.

As soon as they walked out of the apartment building Anton took her hand in his as if he did so every day. Willie was afraid to squeeze his hand back. Maybe this was just a French thing. Even still it made her uncomfortable. She put her hand back by her side when they went through a crosswalk and Anton claimed it again as soon as they were through the intersection. It was a sweet gesture, so she let it go.

The night really was beautiful and it wasn't nearly as hot as Willie thought it would be. She was able to catch a few glimpses of Anton without him noticing. His legs were simply gorgeous. He looked every part the athlete with his t-shirt tucked neatly in his mid-thigh length shorts, showcasing his broad shoulders. His ass was immaculate. She also noticed how women got their eyes full staring at him when they passed. Could she blame them?

"Come on, chérie, let's jog." Anton dropped her hand and they both started a light jog toward the casino. Willie noticed how clean everything was in Monte Carlo. You could almost eat off the streets. It looked like something out of a movie set. As they were idling to cross an intersection someone called out Anton's name. Willie turned her head to look in the direction of the woman's soft, lilting voice. She was tall, thin and impeccably dressed with beautiful, long raven-colored hair and a perfectly made face. It was obvious that Anton was surprised to see her.

"Hello, Monique, how are you?" Anton's voice was cold. This was not a chance meeting that he enjoyed.

"I'm doing fine, considering. Aren't you going to introduce me to your new friend? She is new, isn't she?"

Anton took Willie's hand in his. "This is a very dear friend of mine, Willadine. Willadine, this is Monique."

"Nice to make your acquaintance," Willie said with a polite smile.

"So you're Anton's flavor of the month?" she said with bitterness pouring over her tongue.

"As much as I hate to disappoint you...."

Anton cut her off before she could finish.

"Willadine is my girlfriend and is staying with me at the moment," Anton said, interrupting her. Willie's face turned beet red at Anton's declaration. She knew it was a ruse, but just didn't know why.

"Anton Delacroix in a committed relationship? I'll believe that when you finally tie the knot. Good luck with this one Willadine- you're going to need it." Anton's friend turned and entered a cafe at the intersection where they were waiting to cross.

"What was that about, Anton?"

"I'll explain later, but I need to kiss you while she is still watching us. Is that okay, Willie? Please?"

"Sure, I guess." Willie thought a quick, placid kiss would be innocent enough, but that was the opposite of what she got. Anton cradled her face in his hands, caressing her cheeks with his thumbs, kissing her softly until her lips parted, inviting his tongue in. He turned up the heat, not caring that they were on public display. When Anton didn't end the kiss Willie's hands came up from her sides and swept across his firm biceps. Her body remembered with a low groan what it felt like to be consumed by Anton. Her desire for him had not faded one bit and this was the kind of kiss that would be hard to come back from. He broke with her lips and pecked at her jawline, moving behind her earlobe down her neck. Just as Willie thought her heart was going to pound out of her chest she came to her senses.

"Anton, no. Stop."

Anton brought his eyes to hers and returned another kiss on her lips then rested his forehead against hers, his thumbs caressed her cheeks. She wrapped her hands around his wrists. Both were fighting a desire much greater than their need to breathe. Anton gave her yet another kiss.

"Anton, no," Willie said in a labored whisper.

"Excuse me, Willie...I've....just missed you so much and I got carried away. My apologies," he said as his breathing became impassive. "Shall we continue our run to the park?" Anton asked.

"Yes, let's go."

The park across from the casino was grand. The fountains and lighting were romantic, just as Anton said. If things were only different between them. Seeing the fountain reminded Willie that they left their water bottles on the counter.

"Looks like we forgot our water."

"That is okay chérie, we'll stop by a cafe on the way home and get a drink."

"This is so beautiful," she commented as they ran through the park. As they both came to sit on the side of the fountain catching their breath Anton pulled out a small digital camera and took a picture of Willie.

"What was that for?"

"Maybe I just want a picture of you."

"Then let me get one of you, too."

Willie took his camera and snapped a photo of Anton, chiding him, telling him to work the camera. He obliged and made a silly expression on his face and curled his bicep up like a body builder. Willie giggled and snapped another photo. Anton really wanted their picture together, though.

"Here come closer so I can get our picture."

"I probably smell nasty and sweaty, Anton."

"Nonsense. You smell lovely as always."

Willie leaned in closer to him and he put his arm around her and extended his other arm with the camera, taking the photo of them. A tourist walking by offered to take a photo of them and he handed him the camera. Anton asked Willie to stand for the picture and he guided her in front of him, cupping one arm around the front of her waist, holding her close. He clasped his other hand with Willie's hand that was hanging by her side.

Willie didn't know what to make of his obvious show of affection. Before the gentleman took their photo Willie placed her other hand over his that was holding her waist. He got several photos before handing the camera back to Anton.

They sat down on the side of the fountain and Willie wanted to ask him what was up with Monique. Anton had not volunteered any information and her curiosity was brimming.

"Tell me why you lied to Monique about us. Was she your girlfriend at one time?"

"I dated her on and off for a few months. I would not call her a girlfriend, though. I stopped dating her in April and she's having a hard time accepting that I don't want to see her anymore. I was hoping that if she saw me with someone else she would stop harassing me."

"Don't you think that it's kind of mean to do that?"

"It may seem mean, but she was only ever interested in parties and keeping an outward appearance. I also caught her in several serious lies and it was just unacceptable."

"She is very pretty."

"Yes, but it is all on the surface. You, chérie, are beautiful inside and out."

"Well I'm sure she believed you tonight. Your act was very convincing, but I'd appreciate it if you didn't use me like that again."

"Mon Dieu, Willie, I'm so sorry. I didn't mean to....it was not an act...I just couldn't stop. That's just the affect you have on me. Please forgive me. To be honest with you, I'm not sorry I did it, just sorry that I hurt you. I've really missed you, Willie."

"It's fine, Anton. Are you ready to head back? It's been a long day."

"Of course. Let's get going."

They both sprang up from the fountain and took off in the direction of the apartment. About half way in their journey home she broke the silence. "I've missed you too, Anton." That brought a smile to his face.

She couldn't shake the feeling that Anton was trying to reel her in. The kiss he had given her was all she could think about. With him it was hard to tell if he was putting on an act or if he genuinely felt the kiss like she did. Once they arrived home they both took showers and Willie wondered about the sleeping arrangements.

"Anton do you have a spare bedroom or should I sleep on the sofa again?"

"I have a spare bedroom, but it only has fitness equipment. I never saw the need to fit it with furniture. There is just my bed and the sofa in the office. We are adults chérie, you should sleep in my bed. It is more than big enough for us both and much more comfortable than the sofa. I was going to work some more anyway, so that rules out you sleeping in my office. Go ahead and sleep in my bed. I'll join you later. He gave her a kiss on her forehead and closed himself in his office. Discussion over. Willie dressed in her pajamas and then climbed into bed.

Thoughts of her earlier kiss with Anton were imprinted on her mind. With his show of affection it seemed like he was offering her something different. It was clear they both kept their attraction to each other, but what had changed in terms of expectations? When he broke it off with her she was willing to offer herself to him with no promises. What was being offered and what was being given was diluted by expectations. Could he make any promises to her or would she even want to risk the certain pain that would come when he broke his promise? Willie finally drifted off.

CHAPTER 14

As soon as he parked the car their arms, hands and lips left little to be discovered. Ever and Gabriel made it into his apartment, but had no recollection of how they got there. His shirt was unbuttoned and hanging out of his pants and the shoulder of her dress was draped down to her elbow. The panties that Gabriel bought for her were soaked through. She had never been so turned on. Gabriel wanted to go all night with her so he took pause and changed the pace.

"Chérie," he said breathlessly, "I bought us some champagne earlier. Let's toast."

"Yes, that would be very nice, Gabriel." She said, not really wanting to stop.

He unwrapped the champagne and opened it with much aplomb. An act he likely practiced on a regular basis. With each a glass in hand Gabriel offered up a toast.

"To my dearest, soon-to-be Mrs. Delacroix- you are the most amazing woman and I'm so thankful to have your promise of forever. I love you with all my heart, chérie. Cheers."

"That's so precious, Gabriel. I love you, too. Cheers," she said, raising her glass with his.

"Do you know how much it turns me on to hear you call me Mrs. Delacroix?"

"Why don't we go find out, ma chère?"

They both drained their champagne glasses and set them down before going into his bedroom. Gabriel drew the curtains and set the lighting. It was intimate, warm and romantic. Ever's excitement peaked as she slid Gabriel's shirt off his back and placed it in a club chair near the bed. Love, passion, trust and admiration passed between each glance they shared. She leaned in and kissed his chest while working her fingers around his belt buckle, freeing his pants. She could feel his heat with each exhale on her skin and hair as she dropped his pants. Her face was buried in his chest as her hands graced every part of his body, settling on his mammoth erection over his silk boxers.

"Gabriel you are the most beautiful man I have ever known. I want to share everything with you. I've waited for this my whole life."

Gabriel took his time kissing her neck and slowly slipped both straps of her dress off her shoulders, letting it fall to the floor. He stepped back to get a view of the lingerie he had bought for her and circled around her.

"You are stunning Everdine and I am eager to share everything with you, too." He said kissing the back of her neck and unclasping her bustier, setting it aside. He reached around from behind her, his hands tantalizing her breasts and his mouth carving a path along her neck. "Tell me what you have waited for your whole life," he said as his lips continued on her shoulder.

"I've waited to have someone I could give myself to completely- emotionally and physically. You are the only one Gabriel."

The words made him drunk as he knelt down and fumbled with her garter belt clasps, kissing her thighs, working his way from her back to her front. Ever let her fingers play lightly with his hair as he helped her out of her stockings and removed her garter. His hands steadily removed her panties and he was immediately drawn to her scent. Like a starved animal he grabbed her behind and he thrust his tongue into her hot, wet flesh and she cried out his name. He backed her to the bed and she sat down with her feet firmly planted on the floor. Gabriel continued his assault on her clit with his tongue, using his fingers to spread her sweet liquid around. He took her folds between his lips and tongue and could feel her tension building.

"Gabriel....Gabriel....," she said twisting under his torturous command.

"I want you to come all over my face. Give it to me, chérie."

At his words her pleasure erupted around him. His tongue was as deep as it could be, buried between her clamoring walls and his fingers continued with calming circles over her tight bud.

She screamed his name louder than she'd ever screamed before. When he joined her on the bed she had a dazed expression on her face.

"It's overwhelming what you make me feel when you love me like that. I love you so much, Gabriel."

"I feel the same way, Ever. It was never so with other men, I take it?"

Her eyes gave him a strained look and she was on the verge of telling him.

"Chérie?"

She bit her bottom lip and decided she should tell him.

"Gabriel you should know...I......I've never slept with another man. I've only made out with some boyfriends in the past, but we never did anything like this. You will be my first." She stroked the side of his face as he was laying beside her.

"But I thought you had sex already," he said, confused.

"You assumed I had sex and I didn't correct you. I'm sorry I was evasive, but with the wager we had going I was not going to tell you. Things are so different now, Gabriel. I hope you understand."

"Yes, I understand that. Let's talk about this first."

"Don't you dare break up with me Gabriel....or.." She sounded panicked and worried.

"Stop, Ever. I'm not breaking up with you. Let me explain something to you. There are so may things I've shared with you that I have not shared with any other woman. You are strong, bold, principled, sexy and intelligent. You've managed to wait this long to have sex because you were waiting for the right man or right time. Whether you meant it to be or not, this is a gift. For me the greatest gift you could give me on our wedding night is you. Do you know how much that would mean to me, Everdine?"

"You're asking me to wait until our wedding night to sleep together? Are you crazy? Don't you want to make love to me?" Everdine rolled over on her back exasperated with the dilemma Gabriel presented.

"Oh chérie, of course I want to make love to you- twenty-four hours a day. Do you feel this?" he said, putting her hand over his erection. "Things are just different with you, Everdine. They always have been. Having a relationship like we have is a novelty for me and it has happened at light speed. I'll never have this chance again and I want everything to be as special as it can be with you because you are the most precious person in my life.

I've never wanted such things before, but with you I want everything to be as extraordinary as it possibly can be because I love you so much. If you tell me you don't want to wait then I will respect that, but if you do wait then we can still do other things to satisfy ourselves until our wedding night."

Everdine exhaled and looked around for a few seconds thinking.

"How soon can we get married?"

Laughter filled the room as Gabriel rolled over on top of her and gave her quick kisses. "How soon can you plan a wedding, chérie?"

"Why don't we try for the end of summer?"

"That sounds spectacular. We have a lot to learn about each other still and I'm going to enjoy every minute of it."

"You should know that I will be mad as hell until we have sex and I may even cuss at you or slap you and there is nothing I can do about it."

"Well I think that is a small price to pay for the best night of my life."

"Very good answer," Ever said smiling at him. "Now, about those other things we can do until our wedding night.." Ever planted small kisses down his muscled stomach and pulled his silk boxers down with her, taking him in her mouth.

"Damn, Everdine, you do that so well."

She moved her tongue around his shaft taking him in as far as she could, moving her hands up and down with her mouth. His hands were holding the back of her head, moving with her back and forth.

"Ever, I'm so close. Let me pull out." She kept him firm in her mouth, stroking him again and again with her tongue, as he came in waves. "Oh chérie," he said while she finished him off.

"That was unbelievable."

Ever and Gabriel got ready for bed and spent the next few hours getting to know every inch of their bodies until they were sated in each other's arms. She thought this may not be so bad after all.

Willie woke at 2 a.m. and Anton was not in bed. She padded into his office and he was at his desk holding his head between his hands. He looked dead tired.

"Anton, you should come to bed. Is something wrong?"

"Oh, I didn't hear you, chérie. I was having an issue with an Asian supplier, but I don't think I can sit here any longer." He looked at Willie and gave notice to her dark green silk camisole and matching bottoms. His shorts tightened instantly. If he had known she was wearing that maybe he would have come to bed sooner. Her hair was wild and loose. Willie came around to his chair and lightly massaged his shoulders over his shirt.

"Take your shirt off and I can work on your shoulders and neck. You are so stiff." He was wondering if he should show where else he was stiff and maybe she could take care of that, too. His desire for Willie was about to shatter and he didn't know how much longer he could tolerate it. He unbuttoned his shirt and laid it over his desk. Willie led him around to sit on the ottoman in front of the sofa so she could better reach him.

"I'm going to get my white musk oil and I'll be right back."

"Oui, ma chère." His cock bulged at the sight of her voluptuous ass leaving the room in those silk shorts. He wanted to hold her close and feel the soft silk pressed between their bodies.

"Okay, I have the oil," Willie said, coming over beside Anton. She poured a small portion of oil in her hand and rubbed it along his shoulders spreading the oil around. She started to move her hands around his neck and he tilted his head back in pleasure.

"That feels so good, Willie."

She continued to knead in small circles over his shoulders, upper arms and back. Then she did a move that created wonderful friction at the base of his neck that made him moan in pleasure. Anton bowed his head and reached around with his hand, grabbing her wrist and pulling her around to his front. He hugged her close to his body and relished the feel of her skin underneath the silk. Willie rested her hands on his tight shoulders and continued to stroke him.

"It's late and you should be in bed, ma chère. Thank you for the massage. I owe you one."

Anton took her hand and guided her back to the bed and kissed her on the forehead. He disappeared into his bathroom for a few minutes and then crawled into bed beside her. They both lay facing each other on the king-sized bed.

"Goodnight, Willadine." He reached over and stroked the hair from her face and brushed his thumb down her jaw. She took his thumb in her hand and kissed it.

"Goodnight, Anton." She turned over facing away from him thinking the sooner she was out of his apartment the better. It was too tempting being in such close quarters with him. If she were to act on her desire for him then it may push him away.

His need for Willadine was getting stronger the more time he spent with her. To be in the same bed with her and not being able to make love to her was unnatural. He was taking it slow with her to gain her trust, but all he wanted to do was bury himself in her. Anton thought it strange that the feelings he had for Willie were taking over and making decisions for him. No other woman had commanded his senses like she did. When he first broke it off with her it was because he knew she was the kind of girl you married and had kids with, not the kind for a few hot dates between the sheets. It scared him at first. He did want those things, but saw it as something far off and not so tangible-not so soon anyway. He was wrong.

When morning came Anton woke to find Willie spooning him with her arm wrapped around his waist. He turned over in his sleepy state toward her, not realizing he had morning wood. Willie yawned and awaewness hit her. First, she was nearly on top of Anton, and second, her hand was practically on his full morning salute. She brought in a loud gasp and tore her hand back.

Anton just turned over, facing her and smiled very big. "I can only think of one thing that would make such a wake up even better, but I'll keep it to myself. Good morning, chérie."

"Good morning Anton. Sorry about coming on your side of the bed. I'm just used to sleeping with a pillow."

"It is of no concern to me, Willie. I rather enjoyed it."

"Oh," she said, turning an eyebrow up.

Anton got up and made coffee while Willie just stayed in bed looking out the wall of windows in his bedroom. It was a long way from Appalachia she thought. They both got dressed and were enjoying coffee on the balcony when Everdine texted her.

To Willadine: Do you and Anton want to come to breakfast at 10?

To Everdine: We would love to. See you soon. xo

"Willie, I need to go to the office today to take care of some details for our trip to Paris. Will you be at the apartment after lunch?"

"Yes. Do we need to look at the presentation anymore today?"

"No. I have other business to attend to, but if you could give me a few hours with you tomorrow that would be perfect. Are you able to travel with me Tuesday to Paris to make the presentation? We will stay the night and meet with the bankers at 9am Wednesday morning."

"Sure. I don't think that is a problem at all." The comfort and ease in how they worked and spent time together took Willadine by surprise. It didn't feel awkward at all- as if she's known him his whole life. Anton also felt right at home with Willie. The repose he felt around her was most comforting and he didn't want it to end.

At 10 a.m. Anton and Willie ambled over to Gabriel's for breakfast. He used his key to get in and they soon saw the two love birds making out on the balcony. The way Gabriel kissed Ever gave Willie chills. She wanted that so badly with Anton. A lump formed in her throat as Anton broke up their arduous make-out session. As if he could sense how she was feeling, he comforted her by taking her hand in his.

"Hello you two. It is good to see you kissing instead of fighting." They joined the happy couple on the balcony and jumped into the delicious spread before them. Croissants and an assortment of cheese filled their plates. Everdine was dying to tell Willie about their engagement. She and Gabriel kept making funny faces and smiles at one another and lost the ability to keep their hands off each other. As Gabriel took Ever's hand to his mouth for a kiss, Willie noticed the huge rock on her finger.

"Everdine, where did you get that ring? It is beautiful."

"Ever smiled at Willie and then at Gabriel." Before she could speak Gabriel answered for her.

"We have something to share with you both. I have asked Everdine to marry me and she said yes."

Shock and elation spread around the table. Willie was ecstatic for her sister and Anton was baffled.

"Wow, little brother. Congratulations. When is the big date?" Anton asked.

"I told Everdine to pick a date. We are shooting for end of summer- less than two months."

"You didn't even tell me your plans," Anton said, disappointed.

"It was something I had to do myself."

"I understand. I'm very happy for you both. You have found yourself a wonderful woman. Cheers."

They all lifted their champagne glasses and toasted the happy occasion. Anton clasped Willie's hand under the table in an intimate gesture. After the excitement abated Willie whisked Everdine off to borrow some clothes for her business trip on Tuesday. She was also dying to find out how sex was with Gabriel.

"Ever I am so happy for you." She hugged her sister and they both giggled like school girls. "I am dying to know how sex was with Gabriel. Was it amazing? Well, of course it was amazing or you wouldn't be marring him."

The happy countenance on Ever's face gave way to confusion. "Well, we didn't exactly do it yet."

"Get out! You are kidding, right?"

"No Willie, I'm not. I wanted to and he wanted to, and we were getting ready to, but after he proposed I had to tell him I hadn't had sex before. He got all sentimental on me and said it would be the greatest gift to give him waiting until our wedding night." Willie started to tear up. "That is so precious. He sounds like a remarkable man."

"Oh, he is Willie. I know this happened so quickly, but I love him so much. Now that does not mean we've been keeping our hands off each other. I can just about say we've done everything but had intercourse. He is so passionate in bed it drives me crazy."

Willie just stared at her sister with her mouth agape. "I am so jealous of you."

"What about Anton? Is he coming around?"

"I have no idea, sis. He gave me a magnificent kiss last night to make an old girlfriend jealous while we were out. It kind of pissed me off even though I could barely stand afterwards. Sometimes he acts like he is flirting with me, but he hasn't made any declaration of love. I don't know what to think. He's very hard to read."

"It's time to go on to phase two of our plan. You need to make yourself look irresistible at all times. Don't forget to wear a dab of perfume. We need to go shopping tomorrow and adjust your wardrobe. You do realize Anton is smoldering hot, don't you?"

"Yes, I realize how hot he is. Especially when these women come up to him, flirting while trying to warn me off.

Apparently, he'll screw any woman but me. I just don't know if I can do this."

"Willie I bet you that pair of Louboutins that we saw in Geneva that you'll bed Anton before I bed Gabriel. In fact, if you had those Louboutins it may happen much sooner."

"I don't know about that. We will be in Paris overnight Tuesday and I do need to get more clothes. I left my business suits in Geneva and don't have time to go back. Do you have a suit I can borrow?"

"I didn't bring a suit either. But, I did find a boutique in town that sells last year's designer apparel for a good price. We can look there to start and then go to a few other places I know of."

"Thank you so much, Ever. You are the best!" Willie gave her sister a hug and they joined the men on the balcony who were talking in hushed tone when they saw them.

"I have to make my way to the office now. Willie do you need to go back to the apartment?"

"Yes. I'm going to change and go for a run. The food here is so rich I feel like I could lose a few pounds."

"Trust me chérie, you are perfect. No need to lose any pounds."

"Thanks, Anton," she said and turned to Ever and Gabriel. "Goodbye you two love birds." She gave her sister and her soon-to-be brother-in-law a hug and walked out with Anton. He kissed Willie on the cheek before heading to his office.

While she was running Willie thought a lot about what her sister said in terms of dressing differently for Anton. Playing up her assets is something she never did before. Buying new clothes was one thing, but mustering the confidence to pull it off was another. If Monique was typical of the kind of woman Anton was attracted to, then it would take more than a polished wardrobe to get his attention. After running eight kilometers Willie went back to Anton's apartment and worked on her abs before showering.

At 1:30 p.m. the door buzzed and Willie hoped it wasn't one of Anton's feral girlfriends. She opened the door to see a huge bouquet of flowers.

"I have a delivery for Mademoiselle Crenshaw." An unfamiliar man's voice called out.

"Oh, do you know if it is for Willadine or Everdine Crenshaw."

The delivery man rattled something off in French and finally answered. "It is for Miss Willie Crenshaw."

"Please come in and set them down on the table over here." The bouquet was so big the man had to turn his body to see where to set the flowers. Willie thanked him and sent him on his way. The bouquet was stunning, with beautiful hues of purple, lavender and white. It smelled incredible. She immediately called Everdine.

"What's up, cutie pie?" Ever asked.

"I just got a stunning bouquet of flowers from Anton."

"How nice! What's the occasion?"

"I don't know. Anton asked me this morning if I would be at the apartment after lunch and these beautiful flowers came."

"What did the card say?"

"I haven't even checked for a card. Let me see."

Willie searched the bouquet for a card and finally found it and read it to Ever.

"Okay, here is the card: DEAREST WILLADINE, THANK YOU FOR YOUR HARD WORK ON THE PROJECT AND FOR YOUR UNYIELDING FRIENDSHIP. WILL YOU GO ON A DATE WITH ME TONIGHT? TRULY, ANTON"

"Wow, Willie, that is so sweet."

"I think I'm going to be sick. I'm so nervous."

"You shouldn't be nervous, Willie. After you left this morning Gabriel said that he thinks Anton is in love with you." Willie belted an incredulous laugh at Ever's statement of Anton being in love with her.

"I'm not touching that for all the tea in China. So, did you call your mom or dad about your and Gabriel's engagement, yet?"

"Mother is on a cruise for the next two weeks and then she'll be in Barbados and I left a message for dad to call me. You better hang up with me and call Anton. Have fun on your date tonight. I'll bring you over something to wear later."

"Thanks, sis."

Willie nervously found Anton's number in her contact list and selected it on her mobile phone. Although he had a sexy voice in person, on the phone he was a God. She pressed send and held her breath.

"Oui, Delacroix."

"Hello, Anton. It's Willie," she said nervously.

"You don't say? I know who you are dear girl." Willie knew she would be nervous, but didn't realize just how nervous.

She had no problem talking to Anton when they were just friends, but at the first hint of anything more and she started to shut down. He was drawing her in again and resisting his pull was something she wasn't capable of.

"Thank you so much for the sweet note and flowers. I treasure them both."

"You are very welcome, chérie. I don't know what I would have done without your help the last few days on this project and I'd like to show my appreciation. There is a rustic restaurant up the hill and I'd like to take you there for dinner."

For a moment Willadine was disappointed. She thought he was asking for a romantic date, but it seemed to be about the project.

"So it is more like a business date then?"

"Uh...non, chérie. I don't take business associates on dates and I don't consider you a business associate in this instance, either. Apologies if I confused you."

"Oh...then, yes, I'd like to go on a date with you. What time do I need to be ready by?"

"I'll pick you up downstairs at 6:15."

"I'll see you then, Anton."

CHAPTER 15

Everdine came over and helped Willie get ready for her date with Anton. She blew her hair out as straight as possible and put a smoothing cream on it. She pulled individual strands back and twisted them, folding them under in an inverted pony tail and knot in the back. It looked very elegant. After weeding through some clothes that Ever brought over they put together the perfect outfit. She decided on a short, cream colored pencil skirt and matching short jacket, a black sequined halter top with a bustier underneath and some black sling-back pumps. A spritz of Miss Dior on her pulse points and she was ready. Since the outfit spoke for itself Ever told her she should keep the make up light, but to play up the eyes a bit more.

"Willie, if he does not attack you tonight then you seriously need to move on. You look so hot. I wish I had your legs and boobs. You fill out that bustier a lot better than I do. He is going to flip over your cleavage."

"Maybe it's too much. I've never had so much cleavage before. I should change real quick."

"Don't you dare. This is exactly what you need to wear. I promise you."

Willie thanked her sister and then headed down to the lobby of the building to wait for Anton. She figured at this point she really didn't have anything to lose.

As soon as she exited the building she spotted Anton leaning up against his Aston Martin, chatting on his phone. She was half way to him when he noticed her and ended his call. He had dated many beautiful women, but the affect Willie had on him was astounding. His heart was aching to tell her just how he felt. What he loved most about her was that she had absolutely no clue how gorgeous she was. His eyes graced her from head to toe, leaving his mouth ajar and pulse racing. Her legs could be considered statues of art. Willie was visibly embarrassed at the attention.

"Hi Anton."

"Good evening, ma chère. You look absolutely beautiful, Willie." Anton held her cheek with one hand and laid a lingering kiss on the other cheek.

"Thank you, Anton. I'm very happy you asked me to dinner."

Anton helped her in the car and left for the restaurant, which was a twenty-five minute drive away. They filled the ride with conversation about the upcoming wedding and went over some work details and the trip to Paris on Tuesday.

"So what plans do you have tomorrow, chérie?"

"I didn't bring any business clothes with me from Geneva, so Ever is going shopping with me tomorrow morning- unless you need to meet with me then."

"No, that is fine. We can meet in the afternoon. Willie I have to insist on something. You are taking this trip because of work and I insist on buying your clothes. Do not even try to argue about it."

"Anton you know I have the money to pay for my clothes. Why are you being so difficult?"

"I am begging you to let me do this for you. Besides, you'll need to get an evening gown for our night in Paris since we are attending an event. Please, Willie, let me do this without having to get sneaky or go behind your back."

"Fine, Anton. I'll relent this time, but do know that I'll get you back some way, some how, when you least expect it."

"I look forward to it."

Le Rustic was a very elegant gourmet restaurant with lodge-like decor. It had outdoor seating with several fireplaces and a long concrete circular bar open to both inside dining and outside dining. Anton and Willie were shown to their table on the patio with booth seating so they could enjoy the views of the valley and distant water.

"This is so nice, Anton. What a lovely evening."

"It's very romantic, don't you think?" he said, tilting his head to catch her gaze.

"Yes, it is," she answered with a grin. Anton loved that it took so little to make her blush. At the risk of being brazen Willie wanted to show him how much she appreciated his efforts. She leaned in holding his face with one hand and gingerly planted a kiss on his clean smelling cheek. "Thanks for the flowers," she whispered.

Before she could pull back Anton eased his lips on hers and they kissed laggardly, softly nipping each other for what seemed like a few minutes. His taste and the softness of his lips made her dizzy.

"Mmm....Willie."

She immediately threw back her wine glass; one for the nerves. Anton took her hand in his and wouldn't let go. "Excuse me, Anton, I need to go to the ladies room."

Anton stood as Willie got up and walked toward the inside of the restaurant. When she passed the bar a man caught her arm and stopped her. Dominic Ferrier. If there was possibly a bigger playboy than Anton, then it was Dominic. They were old friends and comrades in the card playing circuit. He looked like he came straight out of the sand and sea with his sun-bleached, orange-blonde hair that was a darker color at the roots and his piercing amber eyes. Anton was amused at Dominic approaching Willie and just sat back to watch the fireworks. Then he remembered if Willie could tame him, then taming someone like Dominic would not be out of the question, either. They were cut from the same cloth.

"Chérie, please stay and talk to me for a minute." If sex could talk then Dominic could speak volumes. His French-littered accent was oozing sex appeal and Willie was on high alert.

"I'm sorry, but I'm here with someone," she said motioning to Anton. Anton caught her gaze and waved at them.

"Oui, I'm sorry you are here with someone, too, but Anton won't mind. He is an old friend. You are American, non?"

"Yes."

"I have to know how Anton snagged such a beautiful woman." Willie took her arm out of his hold and turned to face him.

"For starters, Anton has not snagged me. We are just very good friends."

"I would love to have a friend like you to kiss as you and he just did. If you ever get tired of Anton's ....uh ...friendship, here is my card- call me. I promise you'll have a lot more fun in my bed than his."

"It may be hard for you to believe this, but I'm not sleeping with Anton, nor do I go around sleeping with strange men in bars."

"Anton having a lady-friend as beautiful as you and not sleeping with her is just unbelievable, chérie. But, I can tell you are a fine lady."

"Let's just say I'm not quite Anton's type."

"I have to agree with you. I've never seen him with such a gorgeous woman before." Dominic was unflappable.

"I guess you have not met Monique or Anaïs? They are both beautiful enough to be models. In fact, I would not be surprised if they are models."

"You are the total package, though," he said as placed his hand over Willie's hip and ran it down too close to her curvy butt. Nothing but instinct took over and Willie slapped his face, drawing the attention of everyone around them. Across the room Anton stood up, ready to intervene. Dominic had taken his ruse just a little too far.

"Keep your hands off me," Willie said as she stormed off to the ladies room. When she was safe inside the bathroom she realized she still had his card. Time to teach him a lesson she thought.

An embarrassed Dominic thought he'd better smooth things over with Anton. He had no idea Willie was such a firecracker. "That is quite a woman you have, Anton. I apologize for making her upset, so please beg for my forgiveness."

"You'd be wise to keep your hands off her Dominic. She was able to take care of you herself, but I won't be nearly as kind if you try that again, my friend."

"I acted very poorly and I really am sorry. Too many bourbons. She said you were only good friends, though. You are very protective of your friend."

"Oui, we are good friends, but I'm working towards something more. She is very special."

"I'm not blind Anton. That's not the kind of woman you have a fling with, she's the kind of woman you marry and have babies with. I wish you both the best, my friend. Oh...dinner is on me. See you soon." Dominic and Anton shook hands before he strolled off.

"Thanks, Dominic. Ciao."

When Willie returned from the ladies room she could tell that Anton was worried about her. She also noticed that Dominic was no longer there- to her relief.

"Chérie, I am so sorry my friend was such an ass to you. He felt really bad and came to apologize. We go back a long way and he was very apologetic about his poor judgement. Are you okay?"

"I'm fine, Anton. Don't worry. Dominic will get what's coming to him pretty soon."

"Should I even ask?"

"Nope. You may find out soon enough."

"Mon Dieu! Remind me to never cross you. By the way, Dominic took care of our dinner and sent over this lovely champagne, so let's enjoy."

She felt a little bad about what she had done with Dominic's card in the ladies room, but he really did need to be taught a lesson.

The fire was giving off so much heat that Willie took her jacket off. The last thing she wanted was to be sweating on a date with Anton. Panting, yes. Sweating, no.

He could not help but to steal glances at her copious amounts of cleavage. He remembered how wonderful her breasts looked and felt in the limo the night of the ball when he broke up with her, and just thinking of how she looked at the beach made him hard. Her halter top was backless and he moved to caressing her back while they talked. Her skin was incredibly soft. Willie noticed that since they kissed he always had some kind of contact with her. Whether it was holding her hand or stroking her back, he had to touch her.

Over dinner they talked about their childhood and family. Willie was surprised to learn that he also accompanied his father on poker trips. They had spent one summer in the U.S. when he was a child and he got to play poker with other kids just like her. She loved hearing him tell stories. He was so animated and sexy when he spoke. The way their eyes connected made her heart turn flips. There were so many things she could read in his eyes and it was frightening, sexy and wonderful.

"There was once the ugliest boy I had ever seen. I think he was from Scotland because his hair was bright red and frizzy, and so big it looked like a clown wig. He was a lot younger than me, but he really kicked my butt in poker. The boy had a big heart though." Anton smiled at his endearing memory.

"In fact, that summer I ended up losing all of the toys I brought with me on that trip. I remember my dad having to stop in the department store to buy me more." Anton didn't tell her, but the act of kindness the boy had shown by trying to give him his toys back had always stayed with him. She also remembered losing quite a few of her toys, too.

"Is that where you learned to speak such good English, traveling in the U.S.?"

"Oui, but we also had an American nanny who spoke English to us. Up until my mother passed away I had an ideal childhood. After that my dad never remarried. He just seemed to have a bevy of meaningless women in his life. I did the same.....until now."

His eyes were burning on her as he said it. She returned his look and was hoping- no, willing him to kiss her. He paused for a moment, staring at her lips and then descended slowly, making sure she knew what was coming. Her heart was pounding in anticipation. She wanted him to kiss her, but she knew that one more kiss like the one earlier had the potential to slay her. He took her lips in his and worked them until she opened and invited him in deeper, warm and sensual. His hand gripped the back of her neck, caressing her while he took her mouth. She didn't want to question his feelings or hers, and she also didn't want to broach the topic before they had to travel and work together in Paris. For the first time she didn't need to label what they had.

As Anton let them into the apartment she thought about this coming Friday and the date she had made with Giovanni's brother. After having such a wonderful night with Anton pretending to be interested in any other man would be nothing short of subterfuge. She would need to cancel her date.

"Anton, I need to ask you something. My friend Giovanni in Milan set me up on a blind date with his brother this coming Friday. I've never met him before and was reluctant to agree to it. Should I cancel this date?" Willie looked at him with hope and longing in her eyes.

Anton appeared as though someone had just splashed him with cold water. He could not fathom Willie going out with another man. The thought of such nearly sent him to a fit of rage. "Do you want to go out with him?"

"No, not really. I think any attempt to feign interest in another man would be futile. I guess it depends on you."

"Willie," he said with a solemn expression on his face, "if it were up to me, then I'd say no. I'd tell you that I'd be miserable if you went out with another man with a romantic interest. You are all I've thought about since the night we met on the veranda. I'm trying to make things right between us."

"Then it's settled. I'll cancel the date. I'm not interested in seeing anyone else."

"I'm going to have some wine. Would you like a glass?" he asked with a sigh of relief.

"Yes, I'd love one. I'm going to change and go to the bathroom. I'll be right back."

Willie remembered what her sister told her about dressing up her assets at all times around Anton. She really just wanted to be comfortable, but she could also make it sexy, too, she thought. She grabbed a pair of her small cotton shorts, the kind most girls wore with the waistband rolled down, and a tight, scoop neck t-shirt with no bra. That should do the trick she thought.

Upon joining Anton in the living room she noticed the new sectional sofa. "What happened to the other seating arrangement that was here?"

Anton took pause before answering her, admiring every luscious curve revealed in her snugly fitting clothes. "Well, your sister apparently told Gabriel it was very bad for cuddling and making out, so he ordered us both one of these. Want to try it out?" Anton said, smiling and gesturing to the brown leather sofa he was sitting on.

"Well I can't argue with that," Willie laughed. "It looks very comfortable."

"Yes it is; come join me. You look very comfortable yourself."

"I know I'm dressed like a slob, but it's what I usually wear at home. Should I change?"

"Not at all. I want you to feel at home here. You look very nice in these clothes."

Willie took a seat beside Anton on the couch and he made sure there was no air between them. He noticed immediately that she wasn't wearing a bra. Between sips Anton brought her in for a kiss and pulled her legs up over in his lap and her hands rested on his shoulders. For the rest of the evening his lips explored hers with all the time in the world. She fell asleep in his arms on the sofa until Anton carried her to bed in the middle of the night.

In the morning when Willie woke up Anton had already left for work. The note he left on his pillow was endearing.

My Sweet Willadine,

You were sleeping so peacefully this morning that I could not wake you. Last night was very special and I hope we can do it again soon. I know I'll be missing you terribly by lunch, so please try to come by my office for a visit. I left my Visa card for you on the counter and notified the bank that you will be using it today. Call me if you need any help.

Yours- Anton

A huge smile graced Willie's face after reading his note. Her heart was aching for him. Last night was amazing even though no promises were made. She had completely fallen for him all over again and was willing to go with his terms, which seemed to be very lose. She was just as much afraid as she was in love.

Shopping went by very quickly for Willie. She got most of what she needed for her trip to Paris, including a few items to tempt Anton with. Everdine took her to a boutique where she found a wonderful last season Elie Saab gown and business suit. Both fit like they were tailored just for her. She also bought some silk boxer shorts as a gift for Anton- with her own money, of course.

Willie and Ever also discussed wedding details. Gabriel told Ever that he thought it would be meaningful to have the wedding in Geneva at the palace where she first slapped him. That was a special place for both girls since it's where they met the Delacroix brothers. It was nearly noon and time to visit Anton and Gabriel for lunch.

Ever could tell that Willie was holding back about Anton and asked her on the way to DLC headquarters.

"You've been very tight-lipped about Anton. How was your date last night?"

"It was sublime. He was pretty amazing."

"How did he like your outfit yesterday?"

"He loved it, thank you. In fact he could not keep his hands off me. We kissed so much yesterday my lips are sore."

"Willie that is wonderful! But you don't seem as excited as you should be, though."

"Everdine, I'm so in love with him it makes me sick to my stomach. I'm just worried that he will break it off again. He has been so wonderful since I arrived here. All we do is kiss, but he has yet to take it further."

"Maybe he is waiting for you to take the next step, allowing you to set the pace. Just find a way to let him know you are ready for the next step."

"I'll wait until after Paris so the presentation is not jeopardized." The limo pulled up to a nondescript office building on the outskirts of town, nestled within an office park. They arrived on the 3rd floor reception area to see a very handsome older lady talking on the phone with an English accent.

"Hello ladies! I was expecting you. My name is Sylvia. I'll let Anton and Gabriel know you are here."

"Thanks. Nice to meet you Sylvia." Everdine was always the first to speak. It was just a habit she got into in college because Willie was always the quiet one. Sylvia telephoned the brothers and Anton was first to come out. He greeted the sisters, introducing Willadine to Sylvia as his good friend and then led Willie into his office. Gabriel was right on his heels and came out to meet Ever.

"Sylvia I have some great news. This is Everdine, my fiancé. We got engaged this past weekend."

"Oh my, I can't believe it. In a million years I would have never thought this could happen. Wow."

"Thanks for your vote of confidence, Sylvia. It happened fast, but I knew Everdine was the one the moment I met her."

"I'm so rude. Please accept my congratulations. It makes me so happy to see you finally settling down. Now if we can just get your brother managed."

"He is working on it. In the future when Everdine visits my office I'd like no interruptions, please. The same goes for Willadine and Anton. Thanks, Sylvia."

"Yes, Gabriel. Again, I'm so happy for you both. My job just got easier."

After Ever was safely ensconced in Gabriel's office she asked the burning question.

"So why did Sylvia's job get easier?"

"I was wondering if you would catch that. Well if I'm engaged to be married then there will be no more disgruntled women showing up or calling. Sylvia was the one that usually dealt with that."

"You are telling me that you made that poor woman clean up your messy love life?"

"Not exactly, but she is the one that dealt with the fallout when it would spill over."

"Thank goodness you found me."

"I could not agree more. Now let's try out that no interruptions policy I just told Sylvia about."

Anton's office was very clean and minimalistic. A wall of east facing windows filled his office with lots of natural light. Across from his desk were a couple of chairs and on the other side of his office was a large whiteboard with a long table in front of it.

"I missed you this morning. You should have woken me up."

"I left very early today so I could get off at a decent hour," he said as he took her in his arms. The look he gave her anticipated a kiss and it didn't disappoint. All of their kisses since she arrived in Monaco had been slow and methodical like this one. Willie wanted the fire they shared in Geneva. Keeping a slower pace was safe, but Willie was tired of playing it safe. She deepened the kiss with her tongue and let her hands roam to his backside, pulling his hips flush to hers. That was enough to warrant a small growl from Anton. This time he broke off the kiss and sat back in his chair.

"Chérie, I love your idea of a lunch break. Come here I want to show you something." He pulled her into his lap and picked up an envelope. "I had Sylvia get copies of our pictures from the other night and these are yours." It was then that Willie noticed he had a framed photo of them sitting on his desk. Her heart skipped and did a somersault.

"Anton, thank you so much. I want to see them now." For some reason seeing the photos of them made her sad. That's when she wished their relationship did have some kind of label other than just good friends. They looked so happy together, she thought. Even though she knew he cared about her and kissed her like one would kiss a girlfriend, she felt his commitment issues would keep their relationship stagnant. It's almost like he did everything you would do with a girlfriend but didn't want to be encumbered by acknowledging they had feelings or a relationship.

Anton could tell by her expression that she was having doubts when looking at the photos. If he only knew what she was thinking. This should only make her happy.

When she got to the photo that she took of him she smiled and traced over it with her finger, remembering how playful he was.

"Hey, chérie, I'm right here. Stop pining over my photo and give the real guy a kiss." An embarrassed and amused Willadine dove right in to a kiss with Anton. His taste was familiar to her; home. The closer they got emotionally the more she worried about the heartbreak to come. She couldn't imagine life without him and that was scary.

"Thanks for the pictures, Anton. I love them. Can you also email copies?"

"Of course, I will. For a minute there you looked a little sad. Is everything okay?"

"Everything is fine. Maybe we can talk after our Paris trip, though."

"Talking will be great. I also have some things on my mind."

"When do you want to meet to go over the presentation?"

"Ideally, I will just come home early from work and we can have dinner and go over the presentation there. It's more comfortable working at home."

"Great. I'll go by the market and pick up something to cook for dinner and we can hang in the kitchen tonight."

"That sounds perfect. Don't forget to use my card to buy dinner at the market."

"Please let me get dinner," Willie said, taking small kisses along his cheek. "You are going to pay for everything in Paris and I really want to do this one dinner for you. Please?"

"I will agree as long as you tell me what is in that little bag there."

Willie's face immediately flushed red. She had forgotten about the underwear she bought for him and definitely didn't want to give them to him now. "It's nothing really." Her bright red face gave her away.

"I know the store that bag came from and you are not going to get off that easily. Show me now lady." The store sold high-dollar men's clothing and just about anything that had to do with men. Anton shopped there often.

Confession time. "Please don't take this the wrong way, Anton, but I bought you some boxer shorts. Ever was getting Gabriel some and I just thought these would.....they are just.....well here."

"The cat has certainly got your tongue, chérie. Let me see what you have here that has you so flustered."

Anton dug into the gift bag and pulled out some folded tissue paper. He ripped through the paper and held up the skimpiest silk boxer shorts. They were a pale, celery green color with a shorter inseam than what he usually wore.

"These are very nice, Willie. No woman has ever bought me undergarments before. It's very special. Thank you."

"You're welcome, Anton," Willie said, still flushed.

"I am curious, though. These are a lot shorter than the boxers I usually wear. Why did you choose this kind?"

At this point Willie was just about horrified. "I never should have bought these. I'm so embarrassed. It was just an impulse." She didn't dare tell him it was because his legs were sexy as hell and she wanted to dress them up with skimpy underwear.

A smile lit across Anton's face. "Don't be embarrassed, chérie. It makes me so happy that you were thinking of me today. We just have different ways of showing it. I have a picture of you on my desk and you buy me skimpy underwear. I think I like your way better." Could Willie get any redder in the face? What on earth was she thinking buying him such a personal gift?

"Would you like me to wear these when we go to Paris?"

"Mmm..hmm," was all Willadine could manage. Anton was making a meal of seeing her in such discomfort. He relented and kissed her repeatedly on the cheek. It reminded Willie of the time in Geneva where it felt like he was making love to her face. His hand glided slowly up her leg, from her knee to her thigh, underneath her skirt. Willie was just trying not to sound like Jack the Ripper, getting so lit up from Anton's touch.

"I love it when you wear skirts, chérie," Anton said, trailing his mouth down her neck.

"Anton...," Willie said as she exhaled. "I should let you get back to work. Sylvia or someone else may walk in and see us."

"The sooner I finish here the sooner I can get home, but this kind of distraction is the best. Thank you so much for coming to see me and for the sexy underwear."

"You are so welcome." Willie stood up slowly walking toward the door with Anton.

"Oh, would you like me to take your gift home? I can go ahead and put it in the wash."

"Maybe I want to compare mine with Gabriel's to see who has the best boxers."

"I can already tell you that yours are shorter and prettier, so don't sweat it."

Anton walked back and grabbed the bag off his desk, handing it to Willie who was standing outside the door to his office. She smiled expectantly at him, wishing him a good day before turning to leave, hoping he would have at least kissed her.

"Chérie," Anton said, yanking her by the wrist back to him. He gripped the sides of her head in his hands, backing her against the wall outside his office and planted the mother of all kisses on her lips. Willie's arms went limp and dropped the bag and purse, splaying her hands palm side down for support as she was backed against the wall, her mouth and tongue being consumed by Anton. This was the fire she'd been missing with Anton since Geneva. Only this felt more like a super nova. His tongue was rolling hers and he could not get enough. Willie's whole body was alight with need.

Anton pulled his lips away, resting his forehead against hers, both gasping for air. "Cela me tue. Je t'aime beaucoup," he whispered under his breath. Willie didn't have enough whits left to comprehend that he just professed his love for her.

"And to think I almost got you bikini briefs," she said, breathlessly.

Anton chuckled at her quick humor. She was right, though. If she had given him bikini briefs then he may very well have cleared his desk and taken her right there in his office.

"I'll see you tonight at five, chérie." With a chaste kiss on her cheek, he side stepped back into his office leaving Willie to face a stunned Everdine, Gabriel and Sylvia gawking at her from the lobby.

The twenty feet Willie had to walk to the lobby felt more like a mile. Her face was a beacon of red and her step unsteady after Anton's mind-boggling kiss. How could his demeanor seem inscrutable and unaffected whereas she was left breathless, red-faced and with a staggering step. Willie met with the incredulous smirks waiting for her in the lobby.

"Willie, what did you do to him?" Everdine asked with a huge grin on her face.

"I didn't do anything but give him the boxer shorts I bought for him today."

"Those must be some powerful boxer shorts," she replied.

"Don't say a word, Gabriel," a glowing Willadine said. He just grinned and walked back to his office.

CHAPTER 16

The rest of the day flew by. All Willie could think about was the million-dollar kiss Anton gave her at lunch. Throughout dinner and packing for Paris her mind was elsewhere, and it was hard to concentrate on the presentation. Anton also seemed preoccupied. He was quiet and contemplative while they went over the order of the presentation slides together. The way he looked at Willie was steeped with some kind of weighty sentiment. His ability to turn his emotions on and off frightened her. He kept his distance from her when he got home, which made Willie wonder if he was as invested in her as she was in him. She also realized that the nature of his work took a great deal of focus, something at which he was masterful.

As usual Anton worked late after dinner and Willie went to bed without him. This was a sobering reminder that she was an interloper. He was probably getting weary of having a houseguest. She had become too comfortable in a relationship that had no definition.

Muffled shouting erupted somewhere in the apartment. Willie didn't even know what time it was, but she knew it was clearly too early to be up. As she walked toward the office she heard him in a very heated argument on the phone. His office door was ajar, but she didn't dare go in. She could not recall him ever coming to bed last night, either. Regardless of how their relationship was progressing, she decided it was best to get her own hotel room for the remainder of her time in Monaco. She found that the longer she stayed with him the more she started having expectations.

She finished a small glass of orange juice and started back to the bedroom when Anton charged out from his office and was surprised by her presence.

"Chérie, so sorry I woke you."

"It's fine Anton. This is your home, so please don't worry about me. Sometimes I feel like I'm stepping on your toes here."

"That is nonsense. I enjoy having you here and I want you to feel at home."

"Did you come to bed at all last night?" she asked.

Willie could tell he was wary about answering her question and he looked completely dogged.

"I did come to bed late, but I had to take a call at 4 a.m. You should go back to bed, chérie. We have a big day ahead."

"Will you come to bed, too? Please?"

"Sure. I could use a few more hours of sleep."

Willie took Anton's hand and led him to the bedroom. Before getting back in bed she gave him a heartfelt hug and a peck on the cheek. She couldn't tell if he was just tired or still thinking about the argument he had on the phone, but he looked a million miles away.

"Goodnight, Willie," Anton said after turning out the lights.

"Goodnight, Anton."

After a minute of lying next to Anton, Willie mustered the courage to talk to him.

"Anton," she whispered.

"Oui, chérie."

"It's hard to say this without feeling like I'm intruding, but I'm worried about you."

He caressed her arm and planted a gentle kiss on her head.

"Why are you worried about me?"

"You work such long hours and get so little sleep. You've been looking tired lately. I don't think you've gotten a full night's sleep since I've been here. As your good friend, I'm worried about you."

"I appreciate your concern, but you needn't worry about me. This is just a busy time right now. Gabriel and I have spoken about hiring someone."

"I care about you a lot, Anton, and it's hard to see you like this. Is there anything I can help you with?"

"We can discuss that later. Right now just having your support and friendship is more than enough. If you weren't helping me on this project I would be in big trouble. Goodnight, chérie."

The flight to Paris was short and uneventful. Willie had let Anton sleep in as late as she could before waking him. He seemed a little disoriented when he woke up, not having slept so late in such a long time. On the way to Paris he told her about the benefit gala for cancer research. Gabriel usually attended with him, but he had an important meeting with some foreign business associates at the office. As they were checking into the hotel Anton seemed a bit nervous.

"Chérie, I hope it is okay, but I put us in the same suite."

"Of course, Anton."

When they were shown to their suite, the bell boy put her luggage in a different room than Anton's. Their hotel room was two bedroom suite with a spacious shared living quarters and a balcony with a view to die for. The thought of sleeping in a different bed than Anton knocked the air out of her. It reminded her that their time together was limited and she should get used to it. It was too easy to forget the circumstance that brought them together in the first place. All of the distance Anton was putting between them emotionally and physically made her very insecure in how far she thought they had come. Being with him was like riding a roller coaster, but she also had to ask herself if she truly was ever with him.

"Chérie, I need to go run a few errands before we get ready for the gala, but I wanted to talk to you first."

"Sure, Anton."

"There will be a lot of people at the gala that I've known for a long time. You have already met a few women that I dated before and there may be others at this event tonight. You can expect to receive a lot of attention if we are together tonight. So...."

"You want me to attend as your friend?"

"It will be easier to introduce you as my friend."

"As opposed to what? Your good friend?"

Willie didn't like where this was going at all. She really didn't have to go if her presence was going to be such a chore for him. Maybe he was ashamed of her, she thought.

"I just want us to have a good time this evening, chérie, without so much drama."

"If being with me is going to create such a strain, then I really don't have to go, Anton. I promise you I would love nothing more than to take in the sights of Paris by night. It does not bother me at all. I swear to you."

"You are talking nonsense, Willie. Of course, I want you to come. I would just hate for you to spend your entire evening fighting off jealous, grudge-holding women."

"Anton, am I your girlfriend or are we just good friends? What's going on here? I really need to know."

"Well, I haven't thought about..."

"You know what? If I have to ask then that should tell me my answer. We are good friends and that is what we are at the gala. Silly me for thinking otherwise. Problem solved."

"But you know that's not..."

"Anton, please don't make anything out of this. Let's just have a good time and not get caught up in some kind philosophical debate about what we are."

"Agreed. Do you need anything while I am out?"

"No. I'm going to the salon in the hotel so they can do something with my hair."

"Be sure to charge it to the room. Shall we leave together?"

"Lets' go."

Willie's hair had never looked so beautiful before. The stylist straightened her hair perfectly and parted it on the side, leaving a few cascading waves and styled the rest in a French chignon to the back. Her make up was done a bit more dramatically than she was use to. She wore smokey eyes for the first time and didn't come out looking like a raccoon. Underneath her strapless, eggplant colored Elie Saab gown she wore a matching bustier and g-string. At quarter of seven Anton knocked on her door and asked if she was ready to leave. In Geneva she had worn Kenzo Vintage perfume and it drove Anton crazy. She sprayed it on all of her pulse points and also walked under it. Time to go and be the best damn sexy, irresistible good friend she could be.

"I'm ready," Willie said as she walked into the living room.

Anton's heart sank when he saw her. "Willadine, you look breathtaking; so beautiful. But there is only one thing missing." Anton took out a rectangular jewelry box and explained that it was a family jewel on loan. It had been in the family since his great, great grandmother. He pulled out an egg-shaped black opal pendant necklace. It complemented her dress perfectly. After clasping the necklace together he lightly stroked Willie's arms and kissed her shoulder.

"Thank you, Anton. I'll take good care of it."

"Come, chérie."

As soon as she and Anton entered the ball room of the gala it almost resembled a scene from The Battle of Little Bighorn in seeing which desperate socialite could get to him first. It was almost like every single female eye in the room shifted in his direction. She was about to give him the space he requested earlier in the day, but he held her close around the waist. These women were all gorgeous, Willie thought. They either had paper thin bodies or were made of more plastic than Barbie. Anton marveled that at one time this would be an ideal situation, but now he only felt discomfort with so much attention.

"Hi Anton darling. How are you?"

"I'm doing fine Marlie, and you?"

"Great now that you're here. Who is this with you?"

"This is my good friend Willadine, my date for the evening."

"Nice to meet you, Willadine."

"Likewise," Willie responded.

That scene repeated itself several times. A few women came up to Anton to find out if there was any reason to worry that he was off the market and Anton gladly gave them the satisfactory news that Willie was just a friend. It irked Willie to no end being referred to as his friend. Although they didn't establish to each other that they were committed, in her heart there was only one man for her and it saddened her being reduced to just his friend. She was visibly cold to his treatment of her.

After the buzz seemed to die down around the female-fest that was Anton, two business associates came up to talk to him. They were from Munich and looked very dashing with strong facial features and slicked back blonde hair. "Anton, long time-no see, my friend. I would ask how you've been, but seeing this beautiful lady at your side means you must be doing very well."

"Torsten, it is great to see you. This is my date, Willadine. Willadine, this is Torsten. Torsten and I worked together in the past on a few projects."

"Nice meeting you, Torsten," Willie replied.

"Likewise, Schatz. So how long have you two been seeing each other?"

Anton had a confused look on his face trying to figure out what to say before Willie cut in.

"I got this one, Anton," she whispered.

"Actually, Torsten, Anton and I are not seeing each other. We are only friends-good friends."

"Well then, my night just got better. You must save me a dance later."

"With pleasure."

"We'll talk later, Anton."

"Oui."

Anton had a strained look on his face as he asked her if she wanted a drink. He really shot himself in the ass he thought. Would it have been so bad if he introduced her as his girlfriend? Since the kiss they shared in his office he'd had a hard time coming to terms with how his life was changing; how much he loved Willie.

While Anton was procuring drinks she felt a hand on the small of her back from behind. "Hello, chérie. Do you remember me?"

"Hi Dominic," a flustered Willie said.

"So are you here with your good friend tonight?"

"Yes, I'm with my good friend, still. Thank you very much for buying dinner the other night."

"Well it is the least I can do after I acted so poorly. But, you were swift in your retribution, weren't you?"

Oh shit. He must have heard about what she did to his business card. After Dominic copped a feel of her butt she left his business card on the bathroom counter- not before writing on it that he had a small penis. She blushed a lovely shade of red.

"I'm sorry if that caused you any lonely nights, Dominic, but I'm very particular about strangers touching me."

"Chérie, you were perfectly right in putting me in my place. I deserved much worse. Your good friend, Anton, already told me that he would get involved if I put my hands on you again."

"What are friends for?" she commented, dryly.

"Why don't you share this dance with me and we'll start anew?"

"Anton is getting me a drink, so I'd better stay put."

"Well it looks like Anton found a distraction on the way to the bar."

Willie looked in the direction Dominic was pointing to see Anton dancing very closely with another woman, a very attractive woman. Her heart dropped seeing him dance like that with someone else. This was a game she didn't want to play anymore.

"I'll dance with you, but if your hands go roaming then I'll kick you."

"You are such a spitfire, Willadine." Dominic said, leading her to the dance floor. "Anton better hang on to you."

Willie reluctantly enjoyed getting a feel for how built Dominic was and how delicious he smelled. Dancing with him would not be hard at all.

"I wish I was Anton's to hang on to, but it does not look like it will happen. He has already broken my heart once and tonight has been nothing but a clear reminder of why I should stay away from him."

"Chérie, if you give him some time I'm sure he'll come around. I know he cares for you deeply. I think you know that Anton has never had a serious relationship and it may take time for him to put that into perspective."

"I don't know Dominic. He is so complicated and it seems like part of his past will always be so much bigger than what he and I can ever be together. I don't date around and have some expectations that I'm not sure Anton can meet. At one point I was willing to abandon my own self-belief for him and he was gentleman enough to tell me no."

"It sounds like you are a very sensible, intelligent woman. I can see why Anton is drawn to you and it's refreshing."

"Enough about man trouble! Tell me how you came to speak such good English?"

"Well, my mother is originally from Ireland and as a child I spent a few summers on my grandparent's farm. My dad is from Straßbourg, which is along the border of Germany. My mom would speak English to me until I was about 8 years old and then I resisted. It was enough to give me a good foundation though. Do you speak French?"

"Yes, but I should be speaking more while I'm here. When my sister and I go back to Geneva...." Willie suddenly had a confusing look on her face.

"What is wrong, ma chère?"

"Well, my sister got engaged last week to Anton's brother, so I'm not sure if she'll be coming back to Geneva. Wow. I've been so busy working on this project with Anton that I've barely had time to think so far ahead."

After Dominic got over the initial shock of Gabriel getting engaged, he and Willie continued to have lively conversation. He discovered they both had a love of tennis and discussed plans to play when they were back in Monte Carlo. After spending some time with Willie he thought Anton was a fool for leaving her alone at the gala. If Dominic had met someone like Willie he would not let her out of his sight.

After the second song ended and he wished her a good evening. In return Willie gave him a hug and let him know how nice it was getting to know him. They seemed to spark a very kindred connection.

Since Anton never came back with a glass of wine, she went to the bar herself to get one. She was hoping she would see him there. Looking around the room she got a glimpse of him standing with several ladies talking, well more like flirting. She decided to get a glass of wine and take him one, too. All of these women were monopolizing his time. Before she was able to reach him, he kissed the hand of another lady and led her to the dance floor. Willie was as good as forgotten. Anton didn't even look in her direction.

When Anton wheeled his latest dance partner off the floor, Willie approached him with the glass of wine.

"I could see how thirsty you were from dancing and thought you might like a glass of wine." The sarcasm in her voice was palpable.

"Thank you, chérie. You are the best." Anton sounded like he already had a few glasses under his belt. "I was hoping you would dance with me at least once, Anton."

"Of course, we will dance. Have you been mingling and having a nice time?"

"I guess. Your friend Dominic is here. I don't think he was too happy about the stunt I pulled on him at the restaurant, but he admitted he deserved it. We called a truce, though."

"Once you get to know Dominic you'll find he is a very nice guy and loyal friend."

One of Willie's favorite big band songs came on and just as she was setting down her wine to see if he wanted to dance, Anton was whisked away by another one of his female friends. It happened two more times after that and Willie was just about to leave and go back to the hotel when Torsten grabbed her arm and asked her if he could have his dance.

She obliged him, but kept a close eye on Anton. She didn't like at all what she saw. He was very flirty and way too close when dancing with these women. She felt bad not paying much attention to Torsten. He was very handsome and on any other occasion she would have swooned at his feet. Anton had ruined her for any other men.

"I can tell you have it really bad for Anton. You keep looking his way."

"I apologize, Torsten. I'm worried he has had too much to drink and we both have a very important meeting tomorrow morning. I've never seen him so careless before."

"Yes, he is quite active tonight."

"I'm sorry Torsten, but I need to get him back to the hotel before he does something rash."

"I completely understand. Here is my business card. Let me know if you are ever in Munich or Salzburg and we can meet."

"Thank you, Torsten. It was nice meeting you."

Willie parted ways with Torsten and cautiously made her way over to Anton. He looked disheveled, sweaty and his bow tie was loose and hanging around his neck. He didn't seem to notice her so she tapped him on the shoulder.

"What do you want, chérie?" he asked with his arms still around the other woman.

"Anton we should go back to the hotel. We have an early meeting tomorrow morning. You don't look so well."

Anton stumbled over to her and grabbed her around the waist. His eyes looked wild and his pupils were dilated. "You know chérie," he said, slurring his words, "you're the only woman I've ever loved." Anton's honesty was too much for his lady friend to stay and tolerate. She turned on her heels and left in a huff.

"Anton, please, let's go back to the hotel."

"Only if you'll let me make love to you, Willie. Let's make this relationship official." His hands flew all over her while he stumbled into her. She slapped him across the cheek at his forward behavior.

"Oh, so we went from being friends to being in a relationship now. My status has been upgraded."

"Just a minute. I'll tell everyone here. You slapped me, and according to Gabriel, that has to be a good sign."

"No! Wait, Anton.." Before she could stop him, Anton staggered onto the stage where the band was playing and grabbed the microphone after nearly knocking it over, causing all eyes to peer in his direction.

"Attention, please." He tapped on the microphone. As he did the band abruptly stopped playing. "I have to make a declaration to all of you tonight. I told you all Miss Willadine Crenshaw was just a good friend, when truthfully, she is the love

of my life. I will marry her someday and have a million babies."
He barely slurred through his words before starting to wobble on
his feet.

Willie turned a few shades of red and covered her face with
her hand. When she took her hand away she saw Anton reeling
on the stage. He crumpled to the floor and passed out. Willie
went on the stage and kneeled by his side to try and wake him,
but he was out. She looked up to see Dominic making his way
through the crowd.

"Well I guess that answers any doubts you may have had
about his feelings for you."

"Dominic, I think something is wrong with Anton. This
doesn't seem like alcohol alone. Can you help me get him to a
cab back to the hotel and call a doctor. Or should we take him to
a hospital?"

"You think he may have been drugged?"

"Yes. Just look at his pupils." She felt his heart rate and it
was accelerated.

"I'm really worried about him. Just call an ambulance,
please."

Dominic agreed that something was going on. He and
Anton had drank together many times before and this was a
reaction he'd never seen from his stalwart friend. He called an
ambulance and under ten minutes Anton was being wheeled out
with Willie by his side.

"Thank you, Dominic." She gave him a quick kiss on the
cheek and was gone. She called Gabriel and let him know what
was going on and he got on the first flight to Paris.

The doctor had confirmed what Willie thought- Anton was
given some kind of drug to make him incoherent for the next ten
hours. He had likely been given something like a date rape drug.

At 3 a.m. Gabriel came into Anton's hospital room to see
Willie sitting beside Anton with her head resting on his bed, her
hand in his. She darted up at hearing him enter the room.

"Chérie, you must be exhausted. What happened? How is
he doing?"

"He is fine and will be fine, Gabriel. The doctor wants to
make sure his heart rate stabilizes and there are no bad side
effects before discharging him. Someone must have slipped a
drug in his drink at the gala and he was a little delirious at first
and then passed out on stage."

"He was on the stage?"

"Uh, yes. He made quite a spectacle of himself. I could tell something was wrong with him as I was trying to get him to leave with me back to the hotel. Dominic helped me."

"Yes, I saw Dominic in the waiting room and he told me how poorly Anton acted. He said he would take you back to the hotel so you can rest some. On my way here I spoke with the venue manager and security video will be reviewed to see if any details of the evening help uncover who did this."

Willie had a sneaking suspicion that David was involved in this somehow. Why he would go to such great lengths to get revenge, she didn't know. "Anton and I are supposed to meet with the bank at 9 a.m. I guess I'll have to cancel our meeting."

"No. Anton would be mad as hell if you canceled the meeting. You can do this Willie. Both Anton and I have one hundred percent confidence in your abilities. He brags about you all the time and thinks you would make a wonderful addition to our company. Please, go get some sleep for a few hours and meet with bank officials yourself. You've got this."

The confidence that Gabriel and Anton showed in her made her head spin. There was no way she could let them down now. Then she wondered if Anton had been telling the truth when he said she was the love of his life. Seeing him this way only confirmed how much she loved him. If anything had happened to him she didn't know what she would have done.

"Okay. I'll go back to the hotel. Are you staying here with him?"

"Yes. I won't leave his side."

"When he wakes up his head will be in a lot of pain and he may be sick. And just so you know, he has been burning the candle at both ends the last week. He's been working too hard and not getting enough sleep."

Willie kissed him a few times on the cheek and whispered something in Anton's ear before hugging Gabriel and leaving the room. She hated to leave him, but knew he would want her to take care of business that they worked so hard on the last week. She and Dominic left the hospital and he dropped her off at the hotel.

CHAPTER 17

Nervous could not begin to describe how Willie felt. Sick, wretched and nauseous, came close though. The team that met her at the bank was very professional, courteous and unaware of her spurious confidence. She explained that Anton fell ill last night and was in the hospital. The presentation went off very smoothly and she was able to answer questions without so much as a hiccup. They were very impressed with her business acumen and asked questions about her background. The senior vice president was so impressed he told her to apply for a job after she finished her internship in Geneva. The team at the bank said they would call with their decision after everyone had time to study the prospectus she had left them with.

Outside of the bank she immediately called Gabriel to see how Anton was doing. Gabriel and Dominic were with him at the hotel room where he was resting. She walked as fast as she could to get to the hotel, making her way to the suite.

"How is he feeling?" Willie already knew the answer, but asked anyway. Dominic and Gabriel were sitting in the living quarters of the suite.

"His head hurts, but he really feels bad about how he treated you last night," Dominic said.

"I'm surprised he even remembered."

"Well a little reminder does not hurt, Willie."

"Dominic, that really wasn't necessary. He's been through enough and has had so little sleep this week."

"Ma chère, my brother would want to know that he acted like an ass. And from what I heard, it started before he was drugged. David will go to jail for this if they find he is behind it."

"Gabriel, I have to ask you why David has taken this so hard? Why not just move on to the next opportunity?" Willie asked.

"Maybe you don't understand how much there is to lose with this deal, Willie. David stood to lose millions in return for his backing of the project. Albeit, most of it would not be realized until the next few years, but this is the kind of project that pays long term being part owner of the company. Based on its' success, of course."

"I never thought about it like that. He really does hate me then."

"Don't you worry about him, ma chère. Dominic and I have plans for David. The surveillance camera at the gala picked up enough to make an arrest of his female accomplice. We are going to leave you with Anton now. See you back in Monte Carlo and try to get some rest."

"Bye Dominic, Gabriel. Thank you so much for your help."

"Don't thank us, it's you and your sister who saved our asses. Ever met with my foreign buyers today and took care of loose ends there and you sealed the deal this morning at the bank. We should be at your mercy thanking you."

"I don't know about that," Willie said, nervously.

"Well I got a text message from an old friend at the bank who said you nailed it on the fucking head. Congratulations. Alright, we are taking off now. Don't worry about the hotel room; I extended your reservation a few days. Take some time to rest."

Willie was dog-tired after the night she had with Anton. She wanted to go to her own room and sleep, but she was still worried about Anton. The thought crossed her mind that something much worse could have happened to him if his reaction to the drug was more adverse. For her own preservation she pushed that thought out of her head. Quietly, she opened his door to check on him. He had a glass of water and some pain medicine on the side table. Willie took off her shoes, stripped down to her undergarments and crawled in bed beside him, being careful not to wake him up.

Slowly, Willie woke up, knowing she'd have to face Anton and a plethora of other issues they needed to talk about. She could hear Anton out in the living area talking on his phone. As much as she loved him, she could not continue on this roller coaster they were on together. The uncertainty was too much for her to deal with. He had such a strong hold on her heart that she didn't know where she would find the strength to end this cat and mouse game. A quick glance at the clock and she could not believe it was almost 4:00 in the afternoon. It felt great to get some sleep, but a shower is what she needed. As the water rolled over her she used Anton's soap to wash herself. Just the smell of it turned her stomach over. How could hot water feel so damn good? Would she ever be able to shake her desire for him? As much as she wanted to stay under the warmth and cover of the water, it was time to face Anton. With towel wrapped tightly around her body and one wrapped around her hair, she gathered her clothes and entered the living room. Anton was setting up some dinner he had ordered when his eyes met hers.

"Hey, Anton. How are you feeling?" she said, somberly.

"I'm fine, thanks to you. Why don't you get dressed and we'll eat." She noticed the weight of melancholy in his voice as she sauntered to her room where her luggage was. Her eyes welled up as she got dressed and dried her hair. How she let herself get in this situation with Anton again was beyond her. She was either the eternal optimist or a lover of pain. She put her hair in a ponytail and joined Anton in the living room.

"Are you hungry, chérie?"

"A little, but I'm not sure I could eat right now."

"Come sit at the table and try to eat some. I ordered you a salad with grilled chicken and some tomato soup."

"The soup sounds perfect."

The quietness was gnawing away at her and there was no way she could broach the topic first. She would not even know where to begin.

"Does your head still hurt Anton?"

"Oui, a little bit, but not so bad. I'm feeling much better. After we have dinner and talk some I was hoping you would join me for a walk to get some fresh air."

"Maybe," Willie said in a very non-committal way. If he thought for one minute that she would still want to be with him after he broke it off with her for a second time he was clueless.

"Do you feel rested enough? Gabriel told me you gave the presentation after staying with me until the wee hours of the morning and that you made quite a delivery."

"I have no idea where I found the fortitude to give the presentation, but somehow carried it through."

They both ate quietly and didn't talk the rest of the way through dinner. For some reason, Willie seemed to be at peace if Anton dumped here again. If anything, going through the range of emotions she'd been through the past few weeks had made her stronger.

"If you are finished eating, can we go talk now? I'd like to have your complete attention." Anton's tone was unwavering.

"Sure, let's get it over with."

He took her hand and led her to the sofa and sat beside her. Willie could not look at him as tears fell without care down her cheeks.

"Hey, Willie, don't cry. Look at me."

Willie shook her head from side to side. "I don't want to talk about it. Say what you need to say and I'll listen."

Willie rested her head in her hands and let her tears fall. Anton pulled her into his arms and let her cry on his shoulder.

"Chérie, I am so, so very sorry I hurt you yesterday. I was such a fool. After I kissed you in my office the other day it was clear to me that life as I was accustomed was forever changed. That along with the fact that you would be leaving again at the end of the week made me give serious thought to what I wanted in life. I've been jumping over emotional hurdles since then. What I mean is that I came to the realization that I don't want you to leave. I can't imagine not seeing you every day or not waking up with you in my arms every day. Having you in my apartment this week has been the absolute best. I want you to move in with me and give us another chance at a relationship."

That was not what Willie was expecting to hear, but she wasn't sure how it changed his lofty behavior. Willie looked up at him with her weepy eyes. "Anton, what frightens me most about you is your ability to completely shut down emotionally and turn your feelings off. After you kissed me like that in your office the other day and then hardly spoke two words to me or touched me afterwards, I thought you wanted to break it off with me. I just don't think I can take any more risks with you."

"Please don't say that, chérie. For so long I have carried out the same kind of meaningless relationships and it has taken a huge shift for me emotionally to accept what we have together. I'm just asking you to have confidence in us and please give me the chance to prove that what we have is worth fighting for."

"It hurt me so much to see you pawing all over those women last night. To willingly put myself in that situation again would be like running into a brick wall. I don't know what to tell you."

Anton was trying to think of what he could say to sway her decision, but nothing other than the truth would work.

"I know it would have been messy to come out as a couple last night at the gala, but that is the price I should have paid considering how much you mean to me. I was so wrong to think delaying it would be easier. Do you remember what I said on the stage last night?"

"Yes, Anton. I remember vividly."

"Well, I don't Willie. Dominic told me verbatim what I said and it is the truth. You are the love of my life. There is no other woman who could ever compare to you. Do you remember why I didn't want to introduce you as my girlfriend?"

"Yes. You said that they would react badly toward me or you and ruin the evening. The evening was ruined anyway, so it doesn't matter." Willie didn't know what he wanted to accomplish bringing this up. It didn't seem to matter much in her opinion.

"Let me show you the text messages and voicemails I got on my phone after that declaration of mine on stage."

Anton pulled out his phone and showed her at least 5 vile text messages directed at him after he had made his declaration for Willie last night. She understood why he wanted to distance himself, but it still bothered her. If they were going to make a relationship work, then they would have to make it official eventually.

"What about the next time we attend a function or go out together Anton? I refuse to be relegated to friend status in order to make life easier for you. Up until you swept me off my feet with that kiss the other day I felt myself expecting more out of you. I'm not going to settle feeling like second best or being your girlfriend only when it is convenient for you. If you can't meet my expectations then there is no us."

A look of relief came into his eyes as he realized she was willing to try it seemed. He would damn well meet any expectation she gave him.

"Chérie, I would love to meet your expectations. Tell me what they are. I'll do anything. I promise that from here on out you are my girlfriend, my lover, my best friend, the one I can't live without.....my everything. That is you, chérie. I'm ready to make that commitment. The thought of not waking up with you every morning scares the hell out of me." The urgency in Anton's voice went straight to her heart.

She was an emotional basket case at this point and it was hard for her to talk through her sobbing. Was she finally getting what she wanted out of Anton? It was time to find out.

"What I want from you is to be honest with me. Tell me how you are feeling, whether it is good or bad. Just have confidence that I can handle whatever is thrown at me. I expect you not to hide our relationship from anyone. It's very hurtful and unhealthy for me when you deny what we have. I expect you to treat me like your girlfriend and keep your hands off other women." She paused for a moment, then looked him directly in the eye. "I'm in love with you Anton."

Anton stood and pulled Willie up with him. His long fingers wiped away her remaining tears, followed by ponderous kisses around her face. He laced his arms around her in a bear hug and lifted her up and she wrapped her legs around him. He walked with her to the bedroom and set her down, kissing her along the way.

"Chérie, I love you, too......so very much. You confound every part of my sensibilities."

His eyes were attuned to hers as he unbuttoned her blouse, pushing it over her shoulders, letting it fall to the floor. She was nervous, but what she wanted most in life was about to happen. She was going to give herself to the man she was in love with. She buried her head in Anton's chest, taking in his scent and letting her hands feel his beautiful form before unbuttoning his shirt. His bare skin was an aphrodisiac- his smell, his warmth and sensation filled her. A groan escaped his over his lips as Willie dropped to her knees and unfastened his belt, helping him out of his pants. To Willie's excitement, Anton was wearing the green silk boxer shorts she had given him. His erection was skirting the hem across his leg and she could not take her eyes away.

Willie let her hands glide up Anton's thighs, firm ass and all over his legs before resting on his penis. The thin veil of silk fabric between her hand and his erection was slowly discarded as she took his large cock in her hand.

"Anton, It's beautiful.....and big." Anton chuckled at her vivacity.

"Chérie, you are driving me crazy."

She took his length in her mouth and moved back and forth, finding a slow rhythm. Anton grasped her head and was moving his hands in rhythm with her, his breathing becoming ragged. Her slow, duteous movements brought him close to the edge. "Stop, chérie. It's my turn."

He brought her to her feet and closed in on her. Pushing her curly hair aside, he kissed down her neck. Willie tilted her head back giving him more access. His mouth traveled from her ear down to the nape of her neck and onto her shoulder. He slid her bra straps off her shoulders and rubbed his hands along the bare breadth of her shoulders.

"Anton..," she exhaled, "I want you now."

"Soon, chérie. Let's take our time."

Anton moved his hands to the front of her skirt, pushing it down until it hit the floor. She stepped out of her skirt and kicked it aside. He stepped behind her and unclasped her bra, slipping it off. Reaching around cupping Willie's bare breasts, he caressed them and lightly pinched her nipples with his fingers while sucking on her neck from behind. "You are so beautiful Willadine. Please say you'll move in with me," he whispered in her ear.

A moan of agonizing pleasure escaped through her lips at his touch. One hand left her breast and drifted down her stomach into the front of her panties, sending Willie's head backwards, writhing under his attention. Anton's fingers rejoiced in the hot moisture between her legs.

"Damn, you are so wet already."

Willie just melted at his touch. "Don't stop, Anton. Please."

His fingers held a steady pace between her lips, rubbing her moisture around her clit. His mouth ravaged her neck as he continued pleasuring her with his deft fingers. A few more strokes and Willie came hard under his commanding fingers.

"Oh Anton...," she said as she climaxed, pleasure whipping through her body. Anton supported her with one arm around her waist and she rested her head back on his shoulder while her hands coaxed his legs. "That was... amazing." Anton laughed at how responsive she was. "It's only the beginning, chérie."

Anton turned her around and kissed her hard until her lips parted, inviting his tongue in. He wanted to take her then, but there was still one thing he had to do first- taste her. He backed her up until she felt the bed behind her legs. Anton threw the covers back and helped her get on the bed. Before crawling on top of her he slid her panties off and discarded them. Now they were both naked and Anton relished the way her naked body felt under his. His mouth moved down to her breasts where he gave each one faithful attention, admiring her size. Her nipples puckered between his lips and tongue. He planted small kisses down her stomach until he found himself between the apex of her thighs. He spread her legs and inhaled her scent. Willie wasn't even mortified that he was between her legs, about to go down on her, but everything with him felt like home to her.

"Willie, you smell so damn good."

Anton held her thighs open with his hands as his tongue laved her clitoris. She responded immediately with her hips bounding slightly upwards. He continued to make big strides with his tongue sending her into a state of ecstasy.

"Anton," she screamed. Her back rose up off the bed, gripping his head as she squirmed under his tongue. She was still sensitive from her first orgasm as the second wave of pleasure capsized her body.

"I love it when you say my name, chérie," Anton growled. "You are so beautiful."

He kissed his way back up her body, his thighs resting between hers. Willie could feel his erection pressed against her. He could not wait any longer to be inside her. Anton sidled up on his elbow, running his fingers through her hair with one hand and caressing her cheek with the thumb of his other hand. His soft lips swept across hers and she could smell her passion on him. She couldn't get enough of him, deepening their kiss.

"Are you sure you want to do this Willie? I can wait." He whispered in her ear.

"I want you now, Anton. I can't wait any longer."

"Should I get a condom?"

"I have an implant, so it is fine unless you want to wear one."

"I've never done it without one, chérie, so this will be something very special between us."

That was all the assurance Anton needed. He sucked and kissed his way down her neck and let his fingers tease her clit before pushing one inside her. Willie's heart was racing and her breathing stuttered at his touch. He rubbed his penis at her opening, spreading her moisture over him. Willie couldn't fathom that she was about to lose her virginity to the man she loved so deeply. Everything she had done in her life culminated to this point.

"I love you so much, Willadine. You belong to me, chérie." He spread her legs and lifted her thighs back, plunging into her hot, tight walls. She winced and gasped at the pinch of his length pressing through her. Anton paused to make sure she was okay, allowing her to adjust to his size. He pulled back and drove in again slowly, with Willie moaning as he entered again. His size made her feel full and sensational. Each time her moans became louder her and breathing harder; again and again he pulled back and dove into her. His face was tucked beside hers as the moved inside her.

"You feel amazing, chérie. So wonderful. So right."

He repeated several times how much he loved her and that sent shutters through her body. His fullness and love exploded rampant emotions inside her. He could feel her tensing as his own control ebbed with each thrust.

"Anton..," Willie shrilled, releasing around him. It didn't take her long and he was glad since he had to hold back from the moment her entered her. He gave three hard thrusts, coming furiously inside her with each one before collapsing on top of her. Anton muttered something in French, before raising enough to give Willie a slow, hard impassioned kiss. Until now he had only had sex for pleasure, not love. For the first time it was an expression of love. It had dawned on him.

"That was unbelievable. Nothing will ever compare to this. You're the only girl for me, Willie."

Willie was overwhelmed with all of the emotions coursing through her. Never had she imagined making love to him would be so powerful. Even though she held doubts in the back of her mind whether or not he would stay with her, at this moment everything was perfect. She could only live in the present where he was concerned. Anton was an amazing lover.

"Chérie, are you okay?"

"I'm just a little overcome. It was beautiful, Anton. I didn't know it would be like this." Her eyes welled with pools of happiness as he hugged her close to his chest.

Anton cleaned them both up before tucking her under the covers with him, snuggling up behind her, holding her until they both fell asleep. It was the kind of sleep that can only be achieved when every emotion, feeling and nerve ending had been scratched and sated.

A few hours later Willie woke up with abdominal cramps. She carefully slid out of Anton's hold and went searching for pain reliever. She couldn't find any in her purse and opted for a hot bubble bath instead. A hot soak was just what she needed.

She was enervated from the strains of the last few days, but was too excited to do anything but think about making love to Anton.

With her eyes closed she languished under the bubbles in the hot bath while a huge grin crept across Willie's face. Sleeping with Anton was beyond anything she had anticipated. It was slow, sensual, patient and mind-blowing. Her grin tightened just thinking about his lips on her body and how she could not wait to make love to him over and over again.

Anton stood at the entrance of the bathroom watching her, amazed at how far he had come with Willie. He was certain she had no idea just how crazy he was about her. Everything about her felt natural- waking up with her, working with her, kissing her, sharing a bed with her and more than anything, loving her. He had a deep connection with her before they made love, but now it was animalistic.

"Please tell me what you are smiling about, chérie." Anton walked over to her and sat on the edge of the spa tub. Willie opened her eyes at hearing his voice and gave him a big toothy smile and blushed. If he only knew what she was thinking.

"I'm just thinking about you."

"I like that it brings such a pleasurable look to your face. How are you feeling, chérie?"

"I'm having some cramps, but feel otherwise fine. I couldn't find any pain reliever so I thought a bubble bath would help."

"I'm sorry I wasn't very attentive. I didn't think about this. I'll be right back."

Anton left the bathroom before Willie could say anything. She enjoyed watching his sculpted, naked body move. She didn't mind having some pain since the memory of why she had it was so sweet. He came back quickly with some water and pain reliever.

"Do you want to join me, Anton?"

"I'd love to."

"Here, sit in front of me and lean back."

Anton carefully entered the tub, sitting between Willie's legs and slouching down so his head was laying on her chest and his arms resting on her legs. She cherished touching him in such an intimate gesture. Her hands caressed his chest and shoulders with soap while she kissed his temple. A soft, throaty growl passed over his lips.

"Chérie, your touch drives me wild." Anton hid his raging hard-on under the bubbles.

"You have the best hair, Anton. When it's wavy and curly like this it takes my breath away. I can't keep my hands out of it. You're so handsome."

Willie ran her fingers through his hair, placing gentle kisses on his face and neck while her other hand grazed through his chest hair, coming to a stop on his neck. Anton wanted her in the worst way but knew she was too sore to take him again. Willie continued her assault on his senses and both were soon lost in measured breathing.

"Willie, you are really driving me crazy. It will be hard to keep my hands away from you if you continue that."

"Anton I need you to make love to me now." He sensed an urgency in her voice.

"Chérie you have to let your body rest. I will gladly pleasure you though."

"No, I want you Anton. Now." She was burning to have him inside her again.

He made a guttural sound, indicating the internal debate of her request. "Alright, but we will take precautions so you don't hurt yourself."

Anton stepped out of the tub and helped Willie out, patting them both down with a towel. As soon as he put the towel down Willie gripped his erection and lit into his mouth with hers. Anton steadied himself, stepping back a half of a step at her amorous invasion. She was out of control and he liked it. He had been with countless women, but none of them had ever commanded his body like Willadine; his heart, too. His only regret was that he didn't claim her sooner.

Willie came alive in Anton's arms. He was stunned at the fervor in which she kissed him. Slowly, she backed him out of the bathroom to the bed, never breaking contact and crawled up on the bed with him. This was a side of Willie that Anton had never before experienced: virgin to vixen in 60 seconds. He was sure that if he had clothes on she would have ripped them off already.

"You should be on top, chérie, so you can decide how much. I won't be able to control myself and don't want to hurt you." Anton was so winded he could barley get the words over his defined lips. "I don't know what's gotten into me, Anton. I just need you so badly."

CHAPTER 18

Anton sat up in bed leaning against the headboard, cupping her breast. Willie swung her leg over him and straddled his hips, lacing her fingers through his while bringing his hands to rest against the headboard. He bowed his neck as Willie continued kissing and nibbling at his jaw and neck. She pulled back slightly, looking at him with emotion-filled eyes. Anton could see the turbulence in her gaze. He had no idea what she was thinking, but it didn't last long enough to matter.

Willie mounted him delicately, easing down and braced her hands on his chest. The euphoric feeling of being gorged with him while still tender surged her body as she threw her cascading curls back. She began to move passionately on top of him. Anton had never seen such a beautiful sight than that of the woman he loved grinding herself to a blissful end on top of him. He had the perfect view of her full breasts.

As Willie adjusted to his size she began to rock more wantonly, losing herself thoroughly. She was dizzy, feeling both pleasure and pain. Anton steadied her along, gripping her waist. In the back of her mind Willie knew why she had taken Anton so quickly. She didn't know what would happen tomorrow when they both had to face the light of day. No matter what words were spoken between them that brought them together, deep down she had doubts that he would stay with her. Loving him was easy, but trusting him was not. She put everything she had into making love to him, now with fear of what the future held. Nothing else mattered and she kept nothing back.

"Chérie, I'm so close." Willie slowed her pace so she could devour his lips. Taking, probing, hungry and unrelenting. She left Anton gasping for air and as she continued rocking on top of him. "Faster, chérie. Please."

His words set her aflame and she started moving with the pace of a sprinter. She lifted up just enough so that he was at her entrance and then moved back down with graceful aplomb. Over and over; faster and faster. They were both lost under a cloak of passion and need. The little sounds she made as she came down on him were enough to declare him oblivious. Nothing ever sounded so sweet or sexy. The way her curly hair fell down her back as she was loving him was a sight to behold.

Her body was clenching, pulsating around him as they both fell into a pool of ecstasy. "Anton," she mewled as he finished inside her. He drew her in as tight as he possibly could and her arms were glued around his neck. Both of them were staggered at the level of intimacy they'd just shared.

Anton broke his hold and pulled her back to kiss her sweetly on her forehead. It was then she noticed that they both had been brought to the verge of tears, eyes swollen and misty. She rested her head on Anton's chest and he stroked her hair, neither saying a word until Anton rolled her over to the side and positioned himself on top of her.

"Marry me, Willie." He gave her a quick succession of kisses on her face and stroked her hair back. "Marry me, please. I never want to be without you. Ever. I can't live without you." He skimmed his thumb over her bottom lip and parted a meek kiss upon her supple lips.

"Anton...I..I need to go to the bathroom. Excuse me."

Anton rolled off her and she sauntered to the bathroom to splash some water on her face and clean up. Still shocked by his declaration of matrimony, she wondered why it didn't make her as happy as it should have. There was no question that he was the only man she could ever love so deeply. She was expecting him to distance himself from her not offer up marriage. After pushing her away so many times she doubted this time would be any different.

When she joined Anton he had pulled his boxers on and was laying on the bed waiting for her. He motioned for her to come up on the bed beside him.

"Now how could a proposal of marriage cause such a dismal response? Tell me what you are thinking, Willie. Why don't you want to marry me?" He took her hand, kissing her knuckles.

"I didn't say I didn't want to marry you. I could not imagine my life without you, Anton. It's just too soon. We should just wait a little before we think about that."

"Wait for what?"

"I just need to.......I want our relationship...."

"What are you worried about Willie? Just tell me, chérie."

Willie's eyes became laden with sadness and a little fear. How would he handle the truth? She didn't want to start their relationship worrying about his reactions so she was blunt in her response.

"Anton, I have a hard time trusting that you'll want to stay with me."

There. It was out. She could have never imagined Anton's reaction. His expression sliced through her. Anger laced with pain seemed to translate to bewilderment on his face.

"Why in the hell would you make love to me if you didn't trust me?" Anton was obviously bristled at her lack of trust.

"Don't be mad at me for being honest with you. I made love to you because you are the only man I ever want to give myself to. I truly thought that when you woke up in the morning that you would be running scared and that this may be my last chance to make love to you."

"So you were giving me a goodbye fuck? How sweet of you, Willadine. It's good to know how you really feel." It made Willie uneasy when Anton raised his voice.

"After all the times you pushed me away and how badly you treated me, what do you expect?" Willie also realized that he was a man that was use to getting his way and had a hard time accepting otherwise.

At that he went to the bathroom and took a shower. Willie knew he wouldn't like what she had to say, but never imagined it would be that bad. She knew she would not be able to capture any sleep with the state of her emotions and it being a few hours before it was time to get up anyway, so she went to her room to shower quickly and started packing.

Anton came out of the bathroom with a towel wrapped around his hips. Damp, hot and sexy enough to make her melt into the floor.

"Tell me this, chérie. If you were trusting of me would you agree to marry me?"

"Yes, Anton," her eyes swelled up, "my heart already belongs to you."

"Hey, don't cry."

"I'm just so tired of fighting with you. I'm just tired. If I told you right now that I would marry you there is no way you'd accept that knowing how I felt, right?"

He waited a tad too long to reply. "Yes, you're right. I just want so badly for you to trust that I know what I want and how I feel about you."

"My feelings about trust are based on our experience together and that is not something I can ignore. You've gone cold too many times. All I need is time to cultivate some trust. I love you so much Anton that it scares me. You have the ability to destroy my heart. I just need time."

He wrapped his arms around her, crushing her into his chest. "I will never do that to you, Willadine. Promise you'll never do that to me. Promise me I'm the only man for you."

"I'll never hurt you like that Anton. I promise. You are the only one. In order for me to believe we have a future together I need to trust in what we have. Can you just give me some time?"

Anton crushed his lips against hers. He realized that he was powerless when it came to Willie. He would give her anything she wanted. He was amused that she was the one that felt vulnerable when all he felt like at the moment was a little boy. She was the one with the power to destroy him if she walked out.

His tongue rolled around hers and their hands graced each other. It wasn't enough. It would never be enough. Anton pulled her hair away with his hand and sucked at her neck, tasting her sweet skin. She had the creamiest, smoothest skin that invited passion. Willie could feel his hard cock pressed against her abdomen and it made her crazy. She unwrapped his towel, setting him free. Anton growled at her suggestion.

"I'll never get enough of you, Willadine. Never."

"God Anton I want you again. I need you again."

"No, chérie, you are still sore. It would be too much. We'll do other things instead. Come with me to bed."

Anton laid down on the bed and brought Willie up with him. "I want you to straddle my face so I can taste you."

"What?" Willie was not use to being so blunt about what she thought of as kinky.

"Trust me, chérie."

Willie climbed over Anton and ambled her way to his head, grabbing onto the headboard. Anton wrapped his arms around the backs of her legs, gripping her thighs, keeping them apart.

His tongue lapped between her silky, moist folds and Willie moaned in satisfaction.

"Oh Anton.."

"You taste so damned good. It drives me crazy."

He kept driving his tongue into her and then circled around her clit. She was bouncing all over his face about to lose herself when she pulled away.

"Anton I want us both to do it at the same time. I want you in my mouth."

Oh hell. He nearly lost it hearing her speak those words. Her honesty, he found, was one of the sexiest qualities about her.

Anton scooted down the bed some and instructed her to turn around and straddle him again. "You stay on top and we'll do sixty-nine."

"Oh my goodness, I can't believe I'm doing this." She was excited about performing such an erotic act with Anton. It made her only want to do more with him.

Anton wedged a pillow under her stomach so she would be more comfortable. He started playing with her wet folds, gently inserting his finger. Willie took his rock-hard cock in her mouth and slowly moved up and down his length, savoring the way his steely, smooth skin tasted. Hearing her moan while she swirled her tongue around the tip of his penis made him swell even more. She could feel him getting thicker.

Anton wanted to give her a night she would not forget. As he licked her clit he pushed his finger inside her and then circled it around her anus with the moisture her arousal provided. He did the same with his pinky finger several times. It made Willie lose her mind. All while she was sucking on him she was moaning with him in her mouth. He had no idea what her garbled sounds meant other than she was on the verge of coming on his face and he was also close. He continued his assault with his pinky and when he thought it was lubricated enough he slid it inside her while continuing to lash his tongue over her clit. Willie felt like every pore and hair on her body was electrified. Nothing had ever made her so excited or turned on than what Anton was doing to her at that moment. She cupped his balls and continued to pleasure him.

Anton could tell she was about to come and he plunged his finger feverishly in and out while sucking her clit between his teeth, lips and tongue. With him still sheathed in her mouth she squealed and he felt the vibrations of her pleasure all over his body. Hearing her scream with his cock in her mouth undid him and he came before he could warn her. "Willie," he wailed so loud he was sure the hotel walls were not thick enough.

Feeling completely whipped and sated, she rolled off him, resting on her back. For the next few minutes they lay quiet in contemplation. Willie was in awe of Anton; in awe of the male body. Being with him tonight made her realize that she would not only be making love with him, but also exploring her sexuality. Before she made her way to the bathroom she gave him a soft kiss and sheepish grin. No matter what issues they were having, passion, love and sex were never in question. She had often heard girls in college talk about doing such things with boys, but never imagined it would be her. She could still taste him, striking her as more erotic than anything else.

Willie took a shower and dried and styled her hair. It was getting so long and the layers drew up in soft, taut curls. Without curl cream and a diffuser she would look like a wooly mammoth. She dabbed a small amount of makeup and joined Anton who was checking his messages on his phone when she joined him.

She crawled up beside him and he set his phone down on the bed. He nestled her in the crook of his arm, caressing her face planting tender kisses on her cheek. "Do you know how stunning you are and how much I absolutely love you?" Willie could see the love and sincerity in his eyes.

"You are the sweetest man Anton. Sex with you is just.....I can't put it into words. It was so erotic that I get hot just thinking about it."

He threw his head back in a light laughter. "Oh chérie, have I created a little sex kitten?"

"Only with you Anton. I want to do everything with you." He wasn't sure how to regard her statement.

"So it did not bother you what I did with my little finger?"

She closed her eyes, bit her bottom lip and shook her head from side to side. He closed his eyes and kissed her on her forehead.

"And you would like to experiment some more, chérie?" Anton growled thinking about what he'd like to do to her.

"Yes. You drove me insane, Anton. You have to tell me if there is anything I can do for you. I just don't have the experience and want to know that you are satisfied."

Anton was thrilled at her enthusiasm.

"You are the most sensual woman I have ever met, chérie-and an incredible lover, too. I'm so glad you are adventurous in this way."

The phone beside the bed rang and Anton answered it. "That was room service and breakfast is on the way up. I ordered it while you were in the shower."

"That sounds perfect. I'm so hungry." He went to the bathroom to wash up and finish getting dressed before joining Willie in the dining area of the suite. Anton didn't bring up marriage again and they talked about plans for their last night in Paris.

CHAPTER 19

Everdine was enjoying a seldom rain shower in Monaco. Her and Gabriel still upheld their pre-wedding chastity vow and it was driving them both mad. Although they licked, sucked and grabbed every orifice and protrusion on each others' bodies it still left her yearning for him in the most intimate way. Nothing they did together could satisfy the need to have him between her legs.

She decided to see just how strong Gabriel's resolve was. Her black satin corset hugged and pushed her body in all the right places. The matching panties didn't cover much from behind and gaped in just the right place. She pulled on a pair of sheer, black stockings, held up by the garter on her corset and slipped on her black pumps. Her make up was layered just enough that Gabriel would notice and she dolled up her hair before slipping into her tan trench coat, leaving for his office.

Gabriel didn't have time to go home for lunch. With Anton having been in Paris, and a whirlwind trip back home before going away again on business, he was working long hours, spending most of it on the phone covering for Anton. He also had to join Anton on some of the business trips coming up the next few weeks and was swamped with work. Sylvia was just getting ready to take Gabriel's lunch into his office when Ever walked in. He usually had grilled salmon and greens delivered from a brasserie nearby.

"Hello Everdine. Gabriel didn't tell me you were coming by today. Is he meeting you for lunch?"

"Oh no, Sylvia. This is a surprise visit. I just wanted to stop in for a minute."

Ever was so nervous about what she was wearing underneath her overcoat, but didn't show it in the slightest.

"I was just getting ready to take his lunch in. Why don't you do it? I'm sure it'd put a smile on his face."

"I'd love to, thanks."

She was going to put a smile on his face alright. Hers, too.

Before she walked toward his office she asked Sylvia a question. "Do you usually knock first before you go in or call him?"

"When I deliver his lunch I knock twice before entering and he usually doesn't even raise his head to acknowledge me. He is completely focused on his phone call or work to even notice me."

"Great Sylvia. Thanks."

Ever paused at Gabriel's door and knocked twice in an efficient manner that she hoped would imitate Sylvia's and opened the door swiftly, locking it behind her. Sure enough, Gabriel didn't even lift his head up. He was looking at a spreadsheet and entertaining a phone call at the same time. His chair was swaying back and forth, facing away from her and he was looking toward his computer that had a huge picture window behind it. She set his lunch down on the edge of his desk and slowly untied her sash and opened the buttons on her trench coat. She tossed her hair a little and struck a seductive pose, tucking one side of her coat behind her back with her arm so that the whole side of her body was exposed from the breast down. She propped her leg out slightly to the side, projecting her inner seductress. She just stood there waiting several minutes before he finally ended his call, returning his full attention to his computer screen. Her heart felt like it would beat out of her chest.

"Would you like dessert first?"

A surprised Gabriel jutted his head in her direction. He promptly cleared his throat and let his mouth fall open. "Fuck."

"If it wasn't for Mr. Chastity, then, yes, fuck it would be. I guess we'll have to do...other things."

His erection was growing to new heights. He could not believe how lucky he was to have met someone like Everdine. She stroked every feeling, thought and imagination he had ever had about the woman that would become his wife, only so much more. She was sassy, sexy and was never afraid to put him in his place.

"Do you have any idea what you do to me? How you affect me? How much you turn me on? Everdine you are pure TNT. I can't wait until our wedding night. Not too much longer, chérie."

He started to get up from his chair, but she stopped him. "Stay there."

Everdine came around his desk, untying the sash of her coat as Gabriel's eyes melted on site. She flipped the arms of his work chair up and straddled him. Gabriel called Sylvia and told her to hold his calls and she curtly informed him she was already on it. Ever took Gabriel in a firm, deep kiss while unbuttoning his shirt. Feeling the heavy, warm skin of his chest under her hands and smelling his heated male scent made her moan.

"Gabriel you smell so good I could eat you." His hands stroked up her thighs and when he reached the apex his thumbs caressed over her panties. She tilted her head back allowing the slightest touch of his hands to send pleasure through her whole body. He took the chance to kiss her neck and pulled down her bustier, giving him access to her tight, throbbing buds. The guttural sounds she made when he took her erect nipple in his mouth nearly made him come in his pants.

She turned her attention to his pants and urgently unbuckled his belt and opened his slacks. She slid off his lap and got on her knees before him and pulled his boxers down, freeing his huge erection.

"Oh God, Everdine....I want you so bad I cant stand it." His fingers pieced through her hair in a circular motion as she took him in her mouth. Around and around, her tongue teased his swollen head and shaft, bringing him closer to losing it. She loved the taste and feel of him and purred with him in her mouth. "I'm close Everdine."

Undeterred by his words, she continued to suck him off until he came so hard he saw stars. She took what he had and then stood up and slipped her sodden panties off. She was so turned on she was practically dripping. She straddled him again and took sensual nips at his neck, relishing his taste and warmth. She could feel his erection throbbing underneath her and she started gliding over it using her moisture, taking pleasure in the friction it created.

"You know it would be too easy to take you inside me right now," she said.

"That is my very special wedding gift from you, so please control your urges, chérie. And it is very special to me."

Ever kept moving agonizingly slow, rubbing herself over his penis. "I know Gabriel; It's special to me, too. It's very hard to resist you, but I have to regardless since my birth control needs to be replaced." Her words were tattered and breathless.

"Well that would not stop me. I dream about getting you pregnant, chérie."

"God Gabriel, I can't wait to have your babies."

He growled at her and with a quick jump he stood up, setting her on his desk, propping her feet up. Her heels straddled the edge of the desk, keeping her legs wide open and in place. He leaned down and continued ministrations to her most urgent needs until she couldn't take it any more. She leaned back on his desk, back arching, as his tongue took her over and over until she came. Gabriel just sat back in his chair staring at what was before him. She was utterly breathtaking.

After they finished dressing Gabriel took her over to his sofa and shared his lunch. "So when did you find out about your birth control? Does this mean your mother knows about us now?"

"She called me this morning after a night of gambling at one of the cruise ship ports. She was a little tipsy, but very excited. She can't wait to meet you. In fact, she wants to come a few weeks before the wedding. Is that okay?"

"Wow.. of course, it's great. I can't wait to meet your mother- the woman who raised such a spitfire. I'll be sure to make time away from work."

"Gabriel, my mother is very reserved and proper, so don't expect too many similarities. In fact, I don't think I've ever seen my mother tipsy, so that was quite a surprise. I guess maybe she's loosened up since I've been out of the house."

"So tell me, chérie, how soon after we marry do you want to start a family? You know I'm over thirty years old so my clock is ticking." Gabriel wore that half grin that made her knees weak.

"Maybe we can wait a year at least so we can have time for ourselves first."

"That sounds perfect. We will need some practice, you know."

Gabriel was in awe of how his life had changed in the last month alone. Never had his future or desires become so clear. Two months ago he would have been thrilled to have a long string of women in and out of his bed, but now that idea seemed so foreign. He laughed out loud at his about-face in his attitude about relationships, women and children.

"What's so funny?"

"I was just thinking about how much my views have changed since meeting you. Remarkable does not even do you justice, woman. You really have made my life beautiful."

Ever's eyes began to puddle. "That is such a sweet thing to say, Gabriel. I love you so much." They enjoyed holding each other a few more minutes before Gabriel had to get back to work.

Life became very busy since Willie and Anton came back from Paris. Gabriel and Anton were busy completing details of the new acquisition and Willie and Ever took off in hopes of finding their half-sister, Marva, before Ever's wedding. They split up in their search wanting to cover as many cities as possible. It was a very busy, lonely time for all. Willie ended up in Zurich and Ever was in Dijon. When they didn't have immediate success on the last leg of their search, they left their contact info for Marva at several cafes where she was known to sing. They could only hope she would call and want to meet them when she discovered she had sisters. Both girls were missing the Delacroix brothers something fierce after being away from them for five weeks.

Willie was not feeling too well and decided to stay in Geneva at their apartment instead of meeting Ever back in Monte Carlo. Ever would be coming back to Geneva in a few days anyway. All of the running around had caught up with her and she needed a few days to rest before jumping into pre-wedding details with Everdine and her mother, who would be arriving soon. In another week they would all be in Geneva in preparation for the wedding, including their father. Both of the girls were excited to be seeing him again. Being so preoccupied with the Delacroix brothers, work and their search for their sister Marva, they were only able to participate in two poker tournaments and they both came out with large purses in true Crenshaw fashion.

Although it had been nearly five weeks since Willie and Anton came back from Paris, they had only seen each other for a quick dinner together in Basel while she was waiting for her train. He had begged her to come with him on his business travels, but she was dedicated to finding her sister. Since Anton and Gabriel were traveling so much for work they were unable to meet with the sisters while they were searching for Marva. Both couples had perfected the art of phone sex.

Willie had given a lot of thought about Anton's marriage proposal and she was ready to make the commitment. She was ready to say yes after they had made love in Paris, but gave way to caution instead. He had called her every day they were apart, sent flowers to her hotel in Zurich and sweet text messages. They practically had phone sex every night. She felt very secure in their relationship and finally trusted that this was what he wanted. Being separated from him made her realize that being without him was the most painful feeling she had ever experienced. They were both miserable without each other. Speak of the devil. Mr. Wonderful rang her phone before she was about to go to bed.

"Hi Anton, sweetie."

"Mmmm chérie, I miss you so damn much. How are you feeling?"

"I'm feeling fine, but have picked up a bug the last few days. I miss you, Anton. It's been horrible and depressing without you for such a long time. Are you still coming to Geneva tomorrow?"

"Yes, Willie. I would like to spend the weekend with you. I need some time alone with you before the wedding madness begins. Gabriel and Ever will be very busy and you and I can have some rest and relaxation at my father's chalet in Chamonix. What do you say?"

"That sounds amazing, Anton." She thought a weekend away would be the perfect time to tell him she would to marry him.

"I'll pick you up in the morning then."

"I can't wait. I've missed you so much it's been unbearable. I sleep with your picture beside my pillow every night. I don't ever want to go so long without seeing you again."

"I love you so much my sweet, sweet Willie. You are my world, chérie. See you tomorrow morning."

It had been five long weeks since they first made love and Willie could not wait to enjoy every inch of his body again. She didn't know how Ever and Gabriel remained abstinent. Anton was a sensual and attentive lover and every part of her body ached for him, missed him.

Willadine drifted to sleep with the anticipation of Anton arriving. The last few weeks had seemed like an eternity. The only reason she was able to get some sleep was from being exhausted from all of the travel she had done the last few weeks. The last thing she planned on doing with Anton in Chamonix was sleeping.

Willie woke to the buzzing of the call button to the door of her apartment. After a quick glance to her clock she noticed it was only 6:14 a.m. Excitement abounding, she leaped out of bed and ran to let Anton in the apartment. He swung her around, pressing her so tight against his chest that it took her breath away. Clocks stopped ticking and the world stopped spinning. There were only two people on the planet. They feasted on the feel and scent of each other in their arms for several minutes.

Anton could feel Willie's wavered breathing on his chest and hear her soft cries. He carefully stepped back out of her arms to look at her, wiping the gentle tears from her cheeks.

"Oh chérie, I've missed you so much. Now stop crying."

"I'm just happy to see you. I've never missed anyone like this before and it's a little embarrassing."

"You don't ever need to be embarrassed around me. I love you so much Willie and I promise you we'll never be separated for such a long time again. You should have taken up my offer to fly you in for a visit."

"I know, Anton. I really should have. Being away from you for so long put our relationship into perspective." A fresh wave of tears escaped her eyes. "You mean everything to me and it's important that you know how I feel about you....and us."

Anton embraced her against his body stroking her hair, relieved that Willie was now in the capacity for a marriage proposal. "Willie, I know how you feel and I feel the same. I'm glad that you wanted to give my proposal some time. That tells me what a strong, independent and intelligent woman you are and I value that so much. I have no doubt that we will spend the rest of our lives together. No more crying ma chère."

They stood for a little while holding each other before Anton took her lips softly in his, savoring the feel and taste of her warm mouth on his. He had been up most of the night to make it to Geneva and was in dire need of a little more sleep. He and Willie went back to her bed and slept for a few more hours. Now that Anton was beside her in Geneva she felt worlds better.

At ten o'clock both love birds woke in an amorous embrace with huge smiles plastered on their faces. Anton again was thanking his lucky stars that Willie had put up with his noncommittal, childish behavior and was prepared to move forward with their relationship. He had to run an errand before leaving for Chamonix in order to seal the deal with her and it would be tricky doing this without Willie.

"Chérie, I need to go to my apartment to get a weekend bag and run a small errand. Did you want to come with me or rather stay here and shower and pack?"

"Well I do need to shower and pack. Will I need to bring a dress?"

"Yes, you need just one dress and after that clothes are optional. We'll have a special dinner tonight and we will also go out Saturday night." Anton had a devilish grin on his face. The same one that made Willie melt since the first time she met him.

"I like the sound of that. I don't plan on having clothes on unless absolutely necessary."

Anton embraced her for a pithy kiss and then left the apartment. Willie had a few special things planned for Anton, too. While being separated from Anton for so long her imagination became very active and she bought a Couples Sex Kit while out shopping in Munich one day. She planned on using it this weekend. She also had a special piece of jewelry to give him that she had made. It took a tiny chunk out of her poker winnings, but she wanted desperately to give Anton a token of her love. She had a gold necklace custom made for him. It was a rugged looking, small antiqued chain-link design with an antiqued rectangular pendant that bore the first words he ever spoke to her the night they met. Words she would never forget.

"The most beautiful things in the world can not be seen or touched, they are felt with the heart."

Engraved on the back of the pendant was the date of the night they met and an inscription, "You are my heart and soul - Willie."

She was nervous about giving it him since he didn't wear any jewelry. When she had it made she requested the smallest chain link available and also the smallest pendant possible that would still hold the special words. It would not upset her too terribly if he didn't want to wear it. It was more important to her that he knew how much she loved him and thought about him while they were apart. She felt she made it rather clear that she wanted him to propose again and he hadn't brought it up exactly, which made her uneasy.

Anton made a quick stop at his apartment to shower and pack a garment bag for the weekend. His next stop was at the same jeweler where Gabriel got Everdine's engagement ring. Anton had called their old friend a few weeks ago, letting him know what he was looking for. When he saw the ring his friend had made his heart stirred with sentiment. This was the ring for her and seeing it only confirmed that no other ring would have been right except this one. It was a rather large pear-shaped green diamond, surrounded by a halo of pave champagne diamonds with a band made of the same pave diamonds. In his mind it was as unique and beautiful as Willie. He just hoped he could wait until tonight to propose to her again.

The drive to Chamonix was beautiful and did not lack for excitement in Anton's sports car. They barely had room enough for their luggage. At one point Anton had to pull over because Willie was car sick through some of the curves. So much for the lunch that they enjoyed in Bonneville. They arrived at the chalet in the early afternoon. It was gorgeous. The chalet was not very big, but had excellent views of Mont Blanc and the surrounding peaks. There was a hot tub on the deck and a sauna in the basement. The kitchen opened up to the living area with a huge granite fireplace surrounded by floor to ceiling windows and folding doors that opened to the deck. The design and style of the chalet was very typical of the area with warm wood trimmings. There were two master suites on the main floor and one in the basement. It would make for a very romantic weekend.

"I need to go into town quickly and get a few things for this evening. Is there anything I can get you or would you like to come with me?"

"I think it is best I stay out of the car to let my stomach settle. It's so beautiful here. I'd like to look around some. Could you get something for an upset stomach, please?"

"Oui, chérie."

Anton planted a languid kiss on Willie's pert lips and pulled her close for a hug before leaving. He wanted to get some champagne to celebrate their pending engagement and he also needed to stop by the pharmacy to get something for her upset stomach.

When the pharmacist said the word 'pregnant,' as in "if she's not pregnant then she has a stomach virus," Anton's mind was in complete flashback mode. Paris. Then he remembered his brother talking about how close he and Everdine came to doing it in his office and how he didn't even care if her birth control had run out. Gabriel wanted to start a family with Everdine and that was where his train of thought stopped, not remembering that the sisters had gotten their implants at the same time. He wanted a family with Willie, even though they had never discussed having kids. Secretly he would not mind at all if she was already with his child. For good measure he left the pharmacy with some medicine for an upset stomach......and a pregnancy test.

He was about to crawl out of his skin with desire to make love to Willie, but needed to wait until after he proposed and after he found out if they may be having a baby. It would not be right for him to make love to her without protection knowing that her birth control may be ineffective. He had the perfect evening planned and it could only get better if Willie was carrying his baby.

Anton would not tell her what he had planned this evening-only that she should wear one of the dresses she packed. Willie put on a tea-length, off-the-shoulder powder pink dress. The fabric was stretchy and flowing, molding to her curvy body. She wore her hair down and curly. Anton loved her curly hair. He told her it looked sexy that way. When Anton eyed Willie coming out of the bedroom he could not get past the fact that she wasn't wearing a bra and that dress would be too easy to get into. He had an erection all day and it was making him physically ill. The sooner he proposed, the sooner he could take her to bed.

On the way to the airstrip he thought he should broach the topic of children since they hadn't really discussed it. If there was a possibility she was pregnant then it would be prudent that she feel comfortable with the topic.

"You know, chérie, we are getting very serious and I have to ask you what you think about children. Do you ever wish to have a family?"

"That is pretty serious, Anton. I never really thought about having children."

His heart sank.

"Until I met you, that is. I would love to have children with you. That night I met you was magical for me. It was like every cell in my body awakened. Never did I think in my wildest dreams we'd be sitting in your car discussing children two months later."

"I want children, too. I always knew I wanted kids, though. It wasn't until I met you that I thought it would be actually be possible."

Willie squeezed his hand and brought it to her cheek, kissing his palm and wrist.

When he arranged the helicopter ride he hadn't known about her uneasy stomach. They arrived at the small airstrip and Willie was amazed that he had made such an effort to make their time so special while they were in Chamonix. She was excited about the helicopter ride and didn't feel sick at all. It was close to sunset when they went up. The views were unlike anything she had ever seen. Anton was talking to her through the microphone of the aviation headsets they were wearing, giving her an aerial tour of what she was seeing. Anton sat beside her with his arms wrapped around her while she took in the views.

He tilted her chin between his fingers, turning her gaze to meet his. "I love you so much, Willadine and feel so lucky to have you in my life. You were my girlfriend when we took off, and when we land I would like for you to be my fiancé. Marry me, chérie!"

Although she was momentarily speechless, her eyes said everything. She kissed him like her last breath depended on it. "Yes, Anton, I'll marry you. I love you more than anything. I want you now. Right here." She kissed him and started working down his buttons on his dress shirt. "Uh...Chérie, we are not alone in this conversation. The pilot can hear everything we say." Willie's expression was priceless. She was such a bright shade of red that it looked like someone had flipped the on switch in her face.

"Now don't ya'll mind me. Congratulations on your engagement."

"Thanks, Pike. Bachelorhood is highly overrated." Anton had known Pike since their college days when they met on a study exchange at Cambridge. Pike was from Alabama and never lost his southern drawl. "If all of us bachelors met someone as gorgeous as Miss Willadine, then I would agree."

"So how soon can we land?" Willie asked.

How he loved her enthusiasm.

"It's fine, chérie. We will land as soon as possible. Now, are you even going to even look at your ring?" Willie glanced to Anton's hands, which held open a small, black velvet box holding the most exquisite ring she had ever seen.

"Oh my, Anton.....it's so beautiful. I've never seen anything like this. It's truly amazing."

"Then it is the perfect ring for you. Let me put it on your finger." Willie had little success holding back her tears. She was an emotional basket case.

"Thank you for giving us a second chance, Anton. I was ready to say 'yes' after the last time we made love in Paris and I should have told you then."

"Chérie, you were perfectly fine in taking some time to make such an important decision. I acted like an ass too many times and I'm just lucky you didn't leave me for good."

CHAPTER 20

They spent the flight back to the airstrip exchanging carnal kisses and reading each other's eyes. Fire. Lust. Love. Everything. When they landed Anton said goodbye to his friend and they drove back the chalet. As soon as they were inside Willie threw herself at him and helped him out of the clothes that were encumbering him....and her. She didn't notice that a fire was lit or that the dinner table was set.

Willie pushed him back until the sofa caught the backs of his legs, forcing him into a sitting position on the sofa. She crawled in his lap and kissed him senseless and then slid down and settled on the floor in front of him on her knees. "Oh how I have missed this guy here." She stroked his erection and took it between her lips, savoring his silky smooth skin and masculine taste, moaning with each pass.

"Chérie, I can't hold it. You need to stop."

There was nothing he could do to contain their passionate exchange. Willie ignored him and kept sucking, licking and swirling around him until he released his pent up desire in her mouth. "That was amazing," Anton said, breathless.

"I need to go to the bathroom and we can continue this in the hot tub, on the bed, or in front of the fire." She gave him a sheepish smile and walked to the bathroom.

"Wait, Willie. I need to talk to you about something."

"Sure, Anton. What is it?"

He explained to her what the pharmacist said when he went to get some medicine for her stomach. She had an ashen look on her face that didn't outright deny the possibility she could be

212

pregnant. "I never even thought that could be a reason why I've been ill. Surely that can't be it."

"I bought us a pregnancy test so we can make sure. Will you do it, chérie?" She thought it so endearing how he said he bought the pregnancy test for them both and not just for her.

"Well...I...I guess I should."

"Don't worry about this, Willie."

"I'm just trying to remember when my birth control is supposed to expire and I'm drawing a blank."

"Before you worry yourself, go take the test."

Anton handed her the test and she went in the bathroom. It seemed like she was in there for an eternity, but it had only been a minute. She had a blank look on her face when she came out. "Well, chérie, tell me.."

"It takes a minute for the result to show, so I left it on the counter while we wait. If it has two lines then it is positive. I'm so nervous, Anton."

"Chérie, lets go look together." Anton took her hand and led her to the bathroom. "It will be fine either way, chérie."

On the counter in the bathroom lay the pregnancy stick. Anton tightened his grip around Willie's waist and kissed the top of her head before picking up the stick. Willie closed her eyes, too afraid to look. Anton let out a long breath after looking at the result.

"Oh thank goodness," he said, giving Willie a bear hug. "Do you know how happy this makes me, chérie?" He was on the verge of tears.

"Me, too, Anton. It's way too soon to start a family. I'm just as relieved as you are."

"You misunderstand me, chérie. The test is positive. We are having a baby."

A new wave of nausea hit Willie. She was astounded that this was happening to her. "Oh Anton, I'm so sorry. I really had no idea."

"Willie, stop talking nonsense. I am over the moon with happiness to be having a baby with you and I hope you are too. You can give me no greater gift other than this baby and your hand in marriage. Please be happy about this Willie. This is cause to celebrate. I love you so very much and our baby, too."

Willie fell apart in Anton's arms, tears shedding. He held her close to his chest. Waves of relief, gratitude, love and uncertainty filled her heart. When Anton tilted her face up to his she noticed his tear-streaked cheeks and lifted up to wipe them with her hands. Holding each other's face in their hands they kissed away any worry or concern about being pregnant. "Make love to me, Anton."

Two hours later they emerged from the bedroom and sat down for a late dinner. She felt so much more closer to him and had no doubts about their future. Pregnant sex was simply amazing, too. Anton fed her a piece of bread dipped in cheese fondue and sealed it with a kiss.

"Oh, Anton, I got you a gift for you a few weeks ago in Munich. I almost forgot about it."

"You don't need to give me a gift, chérie, really. In fact, I completely forgot about the present you had Everdine give me after we'd..uh...broken up the first time. I just remembered it is in my brief case, buried under papers. I'm so sorry I forgot about it."

"Well, you had better get use to it. I like to give you presents. I've never had anyone to buy presents for and I'm enjoying it." She went to the bedroom to get the gift out of her purse and joined Anton in the living room.

"I realize this may be different for you, so please don't feel obligated when you open it." Anton stroked her cheek with his thumb. "I'll treasure it. That I promise you."

He unwrapped the small box carefully and opened it, revealing the gold necklace and pendant. His heart could not get any bigger with love for this woman. After reading what was inscribed on the pendant he held it close to his chest and then slipped the necklace over his head.

"It's lovely, Willadine. I'll never take it off. Thank you." Anton swallowed a huge lump in his throat. He seemed a bit melancholy about the gift and Willie wasn't sure what he was feeling.

"You seem a bit sad, Anton. Is anything wrong? I know you don't wear any jewelry and I don't want you to feel you have to wear this." His cerulean blue eyes looked loaded. "I was just thinking that you are the only woman who has ever given me a gift like this. This also reminds me of my mother. Thank you."

"Well the gift in your briefcase is less exciting. It's something very small that use to belong to me when I was a child and I thought you would enjoy it more. At the time I decided to give it to you, it was just a reminder of you after you broke it off with me. That is why I gave it to you, but none of that matters now."

"It does matter, Willie. I'm so sorry I hurt you so many times. I was a fool." Anton walked over to his briefcase and dug underneath the stacks of papers and folders to grab the small wrapped present. It was obviously a book. He joined her on the sofa with the present, giving her a peck on top of the head before opening it. Anton just stared at the tattered copy of Le Petit Prince.

"I had a copy of this book when I was a child. My mother had given it to me."

"Yes, I know, and you told me you lost it. I thought you'd like mine for nostalgic reasons. It seemed to mean a lot to you.

"Yes, it did. It was the last connection I had with my mother before she passed away. And now I can read it to our child." She sat close to him, kissing him on the shoulder. Anton opened the cover of the tattered book and froze. For a moment he stopped breathing.

"What is it, Anton?"

"I don't believe this. It can't be," he muttered under his breath. "Willie where did you get this book?"

"When I was five or six daddy took me to a private card game in Atlanta and I played poker with the other kids while our fathers played cards. One kid in particular ran out of pennies and used his toys instead. I won this book from him."

Anton had a huge grin on his face with moisture pooling around his eyes. "What did you think of this little boy- the one that you stole toys from?"

"I did not steal his toys. He just didn't have a good command of the game. But, I thought he was very cute and I told him I wanted to marry him." Anton bellowed with unbridled laughter.

"Yes, you did. And he probably said something like 'boys can't marry boys,' right?"

"Yes, he.....how did you know?" Willie had a bewildered look on her face.

"I was that little boy, Willadine," Anton said, laughing so hard he had tears rolling down his cheeks. "It was me who lost all of his toys that day. It was me who thought you were a boy and not a girl, with that puffy, frizzy mess of hair you had. It was me whom you said you wanted to marry."

"Oh my God, Anton! How did you know this was your book?"

"In the front cover of the book was a handwritten note: I will always be with you if you look to the stars. Love Maman.

She knew she was dying and left this book as a way for me to remember her."

"Oh Anton. Your mother was very special and it must have been very painful for you as a child to lose this book. I remember you crying, but I thought it was about your toy cars or Rubik's Cube. That's why I gave those back, but kept the book."

"I'm still in shock that it was you....after all of these years. I've never believed in destiny until now. In fact, I never believed in much at all until I met you." Anton spoke through the unexpressed tears that fell. "Do you know Willie, that you are the only one who has seen me cry? Then, when I was eleven and now, as the father of your child and soon-to-be husband, you have kept me in tears. If I think about the significance of this book, it is really what brought us together. It is magical to me that my mother had such a special hand in our paths crossing."

Anton pulled Willie up, fiercely hugging her while laughing and crying at the same time. "You are mine forever, Willadine Crenshaw, and I dare you to even think otherwise. I love you so much it hurts. So, so much"

CHAPTER 21

After a blissful weekend in Chamonix Willie joined her sister at their apartment in Geneva. Ever and her mother had spent the whole day shopping for her honeymoon when they arrived at the apartment. Gabriel would not tell her where they were going, but that she would need summer clothes. Everdine and her mother were so occupied with wedding planning that they didn't notice the rock on her finger. Willie and Ever had barely spent any amount of time talking the last five weeks with all that they had been tasked with. They were both looking forward to some much needed sister time. Willie had yet to spill the beans about her and Anton. She enjoyed speaking with Ever's mother, too. It was the third time they had met- the first time being at graduation and the second time when they left for Europe. She was a very stately lady and somewhat reserved. Willie was sure this had to do with her circumstance of being young, single, pregnant and heartbroken.

The sisters said goodbye to Ever's mom and plopped down on the sofa with a sigh of relief.

"Oh my God, Willie, we have so much to catch up on. I'll get the wine."

"Yes, it's been crazy and not at all what I anticipated for my summer. Maybe I'll just have water instead."

"It looks like Bernard stocked us up on some Italian reds."

Ever poured a glass of wine and water and prepared a plate of cheese and olives for them to nibble on.

"I'll be glad when this week is over. I love my mom, but she's driving me crazy. I should be glad she is totally in love with Gabriel, though. Those two make me sick watching them. He said he loves having a mother to dote on and believe me when I tell you my mom is soaking it up with a sponge."

"Have you and Gabriel decided where you will live?"

"Well, we both agreed to keep things open after you and I complete our internship in Geneva. He is alluding to a wedding gift he has for me that may change my career plans."

"That's scary, but romantic."

"Yes, and I'm sure it has to be over the top knowing the Delacroix brothers."

"Is your gown fitted. Have all preparations been made?"

"Everything is done. It's all gravy from here on out. Oh, daddy will be coming to Geneva on Wednesday and a few of our girlfriends are coming to town on Friday for the festivities."

"That's awesome. I know they will all be swooning over Gabriel."

"I've had it up to here with wedding stuff." Ever motioned her hand well above her head. "Tell me about Anton. How was this weekend? I take it you two are getting closer?"

"Well, that's one way to put it." Willie stuck out her hand with the engagement ring on it and Ever's jaw dropped."

"Oh...my...gosh... Willie. It is stunning. Congratulations! When did he propose?"

"This weekend in Chamonix he arranged a helicopter tour of Mont Blanc and proposed while we were watching the sun set. It was so sweet and romantic. We hadn't seen each other since Paris and I was so miserable without him. After he had proposed to me in Paris I was hopeless after telling him 'no'. I just needed time to accept he was serious this time."

"I was under the impression that things did not go well in Paris after the gala. What happened?"

"No kidding. We had to work through some trust issues. We ended up staying in the hotel making love for several days. He is amazing, Everdine. I had no idea it could be so wonderful." Willie was smiling from ear to ear.

"Willie! I can't believe you didn't tell me. Did it hurt? How was it?"

"It's not something I would tell you over the phone, silly! It hurt a little, but it was a good kind of hurt. He is rather large-large to me anyway, but the cramping a few hours afterwards is what hurt the most. It was incredible. I'm so in love with him. This weekend was a turning point in our relationship and I would do anything for him."

"I'm so happy for you and glad that Anton finally came around. Gabriel still wants to wait until our wedding night for sex. Who knew that he could be so old fashioned? That reminds me- our birth control is ineffective and we should take precaution until getting something in place."

"Yes, I discovered that this weekend," Willie said with a huge smile plastered on her face.

"What do you mean?"

Willie laid her hand on her stomach. "I'm pregnant."

"I don't believe it. Oh no! When did it happen? How is Anton taking it?" Ever's face gave away her being totally shocked.

"Well, when Anton and I were in Paris we didn't use any protection. I told him he didn't need to, so it's my fault. I had been feeling nauseous a few days before our trip to Chamonix. When we got there he went to town to get some medicine for my stomach. After speaking with the pharmacist he bought a pregnancy test just to make sure. When the test was positive Anton was over the moon happy. Me, not so much at first. I was worried about what he would think. He is ecstatic about being a dad and I could not be happier to be having his baby."

Everdine's eyes filled with tears. "I am so happy for you, Willie. You have an amazing man. We both do and I know we'll be very happy in our lives."

"Everdine, I haven't told my parents yet about Anton or the baby. Please don't tell anyone yet."

"Of course."

They both shared a sisterly hug and Willie told Ever everything that happened regarding the Le Petit Prince book she gave Anton and how she had met him when they were both kids. Something magical was happening the night they met the Delacroix brothers.

Willie and Anton stole moments together when they could. With relatives and friends in town for the wedding a few moments was all they had. Willie did call her mother and tell her about being engaged to Anton and also about being pregnant. Her mother was excited, but said she would stop worrying once Willie was married. She also wanted to talk to Anton herself and asked Willie for his number. After giving him the third degree over the phone, she decided she liked him a lot and couldn't wait to meet him.

The hard part was telling her father. He was always very formal with her and had high expectations. Anton wanted to be with her when she told her father and he invited both of their fathers to dinner. Anton's father, Loic, already knew he and Willie were engaged and could not be happier. Dinner was going great and William Crenshaw was happy that Willie chose such a strong-willed man as her future husband. Anton's father and William had known each other casually since before their kids were born from the poker circuit and had a great amount of respect for one another.

"We also have some other news," Anton declared after clearing his throat and grabbing Willie's hand, bringing it to his lips for a kiss. "Willadine and I are thrilled to be expecting our first child next March." He looked over at Willie and sported a smile big enough to light the room, clasped his hands on her face and kissed her sweetly in front of everyone. She was not ready for that kind of public display, which showed with her cherry-red, flushed cheeks. Both of their fathers stood to congratulate and offer hugs. Anton's father was downright jovial about being a grandfather. William seemed contemplative. Willie knew something was wrong when he excused himself to get some air. She soon followed, joining him on the sidewalk in front of the restaurant.

"Daddy, I know we should have waited until we were married, but it happened and we are happy about it. I love Anton so much that I would do anything for him. He is the only man I have ever loved or even slept with for that matter. Don't be upset." William placed his hands up behind his head and was pacing the sidewalk. Willie just stood watching him, waiting for a response.

"For the first time, Willie, I realized what hell I have caused your mother and all of the mothers of my children. Having a daughter who is in the same situation I put her mother in made me realize what her parents went through and what she went through." He was starting to raise his voice with anger and guilt ringing out. "It's not that I didn't realize it before. It's just different when it happens to your own baby."

Inside the restaurant Anton was not liking what he saw. There is no way he would let William hurt the mother of his child and treat her pregnancy other than the blessing that it was.

"I never wanted for you what your mother went through, Willie. Here you are unmarried and pregnant."

"Daddy I have an excellent job, a top-notch education and a man who treats me like a queen. I am happier than I've ever been. You should be happy for me."

"Why couldn't you wait until after you were married? If he is marrying you just for the sake of the baby then it will never work out sweetheart. He will end up leaving you."

"That's enough!" Both of them turned toward Anton who was standing beside the door listening. "I love your daughter more than the air I breathe and we will be happily married and have a big family together. Just because you lived a life with regretful actions doesn't give you the right to project that onto your daughter. She is the most amazing woman I've ever met and we are both thrilled to be starting a family. If you can't be happy for her and appreciate what we have to offer each other, then it is best you keep your sentiment to yourself. Willie do you wish to leave or stay and continue this conversation with your father?"

"We should go. Daddy, I'll talk to you later, but not about this. My life with Anton is not open for discussion. We are happy and that's all that matters."

William went back in the restaurant to talk with Anton's father and Willie and Anton left in his limo. Once inside the limo Willie broke down, upset that her father did not approve of her being pregnant. To her, having this baby was perfect and represented her and Anton's love for one another. Not loving or supporting her baby was tantamount to not accepting her and Anton. He comforted her, wrapping his arms around her. She savored his warmth, support and love. After regaining her composure she straddled him and kissed him hungrily, lightening shooting straight through her body. She wanted him desperately. As her tongue went around, reaching the corners of his mouth, her hands wandered down to his zipper. His arousal was evident as was his labored breathing. "Anton, I want you now."

As he was raising the partition between them and the driver, Willie unzipped his pants and freed him. She didn't even bother to take her panties of and just moved them to the side while she slid down on his penis, taking it in slowly until he was fully sheathed.

"You feel so good," she said between gasps as she was moving up and down on top of him. With each breath, he met her thrust for thrust as she moved skillfully over his cock. Willie picked up the pace, bouncing up and down on top of him. She could not control the visceral pleasure released in unison with fast, sensual movements on his erection. "I'm close, Anton." He helped her along by grabbing her tight ass, aiding in her thrusts. Anton was turned on beyond measure hearing her scream so loudly on top of him, and it was fascinating for him to see her so carried away.

As she became louder it was evident she was about to climax. He put his hand over her mouth as she bounced and screamed her way to the most powerful, slamming orgasm she had ever experienced. Anton was thankful that he was able to muffle her screams somewhat considering his orgasm paled in comparison to hers. When Willie came to a still on top of him she was indeed bashful about how wildly she came.

"I hope I didn't embarrass you. I don't know what came over me."

He chuckled at her candor. "Well I sure as hell know what came over me...hurricane Willadine. Don't be bashful, chérie. I'm sure the driver heard you, but I tried to save your modesty. I love to watch you come. It turns me on more than anything to see you lose yourself while fucking me. In fact, we should go to my place and continue this. Stay with me tonight." Anton squeezed his hands on her ass, massaging her.

"Yes, I'll stay with you. I just need to call Ever and let her know." Willie dialed her sister, but got voicemail. "Hi Ever, it's me. I'm having a hard time keeping my hands off of Anton, so I'm staying over at his place tonight. Must be the pregnancy hormones. By the way dad did not take the pregnancy news too well. I'll see you in the morning."

Before they arrived at Anton's apartment she got a text from Ever.

From Everdine: Haha! Enjoy Anton. Don't worry about Dad. He is here and feels horrible. He is excited for you and Anton & getting ready to go out on the town with A & G's dad.

From Willadine: Tell him not to worry. All is good. At Anton's now. See you in the AM.

When they got out of the limo Willie took notice of the shy grin that graced the limo driver's face. She knew then that she had been very loud when fucking Anton in the back seat, but had come to accept that when it came to him she was lucky if reason made an appearance at all. Her world now revolved around him and his baby.

When she entered his apartment it felt different than it had before. It felt like she belonged there and she also realized it was where she would soon be making a home with him. Overwhelming was not strong enough of a word for how she felt.

"You left one of your bags in the car when we came back from Chamonix, so I unpacked it and made a place in my closet for your items. I also noticed the sex kit you brought. Too bad we didn't get a chance to use it. There are some pretty risqué items in there for a girl like you."

"What do you mean girl like me," Willie smirked.

"Silly, I mean your inexperience."

"Maybe that was the point, Anton. I want to get all the experience I can with you and only you."

"Damn right only me."

She walked over into his arms, gaze searing through him and his playful, but possessive manner. "So you are the jealous type, then?"

"Yes, very much so."

"I've never seen this side of you. I'm intrigued."

"I've never felt this way before either, so it is new to both of us." Then he dropped the tension from his voice and stroked her face with his fingers. "Willie, you know how precious you are to me. You are carrying my child and you agreed to be my wife. I feel very protective over you and that is not something I can readily control." He kissed the tip of her nose.

"I understand, Anton. The night of the gala I also felt the strongest need to protect you even though..." She stopped when she realized what she was about to step into. She didn't want to bring up painful actions from their past.

"Even though I treated you so badly and threw your love back in your face."

"I wasn't going to say that."

"It does not matter because it is the truth. I know I don't deserve you Willie, but I promise I will spend a lifetime trying to."

"Don't ever say that, Anton. It really upsets me. You are everything to me and the father of my child. Your love will always bring me to my knees."

"That is what makes me the luckiest man on the planet. Your faith in me is astounding and I appreciate it more than anything."

Willie crushed her lips to his, backing him against the wall in the foyer. It was then she realized he never re-buttoned his shirt from when they were in the limo. She pulled his shirt down over his shoulders and kissed his neck, sucking and biting her way down. Anton recognized this hunger in her and it was unsettling not knowing what it was from. He detached from her, holding her at the shoulders and took a step away.

"Willie, sometimes you seem to just go wild like this and I have to ask if there is any reason behind it. It feels like you are using sex to cope with something. It's not that I don't enjoy it, but I want to understand it."

A breathless Willadine searched for an answer in his eyes. She had never thought much about it since she had no experience to speak from exactly.

"I don't know really. Sometimes when I'm feeling very emotional it just seems like my preferred way to find some kind of release. Other times I feel like I'm about to explode, out of control with love for you and I have to express it. I guess I get carried away and I don't think I can ever get enough of you. Does it bother you that I get so wild like that?"

"Oh no. Nope. Not at all. I just want to understand. I love it that you feel so strongly about me and feel comfortable enough with me to express it that way. It is a huge turn on."

Anton moved her hand over his erection and she exhaled at his promptitude.

"Now about that sex kit. Let's have a look."

Willie picked up the square metallic case that looked very much like a briefcase and took it to the bedroom. She opened it and set it on the bed. She could already feel the heat pooling between her thighs.

"So have you ever done any of this with another woman before?"

"Uh, yes. It is kind of a mood killer to talk about that though," he exclaimed.

"I don't want to talk about specifics, but can we do some of these things together?"

"You crazy woman I want to do everything your heart desires." He explained what some of the items in the box were and she was curious, yet very turned on.

"Wow, this is exciting."

"You are sure about this?"

"Yes." Willie had a very contemplative look on her face. "Anton, I feel that with the unplanned pregnancy we have limited time to try these things before our world completely changes."

Anton stroked her hair, recognizing concern and fear in her eyes and voice. He realized that life was happening very fast for her and she had never put herself in a situation which she could not control. Willie had excelled at everything she had done in her short life and part of that was keeping control of everything she participated in. He knew that was one reason why she was always pushing the envelope with their budding sexual exploits and he enjoyed it.

"Come on the bed with me Chérie. I want to tell you something." Anton crawled up on his bed and leaned against the headboard and Willie came up with him, resting her head on his bare chest. It was hard for her to concentrate on anything with the energy bouncing off of his warm, scented skin.

"Willie, in the short time you've been here you have had many firsts in your life and at breakneck speed, too: new job, new country, lost your virginity, taken a lover, had a boyfriend and fiancé, and now you are carrying a child. I promise you that after our baby is here our fun will not end. It will only make our time together more precious and as adventurous as you want it to be. I just don't want you to do anything out of fear. It should be because it's something you truly want to do." Anton continued to pull his fingers through her hair and planted sweet kisses on the top of her head.

"You are right, Anton. A lot of things are new to me. You have so much more experience than I do and I just want to try and reach a common ground in some areas. I'm dying to try new things with you in the bedroom. It may seem like I'm rushing it a little, but partly that's because of my temperament. Once I do something I like to do it right and master it. I guess what's surprising to me is that same temperament carries over into the bedroom, as well. I want to be everything you desire in a lover. Being able to please you in bed is very important to me and gives me a huge amount of satisfaction." Willie eased her hand down over Anton's rock hard abs down to his magnificent erection.

"Woman you have no idea how much you please me in the bedroom. I can only tell you it is a pleasure I have never known until you. To share such intimacies with someone I am head over heels in love with, who is carrying my child, is like nothing else. It makes me high just thinking about it."

And just like gasoline on a wildfire they went up in flames in each others' arms on Anton's bed. No matter how hard and deep the kiss was it could never fill the need. They helped each other wrestle out of their clothes. In a snappy move Anton pinned Willie under him on the bed, holding her with by the wrists above her head. She was writhing underneath him as his kisses went further down, settling on her breast. He took the pert bud in his mouth, taking big sucks of her nipples and rolling it between his teeth and tongue. Willie squealed in delight as he did the same to the other breast. Anton moaned as he moved down and his mouth descended on her clit, drawing circles around it with his tongue.

"You are so damn wet Willie. I love how turned on you get. We can start playing with your love kit now."

"Yes."

Anton slid the case toward him and looked at the plethora of sex toys, lube and bondage items inside. There really was a little bit of everything. Anton grabbed some graduated anal beads and lube from the case.

"These are anal beads and the size of the beads goes from smaller to larger and we'll start with these. This will help you get use to the feel of having something down there and also help you train the anal muscles. If you like the feel of this, then we'll try a bigger one. Try to relax if you can." Anton instructed Willie to get on her hands and knees, spreading her legs some. The sight of her on her hands and knees made him ache with desire. He put some lube on her and the beads and continued to play in her arousal with one hand while his other hand carefully inserted the first few beads.

"How does that feel?"

"It is fine. I don't feel much of it."

"Good. I'll slide some more in and when I start sliding them in and out it should feel really good."

Anton massaged her clit while pushing nearly all of the beads in. He didn't have to ask Willie if she liked it. He could tell how close to orgasm she was.

"I'm going to start moving them now. Tell me to stop if you want me to."

He carefully moved the beads out and then back in, slowly. A little faster he moved them again.

"Yes. Oh God, Anton."

"I take it you like it."

"Don't stop."

Anton dropped his hand from her clit and just focused on the beads so she could have that sensation alone. He was amazed at her lack of trepidation and thought they could take it up a notch. He took the beads out at her vocal protest.

"No, don't stop."

"I'm simply going to see how much more you can take. I'll put something a little bigger in and it will feel fuller to you. This will prepare you for me, chérie."

"Oh my."

Anton looked through the case. He could either insert a slender vibrating dildo or a small butt plug that would do more stretching. He wanted to see just how much she could accommodate and selected the butt plug.

"Alright, chérie, I'm inserting a plug since you are doing so well. It's not very big. If it hurts, just tell me and I'll stop."

"Okay, let's do it."

Anton lubed the plug generously and pushed it in with great care. He heard no protest from Willie when he got to the part with the largest girth as she easily took it all the way in inhaling sharply.

"Damn, Willie, you took the whole thing. How do you feel?"

"It feels amazing. There is so much pressure it's driving me crazy," She said through gritted breathing.

"Good girl. Now I'm going to put a vibrator inside your pussy so you'll have both sensations."

Anton swirled the vibrator around her moisture that seemed to be dripping from her perpetual state of arousal. The vibrator slipped in easily and he turned it on a low setting. Willie started to move on all fours trying to find a way to release the pressure. She felt an aching inside begging to be sated by a good, deep fuck.

"You, Anton. I want you. Now. I can't stand it."

"Okay, but be sure to communicate with me."

Anton slid the vibrator out and discarded it beside the bed. He inched his big cock inside her slowly until she was use to the feel of being penetrated by both. Willie pushed back on him as Anton was taking his time to enter.

"Damn, Willie, you are so tight."

"Please. Faster, Anton. Just faster."

Anton started to move in and out with Willie's tightness squeezing him to a frenzy. He pumped harder into her so that his movement would put pressure on the plug, which he could feel through the thin membrane. Willie was practically bouncing off the bed, rocking, meeting his thrusts. One thing he loved about her was how vocal she was in bed. It was so pure and honest and she was being very honest at the moment.

"Fuck me, Anton." She said between gasps of pleasure.

"Damn, Willie."

Anton placed both hands on Willie's hips and rammed into her, stopping deep several times and then quickened the pace until Willie's orgasm shook him. Only then did he let himself find release so powerful that he felt like he would pass out. He pulled out and tucked her in his lap, wrapping his arms around her waist. She let her head fall back on his shoulder and he kissed the nape of her neck while they both floated back down to earth.

"Are you okay, chérie? How did it feel?"

"You have to ask," she joked. "It felt so good that I thought I would fall into a coma. It was mind blowing."

Willie could practically hear Anton smiling behind her. She wondered if it would always be so perfect with him.

"Thank you for giving yourself to me so completely. There is nothing more beautiful than when I make love to you. It's perfect every time. Come with me and I'll run us a bath."

Anton removed the plug and helped her down from the bed, steadying them both after such a demanding love session. A hot bath was the perfect aphrodisiac. Anton calmly washed her as she lounged between his legs in the tub, asking her about her dream wedding, pressing her to setting a date. If Willie wasn't mistaken he almost sounded like he was trying very hard to get her down the aisle as soon as possible.

"I don't really care to have a big wedding or any wedding really. For me, going to the Justice of the Peace in the small town I grew up in would be just as perfect."

"You can't be serious! I thought all girls wanted a fairytale wedding?"

Willie could hear the disappointment in his voice. It sounded like he was the one that wanted a big wedding.

"Well....I do have the fairytale man, so I can see how people may expect such a wedding. Having to get married in front of so many people would make me nervous. I don't know if I could do it. I would even go to Vegas. What do you want, Anton?"

"I only want something small- two hundred people and a really big party afterwards." Willie found humor in his version of small.

"I didn't figure you for a large wedding type. I have to admit I'm surprised."

"For me it is a shock that I'm even getting married, chérie; I never thought it would happen. I want everyone to see what an amazing woman I'm marrying. I feel entitled to some very serious bragging rights, too."

"When you put it like that, then your wish is my command. I'm so excited that I still can't believe it."

"Me, too, chérie. You do't have to worry about any details. Sylvia and I will take care of everything- unless you want to be involved."

"That's perfect. I think having to be involved in the planning will only make me more anxious."

"You'll be fine. Now we need to nail down a date and also talk about our living arrangements. Would three weeks from now be too soon?

"Although I'd like to wait, I guess it's better to do it before the baby starts showing too much. That is the week before Ever and I start our internship in Geneva, so we'll have a short honeymoon."

Anton grabbed Willie's hair and tilted her head to the side, lapping up the warm moisture from the bath from her neck to her shoulder, while his hand slid between her milky thighs.

"Do you know how much it turns me on when you mention anything about the baby? All it does is remind me of how much I love you and how it came to be that you are carrying my child and that you are mine. Hmmm....your skin is so soft."

Willie could hardly mutter a word as Anton slid two fingers inside her hot, wet folds. The tepid water of the bath combined with their earlier lovemaking made her extra sensitive to his ministrations.

"Mmmm Anton." She could feel his length growing against her back. A few kisses and strokes later brought them back to his bed where they rolled with each other until they were listless and contented.

CHAPTER 22

Anton hated to leave the warmth and comfort of Willadine in his bed for a day at the office. He couldn't get over the affect this woman was having on him as he watched her sleeping. They had burned up the sheets several times during the night and just seeing her pale skin in the dim light made him lightheaded.

At the office Anton laid his head on his folded arms on his desk as he waited for Sylvia to bring him some coffee. Transgressions of work, play and no sleep the last few days were coming back to bite him in his cute ass.

"What is wrong brother? That saucy Crenshaw girl keeping you up too late?"

Anton raised his head to his brother, revealing his tired eyes. "You guessed it."

"You look like hell."

"Thanks, but I can guarantee you it was worth it. The woman is insatiable and I love it. Be warned about the Crenshaw appetite in the bedroom."

"You are killing me, but luckily I only have to wait until Saturday to experience the Crenshaw appetite."

"Well, if Everdine is anything like her sister you won't be disappointed, but you will get a good workout." Anton just laughed and shook his head. When he first started seeing Willie she couldn't even touch him without asking and now she can't keep her hands off of him.

"We can't talk about this anymore. I've been taking my share of cold showers and Ever and I decided to wait until the wedding to see each other again. Just wait until the baby arrives, brother, and you'll see how much you miss sleeping. I'm thrilled at becoming an uncle."

"Yes, it's exciting." Anton smiled at the thought.

The brothers discussed work, weddings and honeymoons, taking care of as much business as they could before they started this new chapter in their lives. Since they shared their apartment in Geneva, Anton decided that he would move out and buy a house since they needed more room with a child on the way. Their business was taking off so fast that they lined up a few new top level resources to interview so they could have more time outside of work. Anton also had to get Sylvia started on wedding arrangements for his upcoming nuptials.

Just as Anton and Gabriel were breaking for lunch, Willie waltzed into the office after a quick knock on the door. "Chérie, what a lovely surprise." Anton walked over to her side and kissed her on the cheek.

"Hello, Willadine, good to see you." Gabriel followed suit with a kiss and gentle hug. "So I hear you are to blame for my brother having such a late night."

Bright red blotches graced Willie's face like a beacon. She gave him a bashful grin. "Don't worry, Gabriel, you'll soon be having late nights, too."

"I'm looking forward to it," he replied.

"So what brings you in today, chérie?" She loved the way Anton could smile with his eyes.

"Several things. I got a call from the doctor's office this morning and they have an opening for me this afternoon, so I thought I'd see if you want to go with me."

"Of course, I want to go. I'll clear it with Sylvia."

"I'm also having a very big problem with my bank account. I was checking it online this morning so I can budget for a wedding dress and my account was...."

Anton interrupted her swiftly. "Willie, I will pay for your wedding gown. You needn't spend any money on the wedding. Get the dress you want and I'll take care of it."

"No Anton. No. I am buying my wedding dress and that's not open for discussion. What I was going to say is that there is a boat load of money in my bank account with DLC as the payor."

"Good that it arrived, then. That is your share from the restructuring project. I told you when you started that it was 2.5 percent."

"That is ridiculous, Anton. That is way too much money and much more than 2.5 percent. I can't keep it."

Both Anton and Gabriel chimed in at the same time, "Yes, you can."

"Willie you were paid the term we agreed upon and also my percentage of the deal and a bonus. Had it not been for you, then not only would we not have backing, but my poor condition would have preceded us in the business world. You saved our reputation, as well. And, that is not open for discussion."

"Touché," she replied.

Willie lay nervously on the examination table as she and Anton waited for the doctor to come in. She was naked from the waist down with a sheet wrapped around her bottom half. They were both quiet and Anton kept her hand safely inside his, soothing her. The doctor came in and made introductions and asked Willie questions regarding her sexual history. She was very proud that Anton was her first and only. When the doctor was performing the ultrasound they could not make sense of what they were seeing on the monitor. His excitable exclamation gave them a start.

"Is everything okay?" Willie asked.

"Well young lady, you and your husband are going to be very busy in about seven and a half months. Let's just say double as busy as you anticipated. You are having twins."

Willie had a crestfallen look on her face and Anton was downright jubilant, beaming with laughter. The good doctor let her know that since she was having twins she would be gaining weight at a faster rate than with a single pregnancy- something Willie was not at all excited about. The thought of having twins was thrilling, but frightening. The good thing was that she didn't have to tell anyone about the great news since Anton had called everyone he ever knew by the time he got back to the office. She went back to the apartment to take a nap. Just the thought of having twins was exhausting.

He was caressing her hair, whispering endearments in her ear. God how she loved him. "Come, chérie, wake up or you won't sleep this evening." Anton gently shook Willie as she lay sleeping in his bed. He wanted to come home from work earlier, but with wedding details to take care of it wasn't possible.

"Goodness, what time is it Anton?"

"It is almost seven in the evening. How long have you been sleeping?"

"Since I got back from the appointment at two-thirty. I'm hungry."

"I'll cook us something for dinner and we can stay in this evening. I have something I want to ask you."

She followed Anton into the kitchen where he put on his apron and started dinner. He made his favorite- steamed mussels in a garlic-butter, wine sauce. She loved his cooking. Anton placed a glass of orange juice in front of Willie, remembering the doctor saying she should increase her folic acid intake.

"Gabriele was asking me today if we would want to share their wedding day and have a double wedding. He said Everdine asked if she could offer this to us. He loved the idea and also mentioned how much money we would save by sharing costs. Since we all would invite the same guests it made a lot of sense. How do you feel about it? Would it make your wedding day less special?"

Miracles do happen, thought Willie. "It would be awesome. I wouldn't feel like all the attention was directed at me and it will be a heck of a lot easier fitting in a dress now instead of weeks from now. I would just worry about my mother and other family members coming."

"I called your mother today and told her if she would be able to make it to a Saturday wedding I could fly them over on Friday. I just need to know now so that I can make arrangements. Sylvia has reserved five open-ended tickets for your mom, grandparents, aunt and cousin."

"Then let's do it. That way Daddy does not have to make a special trip back and I also love the idea of getting married on the veranda where we met. That will be so special, Anton."

Anton dropped his wooden spoon on the counter and pulled her in for a passionate kiss. "I was so taken with you the night we met, chérie. I knew you would be mine and it scared the dickens out of me. It was love at first sight."

"Yes, it was. I didn't want to say it, but that's how I felt, too, seeing you from across the room."

After a hearty dinner Anton worked from his home office getting everything prepared for their wedding, which mostly involved people logistics. He let Sylvia take care of most of the details. This also meant that Anton could extend their honeymoon. There was also a special surprise he and Gabriel were working on for the sisters. Due to this certain surprise, the brothers were forced to tell the girls where they were going on their honeymoon. Both had planned unique trips to Italy for their wives. Anton was taking Willie to hit the major cities and spend some time on the smaller islands and Gabriel was going to tour the coastline with Everdine.

The weather could not have been better for an evening wedding. The veranda was decorated beautifully with flowers and tropical palm trees. An aisle was lined on both sides with chairs leading to the veranda were the wedding was to take place. Willie had been able to narrow her wedding gown search down thanks to Sylvia's help and found one in a stunning champagne-colored, silk. Everdine wore a traditional, white gown with a beautiful mermaid cut to it. Both of the girls looked elegant.

Soon after all of the guests were seated the wedding procession started with the help of a pianist and cellist. William Crenshaw walked both daughters down the aisle, one on each side of him. Anton and Gabriel were waiting anxiously for their brides. Bernard was also in attendance. Once the women were delivered to their pining grooms, the officiant guided them through promises and declarations of their wedding vows and delivered a shorter-than-expected ceremony. After sharing kisses, hugs and tears, the newlyweds led the way back down the aisle into the ballroom where a band was setting up. Sylvia was talking to some of the band members and came over to whisper something in Anton's ear.

The brides and grooms were seated closest to the stage while guests were seated at round tables scattered around outer edge of the ballroom. A round of toasts kept the guests entertained as it became apparent it was nothing short of a miracle that the Delacroix bothers were finally married. Willie's mom, Sherry, could not stop crying and she was just as much smitten with Anton as Willie was. They didn't have much time to spend together before the wedding. As dinner was wrapping up Sylvia came to Anton and whispered something in his and Gabriel's ear. They both rose from their table, excusing themselves and walked up a few short stairs to the stage where the band was.

"Excuse me, ladies and Gentlemen. We have something we'd like to share with you. A late arrival, so to speak. This is a surprise Gabriel and I have for our beautiful wives and their father. We give to you your sister, Marvadine Crenshaw."

Both Willie and Ever gasped, bringing their hands to their mouth as Marvadine walked out on the stage and quickly went down to where her sisters were. Tears. So many more tears. The girls could not contain their excitement, nor could William Crenshaw. He wanted as much of a relationship as Marva would give him. He finally had all of his girls together. Anton and Gabriel joined the sisters who were talking non-stop to Marva. It was then that they learned that Dominic was the one who had found Marvadine. Willie went to thank Dominic personally and he told her in very clear terms that he was hot for her sister. Willie could certainly see why. Marva was a drop-dead knockout. Of the Crenshaw sisters her curves would be considered somewhere between voluptuous and buxom. She had dark auburn hair, rosy cheeks and deep blue eyes.

Marva wanted to sing a wedding song for them before letting her back-up singer take over for the evening so she could visit with her newly found family. She also would not mind getting a little closer to Dominic. He had flown back with her from Berlin where her band was playing and they got to know each other a little between his business calls. She got the unmistakeable impression that if Anton were to ever turn up missing, Dominic would be more than glad to take his place at Willie's side. Dominic didn't bother hiding his admiration of Willie, which Marva didn't quite know what to make of.

"Hello everyone, my name is Marva. I'm Willie and Ever's half-sister and I'm going to be singing a wedding song for the happy couples. I was told from a reliable source that Willie and Ever use to belt this song out in their dorm room every Saturday night. Enjoy."

Willie and Ever gave each other a horrified look as Marva started singing Truly by Lionel Ritchie. Willie knew just who to blame for this: Dominic. He was the only one who could have told Marva that juicy bit of humiliating information. Somehow it had come up while they were dancing at the gala in Paris. All of her and Ever's embarrassment was flattened hearing their sister sing. She was a talented songstress. Her voice was somewhere between Joss Stone and Brittney Howard of The Alabama Shakes. There was such a richness to it and not at all what you would expect coming from her. Everyone was blown away, especially a certain Dominic Ferrier. Serves him right, Willie thought.

Desire was taking over between Gabriel and Ever. All he could think about was how soon was too soon to leave. His lips were permanently fixed on hers throughout the song, making them a spectacle. "When can we leave? We've waited so long and I'm about to burst. I need to make love to you now," Gabriel said, looking into her saturated eyes. Ever scattered small kisses on his chest where he had unbuttoned his shirt, getting plastered off his scent.

"Maybe there is a closet somewhere we can go to and have a quickie."

"You daft little vixen, we did not wait this long only to have thirty seconds of bliss in a closet. I need a bed, space and soundproof walls when I make love to you the first time."

"Thirty seconds, huh?"

"I admit I was being generous. Twenty is more like it."

Everdine laughed, her warm breath spilling onto Gabriel's chest. "I love you so much, my sweetheart."

"I love it when you call me sweetheart."

Willie and Anton danced so close they could practically split atoms. Willie didn't know if it was the hormones or if she was just sappy, but she could not help the tears streaming down her cheeks. Anton was wiping them away and kissing her as best as he could while they danced.

"What is it, Chérie?"

"You just make me happy, Anton. You're intelligent, sexy, sweet, caring and you're all mine. I want our kids to be just like you." Now Anton had pools in his eyes. He had done so well not to lose it throughout the ceremony and here was Willie, chipping away again at his heart.

Anton kept one arm around her waist, holding her close and his other at the back of her head resting against his shoulder. "That is the greatest compliment anyone has ever given me, Willie. To have you as my wife, someone who believes in me unconditionally, makes me the richest man on the planet. I promise with all my heart that I will take the very best care of you and our twins."

Dominic was mesmerized by Marva's singing. Watching her made his blood go straight to his trousers. There were times when he was watching her sing that he forgot to breathe. She was absolutely stunning, and sultry, and sexy, and slowly making him rethink his single status. Her voice poured over him like warm honey.

After the newlyweds finished their first dance another song started and they exchanged partners. Anton partnered with Willie's mother, Dominic grabbed Willie and Gabriel and Ever found a corner to neck in. Marva made her way over to William and stole some private time with him on the veranda while her back up singer took over.

"Willie, you look gorgeous and I'm very happy for you and Anton. I'm glad he found you, but I have to say I was secretly hoping I'd have my chance if he blew his."

"Thanks, Dominic. You are very sweet and a very good friend. I know Anton does not have many close friends like you. I can't thank you enough for helping find Marva and bringing her back here. It really is the best present of all."

"Trust me, it was my pleasure. She is quite a woman and just as beautiful as you and your sister. You Crenshaw girls are sinfully curvy." Willie threw her head back and laughed. She had heard many descriptions of the Crenshaw curves.

"You should dance with her, Dominic. Also, after the first week of our honeymoon her band will be playing in Rome and we are going to her concert. You have to fly down and join us."

"Let me get this right. You want me to fly down and hang out with two married couples for a weekend on their honeymoon?"

"That's right, but you'll actually be doing Marva a favor so she does not feel like a third wheel with us married folk."

"I see. If your sister is able to tolerate me, then I'd love to hear her sing again."

The song ended and Dominic gave Willie a kiss on the cheek. They both seemed to enjoy the lightness of their friendship and the ability to talk so freely with each other-especially after having such a rough first meeting. Dominic was looking around the room for Marva and saw her talking with Anton. He grabbed Willie's hand, leading her to the bar.

"Here my old friend. I'll trade you one beautiful woman for another. Marva would you care to dance with me?" Dominic held out his hand for her to take and she gladly accepted. Her band was really good and Dominic enjoyed hearing the old R&B tunes they belted out. They were playing If You Need Me, an old Solomon Burke tune. The back up singer was not as good as Marva, but the imperfections in his voice added character to the tune. Marva was the first one to break the ice as Dominic tested her out on the dance floor.

"So how long have you been in love with Willadine?"

"Excuse me?" Dominic was taken aback by her statement.

"I see the way you've been looking at her all night and it is obvious you feel something."

"First of all, Anton and Gabriel are my dearest friends and I consider them more like family. In fact, they are the only semblance of family that I have here. I am very fond of Willie, but I'm not in love with her. The first time I ever spoke to her she slugged me- something that seems to run rampant with you Crenshaw women. I think what you are seeing is acute jealousy."

Her curiosity was piqued and she had never taken such a familiar tone with a man before. Men were good for one thing. And by one thing, she meant keeping the sheets nice and warm, and hot if she got lucky.

"I don't understand. What exactly are you jealous of?"

Dominic tried hard to ignore the sweet floral scent Marva was wearing and even harder to ignore were her curves. She was wanton by just breathing.

"Anton and I are cut from the same cloth and never once did I think of settling down until he started seeing Willadine. I just didn't think settling down was possible for our kind. Seeing them together has given me...hope."

"Hmmm," Marva exclaimed.

"What is that supposed to mean?"

"It means I hope you don't waste this dress, this song, or this attraction between us by getting all sentimental."

"A lady who speaks her mind. I like it. And just what makes you think there is an attraction between us?" Dominic knew damn well there was an attraction between them, he just wanted to see where she would go with it.

She captured his eyes with hers and smiled graciously. "You really want to know?" He nodded his head. Her hand that was resting mid way up his arm came down, stopping just above his chiseled buttocks. She pulled him forward, joining them together so that his bulging erection was flush against her stomach. Dominic was flummoxed. He was dancing with his evil, female twin and contemporary.

"I think that counts as attraction, don't you? A very big attraction, I might add."

"You obviously know how I...uh...feel about you Miss Crenshaw. How exactly am I to know if this attraction is mutual?" They had just about stopped moving to the music. She closed in on Dominic, bringing her lips to his ears. He eagerly leaned down to capture what she was saying.

"You could take my word for it, but what fun would that be? Since we are surrounded by all of these people it not as if you can just slip your hand under my dress into my panties and feel how wet I am. But make no mistake, Dominic, the attraction between us is mutual. If I didn't think it was I would not be so forward with you."

Dominic closed his eyes and tried to concentrate on breathing as the size of his penis was defying the laws of gravity. Marva felt so good in his arms and would only feel better if naked and in his bed. For the first time in his life he was speechless by the actions of a woman. As thrilled as he was, he was also on edge about her. She was the kind of woman that could chew him up and spit him out and not think twice about it. It was a dangerous proposition, but not one he could easily resist. Ignoring the cold distance in her eyes he acquiesced to her sexual taunts.

"So when would you like to act on this mutual attraction?"

"I'm in room 1610 at the Mandarin. Come by after the party."

Dominic did not answer her, but rather enjoyed holding her until the song ended. Before they parted on the dance floor he planted a kiss at the corner of her mouth and thanked her for the dance. For him it was a goodbye kiss since he had no intention of going to her room tonight. She was clearly on a mission, one that he did not have a good feeling about. He already knew one night with her would not be enough, so better not whet his appetite.

Marva detected a hint of chill in Dominic's eyes as they parted. She had a lot of time to make up with her sisters and wanted to find them before they left for their first night in wedded bliss. Luckily, the Delacroix brothers decided to postpone their honeymoon plans for one day so they could have some time with Marva.

Willie and Ever were excited about their honeymoon to Italy. Knowing the Delacroix brothers, it would be perfectly planned. Gabriel's wedding surprise to Ever was the old perfumerie plantation he'd taken her to on a picnic back in Monte Carlo. He wanted to give her the chance to explore her dream of making her own perfume just as she inspired him to draw again with the art materials she gave him. The plantation had its' own distillery and water source, in addition to crops of suitable plants for extraction. Anton was still tight-lipped about his wedding gift to Willie. Apparently, it would not be ready for several months.

CHAPTER 23

The newlyweds could not wait any longer, calling it a night. Both couples had rooms at the Mandarin since family was staying at Anton and Gabriel's apartment, as well as the Crenshaw apartment. As they were leaving the palace, Gabriel phoned the hotel to let the hotel staff know they would be arriving in fifteen minutes. On the way to the hotel Willie was grinning like a Cheshire cat and Anton finally called her on it.

"My lovely wife, whatever has you grinning from ear to ear."

"I can't believe I'm Mrs. Delacroix now, and that those gorgeous dimples, blue eyes, and sexy dark hair all belong to me."

"That's right, chérie. I'm yours now, but you left out a few other important parts that belong to you, too. Perhaps you should do an inventory when we get to our suite Mrs. Delacroix."

"Why wait?" Willie let her hands roam all over her husband until they pulled up to the hotel. She didn't show it, but she was exhausted and the twins were slowly zapping the last bit of energy she had. When Anton carried her through the threshold of their suite, they walked into a beautifully decorated room. Flowers and candles adorned every horizontal surface and the sounds of a slow-going saxophone filled he air. There was also a selection of delectable food dishes on the dinner table, including chocolate covered strawberries. Anton started their evening off by drawing Willie a bubble bath and giving her a much-needed massage. He then took his sweet time to consummate their marriage.

Gabriel and Ever's ride to the hotel hinged solely on nonverbal communication. They had done enough talking during their courtship and engagement. When their limo came to a stop they were hard to disentangle and practically fell onto the sidewalk. Gabriel grabbed Ever's hand and ran with her into the hotel until they reached the elevator. Urgency to fulfill their needs and desires swept over them like a wave. The air was thin and touch was insatiable.

When Gabriel reached the door of the suite he had one hand in Ever's panties and the other hand searching for the key card. His mouth never wavered, burning kisses into hers the whole time. Once he was able to get the key inserted he slammed open the door and carried Ever over the threshold and straight to the bedroom. Clothes were shed and flying all over the room until they were both naked. Gabriel thought their first time would be something slow and seductive, not like Sherman burning through Atlanta. Flames were jumping and they did their best to roll around on the bed, putting them at ease.

Between hungry mouthfuls of each other Gabriel apologized in advance for the brevity of what would be her losing her virginity. She didn't care and wanted him to take her already. This is exactly what she thought a wedding night should be like. Sucking her tight nipples between his tongue and lips brought her to complete submission. His hand slid between her legs once again and she was wet and ready for him. Each circular stroke of her clit with his thumb sent her into hysterics.

"I need it now, Gabriel. I can't wait any longer. It's too much."

"Okay chérie, lay down."

Gabriel pushed her legs back so she was open to receive him. He played with her opening with the tip of his bulging penis and Ever moaned at this touch.

"Now, Gabriel."

At her demand Gabriel pushed himself firmly inside her and they both gasped at the full, hot feeling shared between them. With only a slight hitch upon entering, he proceeded to find a rhythm to satisfy them both. "Faster, Gabriel, faster."

Her words sent him surging into her faster and harder than he had ever fucked in his life. He could feel her muscles pulsing around him as she practically yelped in ecstasy. "Gabriel," she screamed. She came fast and hard, fireworks and all, and he followed right behind, pounding into her until he came. She could feel the warmth of his seed as he slammed inside her two more times until he was empty.

He bathed her in kisses before collapsing on top of her whispering vows of love in her ear. She affirmed his vows with her own. He was still inside her as they both languished in the love and desire they just shared. "Did you wear a condom?"

"Fuck!"

"I know we talked about waiting to start a family, but I don't mind if it happens sooner, Gabriel. Do you?" Gabriel lifted himself up on his elbows and ran his fingers through her hair.

"No, not at all, chérie. I would have detested our first time to be with a condom. With one time it is unlikely that you are pregnant, so would you rather we use contraception from now on?" The corners of Everdine's lips turned up into a sexy smile and she whispered "no" as she pulled Gabriel down for a deep kiss. A growl reverberated from deep down and he could feel himself growing again as he rolled over, bringing her on top.

"In the shower. Let's go." Gabriel took her hand and helped her off the bed. "Or would you rather have a bath, chérie?"

"A bath would be nice."

"I agree. You get the water started and I'll get us something to drink." Gabriel gave her a pat on her bare bottom and went to the kitchen to get more champagne. When he returned to the bathroom she was already in the bathtub beneath a thin layer of bubbles. Gabriel carefully scooted in behind her taking her in his arms. They made another toast with the champagne. He then took a washcloth with soap and bathed her in the most intimate way.

Gabriel took a sip of his champagne and then grabbed the length of Ever's hair, wrapping it around his hand leaving her neck exposed. He tilted her head to the side, kissing down the soft curve of her neck. As he was kissing her she could feel his erection growing on the small of her back. The quiet sighs she was making only galvanized his need for her. Next she felt a cool liquid on her neck, running down her breasts. Gabriel poured the champagne on her neck and began ravaging her neck with his mouth, taking in the sweetness of her champagne-doused skin.

"Now I'm going to take my time and love you how you should be loved- slow....sweet....tender and hot."

"God, yes."

Gabriel grazed his lips over her shoulders before washing away the champagne residue. He swept his hands firmly over her breasts and and down between her legs while kissing behind her ear, sending her into a state of euphoria.

"Come chérie, let's get out of the tub." Gabriel held a hand for her to steady herself until she stepped out of the tub. He followed behind her, wrapping her in a towel to dry off. As he patted the towel down her legs he stopped at the cusp of her thighs, noticing her bare mound, lustrous with moisture. He knelt down and began lapping up the moisture between her slick folds, sucking her between his lips and tongue. Everdine grabbed the sides of his head with her hands and held him close in place while moaning in pleasure as her head thrust back.

"Gabriel, please."

He continued to coax her clit and between her folds, laving inside as deep as he could go. Ever moved her hands from his head to his shoulders as her legs began to weaken. He could feel the first shutter of orgasm sweeping over her as he buried his tongue deep inside her and circled her swollen bud with his thumb. Ever cried out as she came harder than she ever had before.

A breathless Ever pulled Gabriel up and kissed him hungrily. "That was amazing," she exclaimed. Gabriel returned her kisses, equaling her passion.

"Turn around and hold onto the vanity." Ever did as Gabriel instructed while he closed in behind her, nudging her legs to an open stance. He grabbed her hair, wrapping it around his hand as he did in the bathtub, tilting her head back so he could impart kisses up and down her neck. "You look so fucking hot, Everdine. Mon Dieu!" She loved how he would say her given name when he was excited.

Her hands left the vanity and moved down his hard thighs while his hand came around to her lower stomach, traveling upwards and tweaked her nipples causing her to scream out. She could feel his huge cock on the small of her back. "I'm going to take you from behind now," Gabriel whispered in her ear.

Ever put her hands back on the vanity, spreading her legs more and bending over for Gabriel. Watching him in the mirror of the vanity was so sexy. He slowly played in her moisture with his cock. Both gasped at the full feeling of him penetrating her. When he was completely inside he stopped to savor the fullness. His hands caressed the length of her back while he began to move slowly. Every time he would withdraw from her the head of his penis would tease her G-spot causing her to moan. He kept up his languid pace, driving them both a little crazy.

"Faster, Gabriel." He hastened his thrusts, holding firmly onto her hips and then pulled out abruptly.

"Gabriel, no...."

"C'mon, chérie, I'm taking this to the bed now." Gabriel wanted to prolong their lovemaking as long as possible. He took hold of her wrist and led her into the bedroom and gently kissed her soft, plump lips.

"I want to be on top of you when you come. I want to kiss you senseless and savor every feeling when I'm inside you."

Gabriel nestled between her legs on the bed and held true to his word by kissing her senseless. He laced his arms on the backs of her knees, pushing her legs back and entered her. "You tell me if it hurts, chérie."

"It feels incredible."

Ever's legs were flipped so far back, allowing Gabriel to penetrate her deeply. Every slow thrust he made sent her closer to the edge. "Faster, Gabriel. Harder."

"Oui, chérie," a breathless Gabriel said.

Gabriel was holding back as long as he could, but having her so salacious beneath him was wearing away at his resolve. He began to move faster, making sure to pause briefly after each push. They were both getting lost in the rhythm of his thrusts.

"I love you so much, Everdine," he said between kisses as he pushed harder into her. She could feel him so deep he touched her cervix, vacillating between pleasure and pain. It was more than she could take as a climax ripped through her. "Gabriel...oh my...," she said as Gabriel pounded away before releasing everything he had inside her. He lay limp on top of her, both of them waiting for their breathing to normalize. Gabriel stole a leaden kiss from her before rolling over on his back.

"That was fucking amazing. You are fucking amazing, Ever. You've made me the happiest man on the planet." He held her gaze as he declared his love for her, showering her with kisses.

"Thanks, Gabriel. I feel the same about you. Making love to you is so much more than I could have ever imagined. You are my heart."

They both readied themselves for bed for their first night as husband and wife. Ever laid her head on his chest as they both surrendered to the weight of drowsiness brought on by all of the wedding activities and bedroom activities.

"I need to tell you something Gabriel," Everdine sighed in a nearly peaceful slumber.

"Hmm," he replied in an equally languid state.

"The night we played poker...I threw my hand so you'd win," she said with a contented smile across her face, snuggling close to him with her eyes closed.

"I know," he replied, burrowing her in close. Ever's attention was piqued as she stilled in his arms.

"How so?"

"Because I was playing with a marked deck," he said as a huge grin spread across his face.

EPILOGUE

The newlyweds woke up late the morning after their first night as husband and wife. Never had Gabriel felt so rested and relaxed. Having waited to have sex until after they'd married had caused many a sleepless, frustrated night for both him and Ever. Now they also had the hope of getting pregnant and didn't want to waste any opportunity to hone their love-making skills before becoming parents.

Willie was wondering if the clothes she packed for their honeymoon to Italy would still fit by the end of their two weeks. She was already sporting a tiny baby bump and her breasts were pushing the limits of her bra. Anton was enjoying that part the most.

The newlyweds were meeting Marva for brunch and had postponed their honeymoon for a day so the sisters could visit some more. They had all noticed the spark between Dominic and Marva at the reception and were holding out for any inclination that these two may want to get together. Marva was so excited to finally get some time with her sisters, albeit half-sisters. Although they all had different personalities, Marva sported some very raw qualities they noticed. It likely had to do with her fast upbringing.

Marva was not close at all with their father, William. She had last seen him when she was a child and since they moved around a lot, that didn't leave many opportunities for visits. Marva's mother was a home care nurse and would go where the work would allow her room and board if at all possible. When Marva was a child they moved to New Orleans and were able to get subsidized rent on a shot gun house beside one of her patients. At that time Marva's mother didn't bother to keep in contact with William since he showed so little interest in Marva. These were rebellious years for her and the neighborhood was rough at times. It gave her many opportunities to get into trouble. After she realized her gift of voice she started singing on the street corners with some musicians from the neighborhood and decided abruptly to join the military after a year in college.

After her service in the Air Force she stayed in Europe and found some bandmates that she performed with. They played in cafes across western Europe. One thing that set Marva apart from her sisters was how open and expressive she was. She was every bit as tenacious as her sisters, but there was nothing bashful about her demeanor. She was used to having to fight for anything she wanted in life and what was once a survival skill had become a way of life. Due to some bad past experiences she was determined to always be in control after leaving the military. Although she spoke open and freely, it was never from the heart. That part of her she kept buried very deeply.

While Anton and Gabriel were at the buffet Marva told her sisters about how she propositioned Gabriel, but he failed to act on her invitation. The girls were awestruck hearing how Marva had cornered him on the dance floor. The kind of brazen behavior she exhibited, they had only seen in men thus far. Marva asked Willie to tell her about slapping Dominic the first time she and him had met. Willie recounted that night with amusement as she described the incidence to her sisters.

"If what you say about Dominic is true, then I don't understand why he turned down my invitation last night. How can the consummate ladies man turn down a no-strings trollop in the sack?"

Since Willie knew Dominic best she tried to convince her that even though that may be his past, he is a man of great substance deep down. "Marva you may want to consider more than just a trollop with Dominic. He is a fiercely loyal friend and very protective of those in his circles. He's good looking and employed, too. What else do you need in a man?" Marva got a chuckle out of Willie's boiled down version of the perfect male.

"Men aren't the highest form of species in my experience and it serves me better to treat them accordingly."

"Ouch," Ever exclaimed. "Maybe you need to work through your issues, because that sounds like a very empty reality."

"Yes, but, it's what I know."

Just then Anton and Gabriel joined the sisters with a plate of food in tow and one fine looking Dominic. He greeted everyone at the table and made a point to personally greet Marva with a kiss to the back of her hand. He noticed the blush of awkwardness that swept across her face. Something finally clicked that might explain her motivations. She was used to being the aggressor with men, but when it came to men lavishing her with attention it was clearly a discomfort to her. She could talk with the salt of a sailor, but as soon as the tables were turned she was a fish out of water.

There was no doubt in Dominic's mind that he wanted Marva, but it was hard to relegate it to just a hookup. He wanted to know more about her. Both Marva and Dominic remained cordial during brunch, with stolen glances from across the table. Dominic had yet to have the opportunity to address why he didn't come to her room last night. He wanted to play it cool because he knew if he told her the truth it may push her away.

When the table was cleared Gabriel got up to go to the bathroom. Dominic took his small plate of chocolate covered strawberries and sat down beside Marva where Gabriel had been sitting. He took her hand in his under the table, and although she stiffened, she didn't pull it away. He leaned in closer to talk to her.

"I apologize I was unable to come to your room last evening. I was on a long call with Australia and had no way to contact you. You'll have to give me your phone number before we part."

"Is that so? I'm sorry you were unable to come last night, too." The double entendre didn't escape Dominic. He stroked the back of her hand with his thumb and he could see her discomfort at such a small intimate gesture. "Would you like a strawberry?" he offered.

"Sure." Marva reached for the plate and Dominic stopped her with his free hand.

"Allow me." Dominic grabbed one of the strawberries by the hull and brought it to her mouth. She bit into the berry, grazing his fingers with her tongue in the process. Dominic cleared his throat at her sensual act. If the throbbing erection in his pants was any indication of how attracted he was to Marva then it was huge. As the group chatted about honeymoon plans around them Dominic decided he had better leave while he could still walk.

"Dear friends, I have to go take an untimely business call and want to wish you all the best on your honeymoon. Thanks for the invitation to meet up in Rome for Marva's concert; I look forward to it." Before getting up he leaned over to Marva and caressed her cheek with his thumb, giving her a sweet kiss on the other cheek. As he was about to drop her hand under the table, he brought it to his lap and brushed it over his erection. A nervous giggle escaped from her mouth, which she tried to cover by clearing her throat. They all hugged goodbye and Dominic told Marva to come to his suite after visiting with her sisters so they could exchange contact info.

Ever and Willie didn't make a big deal out of Marva and Dominic, but the looks they shared with each other gave recognition to the palpable tension. After exchanging contact info with her sisters and saying their goodbyes, Marva made her way up to Dominic's room. For some reason he made her nervous, but then again Dominic wasn't like most men she came in contact with. There was such a recondite depth to him that she was afraid her regular modus operandi would not work with him. They often looked at each other as if they shared something-something Marva could not yet place. She smoothed out her skirt with her palms, cleared her throat and knocked nervously on his door.

ABOUT THE AUTHOR

Dare Pender is married and lives in the Carolinas with her family. She enjoys various sports, outdoor activities and being near the coast. Going to graduate school made her realize how much she appreciated works of fiction and decided to make a jump into self-publishing with her first book, Eurotrash.

www.ingramcontent.com/pod-product-compliance
Lightning Source LLC
Chambersburg PA
CBHW050924120626
46552CB00001B/33